Sword and Song

by
Angela Dencklau

SWORD AND SONG
Copyright © 2003 by Angela Dencklau.

ISBN trade paperback: 0-9722349-9-3
Library of Congress Control Number: 2003102008

All rights reserved. No part of this book may be reproduced or transmitted in any form or by any means, electronic or mechanical, including photocopying, recording, or by any information storage and retrieval system, without the written permission of the publisher, except in the case of brief quotations embodied in critical articles or book reviews.

This is a work of fiction. Names, characters, places and incidents are either the product of the author's imagination or are used fictitiously, and any resemblance to any actual persons, living or dead, events, or locales is entirely coincidental.

This book was printed in the USA.

For inquiries or to order additional copies of this book, contact:

Gardenia Press
P. O. Box 18601
Milwaukee, WI 53218-0601 USA
1-866-861-9443 www.gardeniapress.com
books@gardeniapress.com

*To my mother, for always telling me the truth,
and to my father, whose grudging financial assistance
has often kept a poor college student afloat.*

Prologue

A man leaned over a well, his hands resting on the stone rim. Lovingly, his fingers traced the runes that were inscribed in the cold stone. At his touch, light flooded from the water and lit the darkness that surrounded him. Little by little, the stone began to grow warmer beneath his hands.

He pushed his sleeves up as he looked into the water, careful not to let any part of him touch the shining depths. His eyes glinted at what he saw as the water swirled in gentle waves, forming a vortex of light and color. Yes, he was very pleased with the vision the well showed him.

A young girl, her eyes wide with fright, wore a cloak that concealed her from head to toe, though the shadows of night already hid her fine features. Looking from side to side, she peered out into a city street, then ran across the empty expanse to an alley, fear giving her feet speed.

The street was lifeless for a long time, empty of motion or sound. All of a sudden, soldiers burst into the street, torches raised as they attempted to banish the darkness that slowed their hunt. With a nod from their commander, the soldiers split up and went different directions, searching with thorough, deadly vigilance.

The robed man drew back from the well, a satisfied smile on his face. With a wicked grin, he drew his fingers across a new set of runes and watched the events that followed with satisfaction.

The sound of stone grating on stone startled him and he looked up. Cursing, he drew away from the shimmering well and disappeared into the darkness. Soon after he left, a woman appeared, a worried frown wrinkling her brow. She went at once to the well, her eyes wide as she looked down at the image that still shone in the waters.

A girl was fleeing from a city on the bare back of a terrified mare. Behind her, fire licked at several of the buildings within the walled settlement. With a thought, the woman directed the well to shift the focus of the vision, and the girl faded away to be replaced by the frantic residents of the city fighting a massive fire.

Men in armor were staggering from the blazing building. They crashed to the ground with agonized screams as they were burned alive. The coat of arms of a noble house adorned their smoking armor. Struck by a thought, the woman shifted the vision to look again at the fleeing girl, focusing on her face. Although it was obscured by the shadow of the concealing cloak, what she could see was enough to confirm the woman's suspicions.

Her curiosity sated, she looked away and noted the various runes that had been awakened before she had arrived. Whoever had invoked the power of the well had known what he was doing. The traces of the mage's power signature still hung in the air. Who had enough power to creep into the center of the monastery and use the Well of Truth? She did not recognize the taste of the magic that clung around her.

Whoever had aided the girl's escape was very powerful. The question was, who was he, and why had he come here to work spells to benefit the girl? Deep in thought, the woman waved a hand and the spells lighting the well died, leaving the room in absolute darkness. Intrigued, she wandered away into the night.

Chapter 1

Falkris Vilenti kept one hand on the sword hidden beneath her cloak as she walked. Scanning the crowd with caution, she pushed her way through the mass of people surrounding the merchant wagon and the man who stood atop its bench. He saw her over the heads of the people. "Kris!" His voice was colored by a measure of panic, mixed with relief at sighting her.

She didn't attempt to call back to him. Instead, she gritted her teeth and began to thrust her way through the throng of people in earnest. Several of the higher born folk that were edged aside turned on her with righteous anger, but the glint in her eye silenced them in an instant.

As she glanced up again at the wagon, she could see that he was in trouble. People were pushing against the wagon, pressing forward as they tried to either climb into the wagon or reach the man perched precariously atop it. If the crowd wasn't stopped soon, the situation would escalate into a riot.

At last she broke through the stifling crowd of people. Light as a cat, she sprang up beside the man standing on the wagon. A moment later, she drew her sword and held it out for all to see.

Those who saw it first fell silent and drew back a step. The others followed suit when the sudden quiet startled them to attention. They all stared up at the shining sword as it swung deftly in Falkris' hand.

"Now," she said, her ruined voice grating like gravel, "I suggest that you either leave, or show some respect for Master Tahnuil. Do we have an understanding?"

Wary, the crowd backed even farther away from the tip of the sharp, lethal sword. Some of them turned to leave, but others remained, forming themselves into a crude line starting at the edge of the wagon and stretching across the spacious town square. Several of the men and women jostled one another in a vicious attempt to get closer to the front of the line. Falkris sheathed her sword as soon as their raging spirits had died down.

With a nod to the man, she melted into the background, her arms folded across her chest. He nodded his thanks and jumped down from the wagon to meet with the first in line. Falkris kept her eye on the people, watching for more trouble. Her gray eyes were sharp as a hawk's, and she used them well.

At times like this she needed all her senses to guard her lord. Sicuth was far from Hestara, the seat of the royal court, and justice in the area had slipped. She dared not leave him unguarded in such a rough city. She needed to be alert for anything that could happen, especially with her impetuous master, who acted on a whim.

Lord Rhen Tahnuil had a taste for adventure and the money to do as he pleased. His latest plan was to cross the formidable Stormpeak Mountains and enter the land of Jenestra. His foremost reasons for making the journey were his desire to face the unknown and his need to avoid his responsibilities as a nobleman. He wanted to go on wild adventures and see the world before he settled down and took over his family's estates. Having tired of the tame world that was available to him, he had turned to the one known place in the world where no other had gone, Jenestra.

The spreading story of his intentions had drawn these people. Many who heard of his plan had gathered to join him. After announcing his intentions, he had been surprised to discover that he wasn't the only one crazy enough to risk such a journey. Never mind that such an endeavor had not met with success in centuries.

Falkris was one of Rhen's personal bodyguards. He kept her with him at all times, and thus she had been the first to hear of his latest idea, and the first to be invited along. Though aware of the dangers involved, she was also eager to cross the

Stormpeaks. This trip would be her only opportunity to go to Jenestra, the country that lay on the other side of the dangerous, storm-plagued mountains.

She had heard long ago that the Jenestran elite fighters, the Blade Singers, had mastered a powerful technique. They had perfected the ancient art of binding the soul of a fighter to his sword. Those who were successful in completing the bond with their weapons fought with the steel of their will as well as their blades. They were quite formidable, and Falkris wanted to study with these proud sword masters.

The summer afternoon dwindled away. Falkris felt herself drifting and fought to keep alert. For the first time since she had stepped up onto the wagon, she shifted her position. Having forgotten that she was present, those still waiting in line gasped in surprise.

She caressed the scabbard that held her sword. A fine weapon, it had belonged to her father when he was still alive. While she treasured it, the sword reminded her of a time before her days as a mercenary, when she had been the daughter of a noble family, before she had come home to find her family slaughtered in the name of a political statement. She alone had survived. Her old friend, Netria, was the only one who knew who she really was, and Falkris preferred that her past stay buried.

"Falkris!"

She sprang down from the wagon to stand beside Rhen. "Yeah?" she asked, her voice rough. Distracted, she rubbed her scarred throat.

"I think we shall end the day here. Can you see to these people, please?" Without waiting for a response, he walked behind the wagon.

Her eyes followed his noble head of blonde hair until he was out of sight, then she turned to the crowd, her gray eyes spearing them as they looked at her. "The interviews have ended for the evening. You may return tomorrow."

When she heard the first murmurs of protests, she brought

out her sword again, her eyes blazing as she dared the crowd to defy her. Certain they would leave without further intimidation, she leapt onto the wagon and stood watch as the line of people dispersed. Most left without trouble, but Falkris had to convince several that they couldn't sleep outside the wagon overnight. They hurried away with suppressed curses. As they retreated, so did the last light of the ending day.

Rhen watched her escort the last of the lingerers from the square. He smiled with wry amusement. "Great work, Falkris. Are you up for dinner at a fine tavern?" He jerked his head across the open area, towards a wreck of a building that in a vague way resembled an establishment suited for dining. His grin betrayed his amusement at the border town's shady condition.

"What about the wagon?"

Unconcerned, as usual, he shrugged. "Leave it."

Falkris frowned. "The lock on the door isn't enough to stop thieves."

"It will do while we are absent for a short spell. If you like, we can sit outside while we eat."

She grimaced. "Yes, so we can enjoy the fresh city air."

Rhen wrinkled his nose. "It doesn't quite have the most appealing aroma, but it'll do. There are plenty of prospective travelers here, all of them willing to pay far too much for an exciting adventure through deadly mountains that haven't been crossed in years." He grinned.

Falkris fell in beside him, one hand on her sword, as they crossed the cobblestone square and made their way towards the welcoming light of the tavern. She shook her head as she matched her employer's pace. "I didn't realize there were so many fools alive in one place."

"Everyone is a fool at heart," Rhen pointed out. "Many of them just learn to suppress it."

"I take it you haven't, Master Tahnuil?"

He smiled ruefully. "Afraid not. But at least I have a fool to keep me company." He winked at her.

She was about to protest, but they had reached the tavern.

As he swept in with the practiced presence and command of nobility, she shadowed him, her eyes scanning the dining area to look for any trouble. No one met her gaze; they all found something else to engage their attention.

The owner of the tavern bustled up. "My lord, how may I serve you this evening?" He wrung his hands in anticipation.

The noble smiled. "My companion and I would like a fine table out on the square, with candles to light our meal and music to gentle our ears."

The man nodded with enthusiasm, the light of profit glinting in his eyes. "Of course, my lord. It will be done at once." He bustled away to attend to the matter.

Moments later, Falkris found herself sitting across from her master, her wary eyes darting from musician to musician. Their waiter handed her a menu, which she studied with pretended interest. Her eyes saw nothing but a scrawl of strange squiggles and lines.

Rhen glanced at her over his own menu. "You should try the chicken; it's rumored to be marvelous. Or, would you prefer steak?"

Falkris let out a tiny sigh of relief. "The chicken." At least she hadn't had to ask him outright to read the menu to her. She hated nothing more than admitting that she couldn't read. Especially not in the better parts of the city, where being a commoner was like being a slave.

Rhen ordered for them both, as was proper. She waited for the meal in silence while he babbled on about his plans to cross the mountains and the kind of people he was most interested in taking with him. She nodded without interest. The meal arrived at last. Before he could take a bite from his steak, she sampled it for him, despite his protest. She rolled the meat around in her mouth, trying to sense any odd spices. After a moment, she nodded for him to eat.

He stabbed the steak with his fork. "That isn't necessary. Not here." He looked up at her like an errant child, his eyes hooded.

Falkris glared at him, forcing him to meet her stern gaze. "*Especially* here. You never know when an enemy will strike."

"If only I could dispense with nobility and become a merchant," he sighed.

"One doesn't usually curse blessings," Falkris murmured. She took a bite of her chicken, delighting in the taste. A moment later, she glanced across the square. Though she was night blinded by the candles, she could still see that the wagon was as yet unmolested.

He shook his head as he chewed. When he had swallowed, he shook his fork at her. "Nor does one mock one's superiors."

Indulging his attitude, Falkris smiled and concentrated on her food. The entire time that the two ate, her eyes roved, moving from the wagon to the people who passed on the street to the man who played his harp behind her noble master.

At last, the meal ended. Rhen rose to his feet, handed an absurd amount of money to the waiting tavern owner and took his leave with praises of the meal dripping from his honeyed lips. Falkris checked her amused smile as she padded after her lord.

He returned to the wagon at a brisk, energetic trot, his blue eyes bright. "See, Kris, the wagon is undisturbed."

She dipped her head. "So it is."

He grinned at her. "And I trust that you'll see that it remains undisturbed whilst I retire for the evening?"

"I will."

His smile broadened, and she braced herself for whatever mischief he had planned for her now. "I'll expect you to help with the interviews tomorrow as well."

Nodding, she schooled her expression to hide her distaste. She despised nothing more than she did sitting still and listening to the nonsense that other people thought of as important. "Do you need me to walk you to the inn?"

He shook his head. "No, it isn't far. There's no reason for you to make the trip."

"You're sure it's secure?"

"Yes. Keth is waiting for me there."

"Keth?" She managed to withhold her frown.

"Who else? The man may not be very intelligent, but his loyalty to me is flawless." He appealed to her with his eyes, willing her to agree with him for once on the issue.

Falkris refused to relent. "I'll see you tomorrow."

"Right. We'll need to move the wagon to a safer place before the crowds arrive, so expect to be up before dawn."

"I will be."

"Of course." He bowed to her and strode off down the street, whistling to himself as he walked along. She watched him go until he was out of her sight, and thus her protection.

Weary, she leapt up onto the wagon and ducked inside the little cabin, closing the door behind her. With a sigh of relief, she removed her light armor and unbuckled her sword. At last comfortable, she rubbed some of the kinks from her muscular body with strong hands.

When she climbed into her bedroll to sleep, her body was heavy with exhaustion. Her hand slipped under the pillow and closed around the hilt of her sword. She always slept with the weapon close at hand.

Sleep was slow in coming. Though her body was so weary that she couldn't have moved if she had wanted to, her mind was wide awake. Her eyes would not stay closed. Refusing to submit, her thoughts raced in circles. When she finally did drift off to sleep, her dreams were troubled with nightmares from the past and present. She often startled awake at the smallest sound and grabbed her sword, her heart racing, and it soon became obvious that she would have no rest on this night.

Finally, she gave up and climbed out of bed. She lit a lamp within the wagon, careful to keep it away from anything that would catch fire. Then she sat back and stared with weary eyes at the floor.

In the flickering light, her legs looked unnaturally pink and muscular. She squeezed her hard calf once, remembering a time when her legs had been soft and pale, as any respectable woman's should be.

Falkris ran one hand through her long, black hair, which she let down on rare occasions now; it only got in the way in fights and often proved to be a weapon that others used against her. She had contemplated chopping it all off, but Rhen had objected. Inside, she had as well. Her hair, unlike most of her, was still decidedly beautiful and feminine. Longer than ever now, it stretched well beyond her buttocks.

Yawning, she rubbed gritty sleep from her eyes. Her head felt heavy, and there was a dull ache behind her temples. Perhaps if she went for a walk, the night air would clear her head and she could rest at last.

Not bothering to put her armor back on, she dressed and grabbed her cloak. She also took her sword. She never went anywhere without the shining blade. Without the weapon at her side she felt naked. Leaving it behind had once almost cost her her life, and she wouldn't make that mistake again.

Falkris walked the edge of the square, her steps slow and methodical. She had passed the wagon several times when the sound of footsteps, fast approaching, brought her gaze up. Falkris froze and melted away into the darkness, watching as a pair of drunk men staggered past, not even seeing her where she stood without sound in the shadows.

Falkris waited until she could no longer hear their feet echoing off the cobblestones. Shrugging to herself, she returned to the wagon. The lamp had burned down while she was gone, and she cursed at her own stupidity. Why had she left it burning?

She lit it again and looked around the wagon. On one side, a writing desk and a heavy chest rested. On the other, a bed was built into a wall of cupboards. Underneath the bed were several locked crates. Everything was tidy and neat, as Rhen preferred it. Although his personality was chaotic, he was often tedious with details. She blew out the lamp and settled in. For a while, she listened to her breathing and the steady beating of her heart. Finally, she drifted off to sleep.

Chapter 2

Falkris was awakened by the sound of someone approaching the wagon. Her eyes flying open, she rose into a crouch, reaching immediately for the sword beneath her pillow. With her free hand, she drew a dagger from its sheath at her foot.

She crept to the door of the wagon cabin, then moved to the side to await the intruder. The door opened with a soft hiss, and Falkris spun to attack, her sword flashing. Dark, wide eyes stared at her with fright as she pressed the weapon against her opponent's throat. The person who trembled at the end of her blade was a huge ox of a man, and ugly as sin. With a sigh, Falkris lowered her weapon. The big man relaxed and stepped away from her, still wary.

Falkris shook her head as she sheathed her weapons and gestured him into the cabin. "Keth," she rasped, "you should've knocked."

He shrunk into himself as he ambled in. "Sorry." His deep voice rumbled in his broad chest.

Sighing, she shut the door behind him. As it closed, she caught a glimpse of the sleeping city, rosy in the soft, predawn light. The new day was close to arriving. Filled with interviews and details, it would be an excruciatingly long day. She wasn't looking forward to it at all.

Keth cocked his head at her like a dog. "Help me?"

"With what? Do you need to hitch the horses and move the wagon?" She coughed. Her voice wasn't working well. Perhaps it was the dry air. Preoccupied, she rubbed at the scar that riddled her throat with its grotesque paint.

Keth was nodding. "Master's waiting."

She sighed. "I'll help you. Did you bring the horses?" Her voice broke, coming out as more of a hiss of air than a word.

Keth looked concerned, his hideous face creased in a mask of confusion. She waved a hand at him, urging him to ignore her obvious discomfort.

After a moment, his face cleared and he smiled. He nodded with enthusiasm. "Horses. Yes." He looked so proud of his accomplishment. The man had been simple since birth. The innocence that accompanied his mentality was a mixed blessing in light of what he had been deprived of.

As she followed him from the wagon, she reflected on that. Falkris had seen the man fight, and in those bloody moments, he seemed far from innocent. She had taught him how to handle a sword and was proud to see that he had learned much from her. Battle had given him experience. He was lethal. However, he didn't seem to comprehend that his weapons delivered death to others. His mind could not grasp that the people he killed were people at all. Perhaps he didn't want to understand the awful truth. Keth wanted to protect his friends, those he loved. When something troubled them, he went to their defense in the only way he knew how, which was with a sword. His blind love spared him the pain that came with knowing what it was to end a life.

Despite his usefulness, the man sometimes irritated her. He was like an overgrown and dangerous child. She had always felt that Rhen needed a man more intelligent and reliable to protect him when she wasn't there. At the same time, Falkris saw the value in the unfailing loyalty that Keth had for Rhen. He was like a puppy, eternally devoted to his master.

The horses were tied outside. She leapt down from the wagon and began to help Keth hitch them to the front. The morning air was cool in contrast to the wagon cabin, which had been heated by her sleeping body. As she worked alongside her big companion, she felt the stiffness born from sleep melt from her muscles.

When the horses were settled in, she and Keth climbed back onto the wagon. She handed him the reins, and he urged the equine creatures forward. Falkris could only hope that Keth remembered where they were going. His memory was by no means superb, but it was all she had to rely on to find her impetuous lord.

The wheels rattled as he guided the wagon down several long streets paved with uneven cobblestones. The ride wasn't a comfortable one, and it was made even more unpleasant by Keth's company. However simple or kind the big man was, Falkris couldn't bring herself to like him. She had little patience for the simple, but he was oblivious. He whistled to himself, pausing to grin at her with his crooked, gapped teeth.

Finally, the huge man guided the wagon through the side door of a warehouse. Rhen met them, his eyes bright and a bounce in his step. Unlike Falkris, he was a morning person. He smiled at the two guards and directed the wagon to its place with a few energetic gestures. They parked the vehicle just behind a long table.

Falkris jumped down and padded over to the table. She looked down at the papers there and peered with interest at the strange markings that danced across the pages. Though she wished she could understand the words written there, Falkris was too proud to ask Rhen to teach her to read.

Rhen was moving chairs into place around the table. Eager for the day to arrive, he sprang to his tasks with energetic efficiency. Falkris ignored his enthusiasm and focused her attention on staying out of his way. She tugged Keth back so that he was out of Rhen's path as well. The noble strung up lines of rope to outline a path for the crowds of people that would soon begin arriving. When he was finished, he pulled on them, as though to test their efficiency. As Falkris watched with a small smile of amusement tickling at the corners of her mouth, Rhen gestured energetically to Keth. The two men threw open the big doors at the front of the building, opening the warehouse to the street.

Keth retreated, leaving Rhen standing there. His back was to them as he faced the rising sun. Silhouetted against the door, the nobleman was little more than a dark shadow outlined with the first light of the day. Hands on hips, he looked out at the world with a challenge in his eyes.

Turning, he strode over to Falkris, stopping just in front of her and tilting back his head to look up at her. Rhen was short in stature, but big in heart. His cheeks were flushed from his exertions, and his blue eyes danced with excitement. "Are you ready to do your part?"

She folded her arms in front of her, expecting the worst. "What *is* my part?"

"I want you to stand just behind me and pay attention to everything that goes on. If I think someone is a good choice, I'll ask you to offer your opinion as well. Especially with the warriors that will guard our expedition."

Falkris smiled at that. "I think that I should test them out personally." She patted her sword for emphasis.

Rhen was about to reply when the first person wandered in. He spun on his heel and rushed to meet her. With a broad smile, Rhen escorted the cloaked woman up and down the roped paths to the table. With a show of flashy gallantry, he pulled out the chair for her and seated himself across from her.

Falkris walked over to stand just behind him, to his right. In the dim light, she could not quite see the face of the woman beneath the hood of her cloak, though she thought that she could see a flash of cool green eyes. As if sensing her scrutiny, the women threw back her hood to reveal a splash of golden curls. Her face was flawless. Like a challenged feline, Falkris narrowed her eyes. If she'd had fangs, she would've bared them.

Rhen, as she had suspected, was immediately taken with the girl. Falkris wondered why men could never see past a pretty face. Her body tense, she took a step forward and put one hand on his shoulder, cautioning him with a gentle touch. He would understand the silent signal; she never touched him unless it was important.

The muscles in his shoulder tensed and he sat straighter, assuming an air of professionalism. "My lady, may I have the pleasure of your name?" Falkris withdrew from him while he spoke, allowing him to work his charms on the woman now that he had been warned.

The woman ignored Falkris and addressed Rhen politely. "Lianna, Lord Tahnuil." Her voice was cultured, suggesting that she'd been brought up in a house of aristocratic standing. Rhen was noble himself and should know those of refined blood. However, his adventurous endeavors often kept him absent from court, and he didn't recognize this woman.

Falkris watched them both with interest as they continued to converse. The woman was tense, almost nervous, and Rhen did his best to put her at ease. "I'm sure that you've come far. Sicuth is a remote town, unworthy of a woman such as yourself." He paused, perhaps to think, or for emphasis. Falkris couldn't see his face to discern which. "Tell me," the noble went on, "what interests you so much about the expedition that you would journey to this forgotten, dirty town?"

"I wish to leave Ravenia." She lowered her eyes, looking down at the table rather than at Rhen. "I have always been interested in Jenestra." She paused to consider her next words. "I can bring no worthy skills to the expedition, though I do know how to ride a horse." She flushed as she admitted this, for in Ravenia it wasn't deemed proper for a woman to ride. "But that is all." Her eyes flashed up to meet his. "What I *can* offer you is money."

He sat back in his chair. "Well, I am interested in that."

Falkris lost interest as they bargained in hushed voices. Her eyes rose to watch the people who had begun streaming into the warehouse. She sighed, wishing there weren't so many. This was going to be a very long day.

Her eyes returned to the table when Rhen and Lianna stood. Rhen smiled. "If you will return tomorrow, the final decisions will be made then. It will be invitation only."

Lianna curtsied, then departed. Falkris noted the nobility in her bearing and the grace in her step as she walked away. Lianna was not a common girl, nor a merchant. She was a woman of royal blood. But what was she doing here, in a border town like Sicuth, and why would she want to leave Ravenia?

Such a woman should not go unescorted as Lianna did.

Falkris looked at Rhen. He met her gaze, the same questions brewing in the blue depths of his eyes. Shrugging, he turned back to the table. Falkris looked again at Lianna. She watched the girl until she was gone from sight, then wearily returned her attention to where Rhen sat at the table with the next petitioner.

An aged man, it was obvious that this one was without a copper to his name. Falkris could smell him from where she stood. He was probably a beggar. Rhen was turning him away with a few kind words. The old man protested with passion, but when Falkris stepped forward in a menacing stance, he left with no further argument.

As the next man sat across from Rhen, Falkris signaled to Keth. "Did you see that man?" she asked, pointing after the aged homeless man who was departing from the warehouse. Keth nodded. "People like him," Falkris rasped slowly to make certain he understood, "don't have the money or skills to go with us. Can you make sure that they don't take up Rhen's time?" Filled with a sudden purpose, Keth nodded.

Falkris watched with satisfaction as Keth waded into the line. A moment later, he was escorting a bedraggled couple from the line and out the door. Once there, he stood in the doorway, turning away those he judged unworthy. Though his perusal seemed unfair, it increased the efficiency of the operation and cut back on the time that Falkris had to spend observing the interviews.

She turned back to the table, watching in silence. Rhen and the newest man were talking together in low voices. "I can't offer you any coin," the man was insisting, "but I can offer you a solid blade. I am known for my skills as a warrior."

"What's your name?" Falkris asked, her voice grating like gravel.

The man deigned to raise his gaze to her. His chest seemed to inflate as he puffed himself up with pride under her scrutiny, like he was a cock strutting for the hens. She felt a sneer of disgust curl at her lip.

"I am Gregor the Mighty!" he bragged.

Falkris barked a short laugh even as she paced two steps closer to the table. "I've never heard of you. I think you are Gregor the Liar."

The man looked indignant even as he rose to the challenge, coming to his feet in a flashy display of righteous wrath. "And who are you to challenge me?"

"Falkris Vilenti," she offered. Seeing the look of shock cross his face, she smiled to herself. Her name was not unknown among warriors, both mercenary and freelance.

The man collected himself and looked affronted. "I will not allow myself to be baited by trash such as you. Leave your betters to discuss matters of business in private, girl."

Falkris flashed one glance at Rhen. The frown that was growing on his face was proof enough that he was offended. His eyebrows threatened to come together at any moment as he glowered at Gregor.

The mercenary moved forward until she was standing right next to Rhen. She placed her hands flat on the table and leaned forward. "Do you care to put your sword where your mouth is, *boy*?" Her voice was harsh, more a rasp than words. Still, it carried far enough in the sudden silence for all to hear.

The man snapped. Rising to his feet, he drew his sword. A crude blade, it was poorly cared for and ill-used. Falkris wouldn't have been surprised to hear that he used it to chop wood at home. When he swung it in a graceless arc, she countered with her dagger. A moment later, she sprang over the table. He staggered back in surprise, and in the moment that he faltered, she was on him. Her dagger easily knocked aside his poorly wielded sword and came to rest against his throat.

Dead silence engulfed her, cradling her in a world thicker than water and filled with the pounding of her heart in her ears. The edges of her vision were red, and for a moment, she was almost ready to kill the man over his indiscretion.

Rhen's voice cut through her blood lust, and she snapped back to real life. "Falkris." His voice was low and commanding.

She lowered her dagger and turned her back on her opponent. If Gregor struck her now, all would see it as false play. She bent to pick up his sword and handed it to him. "Learn how to use this properly before you get yourself killed."

His eyes, as he glared back at her, were both angry and frightened. He seemed about to challenge her again, but scurried away while he was still alive. Falkris watched him go, then she turned to the crowd. "If you can't face me, you aren't fit to fight by my side!"

The silence stretched as she stalked back to her place behind Rhen. The noble looked both upset with her rash actions and proud of her at the same time. She stared him down. Relenting at last, he turned away with a small smile on his handsome face.

As the next man moved up to sit at the table, some of those who had been waiting in line turned away with some reluctance and trudged from the warehouse. Falkris watched them go, her eyes noting the old swords and battered weapons among them. Their hopes of joining the expedition had been high, but it wasn't to be. Following such dreams without the skills to back them was like extending an invitation to death. Better to be disappointed than dead.

The day passed at an inevitable snail's pace. On rare occasion, Falkris noticed, Rhen extended an invitation to certain individuals to return on the morrow at the noon hour. The others were turned away with kind, but firm apologies.

The interviews lasted well into the night. They had to send Keth out for food to ease their aching stomachs. As the day passed, Falkris grew weary and agreed to sit beside Rhen, though she was less able to defend him from that position. She had to concede that passing out from exhaustion wouldn't leave her in any position to protect him.

Several candles had burned out when the last of the candidates had gone. With tired bodies, the three of them closed the warehouse and blew out the remaining candles. Crawling into the wagon, they slept heavily, asleep almost before they reached their beds.

Chapter 3

A scream cut through the still night air, shattering the calm of the evening. Placid clouds floating overhead obscured the full moon with their phantom breath, undisturbed by the shrill cry. The only movement came from the shadows of the trees, almost indistinguishable in the dim light as they danced in the gentle breeze.

Silence followed, hanging heavy over the farm. Then, a faint whimper carried through the air, followed by a desperate, muffled plea for help. Beneath a tree, a horse snorted, its breath rising in the air to drift away from its long, dark face. Beside it, a man shifted, moving his hand to his sword.

"Daymen," a shadowy figure cautioned the man, "stay out of it. This is no concern of ours."

Daymen Aschton lowered his hand, staring at nothing as the whimpers turned to screams. He clenched his jaw, his teeth grinding together in frustration as the screams went on and on. "Couldn't the King have made it a clean death?" he hissed with malice in his voice to his fellow knights.

A man near him shifted from his uncomfortable position. Somewhere in the background, one of their number was sick. The woman screamed again, but the sound was cut off in a wet gurgle. Perhaps their lord had cut the woman's throat.

From behind Daymen, a knight spoke in a low voice meant just for the two of them. "You know King Jemis, Daymen. He has his appetites."

Daymen thought 'appetites' was a rather reserved word for their King's actions. The man had without a doubt taken his blood lust too far this time. Daymen wasn't certain that he could stand firm in his duties as a knight much longer. At times like tonight, his code of honor and his moralistic reasoning came into conflict.

When the woman had refused to bed the King, she had been breaking the law. Daymen understood that she'd offered something else in payment, but her life was too high a price. Torturing her was uncalled for. Castrating her husband and murdering her children was over the edge.

Daymen could stand it no longer. The knight looked once at his fellows, then, in a determined motion, tore the band declaring him King Jemis' knight from his arm. He threw it to the ground. "I've had enough." Walking over to his horse, he prepared to ride away from the life he had fought to live, to a future as an outcast. If he survived.

"Daymen!" Jemis called as he walked into the clearing. "Sir Aschton! Where the hell do you think you're going?"

Daymen put one hand on the saddle, clenching his fingers in a tight grip around the pommel to help him stay in control of his emotions. If he allowed his rage to govern him now, he would certainly kill the monarch. If he did that, he would be executed for treason. Walking away was all he could do.

"King Jemis," he said in a soft voice, "I don't think I can serve you any longer." His voice was barely controlled, as though it would break with anger at any moment. Trembling at his side, his free hand itched to draw his sword and plunge the shining blade into the King.

Part of him was appalled at the thought. He had worked so hard to become a knight. His duty was to serve and protect the royal family. That he desired to kill one of them was against everything he'd ever been taught, and ever believed in.

Jemis moved closer to him in the dark. Daymen could hear his breathing, heavy and ragged after his recent kill. "You *what?*" the King demanded.

Daymen forced himself to turn and face the man. "Milord, I'm leaving your service."

The moon suddenly appeared from behind the clouds, illuminating the King's face with relentless silver paint, revealing the ugliness that rested in his soul. He was furious; his eyes bulged, and he had a slight twitch in the muscles of his jaw. The veins in his pale throat became visible.

Jemis advanced on the knight until he was standing less than a hand span away from him. Daymen backed into his horse, and the big black stallion snorted and stamped one foot. Leaning against his mount, the knight drew strength from equine simplicity.

"On what grounds?" Jemis demanded in a dangerous voice.

Daymen prayed for the proper words to help him escape the King with his life. "Your Majesty, I leave with the protection of the fifth law of the honor code."

"Which is?" the King hissed. His eyes narrowed, and he leaned in slightly, leaving Daymen pinned against his stallion.

One of the other knights spoke. "The fifth law asserts that any knight may leave the service of his noble with honor if that noble has somehow violated the pact made between the two when the knight entered service."

Jemis glared at the knight who had spoken, but didn't act upon his wrath. The focus of his anger belonged to Daymen. "Tell me," he said, his breath hot on the knight's face, "how I have violated our pact."

Daymen swallowed, though it was not from fear of the King; it was more fear that he would kill Jemis before the night was through. "King Jemis," he responded, "you have violated our pact in that you have ordered me to break the honor code."

"How so?" Jemis demanded.

Daymen noted that he had the full attention of the other knights. "The first law of the honor code states that my duty is to the people above all else. Your actions this evening, my lord, were direct injustices against the people. In asking me to ignore your indiscretion, you've asked me to violate the honor code. The pact we made stated that my duty to the honor code must come before my duty to you as a member of the royal family."

Jemis was livid, suppressed rage screaming from every one of his clenched muscles. His eyes were lit with indescribable fury. Beneath it all was a terrifying layer of calm.

Cold intelligence quenched the fire that burned within the man.

"Very well," Jemis said, "you may go. But, grant me one request before you do."

Daymen's heart froze within his chest. The eyes of his fellow knights were fixed on him. As well as he did, the men knew he couldn't refuse this request and maintain his honor. He longed to say that he was free of the King now that he had made his decision, but that would be seen as the coward's solution. Whatever the King asked of him, he had to accept.

"My Liege," he said. His voice was tight with the war of emotions rushing through him.

"Burn the farm."

Daymen blinked, not certain that he had heard correctly. "My King?" Jemis didn't respond, but the cold amusement that twisted his features into a repulsive mask was answer enough. The knight stared at the King in the horrified silence that followed. Unable to refuse, Daymen couldn't honor the request either. He licked his lips, his mouth dry. King Jemis had left him no honorable way to escape.

The same knight who had spoken earlier once again raised his voice. "Your Grace, you request something that Sir Aschton cannot do. Once again, you ask him to violate the honor code. He must protect the farmers, not harm them."

Daymen let out a sigh of relief. Peering into the darkness, he wondered who had dared the wrath of the King to speak for him. Only shadows met his eyes. The moon passed behind a cloud, and they were left in total darkness.

He could sense, more than see, the rage of his lord. The King had been thwarted in his lethal game. His cold logic was banished and replaced with a flaming pyre of anger. He advanced on the knight who had dared to speak on Daymen's behalf.

"You," he hissed, "if you hold your precious honor code so dear, why do you remain with me? Why have you not betrayed me, as Daymen has?"

The knight answered, his voice strong and proud. "I owe

too much to your father to abandon my post."

"I don't," growled the knight who had spoken to Daymen earlier regarding the King's blood lust. His words were followed by the sound of fabric ripping and retreating footsteps.

As Daymen stood beside his horse, the remaining knights tore the royal insignia from their clothing and mounted their horses. Just the one knight remained, and he faced the King with pride.

Daymen didn't hesitate to make his escape while the proud knight stood his ground before the enraged King Jemis. He leapt up into the saddle of his great black stallion and with a cry, kneed the beast after his fellow knights as they plummeted away into the darkness.

As he rode, he heard the King screaming after him. "Damn you, Daymen Aschton! You will not escape me! You will hang for leading my knights in a rebellion against me!"

As the knights fled through the night, Daymen did his best to avoid branches, ducking his head low over his horse. All he could do, as the men pounded onward, was pray that his horse wouldn't break a leg in the treacherous darkness of the forest. That, and hope he would survive the night.

The knights paused in a small clearing, their horses stamping in trepidation and wheeling in circles as the men waited for everyone to arrive. The moon came out of hiding every few minutes to wink at them. Looking at one another with wide eyes, the men couldn't quite dare to believe that the events of the night were true.

When they had assembled, their breath rising in clouds of hot steam in the cool evening air, they all looked for leadership. Finally, one man spoke, his voice containing a frightened edge. "Well, Daymen, what do we do now?"

Daymen stared at the man without expression for a moment, then he collected himself, forcing his thoughts into a semblance of order. "I'll ride for the border while I'm still alive," he said softly.

The knights looked at him, and one of them spoke. "Then

we will ride with you, Sir Aschton."

Daymen gripped the reins with fingers tense and frozen like iron. "No. If we wish to keep our lives, we must not stay together."

"He's right," a man growled. "Jemis will hunt us all down one by one. If we split up, it will blur the trail."

Daymen nodded. "He'll be after me first. The farther you are from me, the safer you'll be."

In the darkness, the knights saluted him. "Honor be with you," they said in unison.

Daymen bowed his head and pounded his own fist against his chest in salute. "Honor be with you."

The knights wheeled their horses, one by one, and galloped away into the darkness. Daymen set off on his own path, following his internal sense of direction without the sun or moon to guide him.

He'd ridden for some time before he became aware that he was being followed. Reining his stallion to the side, he hoped to fool the person behind him into passing him in the darkness. The moon broke through the clouds at just the right moment, showing him the face of the youngest knight as the boy rode past.

Daymen cursed softly and kneed his horse after him. "Cemil!"

The boy started and drew his sword, turning his horse to face Daymen. When he recognized the older knight, he relaxed. "Sir Aschton."

"You were following me?"

Cemil nodded. "I was."

"Why?" Daymen's voice was harsher then he had meant to make it.

The young knight lowered his eyes in guilt. "I— "

Daymen shook his head. "No need to explain, Cemil. Come on." Without another word, he rode past the boy and continued on his way. After a moment, he heard Cemil follow. At least the boy would keep him company on the long journey ahead. Beyond that, nothing was certain.

Chapter 4

Falkris meant to sleep in, but she was awakened before sunrise by the sound of someone moving around in the warehouse. She glanced once at Rhen. The nobleman was blissfully asleep, his mouth agape as he lost himself in the land of dreams. Keth's snores echoed on the floor beside her.

Cursing, the mercenary rolled to her feet, one hand on her sword, the other drawing her dagger forth with a deadly hiss of steel. On stealthy feet, she crept to the door and pulled it open. With quick movements, she scanned the warehouse, but the pale light streaming through its windows did little to reveal the location of the intruder. Silent as a cat on the prowl, she slipped from the cabin.

Once outside, she shut the door soundlessly behind her. A moment later, she sprang down onto the dirt floor of the warehouse, using the wagon as a visual shield as she listened to discern the position of the intruder.

As soon as she knew where the trespasser was, she sprang to attack. Moving in swift steps across the warehouse, she bore down on her victim with silent, deadly stealth. The cloaked woman didn't even know Falkris was there until a dagger was at her throat.

"State your name and purpose," Falkris growled.

"Lianna!" the figure squeaked.

The mercenary released her captive and the woman stumbled away, falling to the floor. She looked up at Falkris with cool green eyes, and for a moment, the mercenary caught a glimpse of a haughty noblewoman in their depths. No other creature could muster that look of acid contempt and wrath. Falkris' suspicions about Lianna were confirmed. The woman was definitely of noble blood.

The warrior didn't bother to help Lianna to her feet, but watched as the woman picked herself up off the floor. Glaring at Falkris, Lianna brushed the dirt from her cloak and skirts. Falkris returned the stare with cold, baleful iron of her own.

"You're early," the mercenary said.

"You could've killed me!"

"You're early," Falkris repeated with patience.

"Lord Tahnuil didn't specify a time," Lianna returned. She drew herself up, doing her best to assert herself.

Falkris sheathed her dagger. "You'll have to come back at midday, when all the others are coming."

To Falkris' surprise, a moment of fear crossed the woman's face, giving her the look of a cornered rabbit. The warrior was caught off guard by the sudden, feral emotion. Then it was gone, and Lianna was serenity embodied. When she next spoke, her voice was firm, though there was still a quavering undertone of terror. "I refuse to leave."

Falkris cocked her head. "What are you scared of?" Violently, she coughed. It was too early in the morning for her to be speaking so much. She needed some water.

Lianna frowned. "I'm not frightened of anything."

Falkris shook her head and signaled the woman to follow her. She returned to the wagon, where she poured herself some water from a barrel at the back. Throwing her head back and taking a deep swallow, she offered Lianna a drink. As expected, the woman declined.

"Now," Falkris said, her voice clearer, "let's try again. Why won't you leave? It's not your pride, but your fear." Lianna's cheeks reddened with indignation. The warrior pressed onward. "Fear of what?"

The woman stood silent for a moment, obviously considering the mercenary carefully. Falkris wondered if the woman would respond. She stared Lianna down as she waited, determined that she wouldn't lose this battle.

"If I tell you," Lianna ventured, "can you secure my place in the expedition?"

Falkris snorted. "It depends on your explanation."

"Then I tell you nothing," Lianna said in a firm voice. Her green eyes blazed, daring Falkris to argue with her. She set her chin at a stubborn angle. "I'll tell you only that my life will be in danger until I escape the borders of Ravenia."

"Treason, milady?" Falkris mocked. "Is that what brings you here?" She advanced on the shorter woman, her piercing gray eyes slicing into Lianna. "If so, you invite the death of my lord, and I cannot allow that." Anger welled up within her, and her fingers closed around the hilt of her sword in reflex.

Lianna backed up several steps in fear of Falkris' wrath. "No, I'm not guilty of treason." She drew in a deep breath. "I was a witness to something that I should not have been. I must leave the country until it's safe to return and tell my story. Until then, I must preserve my life."

Falkris stared at her for some time, trying to discern the truth of her words. After a moment, she decided that she could read no deceit in the green depths of the woman's eyes. She nodded slowly. "Very well. You may stay."

"Thank you," Lianna breathed.

"If you're lying, I'll kill you," Falkris growled, almost before Lianna had finished speaking.

The woman paled, her smooth skin turning as white as fine china. She swallowed once, then nodded in acceptance. "I trust you will see that I speak the truth."

Falkris was about to respond when she sensed movement behind her. Somehow, she knew that it was Rhen. She half turned to her lord so that she could see him and Lianna both. He smiled at the two women. His blonde hair was tousled from sleep, and his blue eyes were bleary. Running one hand over his head in an attempt to smooth his hair, he succeeded in making it stick up at erratic angles.

Oblivious, he came before Lianna and bowed. "Milady, you're early. Your loveliness, as always, precedes all."

Lianna flushed at the praise, her color returning even as Falkris frowned in distaste. How was it that Rhen always seemed to fall for the dangerously beautiful women? Perhaps it was his roguish charm and his merchant's eye for the best quality in everything. *After all, he picked me to be his guard*, she thought with a wry smile.

"Milord," Lianna said, "you are too kind."

Falkris suppressed a groan as she attempted to fade into the background. Why was she always the one to stand guard while Rhen wooed his women? She hated the duty, but had no intention of leaving her lord alone with Lianna. As far as Falkris was concerned, Lianna was still dangerous.

For once, Falkris was grateful to see Keth when he poked his head out of the wagon. She gestured to him, and he joined her. Leaving him to stand watch, she returned to the wagon, where she dressed herself and strapped on her armor and arsenal of weapons.

When she peered around the edge of the wagon, Rhen and Lianna were engaged in a flirtatious battle of words. Her lord wouldn't notice her absence, and he wouldn't get into any trouble while he had a beautiful woman to occupy his full attention.

Falkris signaled to Keth, and the big man nodded. Letting herself out of the warehouse in silence, she slipped away. Midmorning was near, and the town was bustling. She found herself striding past little shops teeming with life. At a bakery, she paused to buy a pastry and nibbled on it as she made her way to the edge of Sicuth.

Once there, she paused to look back down the street. No one was paying her any mind, and she was grateful for that. Readjusting the sword at her hip, she set off across the small grassy field ahead of her at a light jog. At the far edge of the little open area, she came to a halt. Falkris glanced around at the tall grass surrounding her. Not far off, she could see the foothills of the Stormpeaks rolling gently. The dark shroud of a perpetual thunderstorm hung over the mountains. No plants grew on their harsh slopes, and very few creatures dared to call the dangerous place home.

Falkris stared at the peaks for a long time before the wolf came. Though she had not heard him approach, the cold touch of his nose brushing her fingers didn't startle her. She had suspected that he would come soon. If she waited long enough, he always found her.

The mercenary bent down to hug the wolf. As she ruffled the mottled fur around his neck, he licked her with his insistent tongue, making her laugh. Whining, he knocked her to the ground and stepped on her chest with his large paws. With a keen nose, he detected the treat hidden in her pocket at once.

She pushed him off with a firm word. "Dax." A deep note of command was in her voice. Dax moved back, flattening his ears in apology. She stood again and scratched the wolf behind the ears to reassure him.

"Dax," she said in a softer tone, speaking to him like an old friend, "I'm sick of this place. I hope we leave soon, so you and I can travel together again."

Dax listened, his yellow eyes fixed on her and his tall ears perked. When she finished, he cocked his head to the side. Barking once, he sat back on his haunches.

She smiled. "Dax, you've always been so faithful." Her throat ached. She'd been talking too much as of late.

Falkris reached into her pocket and drew forth a piece of jerky. Dax stood right away, coming forward to nose at it gently, though not daring to snatch it from her hand. Urging him to take it, she watched with fondness as his lethal jaws engulfed the treat. As a parting note, she scratched his jowls, then turned to go. He knew better than to follow her into the town, so he watched her go, and when she paused at the edge of the town, he was still there, sitting with perked ears at the far end of the field. Raising one hand to wave at him, she watched as he bounded away to melt into the tall grass.

When she returned to the warehouse, there was no sign of Lianna. Rhen looked rather refreshed when he met her halfway to the wagon. "Did you go see Dax?"

She nodded. "I did."

He grinned, looking wolfish himself. "We shall be leaving this sorry excuse for a town soon."

"Is that a promise?" she asked, raising one skeptical eyebrow.

"Lianna has agreed to provide most of the funding we'll need. All that remains is to select who will be traveling with us and to outfit the expedition properly."

"Where is she?"

"Lianna?" he asked. "She's resting in the wagon. She's had a most distressing journey."

"I'll bet."

"Falkris," he admonished, "the lady has been through hard times. Why are you so set against her?"

The mercenary looked at nothing for a moment rather than into the pleading blue eyes of her lord. "Rhen, the woman will bring trouble on our heads. I know it."

Rhen was skeptical. "What harm could she do?"

Falkris met his eyes. She could see there was no convincing him. He was smitten with the girl. In a weary gesture, she shook her head. "I warned you." Before he could protest, she walked past him and made her way to the wagon.

After a moment, Rhen followed her. "Kris, please. The people I asked to return will be here soon."

She stopped. "Right."

"I need you to be ready to test the guards for me."

Falkris turned to face him. "How many guards do you want?"

Rhen scratched his cleanly shaven chin as he considered, shrugged and smiled at her. "I suppose it's up to you. We want the best and the brightest. Men and women skilled in all weapons."

"How many wagons are we taking?"

"Seven."

"Will the guards be mounted?"

He cocked his head as he mulled that over. "I suppose it's possible."

"Right." She spun on her heel and started off at a trot for the door.

"Falkris?" he called after her, a note of concern in his voice. "Where are you going?"

She stopped and looked back at him. "You'll see." Then she was gone.

Chapter 5

When Falkris returned to the warehouse some time later, she was mounted on her horse. Misan was a dependable war mare. Her name meant "companion" in a dead language, and it was a name that was true to the horse.

The mercenary guided Misan into the warehouse, several horses laden with mysterious goods trailing behind her. She led them into an empty area in the warehouse and dismounted to survey the people gathered near the wagon. Everyone was looking at her with evident curiosity.

Rhen hurried over to her, a mixed look of displeasure and curiosity twisting his face into a comical expression. "I was beginning to wonder if you were coming back."

She snorted. "You can trust me, Rhen. You know that."

"I know." He was silent for a time as she began to unload the horses. His inquisitive nature got the best of him, and he moved forward to watch her. "What are you doing?"

She ignored him for a while, but she knew that he wouldn't be placated until she answered him, so she grudgingly paused in her endeavors. "I'm setting up my side of the bargain. If you want me to pick our future guards, I will. My way."

When he realized that he could get nothing more from her, Rhen returned to his table and his interviews. Falkris continued to work under the gazes of the people gathered in the warehouse. She set up several targets and a series of roped-in paths and hurdles. When she finished, she stood back to survey her work.

Abruptly, she turned on her heel to regard the gathered people. She raised her voice. "If you are applying for a position as a guard, report to me." Her words rasped from her scarred throat, just loud enough for them to hear, but their attention was riveted on her. She had the presence to command an army, ruined throat or not. In the past, before fate had brought her to Rhen, she had fought in the war with Celestia. During her time as second in command in the mercenary corps, she had not only earned the reputation of a great warrior, but had also learned to command hardened men and women and lead them into battle. Her name was not unknown. Many of them would follow her to their deaths, based on the legends that followed her.

Falkris watched with a neutral expression as about seventy men and women approached her. When they formed into a loose crowd apart from the rest of the people in the warehouse, she issued another order. "Line up!"

They fell into a rough line, and she walked among them, looking them over. As she moved along the line, she recognized faces and reacted accordingly. Several of them were men and women that she had fought with in the mercenary corps before she had signed on with Rhen. Knowing their fighting capabilities as well as her own, she didn't need to test them.

Once she had pulled those she was familiar with out of the line, about fifty people remained. For various reasons, she had already sent a dozen or more of the potential guards on their way. She needed strong, experienced warriors who would follow her without question. Not everyone present fit those guidelines.

She spoke in a quiet voice to those left, meeting their eyes. "If you are here to make money, you won't. Those of you who come with us will earn your way to Jenestra and little more. We will outfit you with a good horse, similar to mine, and we'll give you decent weapons and armor. Those of you who already have no need of equipment or mount will get our thanks."

A scarred woman made a disgusted sound and stalked away. After a moment, a handful more followed her. The rest stayed behind. These were people with a sense of adventure, the ones with a dream of seeing a far and fabled land like Jenestra. These were the kind of men and women that Falkris wanted beside her in a fight.

She nodded to them with respect. "Very well. There are about forty of you left. I want to take twenty with me, so you will compete for your places." She stopped speaking before she had to cough, swallowing to try to moisten her throat. "I've already selected two from among you to help me test you. Give them the same respect that you would give me," she rasped.

Falkris split the group up among the three of them so that the testing process would go as quick as possible. The warriors would be tested at three stations. She left Bendal, a solid man who was lethal with a bow, in charge of the archery section. Her old friend Netria, a woman who was an expert in close range combat, was trusted with testing the ability of the recruits with a sword. Falkris tested their riding skills herself.

Some of the potential guards had never ridden a horse before. She was tempted to send them away the first time they fell out of the saddle, but she waited to hear the opinions of her comrades. Some who were weak in one area more than compensated in another. A specific young girl was terrified of swords, but was an expert shot with a bow. She hit the center of the target without fail, sometimes splitting her own arrows in half. Her name was Amial Ravenelle. Falkris decided to keep her on.

When they had narrowed it down to about thirty warriors, Falkris tested them against one another to eliminate any doubt in her decision. Veteran mercenaries who had fought beside Falkris in the last war went up against young lords who had trained in the art of the sword since they were old enough to pick up a weapon.

When it was all over, there were twenty guards, plus Keth and Falkris. Considering the caliber of the warriors she had selected, it would be more than enough. She signaled for Rhen and Keth to join her, then addressed the men and women who would be serving under her in the weeks ahead.

"This is Lord Rhen Tahnuil, the man in charge of our expedition into Jenestra. Everyone answers to him first, and to me second. If you have a concern, he or I will hear you out. Following orders is important to our survival in the days ahead.

If you're disobedient, you'll answer to Keth—" she put a hand on the big man's shoulder, "—or myself. Do we understand one another?"

There was a chorus of agreement. Proud of her ragged band of elite fighters, she smiled with satisfaction. Rhen nodded to himself, his blue eyes narrowed slightly as he considered. After a moment, he turned to her and grinned. "Good work, Falkris!"

"Do you have gold for me? We need to outfit them and get them ready for the journey."

He looked over his shoulder at the dwindling crowd of people surrounding the wagon and the table set up beside it. He nodded. "I imagine so. I'll speak to Lianna about it right away." Before he had even finished speaking, he set off at a brisk trot towards the wagon.

Falkris watched him go, her eyes scanning the rest of the people still remaining in the warehouse. Netria came up beside her, an easy smile on her scarred face. "So that's your rich boyfriend?"

Falkris glared at her for a moment, a frown darkening her face. Then she grinned, her gray eyes lighting with mirth. "Netria, you know better."

Netria shook her head in mock regret. "He sure is a handsome one."

Falkris, laughing, stepped into her old friend's waiting arms. The two embraced, holding each other tight for a long moment. They stepped away, and Falkris lowered her eyes to hide the tears that shimmered there. "It's been a long time."

Netria nodded. "Five years. When last I saw you, the war had just ended. Then, everything happened … and you had to leave the War Hawks."

Rhen joined them and handed Falkris a pouch full of gold. Surprised at its weight, she looked at him in question. He glanced once at Netria and leaned towards his guard. "She says she wants the best for the guards, to insure safe passage."

"Your benefactor, eh?" Netria put in.

Rhen looked at the woman for a moment, his eyes searching her scarred face. Then he nodded. "I suppose you could say that, yes." He walked away with slow steps, thinking about something.

Netria barked a laugh. "I think I scared him."

Falkris hefted the pouch in her hand. With a smile, she turned to the collected men and women. "Let's go."

They didn't move, so Netria yelled at them. "You heard Kris! Get your asses moving!" she said with a grin that lifted the long scar on her cheek, accenting the pale flesh against her weathered skin.

Falkris smiled as she mounted. She patted Misan on the neck as she rode out, her mixed crew of guards trailing behind her either on foot or on horseback. This was going to be an interesting journey.

That night, the new guards set up camp in the warehouse, deciding to spend a night together, since it was the best way to get to know one another. Eager, the warriors had dug fire pits in the dirt floor of the warehouse before going in search of alcohol. Now they were getting drunk together. Falkris supposed that there would be a couple of fights before the night was over. They had to feel each other out. Hopefully, she wouldn't be forced to assert her authority.

She sat around a fire with Rhen, Amial and a few others. At a separate fire, she could hear Netria and Bendal singing an old song, which brought back memories of her mercenary days during the war with Celestia, a country to the north that bordered Ravenia. That was before she had come into Rhen's service, before she had even met him. Since those glorious days, much had changed. Though it seemed like decades, only a few years had passed.

Rhen must have sensed her thoughts, for he leaned closer to her. "Do you regret it?"

"What?" she asked, though she knew exactly what he meant.

"Coming with me."

She thought about it for a moment. "No. The life of a mercenary is harsh. I loved those days … but I wouldn't go back." She was silent for a time before she added, "I didn't really have a choice, so it's not a decision I can regret making."

He looked at her with his frank blue eyes. "You always had a choice, Falkris."

"No," she said in a tone that warranted no argument, "I didn't."

Frowning, he furrowed his brow. She braced herself for a lecture, but in the end he just nodded, conceding the point to her. "I suppose not," he said. Then, a slow smile spread its way across his handsome face. "You're too stubborn and honorable for your own good."

Falkris said nothing, losing herself in old memories. The war with Celestia had just ended, and Falkris' mercenary corps, the War Hawks, had retired to their base. Falkris had been an officer at the time, the second in command, with Netria and Bendal serving under her.

On a slow night, she was off duty, walking the streets of the town near their base. The future for her had been bright and full of dreams and ambitions. She'd had so much ahead of her before everything had gone horribly wrong.

Falkris had gone to her favorite bar. She sang there sometimes, songs that she had written herself on her journeys with the War Hawks. That evening she sang for a growing audience. Many had heard of her talent, and they called her the songbird.

Her purse filled with tips, she left late that evening. She whistled as she walked, a soft tune full of love for life. On such a beautiful evening, she had walked to town, and now she had a long walk back to the base.

Halfway along the road, she was assaulted. Alone and without her sword, there was little hope for her. She'd been stupid, young and suffering from delusions of immortality. After what had happened to her family, she should've known better than to trust fate. They had hit her over the head.

When she awakened, she had been in a strange room. Lord Dracine Silvian, the man who governed the area of Ravenia that the War Hawks called home, had ordered her kidnapped and brought to his estate. He'd heard her sing and wanted her to become his private musician.

She had refused him. Even when he'd offered her everything that was in his power to give her, she had been steadfast in her refusal of his proposition. Furious, the lord had ordered her killed. He'd wanted her death to be long and painful.

Perhaps it had been his very cruelty that had saved her. When they dumped her on the side of the road, she was still alive, if barely. Rhen had been on his way to visit Lord Silvian when he found her. He had rushed her to a doctor.

Rhen had saved her life. The doctors had worked miracles on her, sewing up her wounds. The gash along her throat had not been fatal, for it had not struck a major artery. But it had damaged her throat beyond repair. She would never sing again.

"Falkris?" the noble said beside her, a note of concern in his voice.

With sadness in her eyes, she smiled at him. "I have no choice, Rhen. I still owe you my life. Even if you release me from my debt, I'll still owe you in my heart. Besides," she added, "I like you. I don't regret my years with you."

He laughed lightly, his eyes shining. "Is that so?"

Somewhere behind her, Netria laughed out loud. "I knew it!" she yelled drunkenly. "You *are* her boyfriend!"

Rhen flushed a deep red. "Oh, my."

Falkris grinned. "Don't worry, Rhen. You're not my type." Rhen just laughed, not certain whether to be offended or relieved. Falkris hoped it was neither.

Chapter 6

The men Jemis had sent to hunt Daymen and Cemil were always just behind the two knights, so the pair rode hard. They rested in turns so that one of them was awake and watching for danger at all times. The days were long and the times when they dared to take a respite far too short.

As the sun set one evening, Daymen and Cemil stopped to rest. The dark red of the sun's rays shone through the forest. A breathtaking sight, it was a sign that the end of the forest was near, and that they would soon be out on the plains. Beyond the plains were the mountains, the border and safety.

Cemil kept watch while Daymen cooked a hare over a low fire. While Daymen didn't want the smoke to betray their location, he knew that they needed to eat a decent meal if they were going to keep traveling at their current pace. They'd eaten many of their meals in the saddle, and it was starting to show in their faces.

When they finally sat down together to eat, both men were tense. Cemil started at the smallest of sounds, while Daymen did his best to remain calm. If he appeared on edge, it would make the boy feel even more insecure.

"Where are you from, Cemil?" he asked, wishing to break the unbearable silence.

Cemil jumped when he spoke, but then relaxed and grinned at his own foolishness. "From south of the capitol, Sir Aschton."

"You can call me Daymen."

Cemil's eyes widened. "Daymen, sir? It seems disrespectful."

Daymen smiled, touched by the boy's blatant awe of him. "How old are you? Sixteen?" Cemil nodded. "Well, I'm only about ten years older than you. I think that we could be friends, if you liked."

Cemil beamed. "I would, sir!"

Daymen nodded, and the knights ate in silence for a time. When they finished the meal, the pair put out the fire and scattered the ashes to obscure any evidence of their presence. After that, they mounted up and rode through the growing darkness to a new campsite.

As they were preparing to settle in for the night, Daymen noted that the younger knight was more nervous than usual this evening. Perhaps it was the strange feeling in the air, as if the forest itself expected something to happen. He spoke to his companion in a soft voice, trying to calm him. "Cemil, why did you become a knight?"

Cemil drew himself up, the shadow of his lanky body straightening with pride. "Honor, sir. I wanted to bring honor to my family. I trained hard so that I could become an apprentice knight."

Daymen smiled to himself, the story not unfamiliar to him. That was why they all became knights, for the honor and the glory. And where was it all now? He thought of King Jemis and his smile died. Everything that he had believed in was gone. Now he was running for his life like a common criminal. What a disgrace.

He banished the dark thoughts and put on a pleasant face for Cemil's benefit. "Why don't you turn in for the night and get some rest? I'll take the first watch."

Cemil nodded and climbed into his bedroll. "Thank you, Daymen." He said the older knight's name with triumph as he rolled his blankets around himself. A moment later, he was asleep. The journey had been hard on both of them. Daymen just hoped that they would make it to the border alive.

Silent and still, he stood watch over the camp. The night passed slowly away, the only sound the soft breathing of his companion and the chirping of bugs in the distance. Daymen fought to keep awake, thinking that it was going to be a long night.

In the depths of night, the sound of men crashing through the undergrowth shattered the silence. Daymen kept low to the ground as he peered through the forest, watching as the shadows of men passed by no more than two yards away. He kept as still as possible, hoping that his presence wouldn't be detected.

He longed for the days when he wouldn't have to hide like a coward. A knight, he was a man trained to be honorable and to fight his foes in the open. Creeping through the forest and running at the first sign of a threat was wearing thin on his nerves. For Cemil's sake, he couldn't make a stand against so many men. He would not have the young knight's death on his head.

He crept over to where his companion slept. Leaning down so that his mouth was right next to the boy's ear, he placed one hand over Cemil's mouth to silence any noise the boy might make upon awakening. "Cemil!" he hissed.

The boy startled awake, his eyes widening as he stared up at Daymen. The knight jerked his head towards the men, indicating danger. Cemil nodded and Daymen took his hand away from the boy's face. Slowly, Cemil rose into a crouch.

They watched as the men searched for them, both praying that they wouldn't be discovered. They didn't even dare to breathe as the long moments inched past. One man sighting them was all it would take. They didn't want to take any more risks than they had to.

They were going to stay safe this time, it seemed. The men had moved on without discovering them. Then, Cemil's young stallion snorted. Daymen's mount, a black stallion of the finest stock named Vesahn, was trained well enough to remain silent in the presence of danger, which permeated the air on this evening.

With falling hearts, the knights saw that one of the men heard the sound and turned, calling to his fellows. In an instant, they were returning. A man lit a torch and held it high. Soon its light fell across the pair of knights where they crouched.

Daymen rose to his feet in one fluid motion, drawing his sword as he did so. Cemil was slower to react, and he fumbled for his sword even as their enemies charged them. Daymen moved in front of the boy to defend him until his weapon was ready. He met the first man with his sword, killing his foe with the first blow.

As he engaged the next enemy to reach them, he could hear Cemil cursing behind him. Then, the hiss of steel that signaled a sword being drawn cut through the air. Daymen focused on his opponent, knowing that Cemil had a weapon in hand and could now defend himself.

The men he found himself facing were good, and it was obvious that many of them had trained hard. They were no match for Daymen, but they were still worthy fighters. King Jemis had hired the best to hunt down his rebellious knights.

The battle ended almost as quickly as it had begun, with several dead and the rest fleeing. Daymen turned to congratulate his young friend on a good fight. His stomach tightened with fear when he saw that Cemil was down, blood darkening his tunic with its vile stain.

He rushed to the boy's side, putting one hand over the wound to staunch the flow of blood. "Cemil?" he queried, the concern he felt creeping into his voice.

The young knight stared up at his hero with eyes that even now were losing focus. He coughed once, leaving flecks of blood on his chin. The wound appeared to be fatal, and it wasn't the only one, either. Daymen could see a ragged cut across the boy's sword arm. He was too young to be engaged in a fight where the numbers were so overwhelming.

"Leave me," Cemil whispered. " Don't let me slow you down." His voice was very weak. Daymen could tell that the boy was hanging on to life by a thread. His throat tightened and his vision blurred.

He stayed with Cemil. The boy lost consciousness, and the ragged breaths that he managed to draw in were soon coming further and further apart. A short time later, he exhaled and the breath shuddered from his body for the last time.

Daymen sat by the boy's side for some time, his head bent as he said a prayer for him. He should never have allowed the younger knight to travel with him; he should've sent him off on his own. His poor judgment had cost Cemil his life.

Perhaps the boy would've died if he'd ridden with someone else, but Daymen doubted it. King Jemis wanted him, not any of the other knights. He had been the first one to walk away, thus he took the blame for the transgressions of all the others. Whether Jemis had to hunt him in this life or the next, Daymen would pay for acting against the King.

Daymen tried to banish the thoughts, but despair was creeping into his bones. Already its heavy shroud hung over his heart. He had to cast away his regrets and move on. Cemil's death would not be in vain. He would see to that.

With some trepidation, he raised the young knight off the ground. The boy's horse snorted with nervous energy as Daymen tied Cemil in the saddle. The smell of blood was thick in the air, and Daymen had to quiet the stallion as it danced back and forth. "I'm sorry," Daymen whispered. Then he smacked his sword against the horse's rump.

The stallion neighed in terror and shot off through the forest. Weighed down by Cemil's body, it would appear as though the stallion bore a live rider. Its hoof prints would leave a false trail for his trackers to follow. Perhaps that would buy him some time so he could get to the border. Cemil would have approved, he thought.

Daymen blinked away a tear that threatened to spill from his eyes. Wearily, the knight saddled Vesahn and mounted his stallion. With a heavy heart and a bloody sword, he rode off into the night.

Chapter 7

Seven wagons rode out of Sicuth painted a fresh coat of pink with the soft light of dawn. The shadows of night were still thick on the ground, stretching across the plains that separated the border city from the treacherous Stormpeaks. As the wagons rolled down the old neglected road, guards circled the train on proud warhorses.

Falkris sat straight in Misan's saddle, her back to the canvas of the rising sun. Dax stood at the horse's side, his gaze attentive as he watched the wagons pass. Misan was one of the few horses that would tolerate the wolf's presence without becoming skittish. The mare and the canine had an understanding that Falkris couldn't fathom.

The warrior watched with silent approval as Netria, once again her second in command, rode a tight ring around the wagons, keeping the guards on their toes and alert. Falkris was glad that her friend had decided to join the expedition. She hadn't realized that she'd missed her old, rough life until it had crept up behind her in the form of the scarred woman she had once fought beside.

Rhen drove the wagon at the very front, despite Falkris' many objections. If he was at the rear, there'd be more time to react to any danger that might strike the front first. She wanted to prevent danger from reaching him, but Rhen was the type who wanted to meet adventure head on, not watch as others dealt with it. He faced the fierce Stormpeaks with a huge grin, his spirit quickened by the thrill of the risks yet to come.

Lianna rode inside the wagon just behind his. Since she had first moved into it, she had not emerged from the wagon. Her door was kept closed, and the only one allowed to enter was a mute servant girl. The night before last, Falkris had called on Lianna to be certain that she'd finished her preparations for the journey. When a loud noise had come from Lianna's wagon, Falkris had stopped short. Green light glowed through the cracks in the shuttered windows, and smoke had poured out from under the door. A moment later, Falkris had heard steps coming to the door and had hurried away to avoid detection. The door of the little wagon had been flung open, and Lianna had peered out into the darkness. "Who's there?" The warrior had crept away silently, her heart hammering in her chest.

Falkris didn't know what Lianna was, or why she was fleeing Ravenia. All she knew was that she didn't trust the woman at all. She vowed to watch Lianna vigilantly, for Rhen's sake, if not for her own burning curiosity. Perhaps as the journey continued, she would be able to draw Lianna out of her shell and discover some of the woman's secrets.

Keth interrupted Falkris' thoughts when he waved up at her. A huge smile colored his face as he grinned like the village idiot, which was what he had been before Rhen had rescued him from the ridicule and scorn of his community. She shook her head as she waved back at him. Though Keth was lacking in intelligence, Falkris had to admit that the man had a big heart and a strong sword arm.

She reached down to rub Dax behind the ears, then urged Misan toward the caravan with a light squeeze of her legs. As the mare picked her way forward through the tall grass, Dax remained out on the plains. The wolf knew without being told that he couldn't come with his mistress. Falkris saluted Netria as she passed. Returning the gesture with bright eyes, Netria continued on her rounds.

Falkris rode Misan up to the front of the chain of wagons. Rhen grinned at her. His enthusiasm never ceased to amaze her, even after the years that she had spent guarding his life with her own. Seeing him so happy, she felt a smile tug at the corners of her mouth.

"Well, Kris? How far ahead did you scout?"

Slowing Misan to an easy trot beside the wagon, Falkris

moved from the mare's back to the vehicle. Misan kept pace next to them, not straying from her duties even while her rider's attention was diverted. She was incredibly well trained.

"Well," Falkris rasped, "we rode hard, almost to the foothills, then turned back sometime around dusk. The ride back was dark, but the way was clear. We just followed this old road."

"Don't you sleep?" he asked through a proud smile.

As she rubbed at her throat, she shrugged. Rhen handed her a canteen and after giving him a grateful smile, she took a swig of it. She hadn't had much to drink. For the entire day and night before the caravan's departure, she and Misan had scouted ahead to make certain the way was safe. Dax had come along. Falkris had not slept the whole time, nor paused for rest or a meal.

Misan was exhausted, though obedient. Falkris wasn't much better, but she wasn't about to rest yet. She planned to unsaddle her mare and attend to several matters before she allowed herself the luxury of sleep. Most important, she needed to have a talk with Lianna.

"Why don't you take a nap?" Rhen suggested, gesturing to the wagon cabin behind him with a jerk of his head. His thick blonde hair ruffled in the wind, making him look handsome in a roguish way.

Falkris smiled as she declined. "No." She didn't bother to explain. Instead, she jumped down from the moving wagon and took hold of Misan's reins. As the caravan moved on, she removed the mare's saddle and set her free. The mare waited a moment, then trotted off to find rest in her own way. When she was ready, Misan would catch up, and Dax would watch over her in the meantime.

Falkris jogged back to the caravan and heaved the saddle onto the back of the rear wagon. She climbed onto the front of the wagon and sat beside the guard posted there for a while, needing to rest. After her long ride, she was a bit shaky and saddle sore. Her stomach was protesting from neglect.

The guard said nothing; he just kept his eyes open and alert. Her guards were trained well, as she had made certain they were. When she rode out to scout, Falkris had left Netria in charge of honing the guards' skills. The day had been well spent.

She watched the guards as they circled around the caravan to scan the surrounding plains. They were doubling as scouts. If danger did manage to penetrate their perimeter, all of them would be ready to ride back to the caravan in an instant. They rotated shifts so that there were always five guards and their mounts resting on the wagons while the other fifteen rode wide.

Falkris liked the system. Very efficient while they were out on the plains, it would work just as well in the foothills. Once they were in the mountains, the guards would have to stay with the caravan as they went through the narrow pass. That was, if the High Pass was still open. No one had dared to attempt the journey in years. The storms had been too lethal.

The archers would truly earn their way once the expedition entered the mountains. Amial, Bendal and three others who were expert shots with a bow had come along. They would spend their time on the roofs of the wagons. From that vantage point, they would be able to keep a wary eye on the road ahead and the cliffs around them.

After a short break, Falkris gave in to her drive to accomplish more before she rested. She leapt down from the wagon and made her way to Lianna's wagon. Climbing up on the seat at the front, she nodded to the man driving the horses and knocked on the cabin door. As she waited for Lianna to answer, she looked down at the man. If her memory was correct, he was a famous artist who longed to go to Jenestra to paint the exotic country. Now he was working for his passage there like everyone else. He seemed to be enjoying it; he looked as eager as Rhen.

The door opened a crack and the mute servant peered out. Falkris tried to see beyond the girl, but the wagon behind her was shrouded in darkness. "Falkris Vilenti to see your mistress," she growled.

The girl looked alarmed at her rough voice. When she started to withdraw, a soft command from behind set her to opening the door. With an almost rough shove, she pushed Falkris into the wagon, then left the warrior and Lianna alone. Falkris caught a glimpse of her sitting down beside the artist before the door swung closed.

As soon as the door shut, the outside light was blocked out, and Falkris found herself in near darkness. She could just see Lianna's outline as the woman moved. Lianna opened the window shutters and light streamed in. The rays fell across her flawless skin and lit her golden curls with a gentle shine. Her green eyes danced.

"Falkris," she said, "I was wondering when you'd come to visit me."

The warrior tried not to look surprised. "Oh?"

"Yes," Lianna purred as she sat down in a chair. She didn't invite Falkris to be seated in the cramped quarters, so the warrior remained standing. Falkris tried not to let her weakness show, though she was certain that Lianna could see her trembling from exhaustion.

Lianna cocked her head as she continued. "You see, Falkris, you and I are very similar. We are predators. We hunt those who oppose what we believe in. The only difference is that we fight with different weapons."

Falkris didn't see the Lianna who had begged to be allowed to go on the journey in the woman before her. This was someone else. The creature who had stood before her that day had been nothing more than a convincing mask. Falkris narrowed her piercing gray eyes. "Tell me, Lianna, what is your weapon?"

"Ah, but I think you know, my proud falcon." The edge in her voice was almost intimidating.

Falkris' heart sank. She'd been right about Lianna all along. If only Rhen had listened to her instead of his heart, this dangerous woman would not be traveling with them. "Your tongue, my lady?"

Lianna smiled, and a throaty chuckle escaped her. "Perhaps. There are many ways to win a war, and that is one of them." Sitting forward, she fixed her eyes on Falkris as though to compel an answer from her. "You know, don't you?"

The warrior put one hand on her sword, almost as a reflex. All of a sudden, she felt as though she should be defending herself from something, but she couldn't tell what. "Know what?"

Lianna rose to her feet and moved closer to Falkris. Her eyes narrowed, glistening dangerously. She raised her hands a little, looking like she was about to attack Falkris. Then, calm spread over her in a wave and she relaxed. "Very well, Falkris. I'll play your game. Until then, please be seated. You need to rest."

Falkris seated herself on the bed. She restrained a sigh of relief even as she pushed herself to stay awake and alert in the Lianna's presence. The woman seemed to think that Falkris knew something. As far as the mercenary was aware, she knew nothing.

Lianna catered to Falkris politely. She poured her a glass of tea and offered her a pastry. Then she sat down in the chair again, her calculating eyes focused on Falkris. In the cramped wagon they were so close they were almost touching, a situation that Falkris did not relish.

Falkris nibbled on the pastry, careful not to upset her ravenous stomach. Then she gratefully drank the tea, which had a somewhat sweet taste. The liquid slipped down her throat, easing the burning sensation that ailed her whenever she spoke.

A few seconds later, she felt very heavy, and somewhere deep inside of her, she realized that she'd been drugged. The rest of her longed to sleep. Her eyes shut, and tiny prickles ran along her entire body as the muscles relaxed. As Falkris lost awareness of the waking world, darkness enveloped her.

Chapter 8

Falkris kept her eyes closed and her body still. Until it was an absolute necessity, she didn't want to betray that she was awake. She could hear Lianna's slippered feet whispering across the floor. The wagon was motionless; they had stopped.

Hopefully Lianna hadn't harmed anyone while Falkris slept the precious hours away in a drugged haze. There was no telling how long Falkris had been lying there, helpless. As it was, she wasn't certain that she had the strength to stand. She wanted to make a complete recovery before she moved against Lianna.

What she couldn't understand was why Lianna had drugged her. As far as she could tell, nothing had happened to her while she slept, so it had not been the other woman's intention to harm her in any way. However, Falkris couldn't tell what the world *outside* the wagon was like. She couldn't hear anything at all, not even the horses neighing to one another or guards calling out. Only silence prevailed in the wagon. Everyone outside could be dead, for all she knew.

She almost jumped at the touch of a cool hand against her forehead. The soft rustling of cloth thundered in the silence as Lianna moved closer to her. "Falkris," Lianna whispered, "you are a very dangerous woman."

Falkris didn't dare to move. She barely managed to take deep, even breaths. Her hand itched to seize her sword and draw it in defense against Lianna. By some act of will, she restrained herself and lay still, feigning sleep. The hand withdrew from her forehead, and she sensed that Lianna moved away from her. She strained her ears for a sound to betray what the woman was doing, but nothing reached her senses.

Then, bright light glowed against the lids of her eyes. The light dimmed abruptly, as quickly as it had brightened. She risked opening one eye to a slit. Lianna was standing with her back to her, cradling something in her hands that emitted green light. As Falkris watched, Lianna leaned closer to the source of the light and whispered something. Light flared once, and there was a faint answer from somewhere beyond Lianna. The voice that whispered back was feminine, but the words were too muddled for Falkris to tell more. Lianna continued to speak to the light for some time. When the conversation ended, Lianna put the source of the green light in a chest on her desk and locked it. She put the key on a chain around her neck.

Falkris closed her eyes as the woman turned towards her and approached. Lianna bent down to speak into her ear. "Aren't you awake yet, my pretty kestrel? I thought you were stronger than that. Perhaps I was wrong. No matter. You'll not leave this wagon until I return."

The swish of skirts and footsteps signaled Lianna's departure. Falkris counted to fifty following the click of the door closing. After that, she sat up slowly and examined herself. Her boots and armor had been removed, but other than that she was untouched. She put her shoes and armor back on and performed a quick search of the wagon cabin.

When she opened the shudders a crack, she looked out on a campfire. Guards who weren't on duty were clustered around it. Falkris could see Rhen's golden curls glowing in the firelight. Keth loomed beside him, a silent but deadly presence.

Falkris located Lianna right away, for she was the only woman in the entire camp wearing a skirt. The rest were all in breeches and were armed to the teeth with weaponry. Falkris watched her to see where she was going. Her path moved around the camp slowly, but it was obvious that Rhen was her final destination.

Falkris closed the shutters again and went to the door. As she reached for the doorknob, a strange feeling swept over her. Her hand kept turning aside from the doorknob, and when she touched it, her fingers slipped. She cursed under her breath, her voice sounding more like a dry hiss than words. With an irritated snarl, she seized the doorknob with both hands and turned it slowly, but she had to fight for every inch that it moved. After several difficult moments, she got the door open and stepped outside. She was only too glad to close the door behind her.

As soon as she was free of the wagon, a world of sounds reached her ears. The strange silence that held sway over the wagon was gone. Falkris looked around to see if anyone had noticed her, then leapt down from the wagon on the side away from the fire. Using the cover of darkness, she circled the fire until she was behind Rhen.

Her eyes scanned the campsite. Lianna had almost reached Rhen. When Falkris stepped out of the shadows behind him, showing herself, Lianna's eyes widened in surprise, but the reaction was so fleeting that Falkris couldn't be certain she had seen it at all.

Lianna diverted her path from her original goal and began making her way towards Falkris. With a grim smile, Falkris turned and faded into the darkness. She was certain, as she jogged a short distance away from the camp, that Lianna would follow her. The woman would hunt her, but Falkris would not make her give chase too long. She looked forward to this confrontation.

A rustling in the grass alerted her to Dax's presence. As he circled close to her, his pale yellow eyes glowed in the darkness. She reached down to scratch behind his ears. "Guard," she whispered. As commanded, he faded into the plains behind her. If Lianna attacked her, Dax would help her if she needed him.

When Lianna caught up to Falkris, the warrior's hand was still moist from the wolf's parting lick. In the moonlight, Lianna's blonde curls looked like fine silver. Her skin was white, all of its color stolen by the moon.

"The kestrel has escaped," Falkris growled.

"So I see," Lianna returned, arching one eyebrow. "And it seems you weren't asleep at all. How clever."

Falkris moved a step closer. On the plains, with Dax behind her, she was in control. She was meeting Lianna on her chosen ground, and she wasn't afraid to display her confidence. "Why did you drug me?"

Lianna smiled. "Do you want the truth, or the answer you expect to hear?"

"Truth."

"Very well. I drugged you out of concern for your health. You were white as a sheet. I can't have my rival weakened by her own frustrated perfectionism."

"Rival?" Falkris spat. That she did not believe Lianna was an unspoken understanding between them.

"Of course," Lianna purred. "You alone can stand in my way. You demonstrated that already this evening when you walked through my warding spell."

Falkris didn't answer for a moment. She considered what Lianna was saying. If it was true at all, the woman had some sort of magical ability. Magic had been dead in Ravenia for centuries, if not longer. Ever since the last dragon had been slain, magic had fled the world. Was the woman insane, or incredibly powerful? "You're talking about magic," Falkris said slowly. "Magic doesn't exist."

"And a wolf can't be trained," Lianna countered. "Both are accepted truths, and yet you and I see them for their faults. Don't deny what you've seen with your own eyes."

"Sight lies."

"So do men."

Falkris couldn't think of any suitable argument. Magic would explain many things. Her difficulty opening the door, the strange bubble of silence within Lianna's wagon, the green light. But she couldn't accept it without changing beliefs she had held for decades, so she fell back on her suspicions. "Why tell me this?"

Lianna smiled. "Because I sense a kindred spirit in you. It's been a long time since I've encountered a woman as strong as I. To meet one at last intrigues me."

Falkris raised her own eyebrows, a mixture of surprise and confusion washing over her. She wasn't certain what to think of Lianna. "Who are you really?"

"Who are you? I think we're both lying. Until you can admit the truth to me, I'll tell you no more than I choose to."

"And what do you choose to tell me?" Falkris rasped. Her throat was drier than a desert. She longed for a drink, yet she dared not take her eyes off Lianna for a moment, for Rhen's sake as well as her own.

"I choose to tell you nothing. But I do ask one thing of you."

Falkris grunted rather than tax her voice any longer. Her throat was already very sore this evening, so much that she could barely rasp the words out. What she needed was water, without the taint of sedative drugs.

Lianna smiled. "Be my friend."

"What?" Falkris snapped in complete surprise. Her mouth turned down in a suspicious frown.

Lianna laughed. "I believe you heard me. At least ... be civil. Perhaps you can learn to trust me, with time."

At that moment, they were approached by a slim figure. Falkris recognized Amial. The young woman had her bow slung over her shoulder. With eyes downcast, she reported straight to her superior. "Falkris, ma'am, Netria and I request your presence at the fire."

Falkris looked to Lianna, wondering what to do. Lianna sent her a reassuring smile. "Don't worry, Kris. Dax will keep me out of trouble," she said in a mocking tone.

With some reluctance, Falkris left with Amial. Glancing over her shoulder, she was perturbed to see Lianna bending down to scratch Dax behind the ears. She was tempted to tell the wolf to kill Lianna, but she shook her head and dismissed the idea. Lianna was far too interesting to die. Yet.

She followed Amial to the fire. As Netria moved over to make room for her, Amial sank down on her other side. Netria leaned in and whispered in Falkris' ear. "She drugged you, didn't she?" Falkris nodded. Netria narrowed her eyes in anger. "I'll kill her."

Falkris shook her head. "No. I want her alive for now. She and I have an understanding."

Netria barked a laugh. "Just like Dax and Misan. I tell you, it's not natural."

Falkris just smiled, not bothering to deign that with an answer. Feeling eyes on her, she turned to see Amial staring at her. "What?"

Amial flushed, her skin turning a darker shade of red in the dancing firelight. "Sorry. Netria has told me so much about you—"

Falkris grinned. "Has she?" She glanced at the scarred mercenary. "What has she told you?"

Amial smiled shyly. "Did you really take an arrow for her?"

Falkris nodded. "That I did." She pulled away her tunic to reveal a round scar marring her skin. Amial's eyes widened. With genuine admiration shining in her eyes, she leaned in to look at the scar.

Falkris shifted her gaze to Netria, who was grinning. Falkris shared a long look with her as if to ask whether bringing Amial had been wise. The girl was obviously unblooded, never having fought or killed before. Netria just nodded, offering some reassurance with her widening grin. Falkris had once been as young and naïve as Amial. Like Falkris, this girl only needed guidance to get her through.

"I could never do that," Amial said. "I could never take an arrow for another person."

"Well," Falkris said, "if you care enough about a person, you'll do some stupid things for them. Netria has almost killed herself for me a couple of times, too. Friends do that."

She looked across the fire at Lianna, who was standing in the darkness just beyond the circle of light. A strange look was on her face, one of incredible loneliness. Had she heard what Falkris had said? Silently, Lianna turned and walked away into the night.

A sharp jab in her ribs brought Falkris back to the conversation beside the fire. Netria was looking at her with a strange expression. "What's wrong with that woman?"

Falkris shook her head and turned her eyes to the fire. She didn't know. As the flames crackled, she stared into their depths. Though she didn't understand Lianna at all, she knew that their fates were somehow tied together. Someday, she would know why.

Chapter 9

By midmorning of the next day, the caravan was in the foothills and the Stormpeaks dominated the horizon. Lightning danced among the peaks, and the sound of thunder rolling down from the mountains was constant. Falkris reined Misan in and shaded her eyes as she peered at the dark, perpetual storm.

Out of the corner of her eye, she saw Dax flicker past, weaving in and out of the thick grass. For her benefit, he had shown himself briefly. She smiled in acknowledgement. Misan snorted a greeting. For a moment, all was still as the three stood together in the embrace of nature.

The warrior had fallen behind the trail of wagons. Without being commanded, Misan galloped to catch up. Falkris urged her warhorse alongside Lianna's wagon. As if on cue, the beautiful woman emerged.

She smiled a bright greeting. Falkris jerked her head towards the mountains. "Do you think we'll make it?" she rasped.

Lianna nodded. "Of course." She knelt down and lowered her voice so that only Falkris could hear her. "No one has managed the journey in hundreds of years. Do you know why?" The warrior shook her head. "Because they didn't have a contact on the other side."

Falkris wasn't certain that she'd heard right. If Lianna was telling the truth, she had somehow managed to communicate with someone in Jenestra. Perhaps she'd done so with magic, but the very concept seemed outrageous. Falkris wanted to question Lianna further, but she was already standing. Smiling mockingly, she turned to a guard riding on the other side of the wagon, ending the conversation.

Falkris urged Misan away from the wagon in disgust. Talking to Lianna was like playing a complicated game of strategy in which the rules were made up as one went along. She wouldn't lose this match by taking the bait and pursuing this latest tidbit of information.

Amial rode in on her own sturdy mare, taking her turn to rest on the wagon for a while. A shy smile graced her face as she passed Falkris. The warrior nodded in return, then rode wide of the caravan to search for any signs of danger. She ended up scouting several miles ahead. Dax loped at her side as she rode.

She could see nothing ahead that was worth worrying about. Signs that others had passed through the area weren't recent. Turning off of the old road, Falkris picked her way between the rolling hills.

Misan crested a high rise and stopped short at Falkris' command. A farmstead was below, nestled amidst the hills. Smoke rose from the chimney, and there was activity near the house. Falkris longed to ride down to the farm and talk with the farmers, but she knew that it wouldn't be wise to approach on her own. She turned Misan and walked her back to the wagons.

When she reached the head wagon, she was somewhat annoyed to see that Lianna had joined Rhen. Once she'd snapped a salute, she told him what she'd seen. He nodded to himself as he considered. "We should send someone to speak to the farmers. They may know something about the mountains that could be useful."

His gaze flashed over the hills, then rose to the mountains that loomed ever closer by the moment. "We should reach the Stormpeaks shortly before nightfall. Why don't you take a couple of guards with you and investigate? You can meet us at the camp at nightfall."

"I'm going with you," Lianna asserted immediately.

Rhen and Falkris looked at her in disbelief. Falkris was the first to recover. "No."

The lord seconded her command. "Kris is right, Lady Lianna. It will be too dangerous."

Lianna ignored him, as though she knew that the decision wasn't his. She looked straight at Falkris, challenging her resolve. "You'll need me." The intensity in her green eyes filled Falkris with premonition. Did Lianna know something about this particular farm?

The warrior nodded reluctantly. "Fine. I'll take Lianna and Netria. Bendal will be in charge."

"He's a good man," Rhen said. From his face, Falkris could tell that he had not expected her to agree. Stunned to think of the delicate lady riding into danger, his hands had a slight tremor.

Falkris gave him a reassuring look. "I'll protect Lianna as I would you, Rhen. I swear it to you."

Rhen managed a smile. "I know your word is more than good."

Falkris nodded with an amused smile as she rubbed at the scar on her throat. She looked past Rhen at Lianna. "Let's go."

The three women rode out less than an hour later. Lianna changed into breeches and a tunic, which were far more practical than her skirts, though the men's clothing revealed more of her figure. The male guards were more than appreciative, much to the distress of Lord Tahnuil.

As they rode through the hills, Falkris was impressed to see that Lianna was an excellent rider. She would have attributed it to part of her noble upbringing, but Falkris knew that it wasn't considered proper for ladies to ride any way but sidesaddle. Lianna must have learned how to ride with a normal saddle. How and why would remain a mystery, like so many other things about the lady.

Misan picked her way towards the farm without any guidance from Falkris. The warmare knew as well as her mistress where they were going, as if the horse could read her rider's mind. They crested the rise from which Falkris had first seen the farmstead. The warrior disliked exposing herself so openly at the top of the hill, but this position gave her a good view of the farm below. Large, it consisted of a main house, several barns and quarters for the farmhands. The lowing of cattle drifted up to meet them.

Falkris flicked her hand as a signal to the others, and the three women rode down the hill towards the farm. As they descended, Falkris made certain that her sword was loose in her scabbard. With a gesture, she directed Netria to take a position on the other side of Lady Lianna, so that the two warriors flanked her.

The farm, as they neared, appeared normal enough. Even so, dread set its icy fingers into Falkris' stomach and crawled up the length of her spine. The sense that danger awaited them was almost overwhelming, yet she saw nothing out of the ordinary.

As they rode up to the front of the house, Netria called out to anyone who might be near. Silence returned her greeting. Falkris dismounted uncertainly. As she walked towards the house, she saw that the door hung ajar. Nervous despite herself, she drew her sword.

Climbing the steps with caution, she strained her ears for any sound. "Hello?" she called out. She stopped for a moment on the porch, then gently pushed the door open further with the tip of her sword. Just inside, a woman lay on the floor, a pool of blood seeping out from under her. The kill had been recent.

Falkris turned to signal to Netria to stay with Lianna and stepped over the dead woman to investigate further. The house was empty of any other sign of life, and it appeared that nothing had been disturbed or looted. Whoever had killed the woman had not stolen from the farm family.

The last room she came to was the kitchen. A fire was still burning and the fresh warm scent of bread baking filled the air. A pot of water boiled over just as she entered the room. The kitchen door banged open in the wind.

Falkris sheathed her sword and put the fire out, not wishing for the house to burn down while she investigated further. Removing the water from the hearth with some towels wrapped around the handle, she clumsily set it outside to cool. The bread would have to stay.

Falkris hurried back through the house to the front door. Standing beside Lianna, who was still mounted, Netria was looking around at the farm, a strange expression on her face. She was very pale, which made Falkris wonder if the pair had seen something during her absence. When Netria saw that Falkris had returned, she nodded to the warrior.

Falkris was about to question them, but the sound of the cattle bawling in terror cut off her words. She turned towards the sound, her heart leaping in her chest. The cattle had to be in the pasture beyond the near hill. Whoever the murderer was, she knew they would find him and make him pay for his crimes.

Without being told, Lianna dismounted and came to stand with her two companions. Falkris knew that Misan would look after the horses, so she didn't bother to tie them in place. The three women rounded the farmhouse and passed by the back door. Falkris bent down to examine the dirt next to the door for clues as to what had happened at the farm. Netria joined her.

"Footprints," Netria said, "a man, judging by the shoe size and the depth of the print." She pointed to a round impression beside the tracks. "A walking stick, do you think?"

Lianna spoke behind them. "A staff."

Falkris and Netria both looked over their shoulders at the woman. After a moment, Netria nodded. "Aye, it could be that, too."

The two warriors rose to their feet, continuing towards the sound of the cattle. A well-traveled dirt path led away into the hills behind the house. As the women followed the path at a brisk walk, Dax loped up to follow them. Passing through the hills in silence, all three of them focused their minds and senses on the sound of the cattle bawling in terror.

They knew that they had drawn near to their destination when they stumbled upon the dead body of a young man who looked like he'd been stabbed in the neck with some form of dagger. Falkris averted her eyes quickly, as did Netria. They both looked at Lianna to be certain that the woman was okay.

Lianna was very pale, and she swayed slightly. Fearing that the lady would faint, Falkris took her arm in a gentle grasp. "Lianna."

With great effort, Lianna removed her eyes from the corpse. She looked at the warrior and smiled. "Thanks, Kris. I'll be fine."

Falkris supported her through the next few steps, but as they left the corpse behind them, Lianna regained control. She moved away from the warrior and walked on her own. They increased their pace.

The path opened up abruptly into a short valley. A stream from the mountains laughed its way across the little depression amidst the hills. The cattle were backed up against the stream. On either side of their pressed mass, hills slowed their escape.

Several men lay dead between the path and the stream. More lay among the cattle, their slain bodies already trampled beyond recognition by the panicked livestock. The smell of blood made the beasts nervous. They could stampede at any moment.

As the women watched, a robed man slit the last farm worker across the throat and tossed him aside. When the murderer turned to look at them, Falkris saw that he was holding a dagger with a hooked blade glistening red with blood in his hand. In his other hand he clutched a long staff.

Falkris drew her sword. Beside her, Netria brought out her bow. Both moved so that they stood in front of Lianna. As Falkris began her advance on the robed man, one of Netria's arrows whistled past her shoulder, heading straight and true towards its target. The missile hit a wall of red energy before it could reach the robed man. Light engulfed it. Fizzling and smoking, it fell harmlessly to the ground. Falkris stopped short, her eyes widening. She had to reassert her grip on her sword, lest she drop it. As it was, her free hand was shaking as she continued her advance.

"Wait," Lianna said from behind her. "Let me handle this."

Falkris paused. "Are you insane?" she growled. Beside her,

Dax echoed her sentiments.

Lianna ignored Falkris as she strode forward to face the man before her. He seemed to notice her for the first time. Perhaps in the lady he at last saw a true challenge. Squaring his shoulders, the man shifted his feet so that he stood with a firm stance on the ground. As Falkris watched, he sheathed his bloody knife and put both hands on his staff.

Lianna took up a position in front of him. She raised her arms, her delicate fingers clenched. Falkris could see that she was shaking slightly. She was afraid. What did she think she was going to do?

The robed man raised his staff and pointed it straight at the three women. Falkris brought her sword up in a desperate attempt to defend herself against what she instinctively knew was coming. Power hummed in the air, molding itself into something new that would come for her and the others soon.

Behind her she heard Netria curse. The mercenary drew an arrow back on her bow and prepared to take aim again, but Falkris held up one hand to halt her. The battle was no longer in their hands.

Lianna had closed her eyes and was whispering to herself. Falkris could almost hear the words. Like a fly buzzing just beyond hearing, at some level the sound registered, though she couldn't actually hear it. As Lianna continued to speak, a green light began to glow around her. The aura did not cast any shadows; it was simply there, coating the woman like a second skin.

The man leveled his staff at Lianna, and a chain of fire snaked out to wrap around her. Falkris sucked in a nervous breath as she watched, helpless to act. The fire tightened around Lianna, but it didn't singe her clothing or hair.

The green light began to expand, pushing the fire away. Lianna managed to get one arm free of the chains of fire, then the other. When both were free, she wrapped her hands around the chain and pushed it from her body. When she stepped free of it, it had already set the grass on fire. With a quick movement, she lifted it from the ground and hurled it at the man.

Not expecting opposition, let alone to have his own fire used against him, he almost wasn't able to deflect the chain. While he was distracted, Dax shot towards him, stretching his long legs to cover the distance between them quickly.

The wolf met the wall of red light that had deflected Netria's arrow and passed *through* it. He was on the man in an instant, his jaws tearing out his enemy's throat. The staff rolled away from them and came to rest at Lianna's feet. The chain of fire dissipated into nothing.

In the silence that followed, Dax rose from his kill and licked his jaws. He turned to look at Falkris, his tongue lolling with joy. Pleased with himself, he ran back to his mistress. When she reached down to pat him on the head, her hand came away from his thick fur bloody.

Lianna turned around to look at them with her beautiful green eyes. She was about to say something, but her eyes rolled back in her head and she crumpled to the ground. Falkris cursed and ran to see if she was okay.

Behind her, Netria stood with her mouth agape and wide eyes. All color had fled from her weathered face, and she looked as though she was about to faint herself. Falkris cursed again. "Damn it, Netria! Help me!"

The scarred mercenary recovered and hurried to help her friend. Together, they picked Lianna up. Falkris found that the woman was light enough for her to carry on her own. "Netria," she commanded, "bring the staff and dagger."

As they walked back towards the farmhouse, the sun began to set in the distance. Falkris cursed again. If they didn't hurry back, she knew that Rhen would come looking for them, and she wasn't certain how she could explain everything to him, especially why Lianna was unconscious. Gritting her teeth, she shifted her burden and increased her pace.

Chapter 10

Falkris carried Lianna up the stairs and kicked open a bedroom door. She lay the woman down on the quilted bed and took a deep breath. Getting Lianna to the farmhouse had been difficult, even with her strength and Lianna's light weight.

Netria stood just behind Falkris in the doorway. "Kris?"

"Yeah?" She sat down wearily on the bed beside Lianna.

"Was that *magic*?"

Falkris raised her eyes to the scarred face of her friend. "I think so."

Netria backed up one step, the dagger and staff limp in her hands. "How's that possible? Do you think she's been possessed or something?"

Falkris turned to look at Lianna. Even in sleep her golden curls framed her face perfectly, but she was very pale. Tiny worry lines marred her normally flawless face. She looked exhausted. "No."

Netria leaned against the doorframe. "But magic's been dead for centuries, Kris. When the last dragon was slain, all magic died."

"That man had magic. Magic is not dead."

Falkris watched as several arguments crossed Netria's mind. Each time she thought of something, she opened her mouth to protest. Then she shut it tight, thinking about it some more. Finally, she deflated. "I don't understand."

"Neither do I."

Just then, Lianna stirred. She sat up and yawned. At first, her eyes were clouded and distant, but they soon cleared to their usual green brilliance. Looking around the room in dazed confusion, her eyes came to rest on Falkris and she relaxed.

"Did you stop him?" she whispered.

Falkris inclined her head. "Dax tore his throat out."

"Yes," Lianna murmured, "I remember now." She raised one trembling hand to her temple and closed her eyes. "I tried to stop him, but I've never been in a magical duel before. I've never even cast a real spell."

She shifted her eyes first to Netria, who was eyeing her with a suspicious expression, then to the floor. "Did I at least manage to break the shield guarding him?"

Falkris shook her head. "No."

Lianna's eyes snapped up to meet hers. "Then … how did Dax kill him? Nothing should've been able to penetrate that shield." Her voice was low, disbelieving.

"I don't know."

Netria sighed and turned on her heel to leave the room. Before Netria stalked away, Falkris saw the light of strong emotions burning in her eyes. Gazing after her old friend, she wondered what had upset the easy-going woman.

Lianna remained oblivious to any offense she might have given. She frowned, her eyebrows almost coming together over the bridge of her nose. Muttering to herself, she stared at nothing. "I don't understand this at all. Dax should not have been able to cross through the shield. I wish I could speak to Alihandre about this."

Deciding that now was not the time to press Lianna for details, Falkris sat still and silent while Lianna puzzled things out for herself. When she realized that the lady would say no more, Falkris swallowed before rasping out, "I'm confused."

Lianna looked at her in surprise, not expecting Falkris to admit her deficiencies with such ease. She smiled slowly after a moment. "About what?"

Falkris stood, her frustration tangible. "You."

"Me?" Lianna rose to her feet as well. Unsteady for a moment, she put one hand on Falkris' shoulder to steady herself. "Why, little falcon, have you run into a trap?" The old cunning was back in her eyes. Her smile darkened. "Perhaps I can set you free."

Falkris jerked her shoulder away from Lianna, refusing to offer her any support. "Come on," she growled. "We can't keep Rhen waiting." Without waiting for a response, she left the room.

Lianna's smile was filled with mischief. "Very well. If you wish to flee from the truth, I won't be the one to stop you."

Falkris stopped short at the stairs and turned to face the other woman. "Listen," she hissed, "if you want me to be your friend, I expect you to treat me with respect. I'm not a bird. And, you're not incapable of answering questions."

Lianna smiled brightly. Falkris turned back to the stairs and descended with quick steps. The other woman followed at a slower pace. "Suit yourself, my little kestrel, but we shall see which wind the bird chooses when the storm blows in."

Refusing to be baited, Falkris didn't reply. All she knew was that the strange premonition that filled her at Lianna's words was not good. She hoped it was unfounded, but she somehow knew, deep inside, that the bad luck that followed Lianna was far from over.

The trio of women rode hard to catch up with the others. By the time they arrived, it was well after sunset. On the way there, they were hailed several times in the darkness by scouts Rhen had sent out to search for them as soon as night had fallen. When the three women rode into camp, their number had swelled considerably with guards.

Falkris picked out Rhen at once. He was pacing in the darkness just beyond the campfire. Keth ambled behind him, matching the nobleman step for step. When Rhen saw them, he broke into a run.

Falkris dismounted and lowered her eyes, expecting to be reprimanded. Instead, Rhen attempted to sweep her up in a hug. Since she was two hand spans taller, it was almost impossible. In the end, her surprised reaction sent both of them stumbling until they crashed to the ground.

"Thank the gods you're okay!" he cried.

Falkris stared at him, confused. "Rhen?" she questioned, uncertain.

Rhen stood and helped her to her feet. "Kris, I was so worried. We've been friends for so long—" His eyes moved past her to a point just behind her. "Lady Lianna—"

Falkris moved aside to let him approach the woman. She watched with some confusion as he bowed to Lianna and placed a gentle kiss on her hand. How could he react so differently? So rough with one and so tender with the other, yet giving each a similar degree of affection. After a moment, she nodded to herself. Rhen loved them both, but in different ways. She preferred it that way.

Netria stood at her side. "Wait until later," she whispered. "That's when he'll remember to be angry."

Falkris chuckled as she turned to her friend. "Well, shall we have a drink together before he does?"

Netria grinned. "I'd like that."

They walked into the darkness together. Netria retrieved a flask of brandy from her wagon and brought it to the fire. The two women sat in companionable silence as they stared into the fire, passing the brandy back and forth.

"Tell me," Falkris said after a moment, "why were you upset earlier?"

Netria took a deep breath, her face betraying that she felt she'd been caught doing something wrong. "I was jealous."

Falkris blinked. "What?"

Netria laughed. "Oh, Kris, I've missed you! You're a special kind of commander, the kind that men and women would gladly die for. After your accident, things weren't the same. So, I left the War Hawks to search for you."

"You did?" Falkris' eyes stung with sudden tears. Knowing that Netria had given up the life she loved for her friend was touching. In a way, the two women were family, something neither had truly known for years.

Netria nodded. "Aye. I've spent the last few years looking for you. When I heard you were going to Jenestra, I wanted to go with you and fight under your command again, just like I used to. When I saw you today, I realized you'd made new friends, and things aren't the same. You and Bendal are the only ones I've got. But you ... you've moved on from all of that. You've changed. That's why I was jealous."

Falkris grinned. "There's no need to be jealous. You'll always be my right hand."

Netria smiled, and Falkris thought she could see tears shimmering in the woman's eyes. "Thanks, Kris." They sat together in silence, words no longer needed between them.

Amial joined the older women, sitting beside Falkris almost tentatively. Netria seemed to return to herself, and she leaned past Falkris to hand Amial the flask of brandy. "Drink up, girl!"

With some reluctance, Amial accepted the flask. She studied the veteran warriors, contemplating whether it would be wise to have a drink. After a moment, she took a swig. A spout of coughing that had the older women laughing followed her daring move.

Netria took the flask from Amial's shaky hands. "Good, huh?"

Falkris smiled. "Where're you from, Amial?"

"I live on a farm in the south of Ravenia."

Netria leaned across Falkris again so she could look Amial in the eye. "Why'd you come here?"

Amial flushed. "Well, when I heard Lord Tahnuil was going to Jenestra, I just *knew* that this was my chance to really do something with my life before I married and settled down. So I –" she hesitated, "I stole Papa's horse and rode here."

Netria clapped her on the shoulder. "Well done, girl!" Amial smiled at the praise. When Netria handed her the flask again, she took it. This time she sipped at it and managed to get the brandy down with only a delicate cough.

Falkris scrutinized the girl. In Amial, she could see something of herself, from the days before her family had been murdered. Just like the young woman, Falkris had wanted to run away from her own, boring life. She'd wanted excitement. When adventure had found her, she ended up in the mercenary corps. Though there had been much pain involved, she didn't regret it.

As she watched Amial, Falkris realized that she wanted to protect the girl. The first year or more away from home had been harsh and painful for her. Though she'd wanted to give up, she'd stayed with it. Her resolve had earned her scars. She wanted to save Amial from the same harsh reality.

"Amial," she rasped, "where'd you learn to use a bow like that?"

Amial lowered her eyes. There was still much of the shy, young country girl in her. "I borrowed Papa's bow when he was in the field and practiced far from the farm."

"Would you like me to train you to use a sword?" Falkris asked her.

Amial almost squirmed with excitement at the prospect of studying with her heroine. She nodded vigorously even as she fought to look mature. "I'd be honored."

Falkris grinned. "Good."

Netria jabbed her in the ribs with a sharp elbow. "Kris, here comes Lord Tahnuil."

She raised her eyes in time to see Rhen striding with a purpose towards her. He pointed at her and Netria. "You two, come here."

Falkris rose to her feet, but motioned for Netria to stay where she was. "Netria was acting under my command, Rhen."

With an impatient shake of his head, he cut her off. "No, I'm not going to discipline you." He blinked hurt blue eyes at her. "You know me better than that. I just want a report."

Falkris gave Netria a hand up, and the two of them followed as Rhen trotted off towards his wagon. "Maybe he doesn't get mad," Netria muttered. She frowned in disapproval. "If he wants his troops to do as he says, he needs to assert himself and discipline them."

Falkris gave her a wicked grin. "That's what I'm for." Netria laughed.

Lianna and Rhen were already waiting for them in the wagon. The two warriors crowded in, finding a place to sit. Rhen looked around at them. "Now, Lady Lianna tells me the farm was attacked."

Netria nodded. "Aye, sir. It was a massacre." Uneasy, she glanced at Falkris. "While Kris was in the house, Lady Lianna and I investigated the barn. We found the children, and—" She swallowed. Even a hardened mercenary couldn't handle the sight of a murdered child.

Rhen nodded, pressing his lips together as he stared at the floor. "Who would do such a thing?"

"It was only one man, Rhen," Falkris assured him, "and he's dead now."

"He was a very sick individual," Lianna whispered. None of them mentioned that he had been a magic user, knowing that the big-hearted noble wouldn't be able to handle the knowledge.

Rhen shook his head, sorrow hanging heavy on his shoulders. "We should send someone back to bury the bodies. I hate to think of them just—" He broke down and began to sob into his hands.

Lianna looked at the other women in alarm and put an arm around his shoulders. He leaned his head against her as he cried. Falkris averted her eyes, and Netria stared at him with strange fascination.

After a moment, Lianna took his hand in hers. "Rhen," she said softly. He seemed to calm at her touch. "Rhen," she continued, "it will be okay. We can send a messenger pigeon out to Sicuth. Let the people of the city take care of it. We can't stop now, or turn back. Not while we're so close." Emphasizing her words, thunder rolled near them, rattling the wagon with its vehemence.

He wiped his eyes and nodded as she smiled. Falkris watched the interchange in silence. Part of her was happy to see the affection budding between the two of them. Another part of her was frightened of the predator in Lianna, and what the woman could do to a man like Rhen. He had such a big heart.

Falkris rose to her feet, not wanting to stay in the cramped wagon any longer. The air was too thick, and she knew that Rhen needed some time alone. As she turned to go, Netria joined her. Lianna stayed behind.

The two warriors slipped out the door with muttered farewells. As the door shut behind them, Falkris could hear Lianna and Rhen whispering together. She lowered her eyes and walked away, Netria beside her. As they joined the others at the campfire, both thought it wise not to say a word.

Chapter 11

Daymen led Vesahn behind him as he picked his way across the plains. The grass was tall; if he walked instead of rode, he could stay hidden. Killing his horse would slow him, so he gave the stallion an opportunity to rest whenever possible. Times when he could walk instead of ride were few. Though he'd ridden hard for days, the enemy was always a step behind him.

As he staggered onward, he had to rub his hand across his face to clear the cloud of exhaustion. When he wanted to stop, Vesahn would give him a gentle nudge with his snout, urging him on. They were so close to the border that he could taste it. If only they could make it.

In a cruel mockery of his hopes, a hunting horn blared behind him. Cursing under his breath, he increased his walk to a jog. He let go of Vesahn's reins, trusting the black stallion to follow him. Vainly, he tried to keep his steps light in hopes that they wouldn't hear his mad flight and give chase.

The crash of mounted pursuers carried to his ears. He'd never escape them on foot. If he tried to run, they would ride him down. Knowing there was no other choice, he stopped. Flinging his leg over Vesahn's broad back, he was barely seated when the horse leapt off at a run. Foaming at the mouth, sweat coating his hide, Vesahn was giving everything for this last attempt at escape. His breathing, usually even, came in deep rasps.

Vesahn's valiant efforts ate away the plains ahead of them, and it seemed that they might make it. The stallion was running hard, as if he knew that an end to the running was near. Then he faltered with a grunt, almost falling to the ground. Right away, Daymen urged him to a stop. He wouldn't kill the horse to save himself. Not for anything. Resolute, he turned the panting stallion to face the enemy. Vesahn hung his head, looking like he was about to collapse.

Daymen stood in the saddle and drew his bow. With the extra height, he could see over the grass. His enemies were some distance behind him. Their horses were no match for Vesahn. If the black stallion had been fresh, there would've been no need to make a stand. As it was, Vesahn no longer had the energy to run. So be it.

Daymen nocked the first arrow and let it fly towards its target. The man tumbled from the saddle, the powerful bow sending the arrow off with such speed that it easily knocked its target from his mount. Daymen let loose three more times with the bow, finding a target each time. After that, he was forced to draw his sword in preparation for close combat.

He roared a challenge as the first man spurred his horse and charged. In the first attack, Daymen concentrated on parrying. The men he was facing had the benefit of momentum. A blow from their weapons now would kill him for sure. One man lost his sword in the first charge, but drew a second weapon.

Vesahn seemed to dredge up some energy from deep inside himself. Snorting a challenge, he wheeled to face their adversaries. As the enemy circled around to make another charge, Daymen dismounted. In the past, he and Vesahn had trained for a situation of such overwhelming odds. Now it was time to see how well they fought as a team.

As the first enemy made a return charge, Daymen jogged away from his stallion to lose himself in the grass. The man rode towards the stallion and stopped short when he saw that Vesahn was riderless. Daymen pulled out his bow again and silently took the shot. The man fell from his horse with the arrow in his throat.

More cautious, the second rider dismounted in one quick movement, using his horse as a shield as he moved close to his comrade to see if he was still alive. With a snort, Vesahn rose up on his hind legs and used his lethal front hooves to attack.

The man went down with a scream.

Soon, two more riders arrived. Both of them stopped and began circling. Neither of them moved close enough to Vesahn to encourage the stallion's wrath. Daymen crept closer. When he whistled for Vesahn, the stallion immediately came to his side. Mounting, Daymen drew his sword. With his other hand, he pulled a dagger from the sheath at his boot.

His remaining opponents had noticed him and were already charging towards him, their swords shining with lust for the kill. Daymen urged Vesahn to pick up speed. Before either side could gain enough speed to have an advantage, the knight and his opponents collided. Shining swords flashed as the warriors lashed out at one another. Daymen cursed as he felt a blade kiss his flank. He took a deep, shuddering breath and turned Vesahn to charge again. One of his enemies had recovered sooner than the other, so Daymen faced the man head on. As he passed, he left his dagger in the man's chest.

The other soldier reached him moments later, and their swords clashed. They both wheeled. The second time they passed one another, Daymen felt his sword connect with the man's flesh. The resulting jolt in his arm made him grit his teeth.

Vesahn, sensing that the battle had ended, slowed. The stallion turned and walked back to the scene of the fight. Daymen dismounted next to the first man he encountered. Picking up the man's sword, Daymen used it to slit the throats of his enemies. He wanted to be certain they were truly dead. Though his actions were dishonorable, he'd do whatever was necessary to insure his survival.

The knight collected his weapons and recovered as many of his arrows as he could. When he had done that, Daymen searched through the saddlebags of the horses. He found some rations and some money. A thick blanket and a sturdy set of flint and tinder were also among the gear.

He packed everything he could salvage onto a mare and led her over to where Vesahn was standing. Daymen patted his stallion on the head. "Good job, boy." Bringing out his canteen, he gave the proud stallion some water.

Vesahn drank it all and proceeded to nip at Daymen's hair. The knight threw an arm around the stallion's neck, burying his face in the horse's thick hide. After a moment, Vesahn snorted, reminding Daymen that they weren't safe yet.

He nodded and wearily mounted the mare, leaving Vesahn to follow as he rode off across the plains. In the distance, he could hear the roll of thunder. They were almost there. The taste of rain was on the breeze. Hair on his arms and neck stood on end from the energy of the storm.

Looking up at the Stormpeaks, a resigned look appeared on his face. He wasn't certain how safe the mountains were. All he knew was that once he was there, King Jemis' people wouldn't follow him. No matter how much money he was promised, no sane man would go into the mountains.

When the first drop of rain fell on his face, he looked up at the roiling clouds dominating the sky. With a tired sigh, he lowered his head as the rain began to fall in earnest. Vesahn snorted and moved up to walk beside Daymen.

Somewhere far behind them, the distant sound of a hunting horn carried through the thin air. The rumble of thunder soon covered it, but Daymen knew that the hunt had begun again. Lightning flashed amidst the Stormpeaks, illuminating the forbidding mountains for a brief moment.

Daymen urged the mare to a greater speed, praying for a miracle. The hair on his arms and head stood straight out, and his skin tingled. Lightning flashed and thunder followed, deafeningly close. The knight looked over his shoulder and saw that the plains were on fire. A sudden wind picked up, blowing the flames back the way he had come.

Daymen smiled at the blessing even as the mare bolted in terror. Cursing, he held on for dear life. Though an accomplished rider, nothing could prepare him for the wild ride on the mare's back, especially not when he was exhausted. He fell from the saddle, landing with a heavy thud on the sodden ground. As the air rushed out of his lungs, he heard the pounding of hooves as the mare fled into the distance, leaving him without food or water.

He lay on his back for a while, struggling to draw breath into his tight chest. His vision darkened, and for a moment, he feared that he was going to die. Soft lips pulling at his hair brought him out of his terror.

Daymen drew in a deep breath and opened his eyes. Vesahn stood over him, enthusiastically nipping at his hair and face. Despite his pain and the stark circumstances, Daymen had to laugh. He laughed longed and hard, his mirth banishing all of his bitter sentiments.

After a brief rest, he sat up. When the world righted itself, he stood, took a few deep breaths and looked down at the ground beneath him. Realizing that the grass was coated with blood, he suddenly recalled that he'd been wounded. With the recollection came debilitating pain.

Vesahn supported him as he leaned against the stallion, cursing in pain. Collecting himself enough to examine the wound, he saw that, though it wasn't deep, it was very bloody. He bandaged it with clumsy fingers. Even though he needed food and rest, he dared not stop until safe in the Stormpeaks. He owed Cemil that much, if not himself. Grim and determined, Daymen started walking.

Chapter 12

The Stormpeaks were waiting for them in the morning. The sound of a loud roll of thunder startled Falkris and she sat straight up in bed. Her heart pounded frantically as she tried to get her bearings. For a moment, the only sound was her ragged breathing and the maniacal pounding of her heart; then the skies opened up and it began to pour. The sound of the rain pelting the roof of the wagon was almost deafening after the oppressive silence that had lasted throughout the evening.

She lay back down, not relishing the thought of getting up and facing the journey ahead of them. If the rumors about the Stormpeaks were at all true, she'd be dead before the day was done. So she would rather spend her last day in bed than fighting a storm.

Someone knocked lightly on the door. Falkris closed her eyes, wishing the person would go away, but the soft knock came again. The warrior rolled to her feet and stepped across the wagon. Preferring not to return to the wagon she shared with Rhen and Keth, she had bunked with Netria and several other guards for the night. Many of her comrades were still sound asleep on the floor, some of them exhausted from the night watch and some suffering from too much alcohol. She'd have to be stricter in the future when it came to drinking. Of course, that would mean not getting drunk herself, the thought of which wasn't pleasant. Netria was a superb drinking partner.

Falkris crept to the door, strapping on her sword as she did so. When she opened the door to find Lianna standing on the other side, the warrior frowned, but didn't say anything. She wondered what the woman wanted.

"Kris," Lianna whispered. Somehow, the familiar shortening of her name seemed wrong coming from the noblewoman's mouth. Falkris shook her head to clear it of sleep. She was overreacting.

"Yeah?" she growled, her voice harsher than normal.

Lianna was unfazed. "I need you to come to my wagon."

Falkris peered past the woman's shoulder at the thick cloud of rain pouring down. Because it was just before dawn, there was an odd half-light. Lightning illuminated the sky in a rapid succession of glorious bolts before fading away. She sighed. "Is this necessary?" She didn't really want to go anywhere in this weather.

Lianna raised her eyebrows, widening her beautiful emerald-green eyes in appeal. "Please?"

Falkris sighed in frustration. "Give me a bit."

Lianna nodded. "I'll wait for you there."

Falkris shut the door and picked her way back to her bedroll. Tripping over someone's leg, she almost crashed to the ground. With a muffled curse, she collected her things. She dressed slowly, and threw her cloak over her shoulders, more to keep her weapons dry than herself. If the weather kept up, the fine blades could be ruined by the constant dampness.

Opening the door and looking out at the downpour, Falkris reflected that it seemed to have gotten worse. Gritting her teeth, she tucked her bedroll under her arm and leapt down from the wagon. A moment later, she was running through the rain, her boots splashing in puddles. Still stiff from sleep, she felt like she was running underwater.

When at last she reached Lianna's wagon, she dashed inside, not bothering to knock on the door. Lianna looked up, her face showing no sign of annoyance at Falkris' unannounced entrance. Instead, she smiled a greeting.

Falkris ran a hand through her wet hair so that it was out of her face and hung her cloak on a peg. Water was still dripping from her chin when she sat down across from Lianna and accepted a cup of steaming tea. She frowned, wondering if this drink was drugged as well.

The mistress of the wagon smiled. "Don't worry, little falcon, it's not drugged."

Falkris' frown deepened, but she took a slow sip. The tea was a delight to her tongue. She could feel its warmth sliding down her throat on its way to her stomach, where it stopped to simmer gently, working its wonders on her body. Cupping the beverage in her hands, she sat back with a grateful sigh.

The two women sipped their tea, neither speaking. Falkris refused to break the silence, and Lianna seemed unwilling to. And so they sat, staring at one another across their cups of tea. Falkris couldn't help but think that she was being evaluated in some way.

"Where did your servant girl go?" Falkris asked when she had finished her tea.

Lianna smiled like a contented cat. "It seems that she and the artist who drives my wagon have taken a liking to one another. I don't mind. I have no need of her now, and she can't tell my secrets."

Falkris' eyes roved to the little chest on the desk. Inside was the mysterious object that Lianna had used to create the bright green light. The mysterious item also served to help her communicate with someone else. *Perhaps that's how Lianna acquired her contact on the other side of the Stormpeaks*, Falkris thought. If the woman was telling the truth at all.

"So you know, do you?" Lianna murmured. "My little kestrel is certainly bright."

Falkris looked away from the chest, focusing the full force of her angry glare on the woman seated across from her. "Well, *kitten*, I'm not an idiot. And, if you want me to stay, I suggest that you stop with the damned pet names." She had fought hard in past days to earn the respect of others. The King of Ravenia himself owed her his life, yet this woman treated her like a child.

Lianna laughed lightly. "Ah, Falkris! You have quite the spirit in you! It's such a rare quality."

"I'm not a damned horse!" Falkris grated.

The noblewoman smiled. "You're right, of course. I will dispense with the pet names."

"That's what you said last time."

"True."

"So what did you want?"

Lianna chuckled, hiding her bright smile behind her hand. Falkris looked away, not being able to stand the waste of such beauty on a viper like Lianna. She could think of kinder women who were plainer than dirt. Perhaps personality and physical allure couldn't go hand in hand. If that was the case, Lianna was proof enough. Still, the woman definitely had some charm. Falkris found herself liking her. Far from the beginning of a friendship, the ambiance came solely from grudging respect. She wasn't certain what role Lianna would play in her life in the days to come, but she did know that she wouldn't be parted from her until the noblewoman chose to end the strange relationship between them.

"What did I want?" Lianna asked in a mocking voice. "Well, I wanted to show you something."

Falkris didn't bother to respond with words. She raised one eyebrow, her own face a parody of the mockery that Lianna was so blatantly throwing at her. A corner of her mouth twitched up in a lazy smile.

Lianna smiled as well, her cool green eyes dancing. Without another word, she reached beneath her chair and brought a knife out into the light. Falkris saw that it was the sacrificial knife that the killer at the farm had been using. Leaning forward, she peered at it in fascination. Lianna had cleaned the blood from the weapon's surface. A fine blade with a slight curve, it was perfect for a quick, clean kill. With the hook on the end of the blade, using it to stab someone would cause more pain to the victim than an ordinary blade. Straight blades went in and left smoothly. Curved blades were more likely to tear the flesh.

Lianna turned the blade so that Falkris could see the hilt. There was a strange symbol engraved there. The noblewoman pointed to it with a delicate finger. "This is a Jenestran sigil."

The warrior's eyes flashed. "What?"

"It is Jenestran. It's the royal sigil of Prince Jemis, the current ruler in power. I believe that the man we saw yesterday was an agent of Jemis' sent to contact my father. A corrupted priest, most likely."

Falkris narrowed her eyes. "How can you know that?"

Lianna allowed a smug smile to grace her features. "All in good time, Falkris. I'll tell you once we are safe in Jenestra, and not until then."

The warrior knew that it would be no use pressing her. Lianna had the patience of a mountain, she guessed. Instead, Falkris lowered her eyes to examine the sigil. She'd never seen anything like it in her lifetime, and she had journeyed to many places.

"If you are so familiar with Jenestra," Falkris said in a quiet voice, "you can tell me how magic has survived there."

Lianna smiled, her expression almost proud. Did she think of Falkris as her pupil? The warrior hoped not. The last thing she needed was a woman like Lianna trying to take her under her wing. She had already been kicked out of the nest, and she had no intention of being babied by anyone. Not even Rhen.

"Falkris, your intellect never ceases to amaze me." Lianna diverted the subject. "Have you ever read Celestian poetry?"

The warrior felt a sick feeling creep into her stomach. How could she tell Lianna that she couldn't read? The last thing she wanted was the woman's pity. She also didn't want her to think that she was stupid.

Falkris gritted her teeth. "I don't like poetry." This was a blatant lie. She loved the way it played games with words. Not that she would ever admit that to anyone and let them live to tell her secret.

Lianna was about to say something, but Falkris rose to her feet. "We'll be leaving soon. I need to make preparations."

"Wait!" Lianna cried. In a flurry, she rose from her chair, nearly spilling the dagger onto the ground.

Falkris ignored her as she headed for the door. Throwing

her cloak over her shoulders and stomping out into the rain, she slammed the door behind her. Once outside, she let the rain wash over her. The water weighed down her long braid of hair as she closed her eyes. Tipping her head back, she let the constant pressure of rain on her face soothe her as she took one deep breath after another. She wanted to dispel the sudden feeling of anxiety that assaulted her. Not being able to read made her feel like an ignorant fool. There was nothing she hated more.

As she stood there, collecting herself, a gentle sound rose over the roar of the rain. Her eyes flew open as she listened, wondering if her ears had deceived her with a memory from the past. Nothing reached her keen ears for a long moment, but then she heard it again.

She followed the weak sound towards its source. A shadow stood apart from the wagons, the identity of the person hidden in a curtain of rain. Falkris stopped, staring through the storm at the figure that haunted her with memories of the past.

The soft notes of the song reached her ears as she drew closer, and she recognized a song that she had sung before Lord Silvian had ruined her voice. One of her favorites, she had sung the piece often. Singing it had brought her such joy.

Falkris moved closer, as though in a dream. The sound of the mud sucking at her boots betrayed her presence, and the singing woman faltered and turned to see who approached. Amial looked at the older warrior with wide brown eyes.

"That song," Falkris rasped. "Where did you learn that?"

Amial lowered her eyes in embarrassment. "I … learned it from you."

"What?" Falkris reached out a hand to shake some sense into the girl, but stopped just short of touching her.

Amial raised her voice to be heard over the roar of the rain. "I heard you sing!" She looked away and the level of her voice dropped so that Falkris could barely hear her. "I wanted to be just like you. That's why I really ran away, to follow you. That, and I wanted to get away from Lord Silvian. I didn't want him to do to me … what he did to you."

Falkris stared at Amial, her mind not quite able to absorb what she was hearing. Had this girl really come all this way to follow her? Why anyone would want to do such a foolish thing was unfathomable to her. She patted Amial on the shoulder in an awkward gesture, having no words for the girl.

Amial leaned closer so that she was speaking into the older warrior's ear. "Do you know who Lianna really is?"

Falkris jerked away, looking at the girl. "Do you?"

Amial nodded, her face grave. "When she looked at me with those green eyes of hers, I knew. Lianna is Lord Silvian's daughter."

Falkris felt as though she had been struck. Lord Silvian was the man who had taken away her voice, a part of her that had been more precious than any other. Without Rhen, she would've died of wounds or a broken spirit. Not being able to sing had scarred her more than anything physical could have. To think that Lianna was Lord Silvian's *daughter* was almost too much for the hardened warrior.

She seized Amial by the arms, shaking her none too gently. "Are you sure?"

Amial nodded. "Yes."

Falkris stood for a time, staring at nothing. She could still see Lord Silvian. His pretty face, his feminine mouth and his cool green eyes leapt to mind. The more she thought about it, the more she could see the resemblance between Lianna and the lord. Both of them were ruthless predators, stalking what they wanted until it was theirs. There was no denying the truth now.

Her eyes became focused again, and Falkris realized that she was still holding onto Amial. The girl's eyes were glazed with pain, but she said nothing. Falkris released her at once, cursing and apologizing at the same time.

Amial rubbed her arm. "It's okay. I understand."

Falkris looked down at the girl, seeing the strength in her tiny form. She was exactly like Falkris had been. Even her voice, like a haunting dream from the past, was rich with the soul and joy that the warrior's once had been.

The rain slowed, only a few rebellious sprinkles falling. Someone splashed down from a wagon behind her. Falkris turned and wasn't surprised to see Rhen trotting towards her through the mud, a huge smile lighting his face.

Happy to see him but uncertain what to do, she smiled back at him. She knew he'd fallen for Lianna and that her friendship with Rhen was something that both of them treasured. How could she possibly tell him that the woman he loved was Lord Silvian's daughter? Making him choose between them wasn't something she wanted to do.

Lianna stepped out of her own wagon. She turned to look at Falkris, her green eyes narrowed. Falkris stared back at her. Behind her, Amial shifted closer. Between the three women, Rhen bounded forward, unaware that he was in the center of a battlefield.

Chapter 13

Falkris drew her sword. The hiss of steel clearing the scabbard brought Rhen up short, confusion in his bright blue eyes. She ignored him as she focused on Lianna, a woman who had now become her enemy. As she advanced on her opponent, she knew that she'd have little time to strike Lianna before the woman could use her magic to slay her.

Behind her, she heard the sound of an arrow being nocked on the string of a bow. "Don't worry, Falkris," Amial whispered. "If you fail, I'll kill her." There was an edge to the girl's voice, a promise of death to come for any who threatened her.

Lianna shifted her balance, spreading her legs farther apart as if she was trying to anchor herself to the earth. "So, you know," she said, her voice calm.

Falkris shifted her grip on the sword and took a few steps closer, moving past Rhen, who was sputtering a protest. "As you have all along," she spat.

"I have," Lianna admitted.

"You said nothing."

"What good would it have done?" Lianna demanded.

"You should've killed me while I was drugged."

"I chose not to."

Falkris moved even closer. The energy in the air around her intensified. She could feel the tendrils of magic brushing over her skin. Something foreign whispered into her body, wrapping its warmth through her arms and legs. Her grip on her sword grew slack as she fought the strange sensations dominating her. The warrior closed her eyes and shook herself violently. The strange feeling fled from her, leaving her cold, but more like herself. She shifted her grip on her sword and continued her approach.

Lianna's eyes widened a fraction, showing a little more white than cool green. Then, they narrowed to deadly slits. A single drop of sweat showed itself on her brow and slithered its way down the side of her face. The air around her shifted, and a whirlwind of energy flew out from her to surround Falkris.

As Falkris continued to advance, her pace slowed to a mere crawl. Time bent around her, freezing until it seemed that a second passed in the space of a minute. Out of the corner of her eye, she saw a horse rear, then cease to move as though turned to stone, its hooves suspended in the air.

Falkris and Lianna alone remained mobile while time turned itself inside out. The noblewoman stepped down from the wagon and with careful steps, walked through the mud to the warrior's side. Falkris found that she could move, but only very slowly. Her opponent was unhampered.

"Well," Lianna said, "you've forced me to reveal the extent of my true powers. Whatever am I to do with you?"

Falkris, realizing that trying to attack the woman now was futile, sheathed her sword, the action taking forever to complete. In slow motion, she watched the shifting play of light along the sword's long, silver blade, strangely fascinated as the angle of the light changed.

As soon as the weapon was put away, Falkris found that she could move as normal again. She backed up a few steps, putting some distance between herself and Lady Silvian. Lianna watched this with cool amusement, one perfect eyebrow raised a fraction higher than the other.

Falkris gritted her teeth, refusing to show her dread. Looking at Lianna, all she could see was Dracine. Her fear gave way to a wave of rage. "I'll kill you, be it sooner or later. Let's end it now," she hissed. She burned to strike out at this woman, and thus at the man who had taken her voice from her.

Lianna laughed. "I can't allow that. However," she purred, gliding closer, "I don't want to kill you."

"Perhaps we shall both have to die."

Lianna stopped, a slight smile gracing her face. She strode

over to stand beside Rhen. The noble was frozen in time, his face a mask of agony as he stared into the space where Falkris had been moments before.

Lianna put a hand on his arm, patting it gently. "What would Lord Tahnuil do without the two of us to watch after him? He needs *both* of us, you know."

Falkris gritted her teeth. Her hand itched to throw a dagger at the woman, but she knew that the weapon would slow to a crawl before it ever reached its target. She could picture Lianna easily stepping aside from death, laughing in amusement all the while.

"Do you expect me to forgive the bad blood between us?"

"Consider that I was also persecuted by my father. Do you think I'd choose to flee from wealth and power without good reason? Do you think I'm such a fool that I'd willingly spurn a marriage to the Prince of Ravenia?"

Falkris narrowed her eyes, not wanting to believe the woman. The animal within her cried out for blood, and her heart for revenge. Logic, however, was winning the battle, and she could feel the cold touch of rational thought cooling her blood lust.

The warrior took a deep breath. "If your father was any other man, I wouldn't believe you."

Lianna nodded as she paced a slow circle around Rhen. "Do we have an understanding then?"

Falkris studied the woman in silence. She knew that Lianna was the daughter of the man who had taken her voice, and that the woman was very powerful. Lianna was ambitious and would do anything to reach her goals. Her drive was matched with a sharp mind, a lethal combination.

Though she was a danger to them all, Lianna was the only one capable of getting them through the Stormpeaks. If what Lianna said was true, Falkris needed her alive as much as she needed her dead. Falkris would have to compromise what was best for herself and what was best for the expedition, it seemed. She wanted Lianna dead, but she couldn't afford to kill her.

"Will you promise to do nothing to harm Rhen?"

Lianna laughed, but her gaze turned serious. Her cool green eyes fell on the lord's face. "I wouldn't hurt him for anything." She reached out a gentle hand to touch his face, but stopped short. "His innocence is so pure." There was a tender note in her voice. Perhaps her affection for the lord was genuine.

"Then I will not pursue this fight."

Lianna glanced at Falkris, her eyes sparkling mischievously. "But there will be another."

"Reaching Jenestra is all that matters now."

"And I shall be your tool in that game," Lianna mused. "Very well. I won't kill you, nor will you kill me ... until we are safe in Jenestra."

"Fair enough."

"Until then, would you like to come in for a glass of tea? You look quite soaked."

The warrior rolled her eyes at the woman's erratic behavior. Her gaze shifted to Rhen. "What about him?"

"Don't worry about it. He'll remember nothing when time resumes."

Falkris was about to protest, but the rain began to fall again. Seeing everything spring back to its normal state in an instant was a shock. The horse resumed its dance on its hind legs, crying out in terror as it lashed out at the storm. Rhen stopped in his tracks, his face blank as he stared around himself.

Lianna took the noble by the arm. "Rhen, did you hear me? Let's go in for some tea. You'll catch a cold in this downpour."

Not knowing what to think, Falkris watched as Lady Silvian casually led Rhen away. She took a deep breath, thankful for the cold reality of the rain. Hearing a noise behind her, she remembered Amial, who was still holding an arrow nocked and ready to be loosed, her bow unwavering and aimed towards Lianna.

The warrior hastened to take the arrow from her, then the bow, bringing both of them under the shelter of her cloak, not wanting either to be ruined in the rain. Amial was shaking, her face white.

"What just happened?" Amial whispered.

Falkris glanced over her shoulder. Lianna was looking back at her, a glint in her eye. The warrior's gaze snapped back to Amial. "Did you see everything?" Falkris demanded. Her heart was beating frantically in her chest at the thought.

"I did," Amial whispered. All of a sudden, she lost her nerve and fell towards Falkris with a sob. "It was horrible! I could see everything and hear everything, but I couldn't move!"

Falkris wrapped one arm around the girl. "Come on," she called over the rain, "let's get inside!"

She half carried Amial with her to Rhen's wagon, thankful to find that Keth wasn't inside when she stumbled in. After removing Amial's cloak, she guided the girl to the bed and dropped a thick blanket over her shoulders in place of the soaked garment. The bow and arrow she placed on the desk, then sat down beside Amial.

"Falkris," the archer whispered, "I'm sorry I ever told you. I'm sorry that ever had to happen."

Falkris threw an arm around Amial's shoulders, pulling the girl close. "It's okay, Amial." That another person had witnessed the interchange between her and Lianna neither relieved nor alarmed her. She wasn't certain what she should be feeling.

Amial wept into her shoulder like a child. "I never should've run away. I'm such a *fool*!"

Falkris looked down at the girl's wet hair, imagining what being trapped in an immobile body would feel like. The loss of control had to be maddening. She remembered what it had been like when her life was in the hands of Lord Silvian. Defiance had been the only choice she could've lived with, and she had clung to it in desperation.

"I won't let it happen again," Falkris assured Amial. Having been hardened and embittered by pain, Falkris would do anything to keep the same from happening to Amial.

The archer sat up, wiping the tears and rain from her face.

"It wasn't your fault."

Falkris smiled. She considered arguing with the girl. "I was the one who tried to attack her. I think you just covered me."

"I shouldn't have told you who she was."

"The truth should always be told, however bluntly."

Amial smiled. "You'd never hold anything back, would you?"

Falkris shrugged. "Probably not."

"I like that."

"Yeah?" Falkris said. "At least someone does." Their troubles forgotten, the two laughed.

Chapter 14

The storm died away around midmorning. As soon as they were certain that the rain wouldn't be returning, the members of the little expedition scrambled to start their journey into the mountains while the weather held. Falkris stepped out of her wagon to watch her guards drying and saddling their mounts.

Misan trotted up just then, her coat matted with water. Falkris breathed a sigh and jumped down to see to her mare. Before she risked journeying into the mountains, she was going to have to dry the mare off and check her over. She complained about it to the horse as she did so, but secretly enjoyed the work.

When finished, she saddled her horse. She mounted up, glad to be in the saddle again, and rode a few rounds to check that everyone was in position. The archers were already on the tops of the wagons, their bows ready and their eyes alert for any sign of trouble. Amial waved down at her from the top of Lianna's wagon. Falkris returned the greeting and rode on.

Netria joined Falkris halfway through her second round. The mercenary grinned savagely. "Are you ready for the battle with nature?"

Falkris smiled. "I think so. What about you?"

"I'm always ready for battle; it's my art."

"I know." The ominous sound of thunder rolling in the distance made some of the horses uneasy. Falkris frowned. She'd handpicked the horses to be sturdy and reliable. That some of them were afraid of thunder wasn't good considering the circumstances.

Lightning flashed near them, and thunder followed it a few heartbeats later. Falkris looked up at the tops of the wagons where the archers were perched. It was well known that lightning struck the highest target, and she hoped that such a horrible death wouldn't befall her brave archers.

Bendal looked down at her from the top of Rhen's wagon, then looked away to stare at the mountains, his bow clutched in his hand. "Bendal!" Netria leered up at him. "At least if you get wet, the lightning will fry you till you're dry!"

Falkris felt an amused smile tug at her mouth, but she suppressed it for Bendal's benefit. Her old comrade from her mercenary days was looking disgruntled. Winking, she reassured him with the same calm demeanor that had gotten them all through one bloody fight after another. He nodded and looked away.

"Netria," Falkris chided as they rode on, "don't tease him."

"He brings it on himself," Netria muttered in defense, but there was a touch of affection in her voice.

Before long, everything was ready. The wagons were in position, and the guards had taken their places riding alongside the clumsy vehicles. Blankets wrapped around their shoulders for warmth, the archers were seated atop the wagons.

Falkris signaled to Rhen. He was at the head wagon, impatiently waiting to set out. When he saw her signal, he flicked his reins with great enthusiasm, and the wagons rolled up the steep path that led to the High Pass. Because it was the only known way through the Stormpeak Mountains, they were all hoping that it was still open.

Keth rode up to Falkris, mounted on his gigantic warhorse, one of the few beasts able to carry him. Smiling at her, his eyes bright with expectation, he was almost as excited as Rhen, though that was hard to imagine. The noble was virtually bouncing on the seat as he urged his horses up the path into the mountains.

"Shall we scout ahead, Keth?" she asked the big man.

Keth nodded with a huge grin. Lit with such joy, his face was almost beautiful. Then the fleeting moment was gone, and the ugly brute was riding up the incline on his beast of a horse. Shaking her head, Falkris nudged Misan after the man.

The sturdy warmare soon caught up with the hulking

stallion. Misan nudged her way past so that she was leading. Raising her head just a bit, she showed her disdain of the big horse and his rider. Falkris smiled and patted her trusty mare on the neck.

They reached the top of the path and stopped short, peering ahead. The High Pass was a long tunnel between two mountains, and looked very narrow in places. Getting the wagons through would be difficult, but not impossible. In areas, the mountains towered overhead, walling the pass in. Falkris could already see some areas that would be perfect for an ambush.

Overhead, the clouds boiled, an angry wind turning them in dangerous swirls. Lightning flashed in their depths, lighting them from within with its deadly energy. Misan snorted to show her displeasure, stamping her feet. Falkris patted her on the neck, attempting to alleviate her nervousness.

As Falkris peered ahead, she saw the fleeting shadow of something moving along the path. A smile split her face. "Keth," she said, waiting to make certain she had his full attention, "go down and tell Rhen that the way ahead is clear. Then stay with him and protect him."

Glad to perform his duty, Keth nodded. There was no one in the world he cared more about than his employer. Protecting Rhen gave the man a sense of importance in life. Falkris knew that she could trust him to do as he was told.

She waited until Keth had turned his big mount down the path, then dismounted. The shadow paused and turned, bolting back towards her at incredible speed. Dax crashed into her, knocking her backward and stepping on her chest in his enthusiasm. She laughed as she ruffled his ears. Misan stuck her nose in, pushing her way between her mistress and the wolf in a show of possession. Dax growled at her, but Misan just snapped at him with her teeth, snorting a warning.

Falkris managed to disentangle herself and pay attention to both of them at once. Dax sat down on her foot while Misan nosed at her shirt. For a moment, she basked in their love.

The roll of thunder in the distance returned her attention

to the present, and she pulled away from her two animal companions. When she peered back down the path, she saw that the wagons were about halfway up. In a fluid motion, she mounted Misan and rode ahead to make certain the pass was clear.

As they rode, Dax shadowed them, his presence always at the edges of Falkris' awareness. They rode for some time, all of them alert to any danger. The pass seemed to be empty of everything but the threatening lightning and the rumble of thunder. An incredible amount of energy was in the air, and the hair on Falkris' arms and neck stood up.

After she had ridden for quite a distance, she turned Misan, and the trio headed back to the wagons. Dax broke away from them halfway back, fading into the shadows to watch over his mistress from afar. Falkris watched him go with regret, then turned her attention to the wagons. They had just reached the top of the path and were starting into the pass.

Rhen was looking up at the mountains on either side of them when she rode up alongside him. A worried frown creased his forehead. "It's like riding through a canyon," he muttered. He turned his attention to her. "Did you see anywhere to take shelter in case the storm returns?"

"No," she admitted. "It looks like a straight shot the whole way."

He sighed. "Then we'd better pick up the pace. The sooner we're free of this place, the safer we'll be."

Falkris nodded. "Right."

Amial called to her from the top of her wagon. "Falkris!"

The warrior rode over to Lianna's wagon and looked up at the archer perched above her. "Yeah?"

"Lady Lianna wants to see you inside." A worried frown pulled at the girl's features. Falkris nodded her understanding, wondering what the woman wanted. She wasn't quite ready to confront Lady Silvian yet, not when they had almost killed one another mere hours ago.

Standing in the saddle, she stepped from Misan's back up onto the wagon. The artist and the mute servant looked up at her from where they were guiding the horses. Falkris nodded to them, trying to banish the worry from her face.

Knocking hesitantly, she poked her head inside. Lianna was sitting in the center of the floor with her legs crossed, eyes closed and face smoothed of cares. A rested feeling was evident in the looseness of her shoulders. In her lap, she cradled the strange green stone. Falkris hurried in and shut the door behind her. "You wanted me?" she asked, not bothering to hide the bitterness in her voice.

Lianna didn't answer at first. When she opened her eyes, just the whites showed. She looked straight at Falkris from their milky depths, as though she could see her. The warrior backed up against the door with a muffled curse.

"I wanted to tell you that I'm beginning my spell now. I'm going to go into a deep trance so that I can use the power necessary to hold off the storm as much as possible. If I don't, we'll all die in its rage. I also must keep in contact with Alihandre to be certain that we're able to pass the barrier that forms the border between Jenestra and Ravenia."

"Who's Alihandre?"

"It's not your concern."

Frowning, Falkris forced herself to look at the woman, despite the unnerving absence of color in her eyes. "Why are you telling me this?"

"If something should happen, I'll be unaware of it. While in the deepest stage of a trance, I'm completely oblivious to the world around me. I need you to wake me up if there's trouble."

"I'll try."

"Don't fail me." The noblewoman closed her eyes, much to the warrior's relief. Falkris stood there a moment longer, wondering if she should leave. Her skin crawling, she hurried from the wagon cabin.

Once outside, she climbed onto the roof so that she could talk to Amial. She explained the situation to the young archer. "If there's trouble," she finished, "and for some reason I can't get to Lianna, I need you to wake her up."

Amial nodded gravely. "I'll do my best."

Falkris squeezed her shoulder. "I know you will." A moment later, Falkris leapt down from the wagon and jumped back into the saddle of her waiting mare. She reached into her pocket and pulled out a treat for Misan to reward her for her obedience, then urged her into a light canter to circle the wagons.

When she drew even with Netria, Falkris slowed Misan to walk. Netria glanced at the sky. "It sure looks ugly up there."

Falkris followed her gaze. The clouds sure were hostile. As she watched, a fork of lightning flashed across the sky, striking a target in the distance. The resulting roll of thunder was deafening, and more than one horse tried to bolt in terror. Nervous, Misan snorted, turning back to look at her mistress as though to ask if she might not change her mind about going through the High Pass.

The warrior shifted her gaze to the sides of the mountains that hemmed them in. She noted that the trees that had once grown there were blackened and charred, many of them split in half by the force of nature. To see any sort of life growing there at all was a surprise.

Cursing under her breath, Netria muttered, "Why did I ever agree to this?"

Falkris nudged her none too gently. "Because you like me."

Netria narrowed her eyes, her face creasing in a frown. "Oh, yeah? Well, I changed my mind." She made as though to turn back, but Falkris, laughing, called after her. Netria made a big show of trying to make her choice as the other guards looked on. After some serious consideration, Netria rode back to her place with a stream of curses that could make even the most hardened warrior's ears burn, much to the applause of her comrades.

Falkris noted that Netria's escapades had eased the tension in the air. Grateful, she wondered if her friend had done it all for just that reason. Netria gave her a sidelong glance, suspecting her thoughts. "You'll never know," she teased. Falkris knew better than to respond. Instead, she urged Misan to make a quick round of the wagons, a tight grin tugging at the corners of her mouth.

Chapter 15

The train of wagons journeyed on without event. During the afternoon, Falkris checked on Lianna. The woman looked very pale. Even her lips, normally full and red, were devoid of color. The gentle touches of rouge on her smooth cheeks looked out of place against her pallid complexion.

The warrior stared down at the noblewoman for some time, trying to decide what to do. Knowing nothing of magic, she wasn't sure if she should interfere for Lianna's sake. Waking her could do more harm than good.

The strange stone in Lianna's lap glowed a faint green, the pattern of light that gave it life pulsating rhythmically. When Falkris looked closer, she thought that she could see the face of a woman in its jeweled depths. She wondered if the image depicted the face of Alihandre, the name that Lianna spoke but refused to explain.

Falkris gave up and exited the wagon. Once mounted again, she surveyed her surroundings. The walls were very close, and they towered high above the chain of wagons, creating a claustrophobic feeling that was not improved by the threatening condition of the sky.

Set upon by a sudden bout of curiosity, Falkris urged Misan into a gallop. The horse and her rider moved at a fast pace through the narrow space, and the wagons were soon far behind them. Finding a small side path, she turned Misan toward the top, an open space with a small ledge that overlooked the High Pass. A cave large enough to house a horse and rider gaped at her from the side of the mountain.

She ignored the shelter and instead looked out over the mountains. In every direction, she could see the dark, distant shadow of pouring rain. Where the wagons traveled, there was no precipitation, just the angry clouds. A few drops of rain spattered down on Falkris, but nothing more. Was this Lianna's doing? She wondered if it was coincidence or the work of powerful magic. Either explanation seemed unbelievable.

She went back down the short path and rode farther ahead. Once she was far from the wagons, Dax joined her. They hurried onward, the tension melting from them as they burned away their anxiety with physical activity. As they got farther from Lianna, the light spattering turned into an honest rainfall.

About half a mile further, Falkris was in the heart of a vicious downpour. Lightning flashed everywhere around her. Misan snorted, balking beneath her rider. With some insane urge guiding her, Falkris kept going and Misan grudgingly obeyed. Dax ran along at her side, his ears flat against his head.

Misan skidded to a sudden halt, Dax beside her. Falkris dismounted and ran ahead to see what had stopped them. She ran headfirst into an invisible barrier. The force of the impact sent her flying backward.

She took a moment to catch her breath, the rain falling on her like mad and lightning flashing around her so often that its strange illumination was constant. When she could breathe again, she moved a few cautious steps forward, one gloved hand reaching out in front of her.

She felt something odd beneath her hand, a strange sensation of pulsing energy. Her other hand came up, and she placed her palms flat against the barrier, wondering what it was. When she tried to push through the barrier, she felt like she was walking through water. Closing her eyes and focusing her will, she forced her way forward. The barrier tried to turn her aside, much as the door in Lianna's wagon had done. Once again, through sheer force of will, she managed to pass.

Dax barreled after her, and Misan followed more cautiously. On the other side, horse and rider regarded one another with wide eyes. Dax moved closer to both of them, and for once Misan seemed grateful to see him. Falkris put a hand on both of them. The rain washed over them, and the howl of thunder was deafening in their ears. A strong wind threatened to knock Falkris off her feet.

She had to go back and warn the others about the barrier. Maybe Lianna would know something about it. Her two companions close behind her, she pushed through it again. Once on the other side, she mounted. As soon as she was in the saddle, Misan was galloping like crazy to get free of the deadly storm. Falkris feared that the mare would slip on the wet stone, but she somehow kept her hooves beneath her.

The rain abated, and Misan slowed her pace. Snorting with displeasure, the mare turned her head to glare up at Falkris with contempt. The horse obviously didn't appreciate being forced to carry her rider into a lethal storm. Dax shook himself, showering his mistress and her horse with a spray of water. When Falkris glared down at him, he grinned up at her with his tongue lolling.

Falkris walked Misan back to the wagons. Halfway there, she remembered that Lianna had mentioned a barrier that formed the border between Ravenia and Jenestra. Perhaps the strange energy she had just encountered was that barrier.

Falkris saw no point in troubling Rhen about it until they were near the area. She would ride ahead again when the wagons drew closer to see if the barrier remained. Until then, she wouldn't worry anyone with tales of evil magic.

She rode around a bend, and the wagons came into view. Standing up on the seat at the front of his wagon, Rhen waved to her. Falkris brought Misan to a halt. Behind her, Dax sprang off to make himself scarce. The presence of a large wolf added to the constant roll of thunder would be enough to make some of the horses bolt; he knew that as well as she did.

Rhen frowned at her, yelling as soon as he was close enough. "Where did you go? Why are you all wet?"

Falkris smiled despite herself. "I scouted ahead. I ran into the storm ahead of us, but it's moving towards Jenestra. We'll be safe." After an extended but fond argument between the two of them, the chain of wagons moved on.

Some time later, they approached the barrier. Falkris rode ahead to see if the wagons could pass through safely. The wall of energy was gone. Intrigued, the warrior waited and watched the wagons pass through, neither storm nor magic hampering them.

After they had gone on, she waited. The rain began to fall after several minutes, and the energy in the air changed. When Falkris put her hand out, she felt the barrier beneath her fingers. Somehow, Lianna had done this for them. Through the lady's efforts, the expedition to Jenestra had so far been able to survive the storm and pass through the border. Their luck would hold, but only if Lady Silvian stayed alive and well.

Falkris nodded to herself. *Lianna may be Dracine Silvian's daughter, but she keeps her word. There's honor in her, but I fear that she may be assisting us only to serve herself.* Whatever the case, they'd be through the Stormpeaks soon. Once there, the truth would be known, and Falkris could at last begin her own quest to study with the legendary warriors of Jenestra.

Night fell, but still the wagons crept on. Lightning was their source of light, and as it flashed, eerie and white, it turned the world into something out of a nightmare. The travelers paused to take a break, giving the horses some rest and feeding them sufficiently. When Falkris checked on Lianna, she was alarmed to see that the woman had slumped over onto her side. Her pulse was faint, and her breathing came in short gasps.

Falkris went to Rhen right away. "We need to keep moving," she said. Seeing the confused alarm on his face, she hurried to explain. "I think the storm will hit us soon if we don't clear the mountains in the next few hours." This was a half-truth, but all she could afford to tell him.

Rhen nodded. Though he was confused as to how she knew that the storm was an imminent threat, he'd come to respect her judgment. "Okay." With a weary signal, he motioned for the wagons to keep moving. There were several groans of protest, but all complied with his wishes. None of them wanted to be caught in the pass if the storm struck.

The wagons rolled on. No one spoke, and everyone was tense. The air hummed around them, portending the disaster to come. Lightning flashed in the distance, and the drone of thunder soon became a constant buzz that they tried to ignore.

The High Pass finally opened up, and a valley spread out before them. Falkris rode ahead to find a place where they could take shelter for the night. At the bottom of the valley, she found the remains of a small forest. Amidst the splintered trees, there was a cave. She rode Misan into it to investigate.

Once inside, she lit a torch. The flickering light revealed a large area, big enough to house a number of horses and their riders. Doing a quick mental calculation, she decided that they could fit all of the horses and people inside, but the wagons would have to remain outside.

Dax came inside and nosed around curiously for some time. Then he stopped and barked at her as though to signal his approval. Nothing had occupied the cave in recent days.

Falkris mounted up and hurried back to the train of wagons. She led the others to the spot, and the grateful guards started moving the horses and people into the cave. As soon as everyone was safe in the cave, Falkris went to wake Lianna.

The moment the noblewoman came out of the trance, the rain came pouring down on them with savage malice. Falkris cursed, picked Lianna and her stone up and carried both from the wagon. Running through the torrents of rain, she ducked inside the cave.

Depositing Lianna in Rhen's arms, she went back to the mouth of the cave. When Dax crept into the cave, she put one hand on his head, letting him know that coming so close to the others was okay in this instance. She wouldn't force anyone into a storm like this.

The rain fell with the vehemence of an angry god. The wind blew it right into the mouth of the cave, plastering her hair to her face. An old, blackened tree bent towards the ground under the wind's fury. With a groan, it fell from its towering position to land on Lianna's empty wagon. The wood of the vehicle shattered, and one wheel rolled away to rest at Falkris' feet.

A hand on her arm tugged her away from her open awe of nature's wrath. Netria pulled her back into the depths of the cave. Dax stayed close to her side, keeping most of his body hidden beneath her rain-soaked cloak. A nearby horse snorted nervously, but seemed unwilling to bolt past the wolf into the rain outside.

Dax licked his chops and darted off into a dark corner away from the horses. Falkris watched him go, hoping that he'd be safe. She could imagine what would happen if someone decided to harm the wolf while she wasn't paying attention. Someone would end up dying, and Dax would most likely follow.

Netria pushed Falkris down beside a fire and started drying her off with a blanket. Falkris stared into the flickering flames as Netria tended to her, taking her long black hair out of its sodden braid and wringing the water from it.

"Is Lianna okay?" Falkris asked in a hushed voice.

Netria nodded. "She is. Good thing you got her out of that wagon. The fool hasn't eaten all day." Netria snorted. "She was probably worried about her damned figure getting ruined. You know these noble women." The trace of irony in her voice wasn't lost on Falkris.

She smiled, wondering what Netria would say if she knew the truth about Lianna's actions. As her old friend draped a dry blanket over her shoulders, Falkris nodded her thanks. Someone handed her a warm bowl of soup, and she devoured it in minutes.

All around her, people were eating. Many of them were already crawling into their bedrolls for the evening. Falkris was content to sit by the fire, her eyes vacant as she considered the day. Netria sat with her.

When Netria stood and left the fire, not a word had passed between them. Falkris rose to her feet a while later and went to her bedroll to settle in for the night. Dax moved quickly across the cave and snuggled in beside her. Indulging in a huge yawn, she threw one arm over his soft flank.

She watched the shadow of the sentry standing near the mouth of the cave for a time. Beyond him, the storm raged. Never having seen anything so incredible, Falkris was hypnotized by its power. The flash of the wild lightning revealed that another of the wagons had been destroyed. After a time, her eyes drooped shut of their own volition, and her mind slipped away into the land of dreams.

Chapter 16

Dawn brought a slight remission in the rain. The members of the expedition took the opportunity to rearrange the wagons to accommodate everyone. Falkris found herself sharing a wagon with Lianna, Amial and Netria; it was a convenient group, for the four of them were the only ones with any knowledge of Lianna's talents with magic.

Lady Silvian ate heartily that morning, making certain that she was more than full for the coming trance. As soon as she was settled with the green stone in her lap, her eyes rolled back in her head. While she sank deeper into her trance, the storm abated until it had died away into nothing.

Falkris and Netria shared a long look. Amial, standing between them, was very white. They turned their eyes to Lianna. All three appreciated the woman's sacrifice, but none of them was certain what to think of her. Falkris especially was unable to decide whether Lianna was a friend or foe. Netria, true to her nature, had deduced who Lianna really was and had the same predicament. Amial had been dealing with the truth longer than either of them.

Outside the wagon, Bendal was shouting orders at the guards to form up around the five remaining wagons. The three women left Lianna to her magic and hurried outside. Amial scrambled onto the roof, and Netria and Falkris vaulted into the saddles of their waiting mounts.

Falkris gave the signal to move out after a quick inspection of the wagon train. The wagons rolled away from the little cave that had sheltered them. Two wagons remained behind in the forest, their crushed and smoking wreckage evidence of nature's fury. With that reminder, the Ravenians increased the pace. None of them wanted to be caught in the storm.

Most of them, unaware of the efforts Lady Silvian was making to protect them, prayed to their chosen god for the good fortune to hold. Falkris could see in their faces that many of them had not expected to make it as far as they had. They were as excited as they were nervous, for they expected to clear the mountains by nightfall.

Falkris said a prayer of her own. She rarely did so, but she thought that the effort might be needed this time to see them through. Looking around, she searched for a sign of the terrible thing that she sensed would happen before the day was done. Unfortunately, her premonitions were often valid.

Netria rode up beside her as they cleared the forest and entered a narrow part of the High Pass. "Cut it out," she muttered.

Falkris looked at her, surprised. "What?"

Netria frowned, the scar on her face leaping into contrast to make her expression even more formidable. "You look nervous. It's scaring the guards."

Falkris blinked. "I just have a bad feeling," she said, her voice harsher than normal.

Netria glared at her. "Keep your voice down. The last thing we need is for the guards to know you're scared. I've heard them talking, and the only thing keeping them at all optimistic is your fearlessness. You're their hero."

"What?"

Netria sighed in exasperation. "Falkris! Everyone here has heard of you. When you were with the War Hawks, you were a legend. You still are. They're following you, and if you look frightened, it's going to break them."

Falkris narrowed her eyes. "They should have better things to worry about than a veteran soldier."

"Suit yourself, Kris." Netria kicked her warmare a little too harshly, and the abused mount neighed in protest as she leapt forward. Falkris stared after her old friend. As she thought about what Netria had said, she realized that the woman was right. She sat a little straighter in the saddle.

Because the others looked up to her, she needed to keep up appearances, even if she did feel the fingers of fate tickling along her spine.

The day waned on. They paused at midday to eat a meal and feed and water the horses from their dwindling stores on the wagons. Much of the feed had been destroyed in the storm the night before. The horses were irritable, as if they also sensed something to come.

Falkris ate by herself, preferring some solitude. She'd ridden ahead earlier and crested a small rise. The path ahead was long. To clear the Stormpeaks, they were going to have to travel into the night.

After she finished eating, she checked on Lianna and was surprised to find Amial in the wagon with her. The archer was sponging sweat from the noblewoman's brow. Taking a damp rag, she squeezed water into Lianna's mouth. Falkris watched, saying nothing. When she departed, she nodded in approval to the young archer.

The day faded into night, and still they pressed on. Several hours after dusk, it began to sprinkle. Alarmed, Falkris looked towards the wagon where Lianna was. She wondered if the woman was okay. If the magic guarding them was failing, it was possible that Lianna's health was as well.

Her thoughts were interrupted when she noticed a faint change in the sound that echoed off the tall walls of the High Pass. Something in the sound of the thunder was wrong. She shifted her gaze, her heart hammering as she wondered if what she was hearing over the roar of the storm was the pounding of hooves.

She urged Misan forward, her left hand clenched around the pommel. Her right hand went to her sword. In the next flash of lightning, she could see a shadow running towards them. Standing in the saddle, she craned to see. The next flash of lightning illuminated the silhouette of a running wolf. Dax pelted over the rise, dashing straight towards the train of wagons. Falkris felt her heart rise into her throat. What could be behind him that would make him run straight towards them?

Amial was perched on top of Lianna's wagon as she squinted through the rain. She was worried about Lianna. When she had last checked on the woman, Lady Silvian had been very pale. As was clearly evidenced in the increasing amount of rainfall, she was having trouble holding the trance.

The archer tried to concentrate on her duties as a guard, though she worried about Lianna's heath, and thus the safety of the entire train of wagons. She strained her eyes to see through the rain. A flash of lightning revealed Dax running towards them.

Looking down to see Falkris draw her sword in alarm, she tightened her hold on her bow. The next flash of lightning briefly illuminated the flash of metal. There was someone else out there in the storm. Amial nocked an arrow and sighted, waiting for another bolt of lightning to reveal her target.

Lightning forked across the sky, followed by a deafening roar. Amial's eyes widened. A troop of guards was heading towards them at top speed. She gasped as she drew her bow taut. From the looks of the armed men, they were no allies of the Ravenians.

When lightning struck again, the enemy was much closer. She saw their leader this time, a man in a black robe. The wagon beneath her came to a halt. Falkris was roaring orders. Horses, terrified by the presence of the huge wolf, were screaming in terror, but Amial was oblivious to all of this. As rain streamed down her neck and ran along her back, she focused on her target. All she had to do was wait for her next chance, and she'd take the robed man out.

Before lightning could strike again, another source of light illuminated the robed man. Fire boiled in a red cloud around him. As she watched, too horrified to loose her arrow, the fire solidified into a great ball. The robed man lifted his hands, and the fire swarmed towards them. The great flaming ball collided with the wagon just in front of Amial. She heard screaming, and a piece of timber flew past her head.

She swallowed and pulled the bow taut again. Lightning flashed, and she loosed the arrow, sending it speeding towards its target through the darkness that followed the lightning. When the storm graced her eyes with light once more, she saw that the lead horse was without a rider. With a joyous smile, she sheathed her bow and dropped down to the wagon seat. Now her first concern was Lianna.

Daymen watched from the top of the cliff in growing horror. When he had taken the hidden path up from the High Pass into the Stormpeaks, he had not realized that he'd be leading the Jenestran troops straight into a caravan of innocent people. He wondered, as he spurred Vesahn back down into the canyon, how the Ravenians had managed to cross the border. As he rode into battle, the pounding of his heart chased the thought from his mind.

Falkris met the troops head on, a scream of rage tearing from her ruined throat. She was dimly aware of the mage, her primary target, going down with an arrow in his throat. The brunt of her wrath shifted to the next target before her. From the corner of her eye, she saw Dax leap for the throat of a second opponent, his powerful jaws tearing the man's flesh as though it was nothing. Her sword glinted in the lightning, its blade silver and shining. When lightning flashed again, her blade was dark with the blood of one of her enemies.

Amial half carried and half dragged Lianna away from the burning wagon. She wished for a horse to help her with her burden, but it seemed that all the mounts not engaged in battle had fled. She saw the shadow of Keth run by. The big man was carrying Rhen over his shoulder, much to the consternation of the noble.

Amial called after the two men, but neither heard her over

the roar of the fire and rain. Even if Rhen had heard her, she doubted that the noble would've been able to sway Keth to come to her aid. Sighing, she shifted her hold on her unconscious charge.

A flash of lightning revealed a dark cleft in the rock. In the next moment of light, she saw that it was a path leading up to a cave in the mountain. Barely daring to hope, she dragged the woman toward the opening and pulled her into it.

The sounds of battle drifted up towards her. After a moment, she heard hooves pounding up the path. Grim and determined, she brought out her bow and nocked an arrow. She had a fairly defensible position. Until someone came to her aid, she'd hold out as long as she could. Falkris, at least, wouldn't forget her.

Daymen pulled away from the bitter battle in time to see a young girl dragging the most beautiful woman he had ever seen up the path in the side of the cliff. Curious and concerned for their safety, he urged Vesahn after them. Behind him, several soldiers broke away from the fight and followed him.

The sudden roar of rain beating down on Falkris brought her out of her battle rage. Fire was burning behind her; she no longer needed the lightning to see. She realized that something must've happened to Lianna if the storm had returned. Wheeling Misan around, she rode back towards the wagons in search of the lady.

White fire licked at the wagons, burning hungrily even when faced with the brunt of the storm's rage. Misan leapt over a body, and Falkris looked down at the corpse. The blank eyes of Bendal stared up into the storm, the light gone from his eyes. In an instant, a thousand memories flashed through her mind. Bendal, a man who had been as near to a brother as she had known for a long time, was dead. As she had learned to do in the past, she bit back her grief and rode on.

The warrior reined Misan to a halt next to Lianna's wagon.

Braving the flames, she dashed inside. Only the green stone was in the wagon, flashing in the light of the fire; there was no sign of Lianna. Falkris scooped the gem up and hurried from the wagon.

She vaulted onto Misan's back and turned the horse, looking for the lost lady. A flash of lightning revealed the shadows of men moving down a hidden passage she had not seen before. Her heart pounding, she kicked Misan towards the little cleft in the rock.

Her warmare charged straight into battle. A man was standing in the mouth of a cave. An arrow was protruding from his right arm, but he fought with his left. Watching him, she knew that it was not his dominant arm. Regardless, he wielded his beautiful sword like an expert as he fended off numerous enemies. Behind him, Falkris could just see the crouching forms of two women. She didn't know who he was, or why he was fighting with them against their enemies. All she knew was that he was in trouble.

Falkris didn't hesitate. Dismounting, she screamed a challenge. The first enemy to turn towards her met with a blade. At least six more were between her and the strange man. She intended to cut her way to his side.

The next man to face her was more prepared, and it took her some time to find a hole in his guard. That rain was streaming into her eyes and the constant flash of lightning made the light inconsistent didn't help. The battle conditions were worse than any she had ever fought in before. She relished the challenge.

At the same time her opponent went down, another man crashed to the ground under the hooves of a magnificent black stallion. Misan trampled the man for good measure. Falkris had her own enemies to deal with, for a new opponent had moved to attack her.

The next flash of lightning revealed a blur of fur and teeth as Dax charged into battle. An enemy went down under his teeth instantly. Falkris finished the man she was fighting and found herself face to face with the stranger. A flash of light revealed dark eyes and hair.

Falkris shifted her blade to her left hand, prepared to fight him on equal ground. Saying nothing, the man stood across from her, his sword in hand and blood streaming from his injured arm. She saw that the arrow wasn't his only wound.

Raising one hand to show she meant no harm, she sheathed her sword. Relief crossed his face, and he sheathed his sword as well. "Who are you?" they both demanded at once. His voice was rich and contained a thick accent.

"Falkris Vilenti," she rasped.

He didn't look disturbed at her rough voice, as some were. "Sir Daymen Aschton, former member of the knights of Jenestra."

"Former," Falkris said. Daymen barely heard her over the roar of the storm. She moved a dangerous step closer. "You're a deserter. You led them to us."

He held up his hands in defense. "That wasn't my intention."

Falkris was about to reply, but a low growl from Dax alerted her to more danger. Someone was running up the path. She and Daymen both drew their swords. For an instant, they stood united in their defense of the two women huddled in the cave behind them.

The ugly face of Keth appeared first, followed by Rhen's more handsome features as the nobleman and his guard ran up the path. Falkris waved them past her and Daymen, then tightened her grip on her sword.

A mounted warrior followed Rhen and Keth. Before Falkris could move to attack, an arrow hissed past her ear to lodge itself in the chest of the approaching man. He fell backward from his horse. The terrified mount, bereft of his rider, turned and bolted back down the path.

Daymen smiled ruefully as Falkris looked back at Amial in shock. "The girl has wonderful aim." Looking at the arrow lodged in Daymen's arm, Falkris nodded.

Bleeding from numerous wounds, Netria was the next to come up the path. At the sight of Falkris, she started sobbing. The warrior helped her friend into the protection of the cave. "Netria, what is it?"

"It's Bendal," she gasped. "He's dead!" Remembering the blank stare of the dead guard, Falkris said nothing. She still felt no grief at the loss of her friend, but knew that it would come later.

Falkris held Netria, trying to soothe her. Netria just sobbed, her hands clenched in an iron grip around her friend's arm. Falkris had to pry her fingers away in order to restore the circulation to her hand.

When she managed to pull away, she looked up to see Daymen break the arrow from his arm and pull the head out of his flesh. He tore a piece of his cloak away and bound the wound. When he saw that she had risen to her feet, he gestured to her. "Come on, let's make certain that there isn't anyone else out there."

She went with him, her sword drawn. Dax shadowed them as the pair scouted the area, cautiously checking bodies for signs of life. The world outside was a field of dead. Only a few horses were left, wandering through the aftermath of the battle.

Falkris caught a few of them. She found Rhen's horse, as well as Keth's. Netria's proud mare was dead, a spear through the brave soul's heart. She stopped to look down at it, grief overtaking her.

Daymen shook her with gentle hands. "Falkris!" he yelled over the storm. "We have to take cover soon!"

She nodded and moved away from the slain mare with an effort. Between the two of them, they rounded up three more mares, herding the horses towards the cave. Thankfully, when they returned, they found that there was enough room for everyone. The wolf was an unwelcome addition, but Falkris refused to put him out in the storm.

She watched as Daymen started a fire. She wasn't certain

who the strange knight was, but was thankful that he'd been there to help. Even if he had led the Jenestran soldiers to the wagon train, he had not done it on purpose. He'd come to their aid, and perhaps even saved the lives of Amial and Lianna.

As they all tried to bed down for the night, Falkris stared into the fire. She kept seeing blood and fire when she closed her eyes, the vision of her dead comrades haunting her thoughts. Somehow, deep in the night, she slipped into sleep.

Chapter 17

Morning found the wet band of survivors still asleep, huddled close together in their little shelter. Daymen was the first to awaken. Looking down at the faces of the sleeping Ravenians, he couldn't help but feel a deep sense of guilt. He had caused the deaths of their comrades. Forgiveness wasn't something he ever expected from them.

Drawing his sword, he began polishing it. His armor would also need some care. The perpetual storm wasn't wearing well on him. At a snort from one of the horses, he looked up. Vesahn, he saw with a vicious pang of guilt, was still saddled. He sheathed his sword immediately and saw to the care of his poor mount.

As he was unsaddling the stallion, the sound of hooves on the path made him spin and draw his sword. Falkris rode up the path on a fine, bay warmare. Water streamed from the warrior as lightning flashed behind her. As she dismounted and led the horse into the shelter, her gray eyes were fierce.

He didn't notice that she'd been carrying something until she threw a bag on the ground. A wet wolf followed her into the cave and bent to sniff at the bag. "Dax," she scolded. Her voice was harsh, coming out more like a feral growl than anything human. He found that it added to the wild, independent aura that the woman possessed.

When he'd seen her the night before, her eyes had been filled with battle rage. Her long braid, coming undone, had streamed behind her as she'd whirled to attack. He'd seen, in the brief flashes of lightning, that she was a formidable warrior. When she'd fought her way towards him, there had been a moment of uncertainty when he'd feared having to fight her. Thankfully, they were allies. For now.

Daymen sheathed his sword and turned back to his care of Vesahn. Behind him, Falkris began tending to her mare, rubbing the horse down with care and speaking to her with a soothing tone. The knight half-wished he could hear what she was saying.

The wolf moved closer to Daymen. He knew that the beast was Falkris' pet, but he still felt uncomfortable with it so close. Vesahn snorted his own contempt for the canine and stamped one foot in protest at having a known predator so close. Daymen edged around the horse, putting some room between himself and the furry menace.

A light laugh caught his attention. Falkris was watching him, an amused expression lighting her face with a strange, wild beauty. For a moment, he was spellbound by her fierce charisma. What would it be like to have a woman like that fighting at his side? His pride banished the amiable feeling. "What?" he asked sharply.

Falkris shook her head and returned to caring for her mare. "Dax," she called. The wolf padded over to her, pushing his way past the mare. The horse snorted a warning to the wolf, and he snapped at her. Other than that, the two tolerated one another.

Daymen averted his eyes and returned to his belated care of Vesahn. He made sure to take extra care with the stallion. With death so close at his heels, he hadn't had the time to look after his mount properly for some time. Checking the stallion's hooves, he dislodged a rock from one and cleaned mud from all of them.

To his surprise, Falkris joined him. As she was grooming twigs and burs from the stallion's tail, she eyed Daymen. Her gaze was enough to pin him in place. He'd never been intimidated by a woman before and found it an interesting experience.

"What have you been running from?" she asked. "You don't seem like the type to neglect your mount, and this fellow's in sorry shape." Coughing after the last word, she took a swig from a canteen at her side. He wondered what had ruined her voice. In the dim light, he could make out a rough scar along her throat.

Daymen took a deep breath and told her of his encounter with King Jemis and his resulting flight from the wrath of his monarch. He talked at some length about Cemil, telling her how brave the boy had been.

"You did the right thing," Falkris said when he had finished his story.

"In leaving the king's service?" he asked.

"That, too. I meant with the boy."

Daymen was surprised to hear her agree. Sending the boy's corpse off on the horse was something he regretted, although he knew that it had been his only option. Cemil would have wanted it. Somehow, he hadn't accepted what he'd done until now, when Falkris had agreed with him. Even though the warrior woman was harsh, he sensed that she was a person with firm morals.

Falkris began to work on the stallion's mane. "What will you do now?"

"What do you mean?"

"You can't cross the border to Ravenia; you'd never survive the storm." As if emphasizing her words, thunder shook their little cave. Vesahn stamped a foot in protest. Falkris waited until the rolling sound died away, then continued with her cool analysis of his options. "You can't hide out here; you'd starve."

Daymen considered that. "I can't go back, either."

"Is there somewhere you can go in Jenestra?"

He thought it out. "There's a monastery at the edge of the Stormpeaks. They'll give me refuge."

Falkris gave him a long look, then her eyes moved to her sleeping companions. Her eyes rested on the face of the beautiful young woman with the blonde curls. "Lianna is not well. Could this monastery ... could they heal her?"

Daymen nodded. "The Priestesses of Truth live there. They can restore her health."

Falkris was about to question him further, but Netria

stirred. Daymen watched the proud warrior go to the other woman's side. Then he shook his head and returned his attention to his horse.

Falkris bent over Netria. "Hey," she rasped.

The mercenary sat up and rubbed at her face. She looked around their crowded cave, her eyes coming to rest on Falkris. A thousand different emotions flashed across her face as grief settled into her heart. "Bendal," she whispered. The brief spark of life that had been in her eyes died.

Falkris said nothing for a moment. Then she sat down beside her old friend. "He chose his death."

Netria nodded. "We all do, when we join the mercenary corps." She was silent for a time. "I thought maybe we were different ... immortal."

Falkris grunted. "I know the feeling." She dug a flask of wine out of her breeches. "Here, this will make reality a little easier."

Netria stared at the flask for a moment before taking it. Slowly, a smile spread across her face. Grinning, she took a long swig. "Damn," she said, "reality tastes good!"

Falkris laughed. She remained a moment longer to be certain that Netria would be okay, then crept over to check on the others. Rhen and Keth woke at her touch. They both sat up, getting their bearings. Amial came awake when Falkris gave her a slight shake. Lianna would not wake, even when the warrior smacked her gently on the cheek.

Rhen joined her, a concerned frown etched across his weary features. Keth loomed just behind the lord. "What's wrong with her?" the big man breathed.

Falkris shook her head. With an arm behind the lady, she brought her up into a sitting position. Rhen handed Falkris a flask of brandy at her request. She opened Lianna's mouth and poured some of the harsh liquid down her throat. The lady coughed, but swallowed. Beyond that, she didn't stir.

Her concern growing, Falkris checked Lianna over for any wounds. She couldn't detect any injuries. "Amial," she growled.

The girl hurried over. "Are you the one who brought her up here?"

Amial nodded. "She was like this when I found her, Falkris."

Falkris let out a deep breath. Rhen voiced the thought that was going through Falkris' head. "We need to get her to a healer."

Keth went to stand by the door, staring out into the storm. Falkris watched him, wondering what he was up to. The big man scratched his head. "It's raining." So much was painfully obvious.

Daymen joined them, his manner businesslike. "We'll need to brave the storm."

Rhen shook his head. "No, our luck has held until now. The weather will die down soon, and it'll be safe to travel."

Falkris put a hand on his shoulder. "Rhen, our luck has run out. The storm won't be calming any time soon." *Not while Lianna is unconscious.*

"If we ride hard," Daymen said, "we can reach the monastery a little after nightfall."

Resigned, Rhen rose to his feet. "Very well. For the Lady Lianna."

Falkris let out a relieved sigh, glad that the noble had not asked any awkward questions. She rose to her feet. "Let's have a good meal before we go. We won't be stopping once we're out in the storm."

Amial cooked what some of them considered their last meal. The bag that Falkris had brought back contained salvaged food from the wagons below. While their breakfast was warming, Daymen and Falkris went down the path to bring up some feed for their horses, as well as anything else useful. The fire or the rage of the storm had ruined almost everything that could've been useful, so they had little to bring back.

They ate in silence, none of them relishing the thought of the journey. The storm outside howled its fury at them, promising them death if they should leave their little cave. None of them wanted to discuss that possibility.

Before they set out, Falkris bundled Lianna as well as she could, trying to cover the woman completely so the storm wouldn't touch her. As much as she hated the woman for her lineage, she didn't want Lianna to die. Falkris had come to enjoy the verbal sparring she and Lianna shared so often.

"Okay," Falkris said before they mounted, "Daymen and I will lead. Netria, Keth, bring up the rear. Amial, Rhen, I want you to see to Lianna. We're going to ride hard, and she might slip from the saddle, even if we tie her securely." They all nodded their understanding.

Falkris led Misan out into the storm. The rain pelted against her, and the wind was strong enough to knock her from her feet. Lightning flashed all around her. After a deep breath, she leapt into the saddle.

When they were all situated, she urged her terrified mare down the path. Once the little group was past the wagons and the corpses still littering the pass, Falkris looked to Daymen. He nodded to her. Both of them gave their horses their head. Misan, happy to be moving, broke into a run.

Lightning flashed as the seven horses pounded along the High Pass. The mounts ran as though death itself chased them. Dax was hard pressed to keep up with the long-legged horses, but he somehow managed to stay near his mistress. On either side of them, high walls flashed past.

Gradually, the horses began to tire, and Falkris brought Misan down to a ground-covering trot. The other, slower mounts caught up, and they were soon riding together through the storm. Falkris squeezed her eyes shut, willing the storm to go away.

Hours later, with the horses walking along doggedly, Daymen yelled to her over the storm. "Look!"

She opened her eyes, almost afraid. Up ahead, she could see a light. She cried out, and the others looked as well. Though her fingers were numb from the cold, and every inch of her was wet, Falkris managed a smile through chattering teeth.

The horses, when urged, called on a last reserve of strength. Slowly, they broke into a canter. The mounts turned from the pass up a path. They halted at a set of tall oaken gates. Daymen dismounted and pounded on the thick wood portal with a mailed fist. "Open up in the name of a knight of Jenestra!" he yelled.

Like a miracle, the gates opened. Light streamed out to illuminate the weary travelers, falling on their pale, shivering forms. Misan, without waiting for a command from her mistress, pushed her way forward.

Falkris crossed the threshold into the courtyard of the monastery. To her utter amazement, she looked up at blue skies. The sun shone down on her from a glorious summer sky. She raised a hand to the light, marveling at the warmth on her fingers. Dismounting, she began to laugh with unbelieving joy.

A robed woman approached her, a worried frown on her face. "You must be Falkris," she said, placing a hand on the warrior's back.

Blinking in surprise, Falkris nodded. "I am. Who're you?"

"My name is Alihandre."

Chapter 18

Alihandre was the High Priestess of Truth, the leader of a sect of the religion common throughout Jenestra. She was getting older as the days passed, but the energy of youth still beat in her heart. The only sign of her advanced years was the fine streaks of white that riddled her dark hair. Her face, round and open, was without wrinkles. Her body, though plump, still had cords of muscles running through it.

Looking up at the tall, fierce warrior before her, she felt her age for the first time. Falkris Vilenti was ageless in her strength, and the spirit that burned behind her gray eyes seemed to bubble with eternal youth and power. Alihandre had to crane her neck to look up at the woman. "Where is Lianna?" she asked.

Falkris stared down at Alihandre, her face a mask of disbelieving shock. "You're Alihandre?"

The priestess swallowed her impatience. "Yes, my dear. Now, where is Lianna?"

As Alihandre watched, Falkris shook herself out of her dazed condition, and control suddenly emanated from her. To see the woman restored to her normal level of alertness and cold intelligence was intimidating. Lianna had been right about this one. Alihandre took an involuntary step back. If Falkris noticed her sudden fear, the warrior didn't show it.

The tall woman looked over her shoulder towards the horses. Without a word, she strode over to a mare and untied a lumpy bundle of blankets from the mount's saddle. A moment later, she was carrying it towards the priestess. "She's here. We need to get her warm."

Shocked, Alihandre stared at the limp pile of blankets in Falkris' arms. Could Lady Silvian truly be cocooned in the wet layers of fabric? The priestess felt suddenly very faint. If she'd looked in a mirror, she would've seen that all the color had left her face. She took a few deep breaths and gestured to Falkris. "Please, bring her this way."

In her haste to get Lianna into a bed and warmed, Alihandre almost tripped over her robes several times. Falkris' steady steps echoed behind her as she dashed down halls, leading the warrior to the chambers that had been prepared for Lianna. She thrust the huge double doors open and led the way to the bed. "Here, put her here."

Falkris laid the lady down on the bed and stood back. Alihandre forgot all about the warrior as she peeled away blankets with gentle hands. Lianna looked very thin, and her face was pale. The skin around her lips was tinged a slight shade of blue. Her heart heavy, Alihandre rang a bell even as she began undressing the girl to get her out of her wet clothes.

Servants bustled in, and a flurry of activity followed. When at last they stepped back, Lianna was dressed in fine clothing, and her skin had been chafed to warm her. A fire was lit in the hearth despite the summer weather, and they moved the lady near to the warmth of the flames. All they could do now was feed her a healing drought and pray for mercy.

Falkris shifted, and Alihandre jumped. She'd forgotten that the warrior was there. Moving to Lianna's side, Falkris looked down at her. "I didn't know what to do. I knew she was ill, but I didn't think I should wake her from her trance."

Alihandre hesitantly patted the woman on the hand. "You did the right thing, dear." With her free hand, she rang a bell. "Go with the priestess. She'll show you to your friends. All of you need to rest, especially Lady Lianna."

Falkris nodded and followed the priestess who answered the summons. Alihandre watched her go, then looked down at her young charge. "Lianna, my dear, I shouldn't have asked you to enter the trance without proper training." She smoothed wet curls from Lianna's face. "I only hope you can survive the night."

The lady shifted in her sleep, moaning softly. Alihandre

held her breath, hoping that the girl would awaken, but Lianna slept on. Putting one hand on the lady's brow, Alihandre stroked it as she would a child's. "You've come far. Let's hope it's not too late."

Falkris woke from a long, much needed sleep. She stretched languidly, working the kinks from her tired muscles. As she swung her legs over the edge of the bed, someone knocked at the door. She stood and answered it.

A servant nodded to her in a brusque manner. "Lady Vilenti, your presence and that of your peers is required in the audience chamber of High Priestess Alihandre."

Falkris, too tired to attempt speech, nodded her understanding. The servant bowed and left Falkris to ready herself. The warrior woke Netria before going to Amial's bedside. She was reluctant to wake the girl, but knew she had to. Gently, she shook Amial.

The girl sat up, her eyes wide. Her hand, Falkris saw with some pride, went at once to the dagger beneath her pillow. When Amial's brown eyes came to rest on Falkris, she relaxed. An expansive yawn followed, much to the older warrior's amusement.

Netria made a show of dragging herself from the bed. "So what'd you wake us up for?"

"High Priestess Alihandre," Falkris said.

Amial sighed as she threw her legs over the bed. "She wants to see us?"

"We're required to present ourselves to her," Falkris muttered with some sarcasm. If there were two things that she despised, they were formalities and pleasantries.

Netria frowned. "Is this supposed to be formal?"

Falkris shrugged. "I think so."

The warrior's frown deepened. "What the hell am I going to wear? I lost all my clothes in the damned fight!"

Amial spoke up behind them, her voice soft. "There are some robes and clean undergarments laid out for us." The two warriors turned to look at her. Sure enough, fresh clothing had been set out for them next to a steaming tub of water. All three of them salivated at the thought of a hot bath.

Netria looked at Falkris out of the corner of her eye. "I think she can wait."

Falkris grinned. "We won't give her a choice." Laughing, the three women piled into the tub.

The women were refreshed and dressed in clean clothing when they reported to the waiting room beyond the chamber Alihandre used for audiences. They sat down on a bench together, none of them too pleased with having to wait. A few moments after Netria had stopped griping, Rhen, Keth and Daymen walked into the room, looking equally clean.

Netria found a new focus for her boundless energy as the men sat down. She jabbed Falkris in the ribs and whispered in her ear, her breath hot against the side of the warrior's head. "If you had to pick one, which would it be?"

Falkris snorted. "Definitely not Keth."

Netria rolled her eyes. "I know *that*. I mean him." She jerked her head towards Rhen. "Or *him*." Her gaze roved towards the Jenestran knight.

Falkris looked from one to the other. Rhen looked as alert as ever, his blue eyes dancing as he peered around the room. His blonde hair, usually ruffled and messy, was combed into obedience for once.

Sir Daymen Aschton sat at the opposite end of the bench, dark eyes staring straight ahead, looking at nothing and yet seeing everything. Tanned skin roughened from travel accented dark hair pulled back into a tight braid that streamed down his back.

Netria didn't wait for an answer. "I think I'd go with Rhen. That knight is handsome, but he is much too *serious*." She raised one eyebrow. "I like men with some spunk." Falkris reflected that Bendal had been the serious type. He and Netria had been companions and nothing more. Still, their bond had been special, something that went beyond common friendship.

Amial leaned over to whisper in Falkris' other ear. "I agree with Netria."

Falkris found herself chuckling as the two women leaned across her to whisper to one another. "I tell you what," Netria said at last, "Rhen may have his eyes on Lianna, but I've got my eyes on *him*. We'll see how long he can withstand my feminine charms."

This time Falkris laughed outright, which drew the attention of the men. She leaned over to whisper into her old friend's ear. "Good luck, Netria. He's fallen for Lianna."

Netria bared her teeth in a vicious, primal display. "I'll hunt him down. We'll see how long he can withstand me."

Just then Keth rose to his feet and stalked across the room. The three women looked up at him as he loomed over them. "Whispering is rude," he asserted, glaring down at them with his dark eyes.

Netria cackled out a laugh. She sprang to her feet and leapt up onto the bench so that she was at eye level with the big brute, leaning forward so that their foreheads were almost touching. "What did you say?" Falkris would've been alarmed, but there was a smile on Netria's face.

Rhen, becoming distressed, jumped to his feet to come to the big guard's aid. "Lady Netria, please ... Keth doesn't mean any harm."

Falkris took the opportunity to slip away from the others and padded across the soft carpets, her footsteps silent. With some amusement, she stood back to watch. Netria was growing louder as she and Keth argued. *Well*, Falkris thought, *if she wanted Rhen's attention, she certainly has it*. Rhen was trying to push between them to no avail.

Falkris heard a small sound and turned her head. The servant who oversaw the room had risen from her desk. Her face written with anxiety, she wrung her hands nervously. Falkris wondered if the servant was actually going to do anything to calm the room's occupants or if she was going to just stand there.

"I think that servant is going to have a conniption," a rich, accented voice said in her ear.

Falkris turned to look at Daymen. She would've been surprised, so silent was his approach, but she'd caught the faint smell of him on the air a moment before he had spoken to her. The warrior woman shrugged. Not feeling the need to articulate a response, she said nothing.

The knight leaned against the wall beside her, joining in her observation of Netria's comical antics. "So tell me," he whispered after a moment, "which one of us *would* you choose?"

A slow smile spread across her face. "You have sharp ears, Sir Aschton."

"An answer?" An eyebrow curved up, daring her to give a response.

Her smile died away. "I believe you've already heard far more than you should have. I'd rather leave you wondering."

"It's appropriate to keep one's enemies in the dark," he observed.

"So, are you my enemy then?"

He smiled. "That remains to be seen, milady."

Just then the door to the audience chamber slammed open. Alihandre stormed in, her eyes blazing with indignation. For a person of such short stature, she was a terror when enraged. "This is a *monastery*!" she yelled. "*Not* a tavern!"

Silence followed her words. She stood fuming in the doorway for a moment, her plump frame heaving. "Now, please come inside. I'll see you now."

Daymen stood away from the wall with a sidelong glance at Falkris. "Come along, milady," he chided her.

For a moment, Falkris dared not move. Black fury swept through her. Who was this knight, to talk to her like a child? With barely disguised rage, she stalked after him into the audience chamber.

The door closed behind the Ravenians and the knight. In

the corner of the waiting room, a wall hanging fluttered as the robed man stepped back from his hiding place. He leaned against the wall in the concealed stone corridor, his thoughts running rampant as he considered what he'd just observed.

Lianna was here, and the others were with her. He'd risked much to get the lady to the monastery. On more than one occasion, he'd crept into the depths of the building to use the well. Its ancient power had helped him aid Lady Silvian numerous times. At last she had reached her destination.

Now that he had her here, where his influence over her was the strongest, he didn't want her leaving. This very morning, he had made certain that she wouldn't be departing the monastery any time soon. While her room was empty, he'd crept in and drugged her with a sleeping drought from which she couldn't be roused, even with the powerful magic of the priestesses. No, she wouldn't awaken until *he* desired her to.

He stole through the passage to peer into the audience chamber. Alihandre was speaking in a low voice to the travelers who had come with Lianna. At the sight of the short woman, the man's eyes narrowed. She, of all the priests and priestesses, was the only one who could stop him. Now that he had Lianna under his power, he could eliminate Alihandre. Once he did, nothing would stand in his way.

The warrior woman glanced sharply in his direction. Beldaris cursed under his breath and withdrew. Falkris was going to be a problem, as was the Jenestran knight. The rest of them were fools. But he would deal with *all* of them later. For now, he had to concentrate on bringing Lianna under his control.

Silent as a cat, he crept along the corridor. When he came to Lianna's room, he peered from behind a tapestry to be certain that all was clear. Then, he darted into the room and leaned down beside her bed. Gently, his hand looped through one of her perfect, blonde curls. "Lianna," he whispered to her, "you and I will rule the world."

From where he stood, the robed man could sense the

power emanating from the girl. Such magical talent would be wasted if he didn't cultivate it. He'd win Lianna to his side one way or another.

He looked up as the door began to creak open. Quickly, he darted back to his hidden system of tunnels. As the servant came into the room to check on Lady Lianna, the tapestry dropped back into place. Oblivious to the world around her, Lianna slept, her dreams darkened by the drug that held her under its sway.

Chapter 19

Falkris glanced over her shoulder, her eyes scanning the corner of the room. Though all she saw was a tapestry fluttering against the wall, she had a strong feeling that she was being watched. She glared at the tapestry for a moment more, then returned her attention to the plump priestess.

Alihandre was pacing a neat circle behind her desk, her round face layered with a dark frown. "Something terrible has happened," she said.

Rhen rushed forward, his hands flat on the desk as he leaned over it to make his appeal. "Is it the Lady Lianna? Is she ... is she—" His voice trailed away. The noble was reluctant to voice the thought that was so evident on his pale face and trembling hands.

Falkris shot a look at Netria, who was frowning, concentrating intently on the nobleman. The plots running through Netria's head showed in her eyes. Now that Netria had set her eyes on her target, nothing would stop her. Even in the face of Rhen's obvious care for Lady Silvian, she remained undaunted. In a way, Netria and Rhen shared the same blind hunger for a challenge.

Alihandre waved her hand at the noble, "No, no ... nothing so dreadful. When you brought Lianna in she was on the brink of death. Exhaustion and the storm had taken their toll on her fragile form, but she was recovering admirably, true to her spirit."

Rhen took a step back. "*Was* recovering, did you say?"

The priestess ceased her pacing and turned to face the assembled individuals. "Lianna has been drugged." She raised her hands to forestall their reactions. "I don't know how or when, but she has been. The drug is very powerful. It renders its victim unconscious until the antidote is applied. Until we find the cure, Lianna will be in a form of stasis similar to sleep. However, she'll be very vulnerable during her ... rest."

"How?" Falkris asked.

"While she sleeps, her mind remains open to the person who drugged her. She's very susceptible to anything that person should choose to implant within her mind. If we don't awaken her in time, her beliefs and thoughts may be twisted beyond repair. We must act now to revive her before it's too late."

Rhen had turned very white. "How can we awaken her?"

Alihandre let out a deep breath. "That's the difficult part. We need a special herb known as Night's Breath. Incredibly rare, it's found only in the southern plains of Jenestra."

"Then we'll find it immediately," Rhen said.

"That's not all," Alihandre cautioned him.

"Go on," he urged her, his blue eyes intent.

"Because of the magical nature of the drug, the antidote must be applied by the person who first poisoned the victim. If that's not possible, a second component is needed, an item from the Temple of Purity. It's a ring that can cure any illness. To obtain it, one must enter the temple and survive the judgment of the guardians within."

Alihandre let out a deep breath. "If I could go myself, I would. However, my place is here, at Lianna's side. My fellow priestesses and I will place a spell on her to protect her mind from invasion. We must remain with her at all times to maintain the spell."

Daymen stepped forward. "You wish us to find these things?"

Alihandre nodded. "Yes. I must entrust the search to you."

Falkris glanced at Rhen. From the strange expression on his face, she could tell that he was very confused. "Wait," he said. "Did you say *spell*?"

Alihandre nodded, her brows forming a slight frown at his question. "I did."

"But ... magic doesn't exist."

The priestess smiled indulgently. "Surely you know that Lianna was the one who kept the storm at bay while you traveled. She is a sorceress herself."

Rhen looked at the priestess, his mouth hanging open in surprise. He wrenched his gaze towards Falkris, trusting her to provide him with a logical explanation. Falkris bit back her guilt at hiding the truth from him. "It's true, Rhen."

"Why didn't you tell me?" he sputtered.

Alihandre cut through his protest. "Now isn't the time. You must all leave immediately. After you have divided into two groups, my priestesses will transport you as close to your separate destinations as possible."

Falkris, seeing the chaos about to ensue, took charge. "Right. Rhen, you head one group. I'll head the other."

Keth shuffled forward. "I'm with Rhen."

Netria moved beside the noble. "I'll go with you as well, Master Tahnuil. You'll need my skills."

Alihandre nodded. "Excellent. That leaves Amial and Daymen with Falkris. You must all leave as soon as possible. Pack your things and meet in the courtyard."

Before any of them could even voice the half-formed protests fluttering through their thoughts, she shooed them all from the audience chamber. Once they were out in the waiting room, the door slammed shut behind them. For a moment, they stared at one another, wondering what to do. "Now!" The sound of the priestess' voice, firm and commanding even through the heavy door, sent them rushing off to prepare for their journey.

Falkris was the first to pack her few possessions and enter the courtyard. Saddling Misan while she waited, she basked in the sun that shone down on her from above. She looked up at the clear sky thankfully, hoping that she'd never again have to see a storm.

The cold touch of a nose on her hand startled her. She glanced down to see Dax standing beside her. As she reached to scratch his ears, he sat down on her foot. In the last rush to escape the storm, she had forgotten all about him. The realization of her neglect didn't inspire the best of feelings.

High Priestess Alihandre bustled out into the courtyard, her followers trailing behind her. She marched right up to Falkris, wolf and all, and peered up at her with round eyes. "So, Lady Vilenti, are you prepared to undergo your journey?"

At first, Falkris was surprised by the title Alihandre accorded to her, but then she realized that the priestess used it only as gesture of respect. Falkris nodded. "One thing bothers me."

"What is it that vexes you?" the priestess asked in a calm voice.

"How are you going to transport us? That sounds like powerful magic."

Alihandre smiled. "The truth, however universal, can be bent. We'll simply alter the truth of the reality that surrounds you so that your matter will shift locations."

Falkris nodded, pretending that she grasped the concept. "And Misan and Dax, as well?"

The priestess looked down at the wolf with some unease. "Yes, well ... the wolf may go, but you'll have to leave your mount here." Seeing the frown spread across the warrior's face, Alihandre hastened to pacify her. "We'll give your horse the best of care."

"Good."

Alihandre changed the subject. "Remember that the truth is a very powerful virtue. One can achieve many things through it." Her eyes scanned the length of Falkris and came to rest on her throat. "For instance, your throat. If one could alter the truth that binds the scar to your flesh, you could perhaps heal the injury and be able to speak normally once more." She was a very perceptive woman.

Then I could sing again, Falkris thought. The very idea filled her with such joy that she trembled. For too long, she had gone without soaring on the wings of the human voice. She swallowed.

The warrior moved a little closer to Alihandre. "Could you heal me?"

The priestess furrowed her brow in thought. "It is most likely possible." She nodded to herself. All the hope that was building in Falkris was shattered with her next phrase. "But, now is not the time. Lady Lianna's health is at stake. The very truth that encompasses her being could be altered if we don't act quickly."

Falkris' heart fell. She hardened her features so that her disappointment wouldn't show. Alihandre must have read her mind, for she reached out a gentle hand to comfort the tall warrior. "Fear not, Falkris. When you return with the ring, we'll see to your throat."

Falkris stood straighter. "Thank you."

Amial entered the courtyard, her quiver slung over her slim shoulder and her bow in hand. She came directly to Falkris and Alihandre. Her brown eyes moved from woman to woman before settling on the priestess. "High Priestess, may I make a request of you?"

"Of course, child."

"Will you please explain these virtues to me? I'm entirely unfamiliar with the concept. In Ravenia, we have no such thing."

Falkris was impressed with Amial's foresight. She'd been curious about the virtues, but had not yet asked about them. Since they were going to a temple of virtue, grasping the basis of the religion was important. The priestess smiled at Amial. "Well, it's a complicated matter, but I will shorten it for you considerably. There are five virtues ... truth, purity, honor, strength and compassion. Each virtue has a religious sect that follows it, and a temple dedicated to it. These temples, one of which you'll be entering, are guarded by sacred beings who can judge whether the virtue in question is found within the being that is tested."

A harsh laugh carried across the courtyard as Netria joined them. "Then Kris is in trouble. If you guys are going to the Temple of Purity, she'd better not set foot inside!"

Alihandre frowned. "There is more to purity than virginity, Lady Netria."

Falkris glared at her friend, giving her ire a source other than the presumptuous priestess. "Who said I wasn't a virgin, anyway?" Amial, standing between the older women, flushed.

"I never did!" Netria growled and proceeded to mutter a stream of obscenities under her breath that made the priestesses gasp. She was obviously more insulted by what Alihandre implied than Falkris was. Order was restored only when Falkris managed to quiet Netria.

Daymen strode into the courtyard as silence descended. Alihandre glared at the young priestesses who were staring at him until they looked elsewhere, then she addressed the assembled group. "Well, the three of you are here, as is your … pet. I suggest that you depart now to save time."

Daymen nodded. "Right."

Falkris bit back a protest. She'd wanted to say goodbye to Rhen, but there was no time for that now. About to nod that she was also ready, she was assaulted by Netria. The mercenary seized her in a powerful hug. "Kris! I'll miss you."

Falkris disentangled herself and stepped back. "Netria," she said fondly, "we'll live to meet again. But you must promise me something."

"Anything, Kris."

"I once swore to protect Rhen with my life. For the time, circumstances dictate that we must part. I want you to protect him in my stead."

Netria grinned. "No need to ask, boss. I'll protect him with my life, and my heart as well." She winked.

Falkris smiled and forced herself to step away. Alihandre herded Netria away so that she stood apart from the three of them. The priestesses loaded the travelers with provisions, then stood back as well. The High Priestess oversaw all of this, her brow furrowed and her opinions critical.

When all was set, she nodded. "It is time. Please hold still while we work the spell."

The assembled Priestesses of Truth gathered around them in a circle. At a word from Alihandre, they all joined hands and began to chant. The sound rose and swelled. Slowly, the women began to circle.

Soon the world around Falkris faded. Her mind was protesting that what she was seeing wasn't logical. Time and space seemed to bend, and for a moment, she was standing in a vast valley. Then she was in the monastery again. Over the heads of the priestesses, she saw Rhen dashing into the courtyard. He raised his hand in farewell. Just as the noble faded from sight, she returned the parting gesture.

A sudden brush of wind against her cheek startled her. Falkris and her group were in a long valley filled with silver-barked trees. The air around the leaves seemed to shimmer, and it looked as though flecks of silver sparkled all around her. She took one hesitant step forward, then turned to look at the others.

The three of them stared at one another. Falkris realized that Alihandre had not given them any instructions regarding their actions once transported. Though she knew that they'd have to find the Temple of Purity, she had no idea how to do that. She didn't even know which direction to go.

Daymen solved the problem. "The High Priestess gave me a map and some instructions to follow. She says here that we are to go north through the valley until we find the Temple of Purity." He looked apologetic. "Would you like to carry the directions, Falkris? You were to head this group, and Lianna is your friend."

Falkris didn't say the first things that came to mind. She couldn't read. Lianna wasn't her friend. Why did he care about any of this at all anyway? Frowning, she fell back on the last rather than reveal the first ugly truths. "Why are you helping us?"

The knight looked surprised at her affront. "Milady, I was the one who caused you all danger in the first place. If not for my flight into the Stormpeaks, the Jenestran soldiers would not have attacked you. I feel obligated to make amends, and I cannot in good conscience betray the wishes of the Priestesses of Truth. They've offered me refuge, and that alone calls for me to repay them."

Just like I want to repay Rhen, Falkris thought. *At least Daymen holds to his word, unlike me. I haven't been the best guard of late.* "I can respect that," she said aloud.

He held the slip of vellum containing the instructions out to her. "Will you take it, then?"

She shook her head. "No, you can keep it."

Daymen frowned. "But, Lady, you're the one in charge, so it only seems right that you bear the instructions."

"My name is Falkris, damn it!"

Amial moved between them. "Daymen, Falkris can't read."

Silence like the calm before a storm descended. For a moment, Falkris waited in stark terror for the mockery to follow. She braced herself for the scorn that she expected to pour from the lips of the Jenestran like a sudden rain.

Instead, he bowed to her. "Forgive me, Falkris. It was an oversight of mine. I never learned to read until I became a knight. I have forgotten, in my years among nobility, that the ability to read is not a gift given to all. Please forgive my stupidity."

She stared at the man, unable to speak. Kindness was the last thing she'd expected. Once more, Amial interceded. "Is that how you learned to speak Ravenian? Through reading?" Again, Falkris was surprised by her quick mind. She asked the questions that needed answers.

Daymen smiled, and the tension in the air broke. "No, Miss Amial. In Jenestra we speak your language, only a different dialect of it."

"Oh," Amial said.

Falkris regained herself and started into the valley. "Come on," she growled to the others, "if the instructions say go north, that's where we need to go." Without a word, they followed her.

Chapter 20

Rhen looked around at the surrounding plains. Even from the back of his horse, he couldn't see over the tall, waving grass. He would've attributed the problem to his short stature, but even Keth's head was below the sea of grass.

The big man loomed beside him, staring at nothing as he awaited instructions. On the noble's other side, Netria hovered, offering protection. Her hand remained near her sword at all times as she waited for orders from the noble.

At the moment, Rhen was wishing that Falkris was there. In the past few years he'd grown accustomed to always having her nearby to give him advice. She had become his crutch, one he desperately needed now, because he didn't know what to do.

"Master Tahnuil," Netria said.

He started at the sound of her voice. The silence before she had spoken had been long. Any sound that covered the emptiness of the plains was welcome. Being at the heart of nature, in an ocean of grass that stretched as far as the eye could see, was almost too much to bear.

"Yes?" he managed.

"Are you okay, Master Tahnuil?"

Distracted, he nodded, running one hand through his thick blonde hair. "Of course, Netria. And please, call me Rhen. There's no need for such formality between the two of us. Falkris calls you a friend, and that's enough for me."

Netria smiled in triumph, as if she'd just won a battle. Rhen wondered what she was fighting for. If it was his approval, she'd won it long ago. He already respected her, not only as a warrior, but also as a woman of superb character.

"Why do you ask?" he said.

She shook her head. "You've been silent a long time. I was wondering if you were feeling ill. Normally you rush into things, ready to face any challenge. Why is this time different?"

He smiled ruefully. "Well, milady, I no longer have Falkris with me. She's been my safety net, and I'm miss her now—"

Keth moved for the first time, turning his big brown eyes on his master. "You got me."

Rhen smiled and patted the big man on the shoulder. "I do, and I'm thankful for that."

"Look," Netria said, "Kris made me promise to protect you in her place. You've nothing to fear while I'm near."

"I should've known that she would find some way to look after me," he mused.

Netria nodded. "So, shall we continue?"

"Of course," he said, brightening already. "Alihandre told me that we must seek out the plains inhabitants. They alone can help us locate the Night's Breath."

"Sounds easy enough," Netria said with a cheerful attitude. "What sort of people are they?"

He shrugged. "I couldn't tell you. Everything was moving so quickly, and there was little time to ask all the questions that I wanted to. There was so much happening at once. I could barely think, let alone get a full report."

He sagged in the saddle. The bustle had been for Lady Lianna's sake. Over the last few weeks, he'd become quite fond of her. She, more than even Falkris, seemed to understand him. "I do hope Lianna's okay," he whispered. Absorbed in his misery over the unconscious woman, he missed the hurt expression on Netria's face.

Netria suppressed a small sigh as she watched Rhen. Falkris was right. The man was entirely smitten with the Lady Silvian. *How could a scarred warrior like me even think of competing with a beautiful, powerful woman like her?* she moped, wishing she'd never fallen for the nobleman.

His heart was so big, though, so full of hope and love. Even when he glanced at her for just a moment, his blue eyes took her breath away. All she wanted was to stare into those eyes, and for him to truly see her.

A moment ago, she had believed that there was still a chance. He'd used a familiarity with her that was a definite step in the right direction, and had even mentioned his regard for her. But that was because of her connection to Falkris, and it was nothing that had sprouted from his view of her as a person.

Netria reached out a trembling hand to touch him on the shoulder. "Cheer up, Rhen. We'll find the Night's Breath for your lady."

Smiling, he placed his hand over hers. "Thank you, Netria." Too soon, he released his hold on her, and she was forced to withdraw her hand from his shoulder.

With that, the noble kneed his horse forward, and they rode through the tall grass. Netria and Keth flanked Rhen, both keeping their eyes open for signs of trouble. The plains seemed to be deserted. There weren't even any trails worn from the passage of animals across the broad area.

Netria had a strange feeling, however, that eyes were on her. She glanced over her shoulder several times. Out of the corner of her eye, she thought she could see the fleeting shadow of something else moving amidst the grass. Always, when she turned her head, there was nothing there but the grass waving at her with an air of mockery.

After they had ridden for most of the day, they dismounted for a short break. Having no way to secure their horses, they let the animals stand with their reins hanging to the ground. The three travelers sat down and had a snack from their rations.

As Netria sat in the grass, apart from the others, she was aware of a strange vibration in the ground beneath her. She shifted her position, wondering if she had sat on something. The faint sensation persisted and then magnified.

The mercenary glanced at the two men. "Do you feel that?" she whispered.

Keth looked at her with an odd expression. Rhen shook his head after a moment of concentration. She tried to ignore the strange feeling, but it was growing in intensity. Soon the men could feel it as well. The slight widening of their eyes alerted her to this, as well as to the fact that she was not insane, as she had feared.

Bending to press her ear against the ground, she could hear a dull roar approaching, like the thunder of thousands of hooves. She cursed as she jumped to her feet. "Something's coming!"

Rhen looked up in surprise. "Are you sure?"

"Yes!" she snapped as she moved to help him up. "Come on, we need to get moving."

He rose to his feet at her behest and began brushing the dirt from his clothing. "Perhaps we should wait here. It may be the plains people, the ones we're supposed to search for."

Now the thunder of hooves striking the ground was audible. Netria listened for a moment, then shook her head. "I don't think so, Rhen."

"What else could it be?" he asked.

She shrugged. "I don't want to know. Let's just go."

He frowned. "No. I wish to remain here. We'll see what it is in a moment."

Indeed, the sound, once distant, had risen to a deafening level. Belatedly, Netria hurried to hold on to her horse. The mare, terrified, jerked away from her touch. The warrior, with a vehement curse, made a last desperate attempt to seize the mare's bridle. Her fingers closed around the rough leather, and she held on for dear life as her horse reared and tried to pull away from her.

As she fought the terrified horse, the grass around her began to flatten with the passage of immense creatures. Shaggy, the beasts had wide feet and lethal horns on their broad heads. They looked like some monstrous breed of cattle.

The mare, with a desperate jerk, pulled free and tore away across the plains, the other two mounts following. Netria yelled after them, terror creeping into the pit of her stomach. How would they survive without food and water? There was nothing out on the plains but grass, and it didn't appear edible.

A rough hand on her arm jerked her out of the path of one of the shaggy creatures. Rhen pulled her towards him and Keth. They dodged another of the strange animals as it charged past them with a deep cry. Its eyes, Netria saw with a measure of fascination, were wide and rolling with fright. The ground was now shaking violently as the herd of great herbivores fled past.

"They're stampeding," she whispered.

Rhen heard her over the pounding of hooves by some trick of the wind. "Obviously."

Netria drew closer to him. "I wonder what made them run."

Just then a terrifying roar split the air. Rhen swallowed. "I really wish you hadn't said that."

One of the creatures running past them stumbled, faltering for just a moment. In an instant, a great, cat-like creature was upon it, tearing at it with lethal claws. The jaws that opened to enclose the head of the terrified beast were huge, with teeth the length of swords flashing white in the sun.

On the other side of the humans, another animal fell prey to the giant predator. Netria, in some insane and desperate attempt to protect herself, drew her sword.

"There's no time for that!" Rhen screamed in her ear. "Just run!"

She sheathed her sword, and the three of them ran as fast as they could amidst the cattle. Behind them they heard the fierce snarling of one of the predators followed by a deep cry of pain. The sound of bones snapping gave them the extra energy to increase their speed.

Netria and the two men ran faster than they ever had before. The strange herd of beasts outdistanced them, but still they ran on. Fear of being caught by the fearsome predators was enough to drive the humans on even when the threat had passed. When they could run no more, the three fell to the ground, drawing in air with huge, panicked gasps.

At last, their breathing slowed to normal, and they strained their ears for sounds of pursuit. Silence descended on the plains. The ground beneath their backs was still, and it seemed that they'd been left alone on the vast grasslands. Without food or water, that made for a very dire situation.

Rhen was the first to rise. Wearily, he urged the other two to their feet. "Come on. There's a little time before dark. Let's make what progress we can before we camp for the night."

Netria rolled to her feet. She swallowed, trying to get some moisture into her wind-torn throat. "Right." None of them wanted to voice the thought that was running through their minds. What if they didn't find the plains people before they ran out of food? If they didn't starve to death, they would certainly die of dehydration. Tired and afraid, they trudged on until dark.

Keth was on watch, guarding his companions while they slept beneath the moon. Their still forms looked like lumps in the darkness, the only thing giving their shape the form of humanity the soft contours of their frames. He cared for them both very much.

So he stood, silent and strong, as the hours passed. Soon the moon would be at its highest, and he could wake Netria to take over the watch. His eyelids felt heavy, and there was a slight sway to his stoic stance. The moment when he could lie down and rest was one that he eagerly awaited.

Behind him, the grass shifted with a soft swish, like that of a woman's skirts as she walked. He turned to survey their surroundings, his hand going to his sword. Keth didn't know what was out there, but he had a feeling that whatever it was did not bode well for his companions. Frowning, he tried to decide whether he should wake the two still forms at his feet.

Before he even managed to consider his options, the swift shadows were upon him. They moved with deadly efficiency, the only visible part of them being their weapons, which shined in the moonlight.

Keth saw the sharp point of a spear descend towards Rhen,

and he no longer needed to consider what to do. Bellowing his rage, he drew his sword. The spears that bit into him as he did so didn't even register in his brain, so filled with anger was he. With the skills that Falkris had beat into him, he cut into his dark opponents, dealing death out with the expert kiss of his blade.

He was happy to see that blood coated his blade, for he had feared that his opponents weren't human. When one of the shadows that he cut into cried out with a normal voice, he was even further pleased. What he had feared to be demons were in fact people, like him.

That didn't sway Keth's blood lust. These people had threatened Rhen, the only man who had ever looked at him with anything other than contempt or pity. No, Rhen loved him, and Keth basked in that light. To see it extinguished would be to die inside. Keth would rather sacrifice himself to save the only person who had ever cared about him than see Rhen die.

As he moved like a whirlwind of death amidst his enemies, he became aware of a sharp pain in his side and upper back. He half-remembered pressure there, and a sick feeling of flesh rending, but he had not felt anything else until now. The warmth on his skin could only be his own blood. Had he been wounded?

As the realization of his own danger dawned on him, he saw that the shadowy enemies were numberless. More than he could count already lay dead at his feet, but still they rose to fight him. Despair gripped him as he fought in vain to save his master.

Netria rolled to her feet at the first sound from Keth. She was lucky that she'd moved so quickly, or the spear that had been coming towards her would've found its mark. She drew her sword as she rose, ready to fight despite the fog of sleep that still weighed on her.

At the sight of so many spears leveled towards her heart, she stopped short. Frightened but filled with grim determination, she stood her ground. The sight of Rhen with a spear against his throat halted any mad schemes to escape that came to mind, so she did nothing.

Escape was already impossible for Keth. The big man was fighting madly, and even in the dark she could see that he'd been stabbed numerous times. The strange men with the spears surrounded him, and in a moment, he went down beneath them, still bellowing as he disappeared in a sea of shadows and spears.

Beside Netria, Rhen cried out in a sound of pure anguish, of pain so raw that it cut straight to her heart. His eyes, dark with the shade of night, brimmed with tears, and one slid down his cheek as she watched. Netria would've moved to comfort him, but the sharp point of a spear at her back persuaded her to drop her sword and raise her hands over her head.

A deep, guttural voice grunted behind her. "Your friend is a fool. Don't make the same error."

Netria glanced at Rhen. The noble was staring in anguish at Keth. The men who had borne him down had moved away, leaving the big man in a crumpled heap on the ground. Oblivious to his own danger, Rhen broke away from his attackers and ran to his friend's side. He pushed warning spears away as he fell to his knees beside the unconscious giant. "Keth!"

Netria moved to his side, keeping her hands raised to the sky as she did so. Kneeling down beside him, she put an arm around his shoulders to comfort him. The moment was lost when an insistent spear again jabbed into her back.

"Come."

She rose to her feet, dragging Rhen up with her. He leaned on her, the strain of grief weighing him down. Holding on to him as tightly as she could, she wished that there were something, anything that she could do to help him.

The man who had spoken moved closer to them, and she could make out the dark lines of his face in the silvery light of the moon. "We'll bring your friend. He may live, if he's lucky, but he may wish he had died. No one kills our people and survives." Her hopes slipping away like quicksilver, Netria stumbled ahead of the spears into the night.

Chapter 21

The valley was beautiful. Where the thick, green grass did not grow, flowers of every color layered the ground like a quilt. Lining the valley on all sides, tall blue mountains stretched up majestically. Their tops were crested with snow, but the air below was pleasant and warm.

Striking down through the trees to create golden beams of light that pooled on the floor of the forest, the sun shone from a flawless blue sky. The silver bark of the beautiful trees sparkled, even when no light touched it. Faultless green leaves graced the branches of these beautiful giants.

Life was abundant on the forest floor. Though there was no sign of any other human having set foot in the valley, the wildlife seemed to be tame. As they walked along the valley, the three travelers were silent. To speak would have been sacrilege. They'd already disrupted the purity of nature with their presence, and they had no wish to damage it further.

Falkris froze as a deer approached her. A buck, he had a full rack of antlers on his head. When he paused to watch her, he looked like something from heaven. An odd sense of intelligence was in his wise eyes as he regarded her. She took one step forward and he bounded away into the trees with a flash.

"What a magnificent creature," Daymen whispered. At his side, Amial didn't dare to speak, though her eyes spoke of the enchantment that the valley had placed on her.

Falkris glanced at the knight, then back to where the buck's fleeting presence had been only seconds before. For a moment, she stood in total awe of nature, her heart quiet as she looked around her at the beauty wrought by a superior intelligence. "Yeah," she managed at last, her voice sounding incredibly harsh to her ears when contrasted with the soft laugh of the breeze.

The three of them walked on, moving with reverence beneath the canopy of leaves. They paused at a stream to drink and rest for a brief moment. As they sat beside the gentle trickle of water, the sun arced down to kiss their skin. The moment would last forever in their hearts, but reality left it too brief.

Falkris was walking a short distance ahead of the others when something soft and cold landed on her cheek. She paused, wondering what it was. Her hand rose to touch the place where her skin had been intruded upon. The tip of her finger came away wet.

Curious, she looked up. As she watched, a white flake of snow drifted down and landed on the tip of her nose. She blinked. The sun shone overhead from a cloudless blue sky, its warmth a gentle comfort. The grass and trees were green, and it was summer here, a virtual paradise. Yet, it snowed.

Walking on, she said nothing. When the snow started falling harder, she stopped and turned to the others in wonder, hoping she wasn't alone in her perception of the strange weather. Amial had stopped as well and stood with one hand outstretched to catch the snow on her palm. As Falkris watched, a flake, perfect and pristine, floated down to land amidst Amial's outstretched fingers.

Daymen was looking around, his eyes narrowed in suspicion as he regarded the trees. "But it's summer," he said at last.

Falkris gestured to them, and they continued. Soon the snow was falling in earnest, and their hair and clothing were coated with white. Despite the summer sun and the gentle breeze, the temperature continued to drop as they walked until all three of them were shivering.

Amial paused and opened her pack. "There's winter clothing in here." She raised her eyes. "The priestesses must have known what we would encounter." Pulling out a long cloak lined with fur, she threw it over her shoulders, adjusting her bow and quiver so that they were still quickly accessible.

Falkris and Daymen looked in their own packs and found

the same. Below the cloaks, there were boots suited for walking in snow. Heavy gloves and scarves were also present. Beneath it all were some rations and basic traveling supplies.

The little group hurried to dress themselves in the warm clothing. Thankfully, the heavy clothing kept the cold at bay. Daymen lifted his pack to his shoulders again. "I wondered why the packs were so heavy."

Falkris cursed, much to the chagrin of the other two. When she looked up to see their eyes on her, she shrugged an apology. "I didn't ever want to be in another storm again, and it looks like that wish is about to be broken already."

She pointed through the trees. Up ahead, the ground was layered with snow. As the forest stretched on, drifts of snow rolled amidst the silver trunks. Exchanging looks that were far from enthusiastic, the three of them continued on.

Falkris looked up. The branches that formed the canopy over their heads were covered with ice. Beneath the clear prison, the leaves were green and perfect. The drift at the base of the tree sloped away from the silver bark. At its lowest, it revealed the colorful heads of flowers.

The warrior bent down to look at the flowers. With her gloved hands, she pushed away the snow. Her efforts uncovered grass and more flowers. She removed her glove to touch the soft grass, which was warm to her fingers, as though the sun still shone on it. The snow, in contrast, was incredibly cold.

Dax bounded through the drift beside her, showering her with a spray of snow. Enthusiastic, he moved forward and nudged her aside to nose at the flowers and grass. As she rose to her feet, he turned to look at her with laughing eyes and a lolling tongue. At least someone was enjoying the strange weather. The wolf, it seemed, was undisturbed.

Without a word, the three of them walked on. Dax bounded ahead, cutting a path through the snow. None of them spoke as they followed in his wake. Standing amidst the summery landscape frozen in a prison of ice was far too unnerving.

Soon their breath was rising from their mouths in a moist

cloud of steam, which rose around their faces, brushing against their skin until it was gone, dissipating in the still air. Falkris watched her breath rise, rather than the strange snow around her.

Daymen was the first to break the silence. "It doesn't make sense," he muttered, his Jenestran accent prominent in his soft voice.

Amial paused, causing the other two warriors to stop as well. She looked around, her brown eyes wide. One hand reached out to touch a green leaf encased in ice. "Snow is so *pure*." Her emphasis on the word wasn't lost on them. "Have you looked behind us?"

They did so. The snow where they'd walked moments before was unmarked. Where they had trudged through the drifts, there remained no sign of their passage, as if they'd never even set foot in the valley.

Falkris shivered from more than the cold. "Why?"

Amial looked around, appraising their situation. "I believe the snow is meant to discourage. This valley houses the Temple of Purity. What could be more impure than humanity? Certainly, our sinful nature is far from flawless. We're the epitome of what's wrong in the world."

Falkris frowned but didn't dispute the girl's logic. *Netria was right when she said that I'm far from pure*, she thought. *My hands are covered with the blood of hundreds.* She could think of no one less suited to enter the Temple of Purity. The moment she set foot inside, she'd probably be struck dead.

Unwilling to voice her thoughts, she walked on. As the day passed, and the storm around them grew more vehement, she began to tire. Forging a path through the snow was hard work. Though Dax bounded ahead of her, the path that he wrought often disappeared with him. She wished that she had a fraction of the wolf's boundless energy.

A touch on her shoulder halted her dogged progress. She turned, grateful for the break. The knight looked at her with his dark eyes. "Milady," he said, pleading with her, "allow me to lead for a time." Before she could manage a protest, he raised a hand to stop it. "We're in this together. There's no sense in allowing you to tire while I'm yet fit."

With a nod, she let him pass. She was content to follow him as he made his way through the smooth drifts. As they moved on, the storm intensified, swirling around them in a deadly tempest of cold. Beneath Daymen's tracks, she saw the gentle heads of flowers encased in ice. Having no desire to linger in the valley any longer than was necessary, she hoped they'd reach the temple soon.

Amial followed the others, walking in the path that they made for her. She admired her companions. The eyes of the two warriors were piercing and ancient, the eyes of people who had seen far too much in their young lives. Neither of them could be a day over twenty-six.

Amial herself had seen little of the world. Her search for Falkris had been her first journey beyond her small farm and the neighboring village. Before then, she had not ranged far from the small box that had made up her life. Her head had been full of dreams and hopes.

Since the day she'd stolen her father's horse and fled her normal life, she had changed dramatically. In the weeks that followed her excursion into the unknown, she'd seen many things and had even killed a man, something that her mind had not yet been able to fathom. She'd gotten drunk with the others, and her ears had burned at what they had told her. A part of her imagined it had all helped her to mature. Another part of her feared she was still the foolish girl who had fled from reality.

Now she was following two of the most amazing people she had ever met. Falkris had a proud heart and a will that could bend iron. Such power in an individual was amazing to see. Daymen was the woman's equal. Amial was proud to have earned some respect from them, which was a miracle to her, a blessing of such magnitude that being grateful didn't seem adequate. As she walked along behind them, she couldn't help but reflect on how her life had changed.

"Falkris," she said.

The woman glanced over her shoulder. "Aye?"

"Why did you decide to become a warrior?"

Falkris didn't answer for some time, and Amial worried that she'd offended her. Then the answer came, as harsh in its message as in its sound. "My family was slaughtered. It was the only way open to me other than selling myself on the streets."

Amial didn't know what to say for a moment. "May I ask why they were killed?"

Falkris nodded, though she didn't look back at the younger woman. "My father was a nobleman. He didn't agree with the policies of the Ravenian royalty. The king, therefore, didn't agree with him."

Daymen glanced over his shoulder at Falkris' answer, which surprised him more than anything else she could've said. And yet, it made sense. The moment the words were spoken, he could see the truth in them. He'd always thought that there was something noble in Falkris' bearing, something that spoke of being high born. *But if she is noble, why can't she read?* he wondered.

Amial's voice rang out again, soft and innocent. "But, if you're a noble's daughter, why didn't you do something?"

Daymen answered for Falkris. "Because she was only a girl, and she didn't want to die with her father."

Surprise tinged Falkris' voice when she spoke again. "Right. My death would've served nothing, so I had to wait for my revenge. I needed to grow stronger."

Silence descended as the three of them continued trudging through the snow. Breaking the trail was hard work. Daymen wondered how Falkris had kept it up for so long without seeming to tire.

Amial, astute as always, asked the very question that was still plaguing Daymen. "But, if you're noble, why can't you read?"

The knight could almost sense Falkris stiffening behind him. Her inadequacy bothered her a lot, though she'd never admit it. He wondered how he could coax her into allowing him to help her, but he doubted that it was possible.

Falkris' answer, when she gave it, was very quiet. "I was a girl, and the youngest in my family. My father didn't see a need to waste money on my schooling." This was a lie, and all three of them knew it.

Daymen looked back at the two women. Falkris was staring at nothing. Amial had a small frown on her face, as if thinking very deeply about something important. "Surely you were given voice lessons," the girl whispered.

"Aye, but that was all I asked of my father. He would've given me far more, but it was all I wanted. Singing was my only true passion. I was foolish." A grudging edge colored her voice. Admitting the truth did not make her proud.

Silence again. Daymen thought about the ugly scar that ran across Falkris' throat. The wound must've ruined her voice. She was lucky she had lived, but the cost to her must have been severe. Naked longing was barely disguised in her rough voice when she talked about singing.

As he tried to think of something comforting to say to her, a building wrought from white, perfect stone came into view through the haze of snow. He paused, wondering what to do. The area ahead of them could possibly be trapped, but he doubted it because the storm was deterrent enough.

Falkris pushed her way through the snow until she was standing beside him. "The sun will be setting soon. We might as well take shelter in there. I don't think we'd survive if we tried to sleep out here in the snow."

He nodded. "Right." Cautiously, the two of them crossed the stretch between the forest and the temple, Amial following in their wake.

Chapter 22

As Lianna's companions were transported across Jenestra, the robed man watched, then faded back into the safety of the shadows. Silent and thoughtful, he slunk away through his tunnels to the little room he kept far beneath the monastery, amidst the crumbled ruins of long forgotten catacombs. Once in his haven, he sank down before the little altar set in the wall. A lamp sputtered beside him, throwing odd shadows as he knelt, head bowed to the floor as he said his prayers. The altar was dedicated to strength, one of the five virtues. He had long pursued the path of the Priests of Strength. Indeed, he had been raised among them, an orphaned child with only the monastery willing to shelter him. From the priests, he had learned the system of beliefs that governed him now.

To follow the way of strength was more than just to temper his body to perfection. He must be strong in his beliefs, unwilling to waver in the face of opposition. Strength of will, heart, mind and soul must be cultivated.

What the priests had not taught him was that with strength came power. Muscled and lean, his body was tireless. He could run for hours, lift twice his own weight and was flexible and dexterous. Those skills had allowed him to gain access to the Well of Truth, the coveted artifact that the priestesses guarded.

Tempering his mind with knowledge, he had learned to think clearly and quickly. To pursue understanding, he'd used his vast intelligence. He had researched and read many books until at last he had come to know himself and his beliefs. The newfound strength in his mind and heart had allowed him to wield the powers granted to him through the Priesthood of Strength with control and incredible potency.

The other Priests of Strength had been disturbed by his

ambitions. Claiming that his perceptions of the meaning of strength were false, they'd cast him out and denied him. He knew that they were wrong.

Thus, he'd crept away into the depths of earth, hiding in the catacombs that he'd discovered through his extensive studies. In time, he made his way here, to the edge of the Stormpeaks, so that he could use the Well of Truth. He had then mastered the powers of the well and learned to use it to his advantage.

Desire to become more powerful was an unquenchable fire within him; he wanted to be the strongest man in the world. The potential to achieve ultimate power was his, but he knew that he couldn't do it alone. He needed followers, people strong enough to stand with him against the combined might of the priests and priestesses of the five virtues.

By eavesdropping from his system of tunnels, he had learned of the existence of a woman who was just what he was looking for. Her name was Lianna Silvian, and she was the granddaughter of an exiled Priestess of Purity. She had grown up in a noble house, oblivious to her origins and to the incredible power that was sleeping within her. Her grandmother had been the most powerful woman alive, and that same power now coursed through Lianna's veins.

Alihandre had learned of Lianna's existence, and of the power she was capable of. Using the Well of Truth, the foolish priestess had contacted Lianna and urged her to come to Jenestra. Alihandre had done so not only because of the girl's power, but also because of the growing threat from Lord Silvian. The priestess had wanted Lianna alive and safe from the lord's reach.

The robed man sat up and regarded the altar before him. Lord Silvian would be an obstacle. The Ravenian noble had mastered his abilities at a young age and was using them to gain power. However, he didn't receive his magic through the virtues or the One God. He called on an older, darker power, the very power for which his ancestress had been exiled. Lord

Silvian would have to be eliminated.

The robed man rose to his feet. With grace and power in his slim frame, he moved to the bed. Sitting down, he folded his legs beneath him as he assumed a position ideal for a trance. He would need to battle the spell the Priestesses of Truth were placing on Lianna now, before it grew in strength. That he would succeed was not something he doubted.

Alihandre and her priestesses sat in a circle around Lianna. The girl was stretched out on the cold floor, her eyes closed. Though Lianna looked like she was just resting, the High Priestess knew otherwise. Alihandre could practically smell the drug that was even now working against Lianna.

The priestesses joined hands, prepared to sit vigil over Lady Silvian until the drug's hold on her was over. Several of the most powerful priestesses were not with those chosen to watch over Lianna. Overseeing the noblewoman could prove dangerous; there had to be someone left alive with the power to transport the six travelers back to the monastery.

Confident that the monastery was in capable hands, Alihandre let herself sink into the depths of a trance. Her followers were with her, and she could feel the soft brushes of their minds against hers. Using their powers, they could fend off any foreign power that would dare to touch Lianna's soul.

Deep within the haze that covered her mind, Lianna walked along a stone passageway. In her thoughts, she was exploring the monastery. In all actuality, she was unconscious, but the truth had no place in her dreams. Oblivious, she continued her unending journey, her feet soundless on the stone as she traveled through the fog of the strange world that held her. Her eyes wide, she explored the catacombs, noting the layers of dust that had not been disturbed in centuries.

She turned a corner and looked up to see a dark figure standing before her. As she watched, he pulled back his hood to reveal a handsome face with dark, flashing eyes. There was strength in those eyes, and power coated him like early morning mist on the mountains. Stopping to regard him in silence, she was uncertain how to react to his presence within the bowels of the monastery.

"Lady Silvian," he said, "I've been waiting for you."

"Do I know you?" she asked.

He inclined his head. "You do not, but I have known you for some time. I've been watching you."

Lianna considered leaving him then and there. She had the power to walk away, but something about this mysterious stranger intrigued her. Perhaps it was the shadows that seemed to cling about him, hiding him from her green eyes. "Tell me your name," she said, "and I'll consider speaking with you."

He laughed then, exposing straight white teeth. "My lady, you humble me with your charm. My name is Beldaris."

"Beldaris," she said, tasting the name. "It's a strong name."

He smiled again, dangerously handsome. "My lady, you do me more honor than you can know." Returning the smile, she accepted his arm. Talking in quiet voices, playing the game of words that Lianna loved so well, they disappeared into the depths of the monastery.

Alihandre's eyes snapped open. Her breath came in short, raspy gasps. She looked to the other priestesses, who were even now coming up from the depths of their own trances. The fear in their eyes was enough to answer the waking dread in her heart.

One of the younger women spoke, fear in her words. "Beldaris ... can it be? Did you hear his name whisper across her thoughts?"

Another priestess nodded. "I did. I heard it clearly. What does it mean?"

Alihandre silenced them all with a raised hand. She was not as calm as she appeared, though she wished that she was. "Perhaps Beldaris has indeed drugged Lianna. He disappeared long ago, and it wouldn't surprise me to have him resurface from his exile at such a crucial time. It's either he who now holds dominion over her mind, or someone who is using his name."

"What will we do?" a woman asked, despair coloring her words.

"We should kill the lady before she falls under his sway," someone whispered. Alihandre looked around, but could not discern the source of the comment.

The High Priestess of Truth rose to her feet, drawing all of the command that she could into her small, round frame. "We'll do no such thing ... until it is absolutely necessary. If Beldaris manages to corrupt her, she must be killed. Until then, we'll guard her and hope that her friends return with the antidote in time." Looking down at Lianna's face, beautiful and peaceful as she rested under the influence of the drug, Alihandre wondered how much time was left.

Beldaris smiled. Persuading Lianna to come to him was easier than he had expected. He'd promised her that he would help her learn to use her powers. Over time, he would win her trust, and perhaps her affection. Once he convinced her that his enemies were hers, and that he loved her, he'd have her fighting for him. One way or another, she would follow him.

With his powers, he had sensed the Priestesses of Truth weaving through Lianna's mind. Before they'd been able to cast the spell that would stop him, he had taken Lianna away from them, back into the core of her mind where nothing could reach her. Nothing but him. He smiled.

Chapter 23

Falkris stood watch in the entrance of the Temple of Purity while Daymen made a fire on the smooth white floor. Amial explored the room they were in as the two warriors worked to secure their safety for the night. Very scrupulous in her examination, the archer nodded to herself when she uncovered the tiny flaw in the wall, which had definitely been placed thereon purpose.

Deciding that caution was her wisest choice, Amial didn't fiddle with it. Instead, she marked its location in her memory and went to sit beside Daymen at the fire. Glancing at the knight, she saw that his eyes were fastened on Falkris. She followed his gaze. The woman stood silhouetted against the storm outside. Leaning against the white stone that constituted the entrance, Falkris appeared to be a shadow. The wolf at her side was as still, like a statue.

"Lady Falkris," Daymen said, "you should warm yourself by the fire. Nothing will threaten us from outside."

Amial nodded her agreement. "If there's any threat to us, it comes from within the temple. The only thing dangerous outside is the storm."

Falkris pushed away from the wall, saying nothing. She turned to regard them, her gray eyes flashing in the light of the fire. A strong gust of wind played with her hair, tugging it loose from her braid so that it blew in her face. Amial was enthralled with the power the woman exhibited.

"Falkris," she managed after a moment, "making yourself sick will serve none of us."

The warrior nodded and stepped from the shadows to the light of the fire. Without a word, she sat down on the side of the fire opposite her companions. Dax trailed behind her like her shadow. He flopped down beside her, pressing himself against her leg. As soon as the wolf was settled, Falkris drew out her sword and began to whet the blade. For a time, it was the only sound in the little room.

While the two women rested, Daymen began preparing a warm meal for them from the rations. He drew out a small pot and poured some water into it, then cut some dried meat into the pot. Amial realized Daymen was going to make soup. Being a farmer's daughter, she had known how to cook for longer than she could remember. "Let me do that, Sir Aschton."

The knight glanced up, but shook his head. "I'd prefer to cook, Lady Amial. It gives me some peace at the end of the day, even if the food is worse for the wear."

Amial smiled and sat back to let him do as he pleased. Falkris continued to draw the stone across the blade, sharpening her sword to perfection. When the warrior spoke, it came as a surprise to the archer. "Amial, sing something."

"Sing?"

Falkris raised her eyes, and for a moment ceased her maintenance of the sword. "That's what I said."

Amial nodded. Suddenly self-conscious, she lowered her eyes and stared at the ground in hopes of inspiration. She almost never sang for an audience, and singing in front of the two hardened warriors was an intimidating prospect. Finally, she collected herself and drew in a deep breath. The ritualistic feel of air entering her lungs, pushing down deep until her stomach expanded, relaxed her. She began to sing, losing herself in the gentle vibrations in her chest as the air moved through her.

Her voice rose as she continued, and she delighted in the feel of her tone resonating higher in her body. She could feel the center of her voice vibrating along the roof of her mouth, extending through her nose and forehead, a sensation that she always relished. The music moved through her, giving her soul a voice.

For a time, she forgot that she even had an audience. Lost in the music, her entire being focused on her song. She let herself soar with the words. When she finally returned to the room, she opened her eyes. The song ended, and she found that her two companions were watching her, spellbound.

"You have a beautiful voice," Falkris said at last. "I would've liked to sing a duet with you."

Amial blushed and lowered her gaze. "Thank you."

Daymen nodded. "The lady is right, Miss Amial. I've seldom heard such a voice."

Falkris spoke softly from across the fire. "You never heard me sing." She was quiet for a time. The uncomfortable silence was filled with the crackling of the fire. "They called me the songbird," she said at last.

Amial didn't know what to say. Daymen did his best to rectify the situation. "Lady Falkris," he said, "sometimes things are taken from us for a reason. If you had never lost your voice, would you be here today?"

She laughed once, deep in her chest. "No, Daymen. You're right there." The knight leaned forward to stir the fire, and for the rest of the evening, little was said between them.

Falkris had the first watch. Daymen and Amial slept on the cool floor while she stood over them, stirring the fire once in a while. As she waited for her watch to end, she couldn't help but wonder where the danger would come from. She had a sickening feeling in the pit of her stomach, a dreadful sense of foreboding that taunted her with its icy touch. Something bad was going to happen, but she didn't know what, or even if it would affect her.

Perhaps something has happened to Rhen. I should never have left him. She tried to shake herself out of her self-doubt as the snowy wind howled outside. Even inside the stone building, she shivered with the cold, for the storm penetrated all the way into the little room she shared with her companions. Dax pressed close to her, but the warmth of his fur against her did little to keep the cold from seeping into her bones.

To occupy herself, she studied her surroundings. The

little room seemed to be as far as the temple went, but that didn't coincide with the outside appearance of the structure. Even through the storm, she had seen that the building was immense. There had to be a way to go further into the temple.

She glanced at Amial, who was sound asleep. The girl had investigated the room thoroughly but had said nothing about her discoveries. Surely if the answer lay within the room, Amial would've mentioned it. She was intelligent enough to discern the answer. If the archer had found naught, Falkris doubted that she would be any more fortunate in her search.

Still, she had the feeling that the way forward was before her. Her growing sense of unease bothered her. That danger lurked in the shadows beyond the fire was certain, not from the storm, but from somewhere within the room itself. Even the pressure of Dax leaning against her leg wasn't enough to calm her.

Falkris finally gave in to her premonitions and nudged Daymen awake. Barely a moment passed before he was alert and on his feet, one hand on his sword. He looked around, expecting danger. When nothing presented itself, he shifted his gaze to Falkris.

She kept her own hand on her weapon. "Something's going to happen." At the sound of stone scraping against stone echoing from the darkness at the back of the room, she fell silent.

Cautious, she drew her sword. The grating sound stopped as suddenly as it had begun. In the following silence, Dax growled low in his throat. Falkris looked to the knight. He had drawn his weapon as well and was staring into the shadows with intent eyes. Turning, she searched for the source of the sound.

Then, flashing out of the darkness, came a monster straight out of a nightmare. A great white creature, it was composed of ice, with outspread wings. Dropping from above them, it landed on Falkris, dragging her to the ground. Sharp claws dug into her shoulders, tearing her flesh into bloody strips.

Falkris struggled beneath the creature's weight, terrified beyond measure. Part of her remained detached, guiding her actions. Tensing her body, she tried to roll away from the monster as it continued to tear at her back. Her body was protected by her armor, but she knew that the leather would be shredded in moments. All efforts to escape the beast were in vain. There was no breaking away from its grasp. Her face smashed into the white stone floor. She heard a low growl, and a shadow darted towards her. The creature shifted, then Dax yipped in pain and fell back. A moment later, a piercing shriek cut through the air, and the weight on her increased, as though the creature was pushing down. Then the icy monster took to the air.

Falkris rolled to her feet, ignoring the pain in her shoulders, and recovered her sword. She took a wary fighting stance beside Daymen, waiting for the creature to drop again. Her eyes followed its path along the ceiling of the room. Although it was shaped like a human, bat wings sprouted from the monster's back. Made of ice, its body was far from flesh. Daymen's sword was stuck in the humanoid's side, and from the wound, a clear liquid dripped to the floor. Falkris realized that the beast was bleeding water.

Awake now, Amial tracked the path of the monster with wide eyes. She rose from her bedroll and grabbed her bow. Her first arrow bounced off the icy fiend, doing no harm. Hissing, the humanoid swooped low over her head.

Falkris moved to the girl's side. The next time the creature dashed at them, Falkris swung at it with her sword. When it pulled up in time to dodge her blow, she cursed. Beside her, the archer thrust one of her arrows into the fire. Amial nocked the flaming missile and let it fly. True to her skills, the arrow found its mark. The missile hit the monster's wing with a sizzle, and the room echoed with screeches of pain. A moment later, the elemental creature plummeted to the ground.

The fiend rose to its feet, wavering where it stood. When the beast unfurled its wings, Falkris saw that one was covered with an ugly black mark. The humanoid didn't move towards them; it just stood unsteadily on clawed feet as it regarded them with glittering eyes. The monster's piercing gaze held Falkris in place, and she found that she couldn't move. The freakish creature hobbled toward her, its clawed hands still wet with her blood.

Amial yelled beside her, but Falkris couldn't understand the words. She was lost in the depths of those dark eyes. As long as the icy abomination looked at her, into her soul, she was powerless to act against it. Mesmerized, she felt her sword slip from her hand to land at her feet.

Risking burning himself, Daymen seized a log from the fire and threw it at the monster with all his might. The sharp pain in his hand was nothing compared to the satisfaction he felt when the flaming end struck the beast full in the chest, and the fiend shrieked in pain. With agonized screams, the creature began to melt, its face burning away and water seeping down to form a puddle on the floor. As the three humans watched in horror, the terrible beast screeched. The last things to melt away were its eyes, still burning into Falkris, malevolent with feral hatred.

The puddle of water disappeared, slipping through the cracks in the floor until it seemed that the monster had never existed at all. Falkris stared at the place where the beast had been and shuddered.

A gentle touch on her arm claimed her attention. She turned to see Daymen looking at her with concern. "Let me help you."

She blinked. "With what?"

He pointed at her bloody shoulders. Amial, looking at the wound as well, turned away, one hand covering her mouth. For a moment, Falkris feared that the girl would lose her stomach, but the archer managed to maintain control.

Daymen sat Falkris down and gently removed her armor. She looked at the torn pieces of leather and chain as he threw them to the side. "My armor's ruined," she whispered.

"Yes, but at least you're alive," he pointed out. "You can

always buy new armor, but a life is lost forever."

As he cut away her tunic, she reflected on what he'd said. How many lives had she ended? Not something she wanted to consider in detail, the thought of all the people she had killed nauseated her. Death was permanent, and she had become its instrument.

Her thoughts were interrupted from their dark cycle when Dax limped over to her. Concerned, she leaned forward to look at him. Seeing no blood matting his fur, she let out a relieved breath. Falkris had not been as fortunate. In shock, she stared at the ragged tears in her shoulders as Daymen pushed the rent skin back into place. Although in tremendous pain, she didn't make a sound as he worked. The part that she hated most was yet to come.

Falkris dug her fingers into her thigh as he brought out the flask of whiskey. Amial had recovered and was watching now. Daymen gestured to her. "Can you sew?"

The archer nodded, her face very white. The knight smiled grimly at her. "I'm going to pour some alcohol on the wound to insure that it doesn't get infected. Can you sew her skin back in place?"

"I can," Amial admitted without enthusiasm. "I gave Papa stitches once, when he cut his hand."

"Good," Daymen said. He handed the girl a needle and thread. "Are you ready?" he asked Falkris, his eyes giving her strength.

She nodded and closed her eyes. Clenching her teeth, she drew in a sharp breath as the alcohol poured into her wounds. The pain was excruciating, an unending burn. For a moment, when her head pounded and her thoughts receded into darkness, she feared that she was going to lose consciousness. Almost, she would've welcomed it.

A rough hand took hers, and she opened her eyes. Daymen was watching her steadily as he held her hands. His dark eyes, as well as the touch of his fingers on hers, gave her strength. He nodded to her.

Her fingers convulsed as Amial set the needle to her skin. With the knight's help, Falkris kept still, despite the pain. His eyes held hers the whole time that Amial stitched her wounds. She could see from his guarded expression that he was still alert to more danger, despite his concern for her.

At last, Amial was finished. The girl bound the wounds with cloth after smearing some ointment on them. Falkris sighed with relief. Daymen seemed reluctant to relinquish her hands, but he did. He helped her put on a clean tunic and gestured to her bedroll.

"You need to rest. I'll take the watch now."

Falkris was reluctant, but did as she was told. Because of the searing pain in her shoulders, she had trouble getting comfortable. Warriors, however, learned to block things out. Especially when faced with death, it was safer that way. Withdrawing her mind from the pain, she drifted off to sleep.

Chapter 24

Netria stumbled into the camp, barely able to walk, as the sun peeked over the horizon. They had been walking most of the night, and with the exertions of the day before still weighing on her, she felt as though she might die from exhaustion at any moment. Not caring to think, she did whatever her captors bid her. She had no desire to contemplate the events of the day. Sometimes the absence of thought was a welcome release. The fleeting emptiness within her was something that she wished she could hold onto forever.

The man who held the spear against her back gestured to her. She stumbled in the direction he indicated. The point of his spear shoving into her brought her panicked thoughts back to reality. Like a common beast, she was herded into a cage of some sort. Rhen was shoved in beside her. The door swung shut and was locked, imprisoning them forever as far as she was concerned.

Inside the large cage, designed to house humans, there was a rough bed against one wall and an area at the back for human waste. Made of thick wood, the bars layered every side of the cage from top to bottom. There was no perceivable escape.

As she watched, Rhen dragged himself to the bed and flopped down on it, staring at the floor in dismay with his head buried in his hands. No light was visible in his blue eyes when he paused to look up at Netria. A strained moment passed, then he returned his gaze to the floor.

Netria paced the cage for a time, wondering what the strange men wanted with her. As she examined her surroundings, she realized that she was in the center of a village of some sort. The houses were primitive, more hovels than homes. She wondered how anyone could bear to live in such places, made from dirt and grass. After years of sleeping under the stars, she preferred the open skies to a home like the ones these people lived in, let alone the cage.

Looking around the village, she realized that she didn't see any form of livestock—no cattle, no poultry, not even any dogs. If these barbaric people didn't eat some form of animal, what *did* they eat? With a swallow, she considered the unthinkable. *Perhaps they're cannibals.* Unbidden, the thought crept into her mind.

She stalked the perimeter of the cage for a time, knowing that her fears would plague her if she dared attempt to sleep. Her pacing halted when Rhen spoke. "Do you suppose Keth is still alive?"

Netria wanted to scream at him. *How the hell am I supposed to know?* Instead of giving voice to her own slow decline of hope, she sat down beside him. "I think he'll live, Rhen. I don't know what'll happen to us, though."

"He was wounded pretty bad," Rhen continued as though he had not heard her, "and there was so much blood."

Frowning, she put an arm around his shoulders. He put his head on her shoulder, much to her delight even under the circumstances. "Look," she whispered, "I don't know what these people want, but I will get you out of here somehow. I promised Falkris I'd protect you, and I will."

Saying nothing, he nodded against her shoulder. After helping him lie down, she settled herself on the other side of the bed. Though he was asleep almost instantly, she stared at the bars over her head for a long time before sleep finally claimed her.

Rhen was already awake when Netria sat up. Rubbing the grime of sleep from her face, she glared up at the sun. By her reckoning, it was some time in the afternoon. As she scowled at the world in general, she wondered which god she had angered to find herself in such dire circumstances.

Rhen turned from his post at the edge of the cage, where he had been observing the villagers. "It seems we've found our plains people."

Unable to verbalize the hopelessness she felt at his words, she groaned. "Damn it all," she muttered under her breath. For his benefit, she forced herself to brighten. "So we have, Rhen."

He trudged over to sit beside her. "All we have to do is convince them that we mean them no harm. Perhaps they'll allow us to go."

At his statement, she had to bite back the bitter laughter that rose in her chest. That thought was a childish fantasy, but she never would've told him that. Under normal circumstances, she would've been annoyed by such ignorance, but she found the quality alluring in Rhen. "Perhaps," she whispered. Inside, she was sulking. *If I ever win this fool's heart, it seems I'll have to be the man in the relationship.*

Just then, several villagers approached, dragging something behind them. Netria realized that it was a litter. Keth lay sprawled out on it, still unconscious. A man opened the cage and they brought Keth in, retreating without a word. As soon as the villagers had gone, Rhen sprang to his feet and went to his friend's side.

Netria came up behind him and looked over his shoulder. "The wounds have been dressed," she said. "At least they're decent enough to care for him. They could've killed him outright." She would have, in their circumstances. As he stared down at the big man, Rhen nodded.

A voice drew her attention. "He will not live long."

Netria turned to face the man who stood outside the cage. She thought that she recognized him as the man who had spoken to her the night before. Dark in coloring, his nose was oddly flat. Facing him, she moved forward and gripped the bars. "You'll kill him after working to save his life?"

The man gave her a wicked grin. "We will sacrifice him. We'll sacrifice you all to our gods."

Rhen came to the edge of the cage. "Please, spare him. He is a simple man; he didn't know better than to fight. He was merely trying to defend me, so the fault is mine." Desperation colored his voice, and his blue eyes were pleading.

The man drew back from the bars, his face closing to them. He spoke again, his guttural voice chewing over the syllables of his words. "I do not know your word. What does this word *simple* mean?"

Rhen cocked his head. "He's not very bright."

"Bright?" the villager asked, and the confusion on his face increased. He lowered his gaze and muttered something in a lilting tongue.

Netria rolled her eyes. "The man is stupid. He's *dumb*."

Rhen was about to protest, but he noticed the look on the villager's face. The man came to the edge of the cage, his dark hands folding around the bars. "Then he is one of those touched by the gods." His dark coloring fled. "We would never have attacked him had we known."

Netria couldn't believe her ears. "What do you mean *touched*?" she asked in a low voice.

The man swallowed. "Those who are born *simple* are intended for a grander purpose. The gods bless them so they may see the way forward when others fail."

The mercenary almost crowed in delight at her good fortune. These villagers were a superstitious lot. In the face of their odd beliefs, she could taste her freedom. She suppressed a grin.

The villager must have read the elation in her eyes, for he frowned. "I said that *he* was blessed. That doesn't mean that our regard for him extends to you."

"So what will become of us?" she asked.

"You'll be given a trial before the council. The big man may go, but you will not." With that, he walked away, not bothering to acknowledge her as she called after him.

After a time, she gave up and flopped down on the bed once more. So much for freedom. She'd be on a sacrificial pyre soon, and she'd have no cause to laugh. Despair set its lethal claws into her heart.

Doleful, Rhen tended to Keth. Neither of them spoke until the villagers returned and shoved food through the bars. Netria snatched it, realizing that she was very hungry. Chewing on the strange wheat cake they had given her, she wondered idly if it was drugged as she swallowed her first bite. Though it was tasteless, it went down anyway.

The nobleman also accepted a cake, but ate it at a much slower pace. She realized that he was saving half of it, and she stopped her ravenous consumption of her own. "Why aren't you eating it all? This might be our last meal." The words were out before she could stop them.

If he heard her pessimistic statement, he didn't acknowledge it. "Lady Netria, Keth may yet awaken. I wouldn't have him starve."

She looked down at her own half-eaten wheat cake, then set it aside. Rhen's eyes widened at her action, and he smiled in approval. "Thank you, Netria."

She grinned. "No problem." She went to stand at the bars. The sun was much lower in the sky now, and night would soon come. Somehow, she knew that something unpleasant would come with the emergence of the stars.

The man came to the bars again. "Prepare yourself," he said.

Netria didn't move any closer to him. Even though he had done nothing to her that would leave a lasting mark, she abhorred the man. The way he taunted her angered the warrior. "For what?" she snapped.

He smiled, his teeth flashing white against his dark skin. "The tribal council will convene tonight. Your fates will be decided then."

"Is there a certain way we should prepare ourselves?" Rhen asked from behind her.

The man laughed, a mocking light shining in his eyes. "Do what you must to prepare yourself for death. That is the only thing you have left." He barked a short laugh and walked away from the bars.

Infuriated, Netria didn't even bother to call after him. Instead, she speared his back with her eyes, imagining the many ways she would kill him once she was free. She was lost in a particularly delightful fantasy when they came for her.

The villagers opened the cage, spears at the ready. Gesturing, they chattered at the prisoners in their lilting language. Netria and Rhen had no choice other than to follow them out. They were led through a cluster of huts to a giant fire at the heart of the village. Seated on benches beyond the fire, women in ceremonial robes waited solemnly. Netria smiled. At least her fate was to be decided by a woman. If it had been a man, all hope would've been lost.

Chapter 25

Daymen took the last watch. Though Amial slept soundly beside the fire, the same could not be said for Falkris. She woke up every time she shifted. Near dawn, she came awake with a hiss of pain, then sat up. Resting her arms on her knees, she stared at the floor, her gray eyes clouded. The wolf emitted a soft whine and nosed her arm. At last, she came back to herself and shifted to make herself more comfortable.

Daymen watched as she let her hair down. He saw that the action pained her even more, but he bit back the protest forming in his throat. Though Falkris was a lady, she was also a warrior, and a proud one at that. Her need to face the pain was something he understood.

She brushed her hair out. Like a mane, it was thick and black. The fire threw shadows over its glossy mass. Daymen averted his eyes, focusing instead on keeping watch. When she gasped in pain, he glanced back at her in concern. She was trying to braid her hair back. Her efforts had caused her wounds to bleed anew, and the shoulders of her tunic were slowly turning red with blood.

"Lady," he protested, "please cease. You're harming yourself."

Defiant gray eyes glared up at him. "No."

Daymen took a silent step closer. "Then allow me to do it."

An eyebrow raised on a brow wrinkled from pain and shined with sweat. "You?" she rasped. Her voice, rougher than normal, was almost hoarse, as though she suffered from illness rather than an old injury.

"I braid my own hair. It's the way of the Jenestran knights." He lifted his braid from his back, showing it to her.

She stared at him for some time, and the silence that filled that moment was oppressive. Then, she relaxed and nodded. "Right."

Kneeling behind her, Daymen unsheathed his sword and placed it within arm's reach at his side. He took her thick hair in his callused hands, feeling suddenly huge and clumsy. Part of him knew that Falkris was a warrior and far from fragile, but she was still a woman.

He focused on braiding her thick hair. When at last she spoke, it startled him. "Why are you no longer a knight? I know you told me once, but tell me again." Something was in her voice, like she was on the edge of figuring something out.

Daymen let out deep breath, then closed his eyes. "My lord," he said, "the King Jemis, was not an honorable man. I couldn't serve him and remain true to what I believed."

"So you left his service," she said.

"He hunted me like a dog. Cemil was with me to begin with. He was killed in one of the first battles. After that, Vesahn and I were alone. We hoped to find refuge in the Stormpeaks."

"That was when you ran into our group." A slight edge of bitterness colored her voice. He was about to apologize, but she spoke again. "Why didn't you go to the monastery first?"

"I didn't want to burden the priestesses."

She sat for a time, lost in thought. "You said you served King Jemis?"

"Yes, milady."

"Lady Silvian—Lianna—mentioned him. We encountered a priest of the virtues on Ravenian lands. Lianna said he was an agent of the king, sent to contact her father."

Daymen blinked in surprise. "What would King Jemis want with a Ravenian noble?"

Falkris grunted. "I was hoping you could tell me."

Silence ensued. He braided her hair tightly so it wouldn't come loose, tied it off when he was done and sat back. Falkris turned her gaze on him, commanding him with her gray eyes. "Help me get this tunic off. We need to redress my wounds."

He did as she bid, trying not to hurt her as he pulled the

tunic over her head. Averting his eyes from her exposed flesh, he unwrapped the blood-soaked bandages with careful movements. Before he could wash the wounds, Dax pushed him aside. Daymen watched in horror as the big canine began to gently lick Falkris' wounds.

"Lady—" he began.

She shook her head. "No, it'll help them heal faster." Her face was white with pain. He couldn't fathom the strength of a person, woman or man, who could stand such treatment without a sound. The only sign of pain she showed was a tiny catch in her voice. "And stop referring to me like I'm nobility," she growled.

Daymen smiled. "But you are."

"Not anymore."

He asked a question to distract her. "What about Lord Tahnuil? Does he know who you really are?"

"No."

"And Lady Silvian?"

She grimaced as Dax continued licking her ragged shoulder. "No." The wolf was very careful in his ministrations, as though he knew not to pull the jagged stitches loose. Fascinating to watch, it was also very disturbing.

Daymen wrenched his eyes from the canine to look at Falkris. He wasn't certain, but he thought that he could see a strange light in her eyes, akin to hatred. "You don't care for her," he stated. Nothing in his inflection suggested that his words were a question.

Falkris shook her head. Her hand curled around the fabric of her breeches, squeezing it hard to banish the pain. "You could say that."

"Then why help her?" he asked.

She looked at him for a time, silent. Her eyes, for a brief moment, were clear and empty of pain. "For Rhen. He loves her."

Daymen wondered what it was he saw in her eyes. Did she love the Ravenian noble? Or was it the fierce loyalty of a devoted warrior? He wished he could unravel this woman's secrets.

Falkris interrupted his thoughts. "You can bandage the wounds now."

Dax had stepped back and was now staring at him. Daymen suppressed the shudder that the wolf evoked in him and set about dressing the wounds. Falkris stared into space as he worked, removing herself from the pain.

"There," he said as he set the last bandage in place.

Remarkably, her hand closed over his. The world slowed, and he felt the heat of her fingers on his. A strong tingle of energy shot through him, and he feared that he wouldn't be able to breathe. Who was this woman?

"Thank you," she said, then her hand was gone from his.

Nodding, he withdrew from her presence, taking his sword and moving away into the shadows. Once there, he kept his eyes from Falkris. He had much to consider before he dared speak to her again.

Falkris frowned and shook her head. "No." She refused to look up at Amial. Standing over Falkris with hands on hips and brown eyes glaring, the archer made Falkris think of her mother, who had often stood in that same manner when she was upset.

"Falkris," Amial snapped, "you need your rest. You can't fight with your shoulders like that! Give the wounds one day to scab."

"No," the warrior growled again.

"Lady Amial is right," Daymen said. Falkris thought that he, at least, would agree with her and had hoped that her fellow warrior would understand. Then again, in his situation, she would've done the same. An injured warrior was more a hindrance than anything. If she tried to fight now, she would certainly slow her companions down and injure herself further.

"Then go on without me," she snarled. "We can't waste any time."

Amial shook her head. "No. We need you in there to fight

with us. If we have to face any more of those things, we'll need your blade."

Falkris, thinking of the ice monster, said nothing. She knew that she was being foolish and stubborn, so she silenced herself. There was no point in arguing when the argument was lost before it began. "Fine."

Daymen moved closer, but it was Amial who spoke. "Good. Get some rest. Tomorrow, we'll enter the temple."

Falkris frowned up at her. "How?"

The archer flushed. "I think I've found a way forward. There's a fault in the wall there," she pointed, "that I believe may trip a door."

"Last night, we heard the sound of stone grating," Falkris said. "Do you suppose that was how the creature got in here?"

Amial lowered her eyes. "I'm sorry, Kris. I should have mentioned it sooner."

Falkris didn't want to hurt the girl, but she knew a valuable lesson when she saw one. "If you had died, we wouldn't have known about the fault in the wall. Next time, report something immediately." Her throat ached. At the moment, she would have given her weight in gold for a drink of water. Daymen must have read her mind, for he handed her a flask. Nodding her thanks, she drank from it gratefully.

When her eyes again sought Amial's face, she saw that the archer understood. Amial wouldn't make the same mistake again. Falkris nodded to her, letting her know that she wasn't angry.

The three of them were silent for a time. Dax panted beside Falkris despite the cold. Shivering, she urged him closer. He settled against her side, almost pushing her over with his weight. As she threw an arm around him, she smiled.

"What shall we do all day?" Amial whispered.

Falkris had an idea right away. "You need to learn how to use a sword. I never had a chance to teach you."

"You can't, not in your condition," Amial said, an angry edge in her voice.

"I'll teach you," Daymen said.

Falkris handed Amial her sword before the girl could protest. "Careful with that," the warrior said. "Not only is it sharp, but it was my father's."

As though frightened that the weapon might attack her at any moment, Amial held on to the sword with a limp grasp. Falkris, frowning, reached out to adjust Amial's hold on the weapon. "Keep a firm grip on the hilt," she cautioned, "or your enemy will knock the sword from your grip in a fight, and you'll be weaponless."

The archer, eager to learn, allowed her fingers to be placed in the proper position, then she held the sword up in front of her. The strength in her arms born from archery helped her to keep the weapon up, but it was still too heavy for her. Falkris and Daymen locked eyes, having a silent conversation in a moment.

The knight nodded and took the sword from Amial. "We'll have to start you with a short sword. This sword is much too heavy for you."

Falkris took her prized weapon back and pointed to her packs. "I have a couple of short swords there."

Daymen went to collect them. Returning with a matched set of short swords, he handed one to Amial. As Falkris looked on, the knight helped his pupil adjust her grip on the weapon. Then he took the matching blade and brought it up to guard himself. "Try to hit me," he said.

Amial's eyebrows shot up. "What?"

Falkris laughed. "You won't get through his guard. Don't worry about hurting him."

The archer stared at the two veteran warriors like they were insane. When she realized that they were serious, a grim expression crossed her face. Lunging at Daymen, she swung her weapon clumsily. The knight parried without effort, knocking Amial's sword from her hands.

Falkris grinned. "Pick it up and try again. Keep your grip firm." Beside her, Dax watched with perked ears, his head cocked to one side. Falkris smiled and scratched the ruff of his neck. He leaned into the caress, the full bulk of his weight moving against her, nearly toppling her onto the floor.

As the archer and knight continued to spar, Amial began to understand something of the sword. Falkris watched as her offensive maneuvers, once wild and uncontrolled, began to take form. Amial was learning the dance of the sword. Though it would be some time before she could penetrate Daymen's guard, her progress was evident.

"Teach her to defend herself," Falkris said.

Daymen nodded and signaled Amial to a stop. "When you're with Falkris or me, we'll be able to help you. What's important is that you protect yourself until we can reach you. I want you to block my attacks." Amial whitened, and the knight smiled. "Don't worry, I won't harm you. If you like, I can wrap the sword with cloth."

The archer nodded. Falkris smiled. Slowly, the day wore on. Outside the temple, the storm raged on. Every so often, a gust of wind blew into the little room, making the fire sputter in a fit of flames. When evening came, the three of them were more than happy to find warmth in their beds.

Chapter 26

Fire played with the women's features. Seated solemnly on wooden benches, dark faces tinged pink and painted robes bathed in eerie, shifting shadows, the trio of judges stared at Netria. She met their gazes, hoping that doing so wasn't considered rude among these people.

At her back, a bonfire blazed. As she felt the heat on the back of her legs, Netria wondered if she'd be burned alive when they sacrificed her to their gods. The smell of burning flesh had never pleased her, and she imagined that knowing it was her own stench would be much worse.

Pushing the thought from her mind, she focused on the tribal council, the three women who were to judge her. Two of them were obviously villagers, one old and gray, the other young and beautiful. The woman in the center, however, was different. She was paler than the others, though her hair was dark. Her eyes narrowed as she surveyed Netria. That she was of the same people as Daymen, the Jenestran knight, was written all over her. Netria sensed that her fate belonged to this woman. Whoever the strange Jenestran was, she held the power among these people. How she had come to be there, in a position of influence, was a mystery that Netria hoped to solve, if she survived.

The Jenestran woman spoke, her voice rich. "Why have you come to our plains?"

Rhen moved to speak beside Netria, but the mercenary silenced him with a warning glare. "Honorable ladies," she said with respect, "we come here at the request of the High Priestess of Truth, Alihandre."

The aged woman muttered something in her tongue. Saying nothing, the young woman just stared at Netria, judging the truth of her words. The woman in the center was calm and cool. "Why would Alihandre send Ravenians to these plains?"

Netria collected herself, praying for the right words. She'd never been the most eloquent of speakers, but adrenaline and the fact that her life was in jeopardy gave her the incentive. "Because, my lady, our companion is in need. She's fallen under the influence of a drug. We seek the Night's Breath to cure her."

"What interest does the High Priestess of Truth have in your companion?"

Something warned Netria against revealing too much. She had a feeling that this woman and Alihandre weren't on good terms. Looking more closely at the woman, Netria wished that the light of the fire wouldn't cast so many shadows. "Milady, I'm not certain of the exact truth, but I believe that our companion has special powers that made her of interest to the High Priestess of Truth."

The woman leaned back, stroking her chin with a speculative hand. "At least you're honest." She glanced at her two companions, then focused her gaze on Netria again, her dark eyes flashing. "Did Alihandre send you here to find help, without suitable offerings for these people, or warnings about their nature?"

Netria shook her head. "We were sent with only ourselves."

The woman nodded. "Then the protection of your companion is urgent indeed. Interesting."

Silence stretched, filled with the crackling of flames. A log fell into the fire with a shower of sparks and the fire roared for a moment. In the shadows, the plains people looked on with dark, glittering eyes. The young woman whispered something to the Jenestran.

A conversation followed in the strange lilting tongue as the three women discussed something. Netria looked at Rhen. Staring around himself helplessly, he looked lost. The shroud of despair seemed to drop its fine cloth over his blonde head.

In a daring moment, she took his hand in her own. He seemed grateful for the human contact, and she squeezed his fingers, letting him know that she wouldn't let him down. The smile he gave her was sad, almost like a farewell.

The woman in the center stood and came into the firelight. Tall, with muscles running through her lean body, she breathed power. Even the high cheekbones of her proud face and her dark, glittering eyes spoke of unshakable control. "We've decided your fate," she purred.

Netria bowed to her, hating every moment of it, but knowing that this woman craved power. Any woman would be kinder towards one who gave her homage than one who spited her. Spitting in the Jenestran's face was exactly what Netria would have done, were it not for Rhen.

The woman continued, "Alihandre and I are rivals, but we must often cooperate in the competitive game of life. I'll grant you aid, but in return, Alihandre will owe me much. I'll see to it that she repays my debt."

Netria allowed herself a moment of daring. "May I ask who you are that you know the High Priestess Alihandre?" She kept her tone respectful.

The woman smiled. "Certainly. I am Yellima, Priestess of Strength. Though my rank is not great, I'm not unknown." In an instant, her gaze shifted from Netria to the noble beside her. Like a predator on the hunt, she stalked closer to him. "And who might you be, to tempt the fates and cross the Stormpeaks?"

Rhen did his best to gather himself. He smiled, a shadow of his old charm, and swept a bow. "Priestess Yellima, I am Lord Rhen Tahnuil."

Yellima raised one eyebrow. "Are you a messenger from the Ravenian government?"

"No, milady, just a foolish man with a taste for the unknown."

The priestess smiled. "An adventurer then. And you?" Her dark eyes flashed to Netria.

"Netria. I'm a mercenary."

"So I see," Yellima said, her eyes marking the scar that riddled Netria's face.

Her caution abating in a flash, Netria sneered back at the woman. "I have other scars, if you find them so interesting."

Yellima laughed, throwing her head back with glee. Even as she lost herself in mirth, the quiet control remained. No wonder she held such power among these people. Netria stood her ground, refusing to show any weakness before the woman.

Rhen moved between them. "Priestess," he begged, "can you help us find the Night's Breath?"

The Priestess of Strength regarded him for a long moment. "I see," she said at last. "You love this companion of yours, do you?"

"I think so," he admitted softly. His eyes shone with his emotions. In the face of the light that lit him from within, Netria felt her own heart sink. How was she ever to claim him as her own when he was so devoted to Lianna? What could she, a scarred mercenary, offer him?

Then again, what did she really want from Rhen? Rather than the target of her affections, he'd become an object of conquest. Netria wanted to prove herself superior to Lianna. Yet, these last days together had made her see deeper into him than she had before. Studying his handsome face and innocent blue eyes made her realize that she did care for him.

Yellima put a consolatory arm around the noble's shoulders. "I'll do my best to help you, but we must wait to begin the search on the morrow."

Rhen nodded, at once businesslike. "Why not begin tonight, milady?"

She smiled. "Patience, Lord Tahnuil. The Night's Breath can only be found on the evening of the new moon, when the sky is at its darkest. I'll send word to the neighboring tribe. The medicine man who lives with them will be able to help you."

Netria trudged after the pair as Yellima led Rhen through

the village. "Tell me," Rhen said, "who are these people? And why are you here with them?"

If his persistent questioning annoyed Yellima, she didn't show it. Instead, she answered him patiently, as a parent would. "These are the plains people, the *Imani*. They lived in Jenestra even before my people came and built our cities and palaces. They've mastered the secrets of nature, and they use their knowledge well.

"As to why I am here, it's my duty. As a priestess of any virtue, I must spend a time serving among the people. I chose the Imani because they fascinated me. They are very primitive to the casual eye, but I've discovered that the core of philosophy that governs their lives is quite complex and developed. We could learn much from them. I have come to study what makes them strong, so that I may learn to liken that strength unto myself."

Rhen nodded as though he had suspected as much. "Is that the mission of the Priests and Priestesses of Strength?"

Yellima smiled. "We seek to become strong in all ways. To be physically fit is important, but the strength must also reside within, in one's character, mind and soul." Her eyes darkened. "With that strength must come understanding of the implications of one's actions. One must learn control. Too often, those who follow our virtue stray from the path and forget to exercise restraint."

"In Ravenia," Rhen said, "we believe in the old gods. I never encountered these virtues before I came to Jenestra."

Yellima laughed lightly. "It's a shame. We teach that one should practice the virtues. When you're at harmony within, you attain a state near to that of the One God. Once you are at peace with Him, you'll receive the blessing of paradise when your soul flies from this existence."

Netria frowned. "I like the thought of a warrior god at my side in battle."

The Jenestran glanced over her shoulder. "The God that I worship has many faces, one of which is the warrior. Battles are fought for us often, even when we're not aware."

Rhen shrugged. "Faith is a personal thing, ladies. To each her own, I say."

Yellima said nothing more until they reached a hut at the edge of the village. "This is my home. You're welcome to stay here until you leave. The large one will be brought here soon."

"Large one?" Rhen said, a smiled spreading across his face. "Do you mean Keth?"

The priestess dipped her head. "I do."

He drew himself up, doing his best to act the part of his noble blood. "Lady Yellima, we are honored."

Yellima waved them into the hut. "Please. I will join you in a moment. I have much to do before I may end my day."

Netria ducked into the hut. Rhen joined her a moment later. Standing close to one another for reassurance, they studied the room. The mercenary eyed the dirt floor, upon which several animal skins were spread. A large pallet suited for a family dominated one wall. In the center of the floor, a cooking fire burned in a shallow pit.

Rhen, ever one to think of the necessities, flopped down on a pile of furs. In a moment, he was asleep, breathing deeply. Netria watched him for a time, filled with jealousy. *How is it that men always manage to sleep anywhere, under any circumstances?* she wondered. Shaking her head, she lay down beside him and sought peace in sleep.

Chapter 27

Morning came. The only visible sign of the passage of time was a slight brightening of the light that streamed through the door. The storm raged on, white and perpetual. Inside the Temple of Purity, Amial, Falkris and Daymen prepared themselves for the day.

Falkris rewrapped her wounds, taking care that the bandages were tight. If she had to fight, she didn't want them coming loose. If her wounds broke open again, the dressings would staunch the flow of blood. She bit the inside of her lower lip to keep from showing any sign of the pain that her shoulders still caused her.

When she finished and pulled her tunic back over her head, she looked up to meet Daymen's eyes. The knight was watching her with a worried expression, and she knew that he was concerned for her. He saw it as his duty to protect those not as strong as he. She would show him that she didn't need that protection.

"Lady—" Daymen began.

She cut him off with a jerk of her head. "I'll be fine," she growled. Suppressing a wince, she rose to her feet, not letting him help her. Defiant, she strapped on her armor and secured her sword at her hip. She also took up the twin short swords and several daggers. They had their place with her gear as well, and she wouldn't feel confident without all of her weapons.

Amial accepted one of the short swords from Falkris. She set it at her hip so that she could draw it easily, as Daymen had shown her. Falkris felt better knowing that the girl had a close-ranged weapon. If the enemy got too close, a bow wouldn't be enough.

When they had cleaned up their camp, packed their gear

and scattered the ashes from their fire, they looked at one another in silence. Falkris was the first to speak, "Amial?"

The archer nodded and went to the wall. She found the fault and bent to examine it. The two warriors waited as she looked it over. True to her intelligence, Amial quickly discovered the secret behind the little fault and reached out to manipulate the wall. In response to her action, a door swung open.

Dax growled a warning low in his throat. Before the trio could react, a white form flashed through the opening. A piercing screech cut the air, deafening the three of them. Falkris drew her sword as Daymen did the same beside her. She had to grit her teeth to bear the pain in her shoulders. Though her wounds slowed her down, she was prepared to fight. She'd fought wars with worse wounds hampering her.

An arrow whistled past the two warriors and found its target in the creature's eye. Although it shrieked, it continued to advance. This one didn't have wings, but instead walked upright like a human, which only made the fiend seem more horrific. The claws it had in place of hands and the icy composition of its body were all that marked it as monster instead of man.

Side by side, Daymen and Falkris moved to meet the wintry monster, which swung at them with razor sharp claws. Even as Daymen sunk his sword into the beast's flank, Falkris parried a blow. Out of the corner of her eye, she saw that Amial had circled to a better position so she could loose an arrow without placing her friends in danger.

The knight tried to pull his sword free, but couldn't. While Daymen tried to get his weapon loose, Falkris distracted the arctic mockery of humanity. After sinking her own blade into the monster's chest, she drew her short sword to continue the battle.

As he tried to pull the sword free, frost began creeping up Daymen's blade. He jerked his hands away as ice closed over the hilt and swallowed the whole weapon in its cold embrace. The sword shattered with a crack, sending shards of ice flying through the air.

An arrow laced in flames thumped into the creature's back, and it screamed in pain. Pulling Daymen with her, Falkris leapt backwards. The monster writhed, its body melting away into nothing. Water dripped to the floor all around the beast as Falkris' sword slid from its body and fell to the ground with a sharp clatter. Then the fiend was gone, and silence descended.

Daymen was the first to regain sense after the adrenaline rush that accompanied battle. He recovered Falkris' sword and held it out to her. She grimaced and shook her head. Pain sliced through her, burning her alive as she fought to remain conscious. Recovering from her shoulder wounds would take longer than she liked.

"Milady?" the knight asked uncertainly.

"Daymen," she hissed, trying to keep her eyes focused on him while the world around her spun, "I can't handle that sword now. I need something lighter. You use it." Though it was her father's sword, the only thing she had left of him, it was no good to her if she died. Daymen would put it to better use than she could. Until her wounds healed, she'd have to trust it to him.

Amial put one hand on Falkris' elbow to steady her. Her brown eyes were filled with concern, but she said nothing. For that, Falkris was grateful. Seeing the objections in Daymen's eyes, she stumbled towards the doorway.

The archer helped Falkris, but she spoke to Daymen. "Come on—there's no sense in waiting any longer. Lady Lianna's life is at stake, and we've already delayed too long. It will take time for Falkris to heal, time we don't have. We must infiltrate the palace now."

"Shouldn't we redress the wounds?" Daymen asked.

Falkris shook her head. "No," she said after a deep breath. As she moved into the next room, her steps wavering, she didn't see the worried look that Amial and Daymen exchanged. Even if she had seen it, she wouldn't have had time to think about it, for the enemy was already upon them.

At the sound of wings flapping, Amial looked up in alarm. Icy figures dropped from the ceiling, falling quickly to land on their prey. She and Daymen were not quite in the room, and thus were able to fall back. Falkris, however, wasn't so lucky. The proud warrior went down under several of the creatures, her short sword flying from her hand.

Dax growled and launched himself into the room. Landing on the back of his first target, he sank his teeth into the monster's neck. The beast collapsed beneath his weight, but quickly rolled to dislodge the canine. A moment later it was upon the wolf, tearing away flesh with bloodied claws.

Amial reacted at once. Using her torch to light the first arrow, she sent the missile to find its target. Daymen stood in the doorway, defending her with Falkris' sword as she worked. Methodically, trying to keep calm, Amial set the arrows on fire and sent them into the enemies.

By the time the monsters were gone, Falkris lay on the floor in a pool of blood. Wet with the watery remains of their foes, her clothing and skin were beaded with moisture. Her entire back was rent open, and a profuse amount of blood gushed from her wounds. Wincing with distress, Daymen ran to her side. Amial wished that she could do the same, but she hung back and kept her guard up instead.

Hurrying to stop the bleeding, Daymen bandaged Falkris' wounds. When he breathed a small prayer of thanks, Amial knew that the fierce warrior lived. As she scanned her surroundings, peering into the shadows, she allowed herself a small sigh of relief.

They were at the base of a grand staircase that led to a second story. On either side of the staircase, set back several yards, were double doors. There was nothing on the walls to the right or left. With three options to choose from, Falkris wounded, and time running out, Amial could only pray that they made the right choice.

She took a step forward and almost fell to the ground when her foot tried to slide out from under her. The white stone floor was covered with a thin layer of ice, as was every surface in this part of the Temple of Purity. Even the walls were painted with ice. With the floor so slick, footing would be treacherous. Amial let out a deep breath and watched her breath rise in the air.

"Lady Amial," Daymen called to her.

She moved to his side, her eyes still wary and watchful. "What is it? Is she okay?"

"She should be fine if we get her somewhere warm and bandage her properly."

"That's not an option."

"I know, but that's not why I called you over. Look at this." He pointed to the floor. Beneath the bloody ice, there was an inscription carved into the stone. Amial checked the room one last time before she bent to look at it.

The way forward shall be unlocked when the three arches are opened by individuals worthy of the virtue purity. Then, the gate shall be revealed and the guardian will pass judgment upon the individual. Only in that way can the relic of purity be obtained.

Amial looked to Daymen for guidance. "You're from Jenestra. Do you know what this means?"

He shrugged. "The temples are reserved for the religious orders and those who bind their souls to their blades."

Falkris stirred just then, and Amial's eyes widened in surprise. She watched with amazement as her heroine struggled to sit up. "I wanted to study with them," Falkris growled, "that's why I came to this cursed country."

Amial knelt down beside her, careful to hold the torch aloft so it wouldn't be extinguished. "You're amazing, Falkris!"

Daymen nodded in agreement. "You have startled me with your strength again, milady."

Falkris glared at them. "Help me up. We need to keep moving." The knight helped her to her feet. Swaying slightly as blood ran from her wounds and dripped down to coat the floor, she looked around. Her eyes fell on the wolf, and she let out a tiny gasp.

Dax must have heard her, for he whined and struggled to

his feet. He crossed the floor to join her, limping and bloody. Tears in her eyes, she patted him on the head. "Good boy, Dax," she whispered, her voice hoarse with tears.

Thankfully, she didn't protest when Daymen picked her up and carried her across the icy floor to the door to the left of the grand staircase. The knight kicked the door open, and Amial followed him into the room beyond. She had an arrow ready for the monster that flew at them. The shot was fired point blank, and the arrow went through the creature. Shrieking, the fiend disappeared in a shower of water.

Daymen set Falkris down on the floor and drew her sword. He held it out in front of him, ready to defend them, as they surveyed the room. Falkris, at his feet, gasped in surprise. An awed expression on her face, she was staring at the floor.

"What is it?" the knight demanded, a worried edge coloring his voice.

Amial felt her heart begin to beat wildly, hoping that it was nothing bad. She didn't think that she could handle anything else going wrong. Moving forward to look over Falkris' torn shoulder, she saw another inscription on the floor.

"I can read it," Falkris breathed. Slowly, her voice grating like gravel, she read it aloud, "Only one whose body is without violation or illness may safely enter the arch and escape immolation in purifying flames. One who fails the test will be returned to dust, from which the One God first made man."

Daymen almost put a hand on her shoulder, but withdrew it before he touched her wounds. "How is this possible?" he wondered aloud.

Falkris turned to look at him, the action clearly paining her. "Maybe it's the magic in the air. Can you feel it?" Dax, sitting beside her, whined his agreement.

Feeling nothing but the bone-penetrating cold, Amial shook her head. She wondered if Falkris was delirious. Having lost enough blood to kill most people, Falkris looked as though she might lose consciousness at any moment.

"I feel nothing, lady," Daymen whispered, echoing Amial's

thoughts.

Falkris raised her eyes to look around the room, unconcerned with their inability to feel what she did. Amial followed her gaze. They were in a white stone room with seamless walls, as if the room had been formed with perfect symmetry when the world was young. At the center of the room was a pure white arch. Blue flames flickered within it, raging in silence as they tempted their prey to enter and face the test.

Daymen approached the arch with slow steps. "Shall I try entering the arch? We must open it to gain access to the ring that Lady Silvian needs."

"No," Falkris said, her voice weak and harsh. "Let's think this through before we act. If we fail the test, we'll be burned alive and turned to ashes."

The knight nodded, paling. He tried to appear in control and prepared, his honor intact and unbreakable. Though he wanted to protect the two women, he was helpless. They all were in the face of death. Why had High Priestess of Truth Alihandre not warned them of the dangers involved in this quest?

Amial forced herself to think of the problem at hand. "Without physical violation ... is that referring to virginity?" She felt heat rise into her face, and her ears grew warm, even in the encroaching cold of the room.

"I believe so," Daymen said. "Are you ... are you yet a maiden, Lady Amial?" He was very uncomfortable.

Amial lowered her eyes. "No."

"Then we're doomed," the knight whispered.

Falkris staggered to her feet. "Am I without honor because I carry a sword?"

Daymen turned several shades of red, each darker than the last. "My lady, forgive me! I thought that—"

"I was a mercenary," she said, "but I stayed in my tent and made certain that others did the same." She glared at both of them. "*I* will enter the arch."

"But your wounds," Amial interjected. "The inscription

says without violation."

"Nothing wrong with blood," Falkris grunted. She staggered a few steps towards the arch. Dax rose to his feet, and she put one hand on his shoulder for support as they approached together.

Daymen moved to stop her, but she pulled her dagger on him. The hiss of pain that followed her action was similar to the sound of the blade clearing its scabbard. The wolf growled low in his throat, baring his teeth in warning. The knight stepped back, more wary of Falkris than Dax. Her eyes glinting almost madly as she held her weapon between them, she looked like a cornered animal.

"Kris," he begged, "please. I don't want to lose you."

Amial looked from one to the other, seeing more than just comradeship in the two warriors. A bond had formed between them, even if they were yet unaware of the connection, as evident in the knight's slip of the tongue as it was in the tears in Falkris' eyes.

"Daymen," she said, her voice almost inaudible, "let me do this." Sheathing her blade, she staggered towards the arch. Dax went with her, his bloodied flank brushing against her leg with each step. Her companions watched as she stepped into the arch. For a moment, she stood there, the fire licking at her body, then she was swallowed up in flames. The wolf disappeared with her.

Amial felt tears streaming down her face. When she took a step towards the arch, she slipped in the trail of blood that coated the floor. Hitting the ground hard, she jarred her knee. The pain she felt was nothing compared to the anguish in her heart. Daymen lifted her to her feet and held her to his chest as they stared at the raging flames.

"What should we do?" she whispered, her voice breaking. "Is she dead?"

Daymen lowered his eyes. "She's still alive," he said stubbornly. Letting out a deep breath, he brought his gaze up to the arch. "She'll come back. All we can do is wait for her."

Chapter 28

Lianna sat in Beldaris' room, waiting for him to return to her. The world around her, only a figment of the fog that draped her mind, was reality to Lianna. She wouldn't have believed anything else. With Beldaris occupying her thoughts, she rarely thought of the outside world, of companions who might be missing her. Though she'd been in the catacombs for some time, days perhaps, the passage of time seemed to mean nothing when she was with her mentor. There was still too much about her powers that she didn't understand. Until she was sure of herself and her magic, she had no desire to return to the upper levels of the monastery.

Once, while Beldaris was gone, she began to worry about the others. As her teacher had taught her, she cast her thoughts out, seeking the presence of others in the ancient stone building. The others were most likely concerned for her, for she had told no one where she was going or why. Rhen, especially, would be frantic.

Drifting upward to the monastery above, her consciousness encountered the thoughts of a Priestess of Truth. Lianna brushed past, continuing her search. Before she was beyond the woman, she felt an icy grip seize hold of her mind. She sensed panic and frantic urgency.

Lianna frowned and tried to jerk her mind free of the priestess. The hold on her thoughts tightened and sharp pain lanced across her forehead. Angered, Lianna lashed out at her captor. Her powers connected with something, and she was free. Quickly, she withdrew her thoughts to the safety of the catacombs. Raising one hand to her temple, she winced. Blood came away on her fingers. What were the priestesses thinking?

A shadow fell over her, and Lianna looked up. Beldaris

stood over her, his dark eyes concerned. He knelt before her and touched her forehead. "It was the priestesses, wasn't it?" he whispered.

She nodded. Beldaris shook his head. "Do you believe me now? Do you see what they're capable of? They don't understand us."

Lianna closed her eyes. "I'm beginning to see why you hate them."

Beldaris drew her closer as he dabbed the blood from her temple. She could feel the heat of his body against her own, and she leaned into him. When he wrapped his arms around her and kissed her, she didn't mind at all.

Alihandre sat straight up in bed. Her heart hammered in her chest, its pounding almost deafening in her ears. Had she imagined the sound that had awakened her? She pushed the covers aside and peered through the curtains that closed her off from the world while she slept. Another scream cut through the monastery. Running feet echoed in the stone hallways.

The High Priestess of Truth launched herself from the bed, making her old bones move faster than they were accustomed to. As she ran into the hall and followed the sounds of the screaming, she wished furtively that she hadn't put on so much weight.

She charged into the room where the screams were coming from. As she had feared, it was the room where Lianna rested in her drug-induced coma. One of the priestesses who had been watching over the girl lay twitching on the floor. Alihandre gasped and rushed to the woman's side. She tried to support the priestess' head so she wouldn't harm herself, but the woman's twitching was too violent. The afflicted priestess' eyes rolled up in her head and she foamed at the mouth.

When the attack ended, Alihandre patiently administered to the girl, hoping that she would survive and regain consciousness. When she did, everyone who had collected in the room breathed a sigh of relief. "Sybil," the High Priestess whispered, "what has happened to you?"

"It was Lady Silvian," Sybil rasped. Her words sounded wet and blocked. Alihandre feared that she was bleeding internally. The woman would not live long. Sybil's eyes rolled back in her head, and Alihandre shook her to keep her awake.

"What about her?" she asked, an edge of panic creeping unbidden into her voice.

"I felt her thoughts." The girl coughed, and blood dribbled down her chin. "I tried to stop her, to hold her at the surface of her consciousness, but she fought me."

"But that's not possible!" Alihandre cried. "She hasn't had the training!"

Sybil's eyes rolled back in her head. Blood ran from her nose and ears, and she rasped out one final breath. The High Priestess pulled her close, tears of frustration and grief running down her face. The silence that surrounded her was deafening.

When she gained enough control of herself, she laid Sybil down on the floor and rose to her feet. She pulled her shift back into place, absently smoothing it; it was wet with blood and tears, but that didn't matter anymore.

"We must give her a proper burial," she whispered.

"What of Lady Silvian?" someone whispered.

Alihandre didn't bother to try and locate the source. "We'll do nothing to her. She lives!"

"She's a danger to us all!" a priestess hissed.

"Then we'll only leave her door guarded, and not her person. She'll rest here, in stasis, until the others return with the cure! No one will be forced to go near her and the danger she represents."

"But—"

"Enough!" she roared, stalking from the room. Without looking, she knew that her advisors followed at her heels. She would need their council tonight, and they were as aware of that as she was. After they scuttled into her room, she closed the door behind them. "Well?" she asked, weariness evident in her voice.

The five women, ranging from very young to impossibly

old, faced her. The oldest hobbled forward. "Mistress, you would be wisest to first discern the nature of the enemy."

Alihandre nodded, knowing this already. "And what are your thoughts on that?" she asked the collected women.

They looked at one another, their eyes wide with forbidden words. At last, the youngest spoke, taking a tiny step forward. "We believe that it is indeed Beldaris who acts against the lady."

"Why?" she asked, needing a confirmation of her own ideas more than an explanation.

"It's simple, really," a third woman said. "Beldaris disappeared perhaps ten years ago, but he was sighted five years ago among the Priestesses of Purity, where he was said to be researching the exiled priestess who was Lianna's grandmother. Not too long after that last sighting, we began having incursions into the monastery."

"You're saying," Alihandre reasoned aloud for all of them, "that Beldaris has come here seeking more power. He'll use Lady Silvian as his tool. Her potential is remarkable, and if he can turn her to his side, the two of them will be unstoppable. He's chosen her to fight at his side, and is currently manipulating her into doing just that."

The five women nodded in agreement. The High Priestess of Truth sighed and brushed loose hair from her brow. "Then what action do you suggest that we take next?"

"Kill her now," two women said at once. The three remaining looked uncomfortable at this suggestion. They glanced at one another, sharing long looks. Alihandre had no doubt that they'd been conferring with one another in recent days, without their two more violent comrades.

The youngest priestess stepped forward again. "We think you should send some women into the catacombs. It's little known that they exist, but they're there. Beldaris, being a well-studied man, will have found them. From their protection, he could've made many raids into obscure parts of the monastery."

Alihandre nodded. "That will work. We'll post guards at

Lianna's door and check the room to make certain it's secure. A team of women will be selected in the morning and sent into the catacombs to search him out."

The oldest priestess nodded her approval. "Send strong women, Alihandre. Beldaris will have grown in power since the day ten years ago when he escaped the Priests of Strength. They'll need to be good women, and they'll need to combine their powers to defeat him."

The High Priestess of Truth nodded wearily. "Yes, I know. I'll go myself."

"No!" all five women snapped in unison.

The youngest priestess smiled. With a nervous edge to her voice, she said, "Lady, we need your leadership here. If you die, there will be a fight over the succession. At a crucial time like this, we cannot afford such a thing. You must live to pick a successor, the new guardian of the Well of Truth and its location."

Alihandre waved them from the room. "I know, I know." Herding them before her, she shoved them out the door. She shut the door to their protests, then stumbled across the room and into bed, not bothering to change her stained shift. Her attire didn't matter in the end, for one never wore true clothing in the land of dreams anyway. Or in the land of the dead.

Beneath the monastery, Beldaris stared up at the ceiling with piercing eyes. He had just left Lianna to return to the waking world. He'd told her that he feared an attack from the priestesses, and that he was going out to meet them. That was, in all actuality, the truth.

Her thoughts hummed at the back of his mind, for he stayed in contact with her at all times. The moment she needed him, or anyone tried to awaken her, he would know. While he guarded his own thoughts, she let hers slip in and out of his mind without restraint, a habit that he would help her break when it was convenient for him. There was no sense in teaching her to protect her secrets just yet.

Beldaris had every intention of keeping her under close guard until he was certain that she would pose him no threat. Once she grew into her remarkable powers she'd be his equal, which was why he didn't want her to become his enemy. If that happened, he would have to kill her, and he didn't want to do that. There was too much that she had to offer him.

Already, he had trained her how to control the latent magic within her. A quick pupil, it took her next to nothing to master the skills that he set her to learn, especially when he taught them through direct mind-to-mind contact. Beldaris was quite confident that she would be able to escape the monastery on her own if it came down to it.

However, one possibility could ruin his plans; she might discover that he had drugged her. If he could convince her that the priestesses had kidnapped her, and that they had been the ones to drug her, he would have nothing to fear. With subtleness, he would lead her to the desired conclusions. Once she deduced a truth on her own, Lianna wouldn't blame his manipulative logic for her false perceptions.

The rebellious nature of some of the priestesses was also a problem. The scheming women wanted to kill Lianna, and that he could not allow. Tonight it would be necessary to stand vigil while Lianna slept. In the morning, he would withdraw to the catacombs to await the coming of his enemies. His resilient body could stand a night without sleep.

Beldaris crept through the system of tunnels. If he became blind, he would still know the way, even with the many winding turns and deceptive doors. Going straight up into the hidden passages that ran through the walls, it didn't take him long to stalk to the room where Lianna slept.

He peered through the spy hole in the wall. The room was dark, but he could see that Lianna was unguarded. Knowing that he could enter without risking detection, he slipped into the room. Reverently, he went to stand over Lianna. Even in the dark shadows of the unlit room, she looked beautiful. In the future, they would make the perfect match. Already, their thoughts and dreams mingled without much effort.

A soft sound alerted him and he withdrew to the tunnels. As he had suspected, a priestess entered the room. She pulled a knife from the sleeve of her robes and moved towards the bed where Lianna slept. Beldaris shook his head in disgust and stretched out one hand towards the woman. When he clenched his fist, she gasped and fell to the ground, clutching her throat. He tightened his fingers and the last of the breath left her. With his magic, it had been an easy task to crush her windpipe.

Standing in the tunnel, he waited out the rest of the night. What would the priestesses say when they found one of their own dead with an assassin's knife in hand? *He* was of a mind to stab her with her own weapon for even thinking of killing Lianna, but he restrained himself. Part of being strong was knowing when to hold back. That knowledge had kept him alive for longer than many wanted, and he intended to keep on living.

Chapter 29

Netria woke, taking her time as she came back up from the many layers of sleep. When she opened her eyes, she was quick to shut them again. The first thing she had seen had been Keth's repulsive features. He was sleeping near her, a thin trail of drool winding its way down from his gaping mouth to pool on the floor.

Before opening her eyes again, she took the precaution of shifting away from the ugly man. On her other side was the much more pleasing sight of Rhen. She looked at him for some time, taking in his boyishly handsome face. Innocent and perfect as he was, Netria thought that she could watch him sleep forever.

Opening his bright blue eyes, Rhen looked back at her. Her heart thumped faster when he smiled. "Good morning, Lady Netria," he whispered, his voice gruff from sleep.

Smiling herself, she suppressed a yawn. "Morning."

Light speared into the hut as someone entered. Netria came fully awake. Her reaction was reflexive as she grabbed her sword and rolled to her feet in one fluid motion. The blade flew free of its scabbard and came to rest at the throat of the intruder.

Priestess of Strength Yellima looked back at her with unfrightened eyes. A moment of tense silence passed, then she smiled. "Withdraw your weapon, Netria."

Netria gritted her teeth. Not wanting to lose face by backing down, she didn't want to lose her life either. She sheathed her sword and ignored the priestess as she rearranged her clothing. Behind her, Rhen rose to his feet.

"Just like Falkris!" he said. "She would've done exactly the same thing."

Netria let a pleased grin cross her face as she turned her back on Yellima to regard the nobleman. "Thanks." To her, it was a true compliment.

He clapped her on the shoulder and moved past her to bend down next to Keth. A worried frown crossed his face, followed by the tender smile of a loving parent. "He's going to be okay."

Yellima nodded. "Your man is as strong as an ox, Lord Tahnuil. He will live. Perhaps he'll even be well enough to accompany us on our journey."

Rhen looked up at her. "Journey?"

"I sent our fastest runners to the neighboring tribe last night. They returned at dawn, bearing news. We are to journey there and arrive before the sun sets this evening, at which point we will begin the search." Her gaze dropped to the prone man on the floor.

"When do we leave?" Netria asked.

"As soon as possible," Yellima answered, still looking at Keth. A corner of her mouth curled down in disdain.

The mercenary moved closer to her, forcing the priestess to look at her. "I don't think it would be wise to leave Keth behind. He's not the type to leave his master's side." *Like a well-trained dog,* she thought.

Yellima nodded in understanding. "Then rouse him. He'll need to have his wounds cleaned and redressed before he is fit for travel."

Rhen stepped forward. "Give me some time alone with him. I'll get him ready. He may be nervous at first, considering what happened to him."

Yellima raised one eyebrow. "Indeed. He wasn't cooperative the first time he awakened. We had to drug him."

The noble frowned. "That won't be necessary again."

Netria put a reassuring hand on his shoulder. "Rhen, it'll be fine. We'll leave you alone for a while. I could use a bath before we go anyway."

"Very well," Yellima said, sounding irritated, "but we must

make haste; the medicine man will not be pleased if he has to wait."

"Right," Netria muttered. *If she would stop making a fuss over everything, we wouldn't be wasting any time.*

Yellima ducked out of the hut, Netria not far behind her. As she left, she heard Rhen talking softly to his big guard. A considerate man, he was always thinking of others and seeing the good in them when no one else would. This was a strength as well as a weakness.

Yellima led her through the village and around a large hut that probably served as a meeting hall. A pond was nestled there. Women and men alike gathered around it, doing laundry and washing dishes. There was even a man cleaning his latest kill. Even a mercenary had learned to do better. Netria's eyebrows rose high on her brow. "You expect me to bathe in *there*?"

The Priestess of Strength snorted. "There is a smaller pool beyond this one that the women use to bathe."

Netria didn't need to be told twice. Leaving Yellima, she hurried past the pond and pushed her way through the tall grass that surrounded the village. After a moment, she came upon the pond. Sparkling in the early morning sun, it shone, inviting her to enter its depths. She was thankful that she wouldn't have to share her bath with anyone, for the pond was unoccupied.

Grateful, Netria slipped out of her clothing, which was torn from the rough journey and soiled in many places with blood and filth. She had not bathed since that day in the monastery, which now seemed so long ago. Even though the water was cool, she moaned with pleasure as she waded into the pool. She had brought her clothing in with her, of a mind to wash the blood and mud away.

Despite her wish to linger, she bathed quickly. When she finished, she climbed from the pool and used her hands to push most of the water from her skin. As she was pulling her wet clothing back on, she happened to glance at the water. Scarred and weathered, her reflection frowned up at her. She leaned over to take a closer look at herself. Her dark brown hair, cropped short for convenience, looked black while it was wet, and her amber eyes were ancient, belonging to a much older woman. She had seen far too much in her life.

Lingering a moment, she stared down at her reflection. She looked like a formidable woman, one who was strong and quick. On a battlefield, she was desirable. At a noble court, she was disdained. How did she ever expect to win Rhen's heart? Love was supposed to cross the boundaries of social status, but why would he ever even look at a woman like her? Her scar was deterrent enough for most men. Of course, some found it attractive, but they were the rare few.

With an exaggerated sigh, Netria turned and trudged back to the village. Some of the Imani villagers eyed her as she passed, speaking to one another in their strange, lilting tongue. Let them say what they would; it didn't really matter in the end.

Rhen met her at the door of the hut. He was still travel-stained, and he smelled bad, but the smudges on his face and clothing only served to endear him to her more. She grinned. "Ready to head out?"

He nodded. "Keth will be fine. As I suspected, he won't leave my side. He is, however, injured. We may to have drag him on a litter."

"We don't have the time for that!" Yellima snapped as she joined them.

For the first time since she had met him, Netria saw anger cloud Rhen's face. "Madame," he said in a dangerous voice, "I will not leave him behind. If I did, he'd only follow us, and maybe kill himself in the process."

"Then we'll drug him."

"No!" he said, his voice rising in volume. "You'll do no such thing! Among these people, Keth is considered a man to be respected. He will not be drugged like some sick animal, but given freedom to make his own choices!"

Yellima's eyes narrowed. Netria could sense that the villagers were moving closer, watching the confrontation between the two. She pushed her way between them. "Look, Yellima, you don't want to lose face with your people. You also don't want to lose your chance to help us and get that favor out of Alihandre. Just let him take Keth, and our lives will be easier."

The Priestess of Strength frowned, and the air around her seemed to darken. Although it was a frightening sight, Netria stood her ground. "Very well," Yellima said in a tight voice, "he'll come with us."

Rhen nodded, looking satisfied with himself. Wet clothing and all, he patted Netria on the shoulder. He didn't seem to mind, but then again, neither did she. "Thank you, Netria," he said. At least he wasn't calling her a lady anymore. Hopefully, that was a good thing.

Chapter 30

Amial stood beside Daymen as they held vigil in the arch room. Several hours had passed since Falkris and her wolf had disappeared into the flames. As much as Amial wanted to believe that the warrior was still alive, she was losing hope with each passing moment.

Suddenly, the flames began to flicker and die away. Amial took one step forward, a mute cry of distress at her lips. As though it had never been there at all, the fire was gone. Falkris had not returned.

"Daymen," she whispered. At a loss, she hoped the Jenestran knight would know what to do.

Daymen turned to look at her with worried eyes. There was pain written across his face, his expression a mirror of her own. Closing his eyes and taking a deep breath, he nodded. "The battle must go on," he said so softly that she almost didn't hear him.

He led her from the room, the sword that had been Falkris' held out before him. Following him in a daze, she reflected on his words. Life was a war, just like their struggle to save Lianna was. Sometimes, to save an ideal or a single life, one had to make sacrifices. This time, it had been Falkris' life that had been the price.

Amial's vision misted over as she walked, and she had to wipe tears from her eyes. There was no sense in letting her grief kill her. Right now, it was important that she remain alert, with her eyes open to danger. Though she couldn't stop the tears from falling, she could keep her gaze forward.

Daymen grieved as well, Amial knew. His pain was as real as hers, and may even have cut deeper. While he hadn't known Falkris well, Amial was aware that he respected the proud warrior. To lose a comrade in arms was a tragic experience that she couldn't begin to fathom.

As she blinked the last of her tears away, she looked around at the temple, which reminded her of hell now, a place where nothing good could happen. Indeed, in hell, one was purified by an eternity of flames that burned away the sins of a lifetime. Wasn't that what this temple was? Resembling a place near to hell, the entire building seemed dedicated to purifying those who dared enter, no matter how destructive or bloody the manner.

She and Daymen moved without delay into the main room and around the staircase to the door on the other side, thankful that they weren't attacked by any more of the strange icy creatures that guarded the temple. As the pair entered the room housing the second arch, they shut the door with a firm click behind them.

"Daymen," Amial said, "what about the first arch? Are we certain that it was disabled?"

He looked harried. The events of the past days were weighing heavily on him. If not for him, the caravan from Ravenia would never have been attacked, Lianna would have not been exposed to the storm and become ill, and Falkris would still be alive.

"Lady Amial, I cannot be certain, but I believe that it was disabled. The flames are gone."

"Must there always be a death to end the flames? There are only two of us left, and there are two arches yet remaining." She hated to sound so cold about the death of her friend and heroine, but she had to be realistic if she wanted to stay alive.

If Daymen was bothered by her assessment of the situation, he didn't show it. "I wish I could tell you, milady, but I just don't know." He looked pained, as though he believed the entire situation was his fault. Taking so much blame on his shoulders was far from healthy.

Privately, Amial wondered if saving Lianna was important enough for others to give their lives for her. The archer knew that she would not die for the Lady Silvian if she had a choice. She was certain that Falkris shouldn't have had to lose her life for one woman. Especially not the daughter of the man who had tried to kill her.

To calm him, Amial put a hand on Daymen's shoulder. "Is there an inscription?" She examined the floor, pushing him out of the way so she could get a clear view. The words were there, as she had expected they would be.

With a heart that is pure and untouched by the ravages of humanity, and eyes unclouded by worldly assumptions, one worthy may safely find the way forward. Those who fail to see clearly, whose sight is darkened, will be forever lost as their souls seek renewal in the heart of cleansing flames.

She looked up at Daymen. When he finished reading over her shoulder, he met her gaze. "Lady Amial, I have fought in too many wars. My hands are too bloody for this arch. It must fall to you."

"Me?" Her heart leapt into her throat. She shifted her gaze to the arch, terror sinking its claws into her stomach.

"Your innocence will save you," he assured her, but she could see the doubt in his eyes, and that frightened her even more.

For Falkris, she would be strong. Lianna no longer mattered, and never had. Amial wanted to do it for her heroine, so that she could know that Falkris' death had not been in vain. Someone had to pass the arches for the way to be opened. If they didn't retrieve the relic, this trip was all for nothing.

Amial stood and took one resolute step forward. After the first step, it was easier. She closed her eyes and moved closer to what she viewed as her death. When she opened her eyes, she was facing the arch. Staring at it for some time, she willed herself to be home, far away from this nightmare.

Vapors of her breath rose in the air. Ice surrounded her, coating everything with a thin sheen. The blue flames that burned within the arch gave off no heat, despite how close she was. Perhaps, if she could not feel a rise in temperature already, she would find that the fire was not hot. She didn't fancy being burned alive. If there was no heat, she would only be turned to ash; even in death, there'd be no warmth for her in this cold hellhole.

Resigned, she stepped into the arch. The fire leapt up to consume her, caressing her with its touch. She felt no warmth, only a relaxing reassurance. Was this what Falkris had felt, just before she died? Had the fire taken her without melting away her flesh, without eating away at her body with ravenous hunger?

Amial closed her eyes, letting the fire wash over her. She didn't feel as though she stood in fire. Rather, she felt like the wings of fairies were tickling her as they brushed against her with their feather-light touch. Smiling, she leaned into the gentle touch of the flames.

Gradually, she became aware of something else with her. She knew that it wasn't Daymen, but something greater. At first, she dared to hope that it was Falkris, but knew it couldn't be. Whatever joined her in the fire was far from human. More than a consciousness, this was the being that would pass judgment on her. She hoped that it was not as thirsty for blood as the icy terrors that infested the temple.

Thoughts slid over hers, prying open forgotten memories and beliefs. In a moment, her entire life was exposed. She felt naked, yet she knew there was no need for clothing in the world that she traveled through. The entity saw clearly; clothing meant nothing to it.

Just as quickly as it had joined her, the being was gone. Amial sensed approval. A sense of warmth washed over her, and she opened her eyes. At her feet, the flames were dying away. She watched them swirl into nothing, then stepped free of the arch.

Daymen met her halfway between the door and the arch. "Amial," he said, relief in his voice, "you've done it!"

She turned back to look at the arch, and a great sadness came over her. "I have," she whispered. "Like Falkris, I've disabled the arch. I, however, came back." At her words, Daymen looked away, but couldn't hide his grief.

Daymen looked over his shoulder to see if Amial was still close behind him. They had not seen any of the ice monsters for some time, but he still feared an attack. The deadly claws of the fiends had nearly claimed Falkris' life. Perhaps it was her injuries that had brought about her death in the end. He didn't want to risk Amial as he had Falkris. The burden of two deaths on his shoulders was not something he could bear.

Ascending the stairs to the upper level of the Temple of Purity, the pair reached a large landing and the third set of doors. Beyond it, Daymen believed, would be the final arch. He hoped to clear it so they could continue further into the temple and retrieve the ring. Once that was done, he would be only too happy to leave.

The half-light in the room flickered without warning, and Daymen looked around to see what the cause was. The main source of illumination, besides the torch that Amial carried, was a strange pale light streaming down from the ceiling. Daymen supposed that it came in from a skylight of some sort, but he wasn't really certain of anything in this strange place.

Near the top of the room, he could see a pale shadow gliding back and forth. His first instinct was to panic and draw his sword, but instead he signaled to Amial. Nodding, she readied her bow. He held the torch so that she could light one of her arrows. A moment later, she took aim. The creature fell with an arrow in its heart. Amial finished it with one final arrow, and it melted away into water.

"Let's keep moving," Daymen said in a low voice, "there may be more of them."

"Why do you think such horrible monsters were left to guard this place?" Amial whispered as they neared the top of the stairs.

The knight glanced over his shoulder at her. Deep brown eyes scanned the shadows as Amial searched for any sign of the monsters. Daymen kept silent until they neared the doors. Thankfully, the door opened and they entered the room containing the third arch without any problems.

He shut the door and turned to face her. "Have you considered how much power there is in the relics contained within the temples? The ring alone can cure any disease."

"And there are five temples, each containing a powerful relic. If a person could obtain all five, they would be unstoppable. These creatures guard the temple to make certain that obtaining even one of the relics is impossible." With her quick mind, she had figured this out on her own once again. Such intelligence was rare in times when so many went uneducated.

"Is there an inscription?" he asked.

She nodded and bent to examine the floor. When she found the words, she read them aloud. "One who seeks only to bring good to others may pass. If the thoughts of the individual facing the trial are colored with selfishness, that person shall be burned alive by the flames of their own self absorption."

Daymen considered that for a time. To pass the test, the person who entered the arch had to be working only for the good of others. He or she couldn't want anything but to aid another.

Amial looked up at him. "It could be either of us. Neither of us really wants this ring; we're doing it for Lianna."

"And the Priestesses of Truth," he said, almost as an afterthought.

"Then shall I face the arch, Sir Aschton?"

"No, milady. You've risked too much already. Also, it's your fire that has kept the enemies at bay. You'll stand a greater chance of survival if you're left alone in this place."

The archer nodded as she stood. "It doesn't seem to be a religious sanctuary at all, unless you call it a sacrificial altar dedicated to hell."

"Be careful what you say, Lady Amial. You never know who might be listening."

She shivered, whether from the cold or fear, he couldn't

know, but he suspected it was a little of both. Resigned, he turned to the beckoning flames of the arch. Without a word, he took the first step towards what could be his death.

The flames, when he stepped into their embrace, were nothing like he had expected. Consuming heat was what he'd imagined. Once, during a battle, he had been pushed into a fire. He had rolled free at once, and his armor had protected him, but the pain had been excruciating. This was different, almost soothing. As a warrior, pain was preferable to this strange sensation. He could deal with pain.

A sudden presence was beside him, but when he turned there was nothing there. When he glanced back at Amial, wondering if she also sensed that someone had joined them, she was gone. Where the archer had been, there were only flames; he was in the center of a pool of purifying fire.

Though he could see nothing and feel nothing when he reached out with his hand, he knew that he wasn't alone. Something slid over his thoughts, touching his mind and heart as it tried to discern his intentions. He felt a questioning gaze turn on him, wanting to know why he had come.

"To help a woman," he said, turning slowly as he tried to locate the source of the strange feelings that wrapped around him.

The presence shifted, moving closer until he felt that he breathed it in. He wanted to take a step back, but knew that he should not. The questioning sensation came again. What did he have to gain from helping the woman?

"Nothing," he admitted. "I don't know her."

"Then why?" This time he heard a voice whisper in his ear. The heat of breath on his skin made him cringe.

"I'm obligated to help her. The Priestesses of Truth have requested it, and I must obey them in return for all they have done for me."

"Then you do this to honor yourself." Disapproval washed over him.

"No!" he said, anger rising within him. "I do nothing to

honor myself! Everything that I do is for the people, and for the One God! I gave up my life and my dreams to become a noble knight, so that I could stand by what is right for the people! Don't *dare* to accuse me of selfishness or working for myself when the life of an innocent woman is at stake!"

There was silence, then the flames faded away. Daymen met Amial's eyes. The third arch had been opened. The sound of stone grating behind him made him turn swiftly. A doorway had opened in the wall. Beyond it, a passageway stretched into darkness. The way forward was open.

Chapter 31

The morning following Alihandre's decision to send priestesses into the catacombs after Beldaris, the High Priestess awoke before dawn. She sat up in bed, a slight tickling along her spine warning her that something was amiss. The smell of discord within the stones of her home reached her nose like the tantalizing allure of the cook's special dessert. Rising from the bed, she threw on her robe.

Her feet were carrying her down the hall to Lianna's room before she had even fully awakened. With sluggish steps, she swayed from lack of sleep. The incident involving the death of the priestess had deprived her of the rest she needed to keep any semblance of energy running through her aged body.

Without bothering to knock, she thrust her way into the room. A priestess lay in the center of the floor, a wicked knife clutched in her hand. Alihandre stooped to turn the woman over. Eyes bulged from a deathly pale face. The woman's throat was bruised, as though someone had strangled her.

"An assassin sent to kill Lianna," Alihandre whispered to herself. "I wonder who protected the lady—" She had her suspicions that it had been the person who lurked in the catacombs. Whoever it was wanted Lianna on his side. For that, he needed Lianna alive.

The door creaked open, and another priestess bustled in. Stopping short at the sight before her, a strangled gasp escaped the girl's throat. When she lost her grip on the tray in her hands, it crashed to the floor. The clatter of broken dishes echoed with enough sound to wake the entire monastery. Soon, all would know of the assassin.

Alihandre dismissed the girl with a glance, then rose to check on Lianna. She'd have to act now, before the priestesses decided to take matters into their own hands. Those who hungered the most for blood would be sent into the catacombs. That would satisfy the most rebellious ones and pacify the others. Politically, the action was sound. Alihandre herself would stand watch over Lianna until she could select a trustworthy set of guards. Only then would she consult the Well of Truth, for she needed its powers now more than ever.

Leaving the dead woman on the floor, she went out into the hall. "See that all of the priestesses are assembled in the courtyard right away," she ordered the first woman she encountered.

Then, the High Priestess of Truth turned on her heel and stalked back into Lianna's room. With her magic as well as her eyes, she examined the dead priestess. She wanted to know the truth behind the death. Any number of things could explain what happened, including a staged assassination attempt. *Truth is my virtue,* the priestess mused, *and I intend to discover the entire truth behind this incident, no matter what.*

When she focused her powers, an image of the assassin creeping into the room flashed before her eyes. As she watched, the woman stopped in mid-stride and began to choke. Magic had slain her, though no power trace was left behind. Whoever had killed the woman was good at hiding his trail. The man was a fugitive. Alihandre's belief that Beldaris was the suspect solidified.

Until a priestess came to notify her that everyone was assembled, she sat in silent contemplation. Wearily, Alihandre rose to her feet and followed her priestess down the halls to the courtyard. Before emerging into the growing light, she paused in the doorway. Her women filled the little open space, tugging their robes into place and suppressing yawns.

After saying a silent prayer for courage and truth, Alihandre stepped out and assumed her place before the women of the monastery, waiting for absolute silence before speaking. "The truth must be known," she stated. That, more than anything she could have said, got the attention of the women. Truth was sacred to them; it was the virtue they lived by.

"Last night, someone tried to assassinate Lady Silvian. Thankfully, Lianna was spared due to the interference of a second individual. I can only assume that it was the very man who has drugged her. As to the woman who was to assassinate Lianna, she is no more. I would like to know who helped plan and attempt the assassination. The truth will be known, one way or another."

Absolute silence met her words. When she drew in a deep breath, she was certain that everyone present could hear it. "Then I must extract the truth from you. Those of you who have not stepped forward will find this painful, but it's the only way." She searched their faces for anything that would betray those guilty. All remained silent and calm.

As Alihandre closed her eyes, she called on the virtue that dominated her life. Truth rang through her, absolving her of her doubts. She didn't attempt to mold it as she let it leave her body and fan out to cover her women. Like fine dust, her power settled on heads and shoulders, coating robes with its fine touch. Still, no one stepped forward.

"If you're guilty of participating in any part of an assassination attempt on Lianna Silvian, say so now or let the truth speak for you."

Silence stretched for several heartbeats, then the screaming began. Five women crashed to the ground, brushing at their heads and clothing as they tried to remove the spell from themselves. Alihandre gasped when she recognized the women as her own advisors. Had they really acted against her? *I dare not trust anyone.*

Alihandre waved a hand to banish the spell before the women were burned alive by their lies and the ugly truth within them. As soon as her advisors were able to stand, they were seized and put into custody by other women. Alihandre faced them with a heavy heart. "There's no denying the truth," she told them in a soft voice. She turned to her priestesses. "Carry out their executions now. They've worked against me and the truth, and must be punished as is written in the law."

The youngest of her advisors was the only to protest her fate. "Those of us who follow truth learn that we must be true to ourselves! In arranging the assassination, we were doing just that!"

Alihandre gave her a sad smile. "We must also be true to the law, and that which is best for the whole. You've not only broken the law with your actions, but you've also risked the life of Lady Silvian. As you all know, she may be the only one capable of standing against the growing threat of evil that comes from beyond Jenestra.

"Much evidence exists that Ravenian nobles have unearthed the dark powers of ancient times and are using them to gain power. Lord Dracine Silvian, Lianna's own father, is surrounded by foul energy. If his power continues to increase, he'll soon be a definite threat to the peace that holds the world."

The advisor who had spoken bowed her head. "You are wise, High Priestess Alihandre." She raised defiant eyes to the women who surrounded her. "Let it be known that I support her, even in my death. We'll face the truth of our actions now, and pay with our lives! As we pass, we will do so in honor of her, the only one fit to lead us!"

Alihandre turned away and fled the courtyard rather than watch the women she had trusted so intimately die. She went to her rooms and threw herself on the bed, purging herself of her pain and sins with tears. Without anyone she could trust, she felt alone. In the hours to come, she hoped that she would make the right decisions. So much depended on keeping Lianna safe from harm.

Beldaris waited deep within the monastery. Going into the trance that let him communicate with Lianna was not a risk he dared take. The priestesses would be coming for him today, that much he knew. Young and strong, his powers were more potent than ever. Still, if there were many of them, and if they successfully united against him, he would fail.

Beldaris shook his head to clear it of his doubts and concentrated on monitoring the catacombs. After checking all of the traps that he'd set for the priestesses, he risked sending his thoughts higher to see what transpired above. Peace and joy radiated from Lianna. Overshadowing the pocket of serenity were grief and confusion. The assassin had been found.

The priestesses would be hot for revenge now. Alihandre would have no choice but to send some of them after him, or they would kill Lianna. They wanted blood to account for the deaths amidst their small numbers, and Alihandre would give them his rather than sacrifice Lianna.

He didn't want to lose Lianna, not when she was the only person with enough power to support him in his quest. When she fought for something she believed in, she could be ruthless. *His* cause was the supreme one; he had to make her see that. Anything that stood in his way would have to be eliminated.

As he considered, he raised his eyes to the ceiling. When the others returned with the antidote to awaken Lianna, he would take her away. He'd make her believe that *he* had rescued her from the priestesses.

Alihandre assembled the ten priestesses she deemed most likely to rebel if action wasn't taken. She surveyed them as they stood in her office. Of them, two weren't powerful in magic, but they made up for it with their quick minds. The rest were balanced with powers and other skills. Only one of them had a true aptitude for the power within.

"Listen carefully," the High Priestess of Truth commanded. "If your enemy is really Beldaris, he will be very powerful. If you wish to defeat him, you must do so as a group. Only with your combined powers can you hope to overcome him.

"If you do defeat him, bind him with your powers, and bring him to me. I want him alive to administer the antidote to Lianna in case Falkris doesn't return from the Temple of Purity with the relic. The temple is well guarded, and the path through it is dangerous. I would have gone myself, but I was needed here." She eyed them. "Do you understand? He is to be left *alive*."

Nodding, they headed towards the door without being dismissed. With a word, she halted them. "*Wait*." They turned to face her, some of them impatiently, others filled with guilt. "I asked you if you understood my orders." As one, they nodded. "If he's killed," Alihandre warned in a low voice, "I will be *very* upset." She stared all of them down until they could no longer meet her eyes, then dismissed them. As the last of them closed the door, Alihandre whispered a prayer for their success.

Chapter 32

At first, there was only nothingness. Then, sensation returned. Flames filled the air with cool smoke that drifted across her lungs like mist. Cold air clung to a gray world with an icy grip. Solid stone below provided stability. Fire everywhere kissed skin with gentle touches.

A step forward, and fire began to redouble its assault on flesh and clothing. Colder than death, flames burned with the same hot intensity as normal fire. Cloth and skin alike were scorched in the ferocity of their hunger.

Human sensation returned with a scream of pain. Desperate hands clawed at the air as her knees gave way, and one cheek touched blessedly cool stone. Something cold and rough brushed against the other cheek ... a tongue.

"Dax." The rasping sound of her own voice brought Falkris back to herself. She opened her eyes to peer through the fire at the wolf standing over her. He looked at her with pleading eyes.

Somehow, Falkris found the strength to rise and crawl from the fire, but collapsed just beyond the flames. Feeling stone the entire length of her body, she realized that she was naked. Her clothing had been burned away. Horrified, she raised one hand to see if her skin was still intact. A whole hand trembled before her eyes, the skin firm and smooth. Why had her skin not burned if her clothing had been destroyed in the fire?

Unsteady, she rose to her feet, assessing her surroundings. The arch was gone, as were the flames. She was standing in a cloud of thick, swirling mist. There was no sign of Daymen or Amial. As she stumbled a few steps, Dax at her heels, pain lanced through her entire body. If she didn't find a place to rest and put a proper dressing on her wounds, they would kill her.

Hopefully, the mist would end. She wanted to be free of this place.

A rich male voice came out of the mist, whispering across her mind. *"I am Shai. If you wish to claim me, show me that you are as strong as my steel, and that your mind is as sharp as my blade."*

A rattling in the mist reminded her that she was alone and weaponless. Falkris turned in the deceptive fog, trying to discern the origin of the voice. Her own pained delirium was deterrent enough to render her nearly blind. Having no idea whether the other was a friend or foe, she didn't call out. That she even had the strength to vocalize was doubtful.

A shadow emerged from the mist, the outline of wings alarming Falkris, for she was weaponless and had no way to defend herself. She didn't even have any fire with which to melt the fiend. Panicking, she fell back. Dax moved with her, his hackles raised and a menacing growl issuing from his throat.

When the monster launched itself into the air, Falkris broke into a lurching run. Her heart leapt into her throat as she sensed the air currents in the fog shift. She knew that the creature was about to drop onto her back, as it had done before. At the last moment, she dodged to the side. The shrieking noise of claws on stone told her the beast had hit the ground. She staggered through the mist, hoping to cloak herself in its concealing embrace until she could find a weapon.

"Your opponent is a water elemental. You cannot hide from it in mist," the voice whispered to her. A strange presence moved among her thoughts. The sensation alienated her and intrigued her at the same time. Somehow, she knew that whatever spoke to her wanted to help her. Even as it aided her, it was studying her.

Falkris focused on the task at hand. For all she knew, the voice in her head was a delusion. Her first concern was staying alive. If she survived, she would deal with whatever spoke to her then. Laughter echoed through her mind. She shook her head to clear it and looked for a way to defend herself.

"Dax," she whispered. The wolf looked to her for direction. "Distract it while I search for a weapon."

The canine seemed to nod, and moved away into the mist, quick and deadly despite his own injuries. *"Anything for you, milady."* The voice that reached her mind this time was cultured and strong. Had she really heard the wolf speaking to her? What was this strange place?

Falkris moved through the mist, seeking anything that she could use to defeat her opponent. To go against it with only her human body would be as good as giving death a formal invitation. Besides that, she was already wounded grievously. Her back burned with every step she took. Even if she survived the fight, it was possible she would bleed to death. There had to be something that she could do to save Dax and herself from certain death.

"Why fight at all? Why not flee and leave the wolf?" the voice asked.

"Because he's my friend."

"Isn't he naught but a mere wolf?"

"That's what you think."

Again the rich laughter penetrated the depths of her mind. *"But why did you come here at all? Why risk yourself and your companion?"*

"I'm doing it for someone." An image of Rhen flashed before her eyes. He loved Lianna, and Falkris loved him, in a way. To see him happy, she would do almost anything, for he was her family. If it meant risking her life to save his lady love, she would do it. She owed him for more than saving her life.

While the owner of the formless voice contemplated her answer, she ignored it and searched for a weapon. The sound of Dax yelping in pain sent her stumbling back through the mist, heedless of personal danger. She had to save him. Loyal and loving, the wolf would die if she ordered it. That, she couldn't bear.

Suddenly, a pedestal loomed before her, and she managed to come to a halt just before she tripped over it. Time slowed, and the fog ceased its lazy swirling. A bright light surrounded the pedestal and arced up to the ceiling, banishing the mist.

Looking around, Falkris found herself in an endless room. Dax lay on the ground not far from her. Over him, still poised in the air, was the icy monster. Once time resumed, the fiend would fall upon Dax and kill him with its lethal claws.

Her gaze returned to the pedestal. Over the center a sword levitated, the polished white blade flashing in the strange light. Ancient sigils ran the length of the deadly weapon. The hilt was silver, with a sparkling sapphire set in it.

"I have chosen you," the voice said.

Falkris stood still for a second, her mind attempting to grasp what was happening. Then, she reached out her hand to take the sword. As soon as the light fell on her skin, she felt blinding pain that shot up her arm and filled her entire body. Despite the agony, she plunged her entire arm into the light and retrieved the sword.

Just before she blacked out from pain, she jerked her arm free. A moment later, she fell to the ground, writhing in agony. Long after she had removed the beautiful weapon from its pedestal, pain lanced through her body. So intense was the agony that she might as well have been standing in the fire. Every inch of her skin was immolated in the flames of unending pain. She felt as though her entire body was being molded in a blacksmith's fire.

The pain began to fade to a dull ache, then it was no more than a memory. As soon as she regained control of herself, Falkris rose to her feet and brought the sword up; it fit perfectly in her hand, as though it had been made just for her. Time resumed and the monster continued its assault, but she was already there, preparing to slay her enemy. The fiend reared back in surprise just before the blade penetrated its icy hide, but death was already delivered.

Her father's sword had not harmed the creature, but this weapon slew the monster with its first strike. She could feel power running from the sword into her body. As the watery remains of her opponent splattered her, she knelt beside Dax. He whined softly, pained, and strove to reassure her with a gentle lick. Weakened, he couldn't even lift his head.

Falkris set the sword down beside him as she bent to look at his wounds. A gentle blue light made her look up. The sapphire in the hilt of the sword was emitting a soft glow. With caution, she reached out to retrieve the weapon. The voice spoke again into her mind, *"Touch your companion, and he will be healed. I will purify his flesh for you, while we are here, in this place of power."*

Hesitant and disbelieving, Falkris did as the voice bid her. As soon as she laid her free hand on Dax, the sapphire in the hilt of the sword flared, lighting the room with brilliant blue light. The wolf whined, but didn't move. When the light died away, leaving the room feeling dark and empty, Falkris examined her companion. Dax was fully healed. In demonstration of this, he jumped to his feet and ran over to lick her.

"At least one of us will live," she whispered. She stretched to touch her back, and her startled fingers encountered rich cloth. Beneath the fabric, she found smooth skin. There was no sign of the wounds that had rent her flesh just moments before.

Falkris rose to her feet, still holding onto the sword. "What's going on?" Her heart almost stopped. The voice that came from her throat was an echo of the past, a sound that she had only dreamed of over the long years. Rich and musical, hers was the voice of a trained singer.

Her laugh was nervous, but even that sound was melodic. Opening her mouth to speak again, she wondered if she had heard wrong the first time. "Can it be?" The same voice spoke, dancing through the words with a rich grace that many would envy and adore.

Hesitant at first, then with growing joy, she began to sing. Because of her excitement and lack of practice, it took her a moment to draw sufficient breath into her lungs. The first notes were weak at best, but it was a wonder to be singing at all when she had lived so long with a ruined throat. As she gained confidence, her voice echoed through the huge room, filling it with the haunting sound of her pure soprano. She reveled in the echoes that came back to her, tears of happiness running down her cheeks. Dax sat at her feet with his ears perked, watching her with something akin to human happiness in his yellow eyes.

"How can this be possible?" she asked, wondering what she had done to inspire such a miracle.

"I, Shai, have chosen you. As my warrior, your body has been purified and renewed."

Falkris looked down at the sword. With a trembling hand, she examined it. Was the weapon speaking to her? Such a thing didn't seem possible. Even so, she had never believed that she'd ever be able to sing again. "Shai?" she asked hesitantly, thrilling in the sound of her own voice. In answer, the sapphire set in the hilt pulsed once.

Falkris shifted her gaze to the wolf at her feet. "Dax? What do you think of this?"

The wolf looked up at her with earnest eyes. *"Anything is possible, milady,"* he answered with the same cultured voice she had heard earlier.

"Now I know I'm insane," she said. Or dreaming. She hoped not. Such a dream would be nothing but pain and torture once she awakened.

The sword warmed in her hand. *"It's only because we're in this place of power. Once we leave, this will no longer be possible."*

Her heart fell. "Then, am I to lose my voice again?"

She sensed a strange warmth, akin to affection. *"No, Lady. Once your body is renewed, it cannot revert to its former state. You can acquire new scars, but old ones will never return unless you stray onto the path of darkness."*

"Then what are you talking about, Shai?" she demanded, still not believing that she was talking to the sword.

This time a sense of offense washed over her. *"I'm not just any sword. What I mean is that once we leave this place, your magical abilities will become latent again. They will not fade, but they will lessen in power. You'll no longer be able to commu-*

nicate with your companion, or me."

"What? I don't have any magical abilities!"

The sapphire flashed. *"You can read words written in magic, and you're capable of advanced telepathy. More will come with time, but enough. There is no time to speak of this now. Your friends are in danger."* With that, the light around her began to grow dim, and the voice of her sword faded.

Chapter 33

Netria kept a careful eye on Rhen throughout their journey across the plains. Brooding, the noble often looked back to see that Keth was well, and that his litter still dragged behind them. Rhen was so preoccupied that he didn't bother to look out for himself. Netria had to tug on his sleeve numerous times to prevent him from stumbling into a puddle or tripping on an obstacle that he failed to perceive.

He always looked at her when she did so, his wonderful blue eyes wide and confused. Then he would smile, and any irritation she felt at having to look after him melted away as her heart raced in her chest. She had fallen for him. *As he's fallen for Lianna, damn her to hell,* she thought darkly.

"Look, Netria," Rhen whispered.

Her hand went straight to her sword, and she glanced around with wary eyes. "What is it?"

He pointed towards the horizon. "Look at the sky." The sun was beginning to set; they had spent the whole day walking towards the neighboring village. On the horizon, a large cloud was shielding the sun from sight. Light shone around the edges of the clouds, tingeing them gold and painting the entire horizon a thousand colors richer than could ever be reproduced in cloth or silk.

Netria's breath caught in her throat. "It's beautiful."

He nodded, then smiled at her, his eyes holding her still. "It's the most beautiful thing I've ever seen," he whispered. He didn't mean the sunset.

Netria was certain that he could hear her heart thudding in her chest. His eyes weakening her, she was at his mercy. With a word, he could crush her heart. A single syllable uttered by his lips could shatter her world. He had so much power over her, yet he was so incredibly weak.

The world reasserted itself the moment she sensed movement behind her. She drew her sword and whirled to defend herself. Flashing in the sun, her blade arched with absolute perfection towards its target, halting in mid-swing as she recognized her foe. With wide eyes that betrayed only a trace of fear, Yellima stared at her. She hid her weakness well.

Netria grinned, happy to have caught the cocky woman off guard, and sheathed her sword. "Never sneak up on a warrior," she said.

"Especially a mercenary," Rhen added, coming up beside her. He put one hand on her arm, rubbing it affectionately. Trying to ignore the warm shiver that traveled outward from where his skin touched hers was futile. When he didn't withdraw his hand, her heart increased its mad fluttering until she was certain it would give out.

Netria swallowed once to regain her voice before speaking. "What'd you want, Yellima?"

The Priestess of Strength did not betray an offense at the casual way with which Netria addressed her, but her eyes flashed. "We'll reach the village soon, despite the delay." Her eyes moved to the litter where Keth lay, dozing fitfully.

Rhen squeezed Netria's arm, then moved forward, a bounce in his step. "Then let us continue on! I wish to find this plant and return home before Lady Lianna falls prey to foul influence."

Yellima frowned and stared at him until he took a step back. She folded her hands into her long robes and regarded them both with serious eyes. "Do nothing to offend these people. If we anger them, all of our lives may be forfeit, even mine. I will not risk myself to save you."

Rhen nodded, excitement still dancing in his eyes. "Of course. We'll follow your lead, Lady Yellima."

The Priestess of Strength shifted her dangerous gaze to Netria. "And you?"

Netria let a bitter smile grace her face. She inclined her

head in acceptance. "Aye, as long as you do nothing to harm Lord Tahnuil or his guard. I've sworn to defend them with my life." Her mood darkening, she frowned. "If anything happens to them, well … just remember that I'm a mercenary. I specialize in cutting people up."

Yellima smiled, amused and far from unnerved by the blunt threat. "Very well." Turning to Rhen, she ignored Netria as she spoke on. "The guards that have accompanied us must leave now. Only the four of us, including the big man, may continue. Any others who dare approach risk death at the hands of these people." She moved over to Keth, and after looking down at him, raised disgusted eyes to Rhen. "Rouse him. We still have a good distance to cross before the sun sets."

As Rhen bent to tend to his friend, Yellima joined Netria. "What does he see in that ugly brute?" she muttered.

Netria glanced sidelong at Yellima. "I think Rhen has little use for appearances. He looks into the heart." *And a good thing, too, with my scar.*

"Let's hope that the medicine man does the same. He has no care for outsiders. Even I receive no welcome among his people, though I've been here for several years."

"Is this man really so dangerous? Surely the power of a priestess like yourself could counter him."

Yellima snorted. "I derive my power from one virtue, but he draws his from all that surrounds him. He uses pagan magic, linked to the elements. I worship the One God, and he worships the old, dead gods. His power is more flexible."

Netria considered. "What's the advantage in your way?"

"We can combine our powers to defeat any one powerful mage or hedge wizard. Our strength lies in our unity and our ability to work towards a common goal. Alone, I am nothing to this medicine man. With two others at my side, he is nothing to me."

Just then, Rhen and Keth joined them. The noble looked as alert as ever, and he teemed with energy, ready for any challenge. Beside him, Keth looked groggy, but ready for travel. Without wasting time, Yellima gestured to them and they headed out into the plains and away from the others. Their quest was almost at an end.

Just before the sun sank below the horizon and night began, the travelers arrived at the village. They were met at the edge and taken to a small hut similar to the ones in the Imani village. Under the watchful eyes of silent guards, they waited there until the penetrating darkness of night descended.

With the coming of the hours of darkness, the medicine man made his appearance, sweeping into the little hut without preamble. A fiercely barbaric mask painted with wild colors hid his face. Just his dark glittering eyes showed, and they were almost as terrifying as the mask itself. Strange symbols swirled across his flesh. When Netria looked closer, she realized that his entire body was tattooed. Naked except for a loincloth made from the skin of an animal, he was like something from the past, come to haunt them with his strange ways.

He began speaking in his native language. The guttural syllables danced off his tongue like water, streaming over the Ravenians. Yellima listened to him closely, nodding several times. The others kept silent while she listened, watching her rather than the medicine man.

When at last he finished speaking, Yellima turned to them. "We are to follow him now. He'll lead us to the place where the Night's Breath grows. We're to harvest only the leaves of the plant, and no more than one from each. He doesn't want to risk the death of such rare plants."

The medicine man ducked out of the hut, not waiting for the others. When Rhen didn't follow right away, Netria took the opportunity to grab his hand and drag him after her. She was even happier when he didn't relinquish her hand, even as they left the village. Perhaps her time alone with him had cured him of Lianna's charms.

The medicine man moved with almost inhuman speed, even in the darkness that came with the new moon. He led them out into the tall grass of the plains without hesitation, quickly leaving the village behind. A gentle breeze lifted Netria's short hair, and its cool touch was welcome after the growing heat of the summer day. Sounds of animals in the distance wrapped around her, surrounding her in a cocoon of nature. With only the medicine man to guide her, she was truly isolated from any form of civilization. Of course, the only people who lived anywhere near were the Imani, and she didn't consider them at all civilized.

As fast as he had begun the journey, the medicine man came to a halt. Without a word, he pointed. Nestled amidst the grass, sparkling in the starlight, was a tiny silver flower with eight shining petals and a black center. Silver veins ran through the triangular leaves, pulsing. In the darkness left by the absence of the moon, the flowers seemed to give off more light than the stars.

The medicine man whispered something, which Yellima translated quietly. "He says that the flower only blooms on the night of the new moon. We are to harvest the leaves and keep them in a black jar. Exposure to bright light can cause the leaves to wilt and become useless. They will keep for several days, so you must make haste once you harvest them."

"How do we harvest them?" Netria whispered.

"Watch the medicine man. He'll pick some for his rituals now," Yellima answered.

The strange man bent to pluck a leaf. Netria watched with interest. Picking the leaf at a point right next to the stem, he was careful not to touch the flower or the other leaves. Netria wondered why, but said nothing. She supposed that he was trying to protect the plants from harm.

The medicine man moved away from them, muttering to himself as he selected plants. With some reluctance, Netria relinquished Rhen's hand and bent to examine one of the flowers. She reached out to caress a leaf. The moment she touched the edge of the leaf, sharp pain lanced through her fingers. She jerked her hand away and was startled to see blood on the tips of her fingers.

Rhen bent down beside her and gently took her hand.

"Netria, are you all right?" he asked. His big blue eyes, almost black in the starlight, were filled with concern.

She grinned at him. "At least it wasn't my sword hand. I'll be fine."

Raising her hand to his lips, he placed a gentle kiss on her injured fingers. Her eyes met his, and the world froze around them. Yellima cleared her throat, and Netria forced herself to look away.

The Priestess of Strength glared at them as she thrust a black jar into Netria's hands and handed her a knife. "Harvest them before the medicine man angers. We don't want to waste his time."

Rhen took the knife from Netria. "I'll harvest them, Netria. You hold the jar. I don't want you to cut yourself again."

She smiled again and shifted closer to him as she held the jar ready to receive the leaves. "How many do we need?" she asked.

"High Priestess of Truth Alihandre said five, I think, but I'm not sure."

Yellima knelt beside them, adding her harvest to theirs. "If you tell me what ails your friend, I can help you."

Netria didn't know if it would be wise to share such information, but Rhen was already talking. "She's been put into a deep sleep by a drug. We need to awaken her before it's too late. If she's left in stasis too long, her mind could be damaged."

Yellima nodded. "I've heard of this before. You'll need five leaves, one for each virtue, and seven more, one for each element. That makes twelve. Then take some more to ensure that you won't be forced to use damaged leaves. If the medicine man would let us have the flowers, we'd only need five, but we can only have leaves. They're not as potent."

A moment of silence passed as they worked, then Yellima spoke again, glancing at them with hooded eyes. "Who is this woman? She must be someone important to have been drugged in such a manner."

Netria seized Rhen's hand, trying to warn him against

speaking, but he must have misinterpreted her signal, for he prattled on. "Lady Lianna Silvian, a Ravenian noble."

Yellima started to rise, her eyes widening in surprise, but she contained herself. "Interesting."

"Why is that *interesting*?" Netria spat.

"Lord Silvian has come to the attention of the priests and priestesses of all virtues. I've heard that he dabbles in the darker arts. We feared his influence over Lianna; she has the potential to be very powerful. Alihandre must have taken the steps to bring the girl here, where she can be safe from her father. It seems that she has enemies in Jenestra as well."

Yellima smiled and looked at Netria and Rhen. Her gaze expanded to include Keth, who stood watch several feet away. "I wish to return with you when the Priestesses of Truth transport you back to their monastery."

Netria frowned. "No."

Rhen looked from one woman to the other, his eyes filled with confusion. He still hadn't figured out that Yellima was a danger to them all. Netria moved closer to him, wanting to protect him from the priestess. If the nobleman read Netria's body language at all, he didn't understand it. He jostled Netria a little so he could be closer to Yellima. "Why would you want to come to the monastery?"

Yellima smiled. "I'm interested in meeting this Lady Silvian." She opened her hands in a disarming gesture. "I will not harm her in any way. I merely wish to meet her."

Rhen nodded, much to Netria's alarm. "Of course," he said. "We'd be only too happy to have you join us."

"Excellent," Yellima said, shooting a triumphant look towards Netria.

Netria ignored both of them and focused on harvesting the leaves. The sooner they could gather the plants, the sooner they could get back to the monastery and end this travesty of a mission. She'd be only too happy to get away from the plains, even if it meant braving the perpetual storm that guarded the Stormpeaks. Anything was better than this.

Chapter 34

Daymen stepped free of the arch and crossed the distance from it to the opening in the formerly seamless wall. Amial followed close behind him, an arrow taut on her bow. Daymen drew Falkris' sword as he passed into the darkness that shadowed the opening. The archer was right behind him. The moment she entered the passage, all of her senses dimmed and blindness overtook her. When she lit the torch, she felt the heat of flames near her fingers, but saw no light.

She blew out the torch and reached out to find the knight. When she said his name, no sound escaped her lips. Her questing hand at last contacted his shoulder. He jumped, as frightened by the contact as she had been. She moved closer to him, keeping one hand on him at all times.

After a long, silent moment, he moved on. She stayed with him, her only comfort in the strange passage the feel of another human being beneath her fingers. Their progress was slow. To scream, to make something in the dark world come to life with sound or light, would have been like heaven on earth. Though she wanted the nightmare to end, Amial knew that caution was best. She didn't want Daymen to falter and lead them both to death at the bottom of a pit. Just thinking about death in this place made Amial tighten her grip on his shoulder. With one rough hand, he reached up to pat her fingers, reassuring her.

As the journey continued, Amial became aware that she and the knight weren't alone. A great presence was there in the dark, touching her and teasing her with its feather-light touch. While she knew that the being meant her no harm, fear of it consumed her. That the entity was testing her for something she was certain, but she couldn't fathom what. The gentle probing she felt now was similar to what she had felt briefly in the flames of the arch.

After what seemed an eternity, they emerged into light. Amial closed her eyes to protect her vision, but pain lanced through her forehead as soon as light touched her. When she was certain she could open her eyes without further pain, she did so.

In a large room filled with snow, light streamed from the ceiling to illuminate great drifts towering on either side of the pair. Amial felt like she was standing at the heart of an ocean during a storm. The drifts were like waves that could crash down upon her and slay her at any moment.

Where there wasn't snow, white stone covered with ice dominated. The ice was thicker here than it was in the rest of the temple, and everything seemed to be on a larger scale as well. Even the cold temperature of the place was more intense. In reaction, the archer's teeth began to chatter.

Daymen moved away from her, the sword held out before him. Still fumbling for her bow, Amial didn't follow him immediately. Fingers nearly frozen solid, she had a difficult time nocking an arrow. Her hands shook, making it hard for her to keep her weapon ready.

When at last she managed to gain sufficient control of her hands, Amial saw that Daymen was far ahead of her. He was moving at a slow pace, but it seemed to take her forever to catch him. Trying to ask him to wait for her, she discovered she couldn't make a sound. The air around her thickened, impeding her progress.

When Amial looked over her shoulder and saw that she had not gone more than a few feet after several minutes of running, she stopped. Her heart hammering in her chest, she looked more closely at the room. Something was wrong.

Wishing to allay her fears, Amial scanned the snow. Meanwhile, Daymen moved out of sight and disappeared around the edge of a large snowdrift. Amial swallowed, trying to figure out what felt so out of place about this room. Fearing that she wouldn't find the answer in time, she decided to climb the nearest snowdrift for a better look around.

The snow was powdery beneath her boots. She sank to the knee with each step, but she was making better progress than she had before. Snow slid beneath her breeches and penetrated her boot with its icy touch. When the cold substance slid along her ankle, she gasped at the sharp sensation. The whole situation added to her sense of unease; beyond this temple, where the world was still sane, it was summer.

When she reached the top of the drift, she turned in a circle to survey the room. Drifts of snow stretched for what seemed to be at least a mile. In places, the powdery ocean of white appeared to have been disturbed by something rather large. Alarmed, Amial searched for Daymen. The knight wasn't far from her. Only one large drift separated them. Calling out and waving her arms, Amial hoped that he'd see her. Again, no sound escaped her throat, but the frantic movement attracted his attention. His eyes met hers, and she saw a relieved look cross his face; he'd been looking for her. Signaling for him to wait, she scrambled down the snowdrift, leaving a chaotic trail behind her.

Her feet touched ground, and she was climbing the next drift. About halfway up, her feet connected with something solid beneath the snow. She froze in place, too panicked to take any other action. When she regained her ability to think, she bent to dig her way down and investigate. Her fingers uncovered something smooth and white as the snow.

Amial contemplated the object for a moment before deciding it was best to keep moving and continue her awkward journey over the drift. When she reached the top, she paused to rest and catch her breath. Daymen waved at her from below. Smiling, she waved back. Just then, something beneath the snow shifted and the archer lost her balance and fell. She slid back down the drift, landing on her butt on the side opposite Daymen. Pain shot through her spine, making her gasp, the sound echoing in her ears after the silence. A heartbeat later, she heard Daymen screaming her name.

Daymen backed up as the snowdrift heaved and Amial slid back the way she had come. "Amial!" he shouted after her. He would've climbed the drift to reach her, but it was rising rapidly, moving as no snowdrift should.

When the knight didn't hear a response, he feared the worst. Holding the sword ready, he kept it between himself and whatever threatened him. Something huge and white emerged from the snowdrift, sending a shower of snow down to land on him. Struggling to stay free of the powdery mass, he hoped for a clear glance of whatever had emerged from the snow and feared it at the same time.

He brushed snow from his face, clearing his vision. Over his head, a white canopy was spread, held up by white ridges that ran diagonally through it. As Daymen looked on, it fluttered slightly then folded and unfolded itself once.

Daymen's bladder almost emptied when he realized that he was looking at an enormous wing. Following the wing came a long, scaled flank. The head, resembling a lizard with wicked horns, reared out of the snow. A reptilian eye focused on the knight and blinked once.

He was looking at a dragon. Even as it stepped free of the snow and shook its wings, its lethal tail flicking back and forth, Daymen had trouble dealing with this realization. In the past, he'd heard of the dragons that were rumored to haunt Jenestra, but he never thought he'd ever see one, let alone in the Temple of Purity. Could this be the guardian that Alihandre had spoken of?

"Daymen!" Amial's cry reached him. By looking underneath the dragon's stomach, he could just see her. The churned up snow hid most of the archer, but her frightened brown eyes gazed into his. He had to get to her and protect her somehow, though he had no idea how he should fight off a dragon.

The knight said a quick prayer and dashed beneath the monstrous serpent. At least, that was what he intended. In reality, he stood there, rooted in place by sheer fear. Such overwhelming terror had never claimed him before. Even in his nightmares, he'd never dreamed of fighting something so huge, so ferocious. Compared to his new opponent, the icy monsters that infested the rest of the temple seemed an attractive alternative.

"Human," the dragon said into his mind, *"do not fear me."*

Daymen could not have responded even if he had known what to say. He had to settle with silence born of his paralysis. Even if he did have something to say, he doubted that the dragon would listen.

"The three of you have been found worthy, and the way has been opened. To claim the artifact that I guard, you must now prove that you'll be able to protect the item from harm. If it falls into the wrong hands, great evil could be done. I must test your strength."

Did that mean that Falkris was alive? The dragon had said that *three* of them had been found worthy. The knight looked around, half expecting to see the warrior woman standing beside him with her faithful wolf. Before Daymen could contemplate this any further, the fear that rooted him melted away. In that instant, the dragon opened its jaws, exposing a set of incredibly sharp teeth, and hissed a challenge at him. Like a snake, it struck with lightning speed. By some miracle, he managed to roll to the side and save himself from certain death.

As he picked himself up from the floor, Daymen caught a glimpse of Amial loosing a flaming arrow towards the dragon. While he found his balance, the dragon shrieked in pain and whipped its head around to face the archer. The knight took the opportunity to distract it by placing his sword in its side. If he had not put all of his strength behind the blade, he wouldn't have been able to penetrate the dragon's thick hide. After a moment of resistance as steel kissed the dragon's leathery scales, blue blood sprayed from the beast's flank.

The injured dragon roared again, this time in pure rage. Daymen struggled to pull the sword free, and in doing so made a drastic mistake. The dragon twisted and tried to bite him, and even at the awkward angle managed to injure one of his legs.

As he pulled the sword free, Daymen fell to the ground with a cry.

The majestic creature took to the air then, buffeting him with its wings as it rose to hover near the high ceiling. The knight tried to stand, but could not put any weight on his ruined leg. Not far from him, Amial lay on the ground, stunned. Daymen guessed that she'd been struck by the dragon's powerful tail.

Trying to stand again, he was stopped short by a strange sucking noise. He looked up and saw that the dragon was taking in a huge breath of air. If the tales of Daymen's childhood proved true, the dragon was about to breathe fire on him.

"Dear Falkris," the knight whispered, "I'm sorry that I have let your death be in vain. May your soul find peace."

Daymen prepared to meet his death with open eyes. As the dragon sucked in the last of its breath, he stared up at it. Time slowed as the dragon opened its mouth. Blue light lit the back of its throat and began to expand. A stream of ice arched down to capture the knight in a frozen prison. As the ice closed around him, he knew that he would be imprisoned forever, never to find the peaceful release of death.

Chapter 35

Beldaris set his mind free the moment he sensed the approach of the priestesses. To know the moment his traps failed and he was in danger, he had to be entirely receptive to them. From the way the holy women huddled close to one another, he could tell that Alihandre had warned them that unity was the key. He could only pray that few of them would survive long enough to find him.

As they moved deeper into the ancient foundations of the monastery, his projected thoughts followed the priestesses through the catacombs. When they came to the first major crossroads, he was with them. There the women stopped, milling about like lost sheep. If he dared, he would be their shepherd. All he had to do was slip between their thoughts, convincing them that the thoughts he planted in their minds were their own.

Their leader, Kamus, faced the other nine women. When she spoke, her words flashed across his mind, echoing around his astral self, an effect of the separation of mental from physical. "We must divide into two groups of five." He felt Kamus' gaze fall on him, then move on without noticing him. In that brief instant of connection, he whispered into her mind, convincing her to take the entire group down the right pathway. Right, after all, was considered lucky, which was why he had placed the most lethal traps down that passageway.

Kamus shook her head, freeing it of his whispered suggestions. Beldaris couldn't be positive why he'd been rejected from her mind, but he was certain that it was related to her strong connection with the truth. Alihandre would have told them to fear his powers, for she was well aware of his capabilities. Kamus must have sensed his presence and put herself on guard against his suggestions.

She spoke again, looking around as though searching for something. "On second thought, we'll stay together. We go left." That she had sensed him was no longer a question. From now on, she would avoid his suggestions.

The priestesses continued on, heading down the left fork of the winding tunnels. Watching with interest, he followed. He wanted to study their movements and watch how they reacted to one another. With understanding of their character and motives came the ability to defeat them easier. Knowing the weakness of his enemy gave him a distinct advantage over them.

The little group went straight for some time, keeping to their quiet path with its gentle downward slope. When it ended, they came to a halt, looking at the three tunnels that lay open to them. Beldaris hovered near, wondering whether he should give the leader another suggestion. He could tell her the opposite of what he wanted and hope that she went against it. She seemed intelligent, perhaps enough to know that he would try such a thing.

Grinning wickedly, he moved closer to her and whispered into her ear. "Take the left tunnel." This was exactly what he wanted her to do.

Kamus froze, then glanced in his direction. Her pretty green eyes looked straight through him. Lianna had green eyes, though hers were far more beautiful, like the cool green of summer shadows; they were eyes he could fall into. The eyes of his opponent were like cheap baubles in comparison to the jewels that adorned his love's face.

Shaking himself from his reverie, Beldaris focused on the present. Now wasn't the time to be distracted by foolish fantasies; he needed to focus on staying alive. In these crucial moments, he was buying himself the time he needed to take Lianna from the monastery, to a place where she would be safe. Then, she'd come to love him if she didn't already.

Kamus shook her head again, and stared down at the floor. Beldaris could see the thoughts spinning in her dull green eyes.

What would she choose? Studying her expression, he looked for the flicker of an eye or tightening of a muscle to betray her.

Raising her head, she stared into the shadows as though to banish him. "We go left again," she stated in a firm voice. Before moving on, she lingered, her magical senses extended, searching. Beldaris kept his glee contained within himself. If he let her sense that she'd done as he wanted, his ploy would fail. To disguise the truth, he forced a sense of disappointment to the surface of his emotions, mingled with a little frustration. Kamus smiled in triumph when her magical senses brushed over him. Actually believing she'd outwitted him, the priestess had made a fatal mistake.

Leading her little band of priestesses down the left tunnel, she took them into one of the largest traps in the entire system of catacombs. In the lead, she was the one to spring the trap. The floor gave way beneath her, the ground several feet in either direction crumbling. Because the priestesses were walking so close together, several of them were caught in the trap. The three or four rearmost managed to snag some of their friends and drag them back before they fell into the pit.

Of the ten priestesses, four weren't fortunate enough to escape the lethal fall into the trap. They crashed down a tunnel lined with spikes into water at the bottom. The rusty spikes rent their flesh, and evidence of this showed in the water, which was quickly developing a red tint. As they screamed for help, their blood attracted the reptilian creatures that dwelled in the water. Their screams turned from pleas for help to ones of pure terror, soon cut off by death.

Shaken, the remaining priestesses rushed back down the tunnel. When they returned to the intersection, they collapsed against one another, their rapid breathing loud in the damp tunnel. A younger woman stood tall, supporting her friends. "We must not let that happen again," she said as she fought back tears. "From now on, we'll use our magic to find where the stone around us doesn't ring true." She dragged the others to their feet. "Come, we must make haste."

With some reluctance, the other priestesses staggered to their feet. The young woman helped them, her spirit and fire giving them the effort they needed. "Come," she said, "we must not let the deaths of our sisters be in vain!"

The others nodded in agreement. As Beldaris watched, they were filled with renewed purpose. At that moment, he felt his physical body sag and returned to it. He drew in a deep breath, and the walls of his room came into view. A pounding headache assaulted him, and his stomach growled in protest. He also discovered, much to his disgust, that he was shaking.

He hadn't slept or eaten in several days. Though he cherished each moment, he'd spent too much time with Lianna. The vigil the night before had deprived him of much needed sleep. Now, he didn't dare rest or search for food. He had to meet the priestesses.

Beldaris rose to his feet and walked around the room, stumbling after the first few steps. The world around him swirled dangerously, and a curtain of black descended over him. Falling backwards, he landed in an awkward position on the bed, grazing his back on the wood. As he faded from consciousness, he realized that all of his strength wouldn't be enough to save him now. He could only hope that Lianna would be safe.

Beldaris didn't awaken again until he felt cords of foreign power snaking over his skin. His body's natural defenses against the strange magic jolted him awake. When he reached for his own power to defend himself, his senses reached into a dry well and met nothing. He was far too weak to work even the simplest spell.

Opening his eyes, at first he could see only the shadowy representations of people standing over him. He blinked several times, and color returned to his world. A trio of women stood over him. One of them was wounded, but the other two remained unharmed. The woman at the center stared at him with hate-filled eyes.

Beldaris closed his eyes again, waiting for death to come.

After what he had done to these women, he deserved it. With a pang, he realized that he regretted killing their comrades. Once, he had been a member of the Priests of Strength. Knowing what it was like to be part of a community of faith, he comprehended how grief-stricken the priestesses were over the loss of their friends.

He contemplated his failure. The moment that the priestesses came for him, he should've withdrawn from the monastery. However, circumstances kept him here. Lianna was still alive up there, and in need of healing. To live long enough to see her safely out of the monastery was all that mattered to him. Everyone wanted to use Lianna's powers for their own gain, as he once had. As he still did. Now, though, he wanted what was best for her.

The realization startled him. Always in his life, he had sought what was best for *him*, never thinking of others. He'd pushed aside everyone dear to him in his quest for power, and he hadn't regretted it. Now, faced with his failure and the possible loss of Lianna, he knew regret at last. He didn't want to lose her; he could not *bear* to.

And in that moment, he knew his first and only weakness, a blonde woman with green eyes that shone like emeralds and skin that smelled of flowers. Power breathed from her, wreathing him with its intoxicating allure. He *needed* her at his side, but no longer as a mere tool of power. Lianna Silvian was his match, the one woman who could stand with him, fulfilling all of his needs and desires.

Knowing that she was his weakness, he realized that he couldn't allow her to fall into hands other than his own. His enemies would use her against him, making her into a mere tool in a complicated game of power, as he had once desired to use her. A single option was left to him. She would join with him in life, or in the eternity of death.

Before either path could be taken, he had to survive the challenge before him now, when death seemed so imminent. When the killing blow didn't come, Beldaris opened his eyes again. The bright glow of magic made him squint. Each of the three women had cast binding spells on him. Cords of their power extended from their hands and came down to wrap around him. Testing the bonds by flexing his weak muscles, he discovered that he would not be escaping these ropes anytime soon.

The young woman in the center pulled on her rope, jerking him to his feet. He recognized her as the fiery priestess who had rallied her friends. When he opened his mouth to apologize, whatever it was worth, the only sound that he made was a slight croak. He was dehydrated.

The girl sneered at him. "Have you been spending too much time corrupting Lady Silvian, Beldaris? It was all in vain. Once she's cured, we'll restore her mind to what it was before you warped it. In the meantime, you'll be kept under restraint until High Priestess of Truth Alihandre orders your death."

He still had some time. If he was left alive long enough to rest and regain some of his strength, he could contact Lianna one last time and tell her the truth. Maybe he could even use his powers to see that she escaped the priestesses. More than anything, he wanted her freedom. He knew what it was to be forced into something. The Priests of Strength had tried to force him to give up his powers once, years ago.

The three women jerked him from the room. Not expecting the sudden movement, he stumbled. They didn't bother to check his fall and he crashed into the wall of the hall, hitting his head hard against it. The floor rising up to meet him was the last thing he saw before he lost consciousness.

When Beldaris woke again, he knew that a great deal of time had passed. Using all of his senses but sight, he gleaned what he could of his surroundings. He was lying on a bed of some sort, more like a rough palette. Ropes, both physical and magical, bound him. Even if he had been at full strength, he wouldn't have been able to break free of the bindings that held him.

Magic permeated the air. Drinking it in, he sifted through the various power signatures. He sensed that Alihandre stood near him. Beyond the High Priestess of Truth, he could taste a trace of Lianna's powers. The air smelled of her perfume as well. Breathing it in with his mundane senses, he smiled to know that she was near.

At last, he opened his eyes. Alihandre stood over him, staring down at him. "Tell me," she said, "What interest do you have in the girl? Do you seek to subvert her to your will and use her powers?"

Beldaris swallowed, trying to moisten his dry throat. He didn't know what he could say to the priestess. The truth would seem as nothing but a lie to her. And yet, she worshiped the virtue Truth. She'd know if he lied or not. "I wish only to care for her and see that she comes into her powers unmolested," he rasped.

Alihandre stared at him for some time. He felt her magical senses scanning him, testing his sincerity. "I believe you." She turned her back on him. "I ordered you placed here. I knew that you'd cause the least trouble if you were near Lianna. After all, it was you who saved her life. I need you to cure her when the antidote arrives. Once that is accomplished," she turned to look at him, "I'll have to turn you over to the Priests of Strength. They'll hold your trial and decide whether you live or die."

"That's as it should be, Lady."

She smiled. "You've a good heart," she said. "It's just buried beneath all of your ambitions and your drive for power." Before Beldaris could contemplate the truth in that statement, she waved her hand over his eyes and sent him back into oblivion.

Chapter 36

When her balance returned and the world ceased spinning, Falkris found herself in a room filled with snow. Light shone from the high ceiling to fall on white drifts. At the heart of the pristine field, a dragon rose into the air, flapping its wings awkwardly as it shook snow from its massive body.

In the brief seconds that passed following this vision, a thousand things went through her mind. The last dragon had been slain centuries ago, and with its death, magic had fled the world. Yet, a magnificent beast that could only be one of the mythical dragons of yore was standing before her. Magic still existed in the world, as did dragons, but how?

Falkris would have stared in awe at the dragon, but a sharp pain in her hand jolted her from her musings. The sapphire in Shai's hilt pulsed, urging her to act. She felt a tiny buzzing in the back of her head and realized that the sword was speaking to her, though she couldn't make out any words.

Dax didn't have to wait to be told. Launching himself over the snow, he howled at the dragon as the great beast breathed ice on the area beneath it, enraged. Dreading she knew the answer already, Falkris wondered what it was attacking.

She skidded down the first drift. As she ploughed her way through the snow, she feared she'd never get there in time. Hurrying on, her feet began to burn with the cold, but she dared not stop to rub feeling back into them. She had lost her boots in the fire, but she would live without them. Whether her friends would live at all was questionable from the way the dragon was bellowing in rage.

What am I doing, fighting a dragon? she wondered. All she knew was that she cared about both of her friends, especially Amial. The little archer meant much to her. She'd vowed to protect the girl, and didn't want to fail now. "We have to sing that duet together," she said to herself. Tears stung her eyes as she hurried on. If the girl died, she couldn't live with herself

Falkris reached the top of the last drift and found herself beneath the dragon. A quick glance at the snow below her revealed Amial lying on the ground at an awkward angle, and Daymen frozen to the ground. Falkris didn't have time to see if either of them was still alive, though she feared the worst.

"Dragon!" she yelled, her voice projecting farther than it had in years. Torn vocal cords had made yelling too painful, but that was all behind her now. Hopefully she'd live to share her elation at being healed with her friends.

The dragon turned its head to glare down at her, eyeing her for a moment, before it began to suck in air. In a moment, it would breathe ice down on her. She didn't know how to escape the beast's attack, but she had to find a way if she wanted to save her friends.

When the stream of ice shot down towards her, she raised her arms to defend herself. The sword twisted in her hand so that the brunt of the ice hit the blade. A blue light surrounded her as the ice melted away, never even touching her. Shai had protected her.

The dragon spoke into her mind, almost deafening her with its mental voice. *"I see that that pesky sword has at last chosen its warrior. Let me see if you're truly worthy to wield the sacred blade."*

Saying that, the mythical beast dropped down to the ground, keeping its wings unfurled as it swarmed towards her. Grim and determined, Falkris held Shai ready, hoping that by some miracle she'd be able to stand her ground. The dragon was upon her before she had the time to think, wings spread to buffet her with a gust of wind, knocking her backwards. She lost her balance and tumbled down the drift, sliding to halt on the other side. The dragon followed, unhampered by the snow.

Falkris rolled away from lethal jaws as the dragon struck at her with lightning speed. She came to her feet in time to block the claws that slashed at her, though the force of the blow sent her stumbling backward. As she dodged and parried, she realized that her only hope was to get close to the dragon and attack from within the creature's guard.

When next the dragon raised its head to strike, she rolled towards it instead of away. She came to her feet under the huge serpent's head and jabbed up with her sword. Shai's blade cut through the dragon's thick scales with ease, piercing it on the side of its neck. The dragon roared and lashed about until the sword came free, then backed away.

"You can't hope to kill me with such a pathetic blow, but you've proven your worth. I have not been truly wounded in centuries. I'll spare you for now, and entrust the ring to your care."

Falkris fought to catch her breath. When she could, she spoke. "What of the others?"

"Take them. When they've recovered, go to the room beyond this one. The ring awaits you there." So saying, the great dragon moved away over the drifts, quickly disappearing amidst the snow. If Falkris had not seen it there a moment ago, she wouldn't have believed that it existed. Dax, standing beside her, whined his agreement.

Falkris wiped Shai clean and sheathed the blade. She was shaking so hard she feared she might collapse. Taking a deep breath, she looked for the dragon one more time, then went to see to her friends, her heart still hammering in her chest. Amial was unconscious, but didn't seem to be injured or have any broken bones. She'd just been knocked out.

Knowing that the archer was safe, Falkris went to tend to the knight. He was covered in a thin sheet of ice. His eyes were open, but he didn't seem to be able to see her when she moved her hand in front of his eyes. Though she knew that she needed to get him free somehow, she wasn't sure how she'd accomplish such a feat.

Shai spoke in the back of her mind. His voice was very faint compared to the strength with which he had addressed her before, but she could understand him nonetheless. *"You must break the ice."*

"Of course," she muttered. "The question is, how?" She unsheathed the sword and thrust it into the snow at her side where she could see it clearly.

"Use your powers. Keep one hand on me. Imagine heat melting the ice away, and place your free hand on him. It's a minor spell, but one that you can work with success."

Falkris did as he bid, at the same time wondering if she really was insane. Not only did her sword talk to her, but she heeded his advice. As though an inanimate object could truly be male or female anyway. When she opened her eyes, the ice was gone and Daymen was blinking at her. Lacking anything else to do, she smiled.

"Falkris?" Daymen whispered. "Am I in heaven?"

She stood over him, clothed in a beautiful white dress. Cut low in the front, it revealed a good deal more of her flesh than he was accustomed to seeing. The skirt that covered her muscular legs was slit up both sides almost to her waist, revealing a tantalizing amount of thigh. A beautiful sword was thrust into the snow at her side, the sparkling sapphire in the hilt seeming to wink at him. But he didn't look at the weapon long, not when Falkris was there, so prominently in front of him.

When he'd had enough of her body, he looked up at her face. Years of worry and pain had been stripped from her. Her face filled with joy, she seemed to have at last found peace. Thick black hair streamed around her face like a halo. She was angelic.

"Daymen?" she said, but it wasn't her voice. The rasp was gone, replaced by a melodious sound that was beautiful. "Daymen, what's wrong?"

"You're an angel," he said, struggling to sit up.

Offering him a hand, she pulled him to his feet. He jerked away to keep from stumbling into her. When he stepped back, he put his weight on his injured leg. Expecting debilitating pain to cut through him, instead he felt nothing. Looking down, he saw shredded clothing, but smooth skin underneath. His eyes rose to take in Falkris. Had she worked this miracle? Suddenly a stunning woman as well as a lethal weapon, she seemed a miracle herself. Seeing her in the white dress with her hair down and her eyes so bright gave him a whole new perspective on his relationship with her. He could never think of her as just a comrade in arms again.

"We're not dead," she assured him, gazing into his eyes, "but I'd not be surprised to find out this is just a dream." Her voice was so rich, so musical. He had a sudden longing to hear her sing. His eyes strayed to her throat. The scar was gone. What had happened to her?

"If we're not dead," he said, trying to focus on the task at hand, "then where is the dragon?"

She shrugged, for the moment looking more like Falkris. "It left."

"Did you defeat it?"

She jerked the sword out of the snow and wiped it on her skirt before sheathing it. "With some help." Dax moved up beside her.

"You killed that thing?" he asked, incredulous.

Falkris laughed as though he'd told a joke. "No, but I wounded it. It was impressed enough with me to entrust the ring to me." She looked around as though expecting the dragon to return. "But I don't think we should linger here any longer than we must. We need to get the ring and leave."

Daymen nodded and forced himself to look past her to where Amial lay on the ground. "What about her? Is she—?"

"No, she's still alive. She's just unconscious. Thank the gods for that. I couldn't live with myself if she died." Falkris spoke quickly, her voice clear and strong, and it was refreshing to hear her talking so much without paining herself.

Daymen nodded. "Nor could I, Lady."

"Call me Kris," she said over her shoulder as she walked over to Amial. Without another word, she picked the archer up and threw her over her shoulder. Although Amial was small, she was by no means an easy load, but Falkris was more than strong enough for the task.

Daymen moved to take the archer from Falkris, but the warrior shook her head to warn him away. Dax moved between them, making him take a step back. Falkris shifted her burden so that it was more comfortable, then set off across the snowy room. Without any real choice in the matter, Daymen followed.

Falkris' feet lost all feeling by the time they reached the door at the far end of the snowy room. At her touch, the door swung open and she stepped through onto stone. The floor was still cold here, but it at least was more bearable. She looked around quickly, checking for any sign of danger.

Daymen came in behind her, but didn't close the door. Perhaps he feared that once the door closed, it wouldn't open again. She nodded to the knight and stooped to lay Amial down on the floor. After she had relieved herself of her burden, she sat down and began to chaff her feet in hopes of regaining some feeling.

"Why a dress, of all the impractical clothing?" she muttered under her breath.

She felt laughter in the back of her mind. *"If you want to be my warrior, you should at least look the part. I suppose I could provide you with some decent shoes, if you insist."*

"Shai, if we survive this," Falkris promised the sword, "I will kill you myself."

"Do you mean break me? Try it. It isn't possible."

"Where there's a will, there's a way." Falkris looked up to find Daymen's astonished eyes on her. She managed a smile. "It's the sword," she said. How could she tell him that her sword talked to her?

He nodded. "I believe you. I've heard of such a thing, but I've never seen it before. They say that warriors who carry intelligent weapons are the only ones capable of achieving the highest level of swordsmanship."

Falkris felt her heart quicken. "Do you mean the Blade

Singers? The ones who bind their souls to their blades?"

"The same."

She rose to her feet. The sapphire in Shai's hilt flashed bright blue, blinding her. When she opened her eyes, white boots covered her feet. She bent down to touch them in disbelief. Fine leather, they were soft to the touch, and very warm on her feet.

When Falkris moved to lift Amial, Daymen stopped her. The knight picked the archer up himself and gestured to Falkris to lead. She drew her sword and moved on. The little room narrowed into a long hallway. At the end of it, they found another room, at the center of which was a pedestal. The ring was suspended in the air over the pedestal, rotating in a slow spin.

Remembering the pain she'd had to endure to remove the sword from its own pedestal, Falkris was hesitant to retrieve the ring. Shai pulsed in her hand, reassuring her. Then she understood. The pain that she'd felt had been her body reworking itself as the healing process had been accelerated beyond normal bounds, causing scars and dead tissue to fall away. Her pain had been a result of the unnatural reaction her body had to the sword. To make her the pure warrior the sword required, Shai had healed her. The light that surrounded the ring wouldn't harm her because she was already restored.

When she reached out to snag the ring in her free hand, the only pain she felt was in her feet as her snow-burned flesh was restored. Bearable this time, it didn't encompass her entire being. On a whim, she slipped the ring onto her finger. The band was silver, like Shai's hilt, but the jewel was white. A diamond.

"Now what?" Daymen asked behind her.

"Now we leave this damned place," Falkris answered. Together, the wolf at their heels, they turned and began the journey out of the Temple of Purity.

Chapter 37

Alihandre checked the room and hallway thoroughly. When she was certain that she was alone, she went to the wall behind her desk and manipulated a false panel. The bookcase swung open, revealing a stone passageway that led down into the depths of the monastery. Glancing over her shoulder, she entered the hall and closed the wall behind her.

When she had first stepped into her position as the High Priestess, her predecessor had shown her this passage, and the well to which it led. Back then, Alihandre had been young and thin. As the years passed, she'd become quite plump. The corridor that had once been a little cramped was a tight fit for her now. She wished, not for the first time, that she'd worked harder to keep the figure of her youth.

Somehow, she managed to squeeze her way down the long passage. The close walls opened into a tall, circular room. At the center was the Well of Truth, a powerful artifact that the priestesses had guarded and kept secret for many years. Ancient runes covered the stones that constituted the well. If she activated the proper ones, the well would come to life and show her what she desired.

Not wanting to risk the intense power that it emanated, she rarely consulted the well. Every time she used it, she risked drawing the attention of the wrong people. She feared that its power had already been tapped by someone else, most likely Beldaris.

Alihandre remembered a night, perhaps a little over a month ago, when she had sensed the power of the well humming beneath the monastery. She'd rushed down to discover who was abusing the well's power but had found nothing upon arrival except evidence that the well had been used; a vision of

Lianna had graced the waters. Alihandre should've taken action when she first knew an unauthorized hand had tampered with the well, but she'd decided to wait until the trespasser dared to use the well again. Now it was too late, and Lianna's life was endangered.

The High Priestess was loath to use the well again, after all of the trouble that it had caused her and her young charge, but she had no choice now. If she wanted to save Lianna, she had to use the Well of Truth to check on the progress of the two groups that she'd sent to recover the antidote. The well would show her where they were and reveal whether or not they'd completed their missions.

Sending the young people out on such dangerous tasks made her feel guilty. She could only hope that they hadn't been harmed in any way. If something happened to them, she would feel horrible. However, she had to admit that their lives were worth risking if it meant saving Lianna. Lady Silvian was the only one who had the potential to defeat the growing threat from Ravenia. In that country, evil magic had been awakened, magic that left behind power signatures reeking of power and blood. The priests and priestesses would be powerless to stop the momentum of the evil powers spreading across the world if action wasn't taken soon.

Alihandre approached the Well of Truth with cautious steps, fearing it almost. Not wanting to touch the runes that would show her what she sought, she couldn't avoid the task either. This was something that needed to be done, no matter how much she loathed the danger it put her monastery in.

Gathering her courage, Alihandre reached out and touched a series of runes, putting a light touch of her power into her fingers as they contacted the stones. Runes flared to life, shining with the bright, eerie light of magic. The water in the well began to churn, spinning rapidly and yet not flowing over the edge of the well. Instead, it spiraled up into the air, forming a tornado of water that cast light into the deep shadows of the room. Alihandre couldn't recall a time when the well had reacted to her touch with such turbulence.

The High Priestess raised a hand to shade her eyes from the bright light. She had to watch the water or she'd miss her requested vision, and her time would be wasted. "Show me Rhen Tahnuil," she called to the well. The water reversed its spinning abruptly, shifting directions so quickly that she didn't even see it slow. Out of the water came a vision of the Ravenian lord. He was speaking to someone, but the person's identity remained shrouded in mist; the well had chosen not to reveal this person for some reason.

Alihandre felt the power of the well begin to stir. Latching her hands onto the stone rim, she tried to keep herself from being blown backward as the magical energy in the room amplified. Never before had the well acted like this. Alihandre feared it was due to major events happening in the world. She wished to investigate the matter further, but first had to attend to Lianna's friends.

"Lord Tahnuil has harvested the Night's Breath," Alihandre said. In response to her statement, the well pulsed a bright blue light. Truth. If it had shone red, she would've known that her statement was incorrect.

"Then, please," she said to the well, keeping her tone as deferential as she could and still be heard over the roaring of the spinning water, "bring him and his companions back to the monastery. He bears that which will heal Lady Silvian." Her predecessor had told her many times that it was important to treat the well like a sentient being. If she abused its power, it would turn against her. She had to *ask* it to do things, or it might refuse her its power.

In response to her request, the well flashed bright yellow. Alihandre could only hope that the well had transported the young noble and his precious plant back. If not, she'd have to gather her priestesses and cast another transport spell. From experience, she had learned that it was difficult to bring a person to her; it was much easier to send them away, to a place she was familiar with and could see clearly in her mind. Forcing her mind to see the person standing beside her was much harder than seeing them elsewhere.

The vision in the water faded. Before the well withdrew into itself, Alihandre called out to it again. "Please, show me Daymen Aschton!" An image of the knight came before her eyes. He looked very worn, and might have been injured. The archer was thrown over his shoulder. A blinding white light surrounded both of them. What caused the light? Where was Falkris?

"Daymen has the ring," she said, hoping that the mission had been successful. To her despair, the well flashed the color of fresh blood. They had failed. Her heart fell. If that was the case, they'd have to force the person who had poisoned Lianna to administer the antidote. Though she had a feeling that Beldaris would do so without much persuasion, she couldn't guarantee it.

The water began to spin lower, withdrawing into the well. Quickly, before it closed itself to her, Alihandre called out one last request. "Tell me what disturbs you!"

The Well of Truth hesitated and the water descended back into the well. Alihandre feared that she had offended the artifact, but then the light in the room changed. The waters calmed, and over their placid surface, the image of a sword shone. Alihandre gasped as she recognized the weapon. "Vihenushai," she whispered. Who had awakened the ancient weapon?

As though from a great distance, there came voiceless words. *The being whose blade is as music shall become a warrior blessed by five and guarded by three. With power unlocked shall this one seal the gates when the twelve are gathered.* The well went dark abruptly, leaving her without any light. She wanted to ask so many questions, but the Well of Truth had finished with her. Standing in the dark for a time, she thought about what had just occurred. Then she recalled that she'd asked to have Rhen transported back, and her musings were banished in face of a greater concern. Daring to hope, she ran to see if her wish had been granted.

Finding her way to the passage by feel, she squeezed her

way through as quickly as she could. Pushing the wall open, she didn't bother to listen for people on the other side. She heaved herself free of the secret passage, and shut the wall, thankful that no one had entered her office during her absence.

After such exertion, she had to pause and catch her breath. The sounds of many feet approaching the door caused her to take action. Something was happening beyond her office, and she intended to find out what. Bursting into the hallway, still breathing heavily, she came face to face with a tall woman she'd thought never to see again.

"Yellima!" she hissed. If she had been a cat, she would have raked the woman with her claws.

Yellima smiled. "Alihandre. You and I have much to discuss, especially a little favor that you owe me. First, let me see the girl."

"What?" the High Priestess sputtered.

Yellima frowned. "The *girl*. Where is she?"

Alihandre, still trying to fathom how Yellima had gotten into the monastery, pointed down the hall. The Priestess of Strength pushed her way through several gawking priestesses and made her way down the hall, leaving Alihandre standing in the center of the hall with her mouth hanging open. Had the well brought the wrong person?

Someone tugged at her sleeve. "There's an injured man in the courtyard," the priestess said.

Alihandre, her mind reeling, allowed herself to be dragged into the courtyard. Rhen was kneeling over a prone man, his eyes worried. Netria was beside him, a reassuring hand on his shoulder. Neither of them looked up as Alihandre approached, not even noticing her when she knelt on the other side of the man to examine him. Recognizing the ugly brute as Lord Tahnuil's personal bodyguard, Alihandre couldn't think of his name for the life of her.

"What ails him?" she asked, unable to see anything wrong with the man from his appearance alone and wishing to save time.

Rhen looked up, his eyes widening in surprise as though he hadn't expected to see her there. "He was wounded in battle. The Imani healed him, but he didn't stay in bed long enough. I think his wounds have reopened."

Alihandre nodded. He was suffering from blood loss, she guessed. If not that, an infection. The Imani were still primitive, despite all of their philosophy and ideals. Most likely, they had used dirty knives or some other such barbaric thing. Not wasting any time, the High Priestess signaled to her waiting followers. "Here, take him inside and check his wounds for infection. Give him plenty of water, and something that will help restore his strength." They did as she bid. After a sufficient number of the priestesses were recruited to carry the big ox of a man, the courtyard was left almost empty.

Alihandre kept Rhen from following after his friend with a warning gaze. Before she spoke to him again, she took a deep breath and tried to collect herself. Struggling to her feet, she looked around. Suddenly, vertigo overwhelmed her and she swayed. Netria's steady hand under her arm kept her from fainting.

When the world cleared around her, she blinked and raised a shaking hand to her brow. With some surprise, she noticed that there was little light in the courtyard. Was it nearing nightfall already? "What time is it? Is the day gone already?"

"No, Lady," Rhen said, "it has just begun."

"Have I truly worked through the night?" Alihandre whispered. "I'm going to work myself to death."

"Pardon, milady?" Rhen said, looking at her with a worried expression painting his face. She noticed the dark circles beneath his eyes and realized that he'd been through much.

"Come," she said, taking his arm as much to support herself as to draw him with her, "let me escort you to your quarters. I think we all need some rest. The antidote can wait several hours. By then, we will have contacted Sir Aschton and his companions."

She led the two Ravenians from the courtyard and down

a hall towards the guest quarters. "Tell me," she asked Rhen, "how did you come to have Yellima join you?"

Netria answered for the noble. "She was the one who kept the Imani from sacrificing us. She also helped us get the plant from the medicine man."

Alihandre nodded. "I should've anticipated your difficulties with the Imani. They're a gentle people, but their primitive lifestyle can make them seem quite hostile. I'm grateful that Yellima was near enough to aid you, and I apologize for my own lack of foresight. I only wonder what my error in sending you unprepared will cost me."

Netria chuckled. "Knowing Yellima, as much as she can possibly get out of you."

Alihandre tried to smile but failed. "My dear, you are more right than you'll ever realize." This time, Netria didn't laugh.

Chapter 38

Falkris and Daymen trudged through the last stretch of snow, leaving the wintry nightmare behind as they emerged into the paradise of summer. Dax bounded ahead of them, happy to race beneath the sun again. The two warriors, exhausted, followed at a slower pace. They shared a long look, then shifted their gaze to Amial's unconscious form. Saying nothing, they moved on.

"Do you remember the little clearing near the brook about a mile from here?" Daymen asked after a moment.

Falkris nodded. "I do," she answered, her voice still rich and musical. She had expected the miracle to fade away as they left the Temple of Purity behind, but it didn't. The dress remained as well. In clothing that was so foreign to her, she felt odd, but she was fortunate that this dress didn't hamper her as others did. She made a mental note to examine it in more detail later, to see what it was about this particular dress that left her free to move quickly in a fight.

They walked for what seemed an eternity before they reached the clearing. Dax was waiting for them there, napping in the sun. Daymen laid Amial down beside the wolf, heaving a sigh of relief now that he was free of his burden. By now, the sun had risen over the horizon and was making its climb into the sky.

Falkris sat down and leaned against a tree. "We need to rest before we move on, but what are we supposed to do now? Alihandre said that she'd transport us back, but how do we contact her?"

Daymen sat down against a tree opposite hers. "I don't know. I suppose we should go back to where we arrived and wait there. Alihandre wasn't very clear on how we would return."

"The whole adventure seemed rather spontaneous to me." Falkris rearranged the folds of her dress, leaned her head back and closed her eyes. "A good campaign, a successful one, is meticulously planned in advance." When she opened her eyes again, she found Daymen's eyes on her. "What?" she asked.

He shook his head. "Nothing. I just wondered ... what happened to you?"

She shrugged. "I'm not really sure. I was swallowed up in the fire, then I woke up and there was this strange mist all around me. I was attacked, but I had nothing to defend myself with. All of my clothing and weapons had been burned away. And ... Shai was there."

"Shai?" Daymen said, sitting up. There was an alertness to his posture that told her he knew something.

"Have you heard the name before?"

Coming to his feet, he moved across the little clearing until he was standing less than a foot from her. "Yes. Vihenushai, the legendary sword. It's an elemental weapon, bound to water, and said to be intelligent."

Falkris bit her lip as she thought. "But Shai said that if I was his warrior, I'd need to be purified. I thought he was a sword of the virtues."

"No," Daymen said, "but think about it. Water purifies."

"He does seem to be a devious sword." She rose onto her knees and unsheathed the sword, noticing the scabbard for the first time. Silver, it had etchings that depicted an ocean. Water. The scabbard was secured at her waist by a simple silver chain.

When she held the blade aloft, Daymen leaned closer to look at the weapon, but didn't take it from her hand. "These runes are very old," he said after a time. "You would need to research them in a library." Apparently, he'd forgotten that she couldn't read. "I think this one stands for the sword's name, which means something like blade of songs."

With a small smile, she watched him examine her sword. "Would you like to hold it?"

His eyes widened. "I'd be honored." He paused, not taking it from her. "I've always been fascinated by ancient weapons, and to know that this one really exists and is in such perfect condition—" Trailing off, he reached out a reverent hand to accept the sword from her.

The moment it left her hand, he cried out in pain and dropped the sword. Thankfully, it landed across her lap, not cutting her with its sharp blade. Her eyes, however, remained on Daymen's hand, which was covered with frost.

"I should have known better," he mumbled. He went at once to kneel by the brook, putting his trembling hand into the water and holding it there.

"What do you mean?" Rising to her feet, Falkris went to join him with sword in hand.

"Vihenushai is a special blade, the kind that binds itself to its owner. It won't accept the touch of any other person but you."

Falkris looked at the sword. "I don't know if I want it if that's the case."

Daymen managed a smile. "Well, at least this way no one can take your sword from you."

He withdrew his hand and dried it carefully, looking at the flesh. Falkris looked as well, and was happy to see that no real damage was done. "Does it still hurt?" she asked.

"No. I think the sword was just warning me."

Falkris contemplated Shai for a moment, then stuck the blade in the water. She watched, fascinated, as the water surrounding the sword began to thicken and freeze. When she withdrew her sword from the brook, she reached out a tentative hand to touch the blade. Warm to her touch, it was incredibly cold to anything else. After drying it off on her dress, she sheathed it, ready to think about something else.

Daymen chose that moment to rise to his feet. Looking down at her for a moment with a strange expression on his face, he unsheathed the sword she had loaned him. "Here—I should return this."

Falkris blinked in surprise. "No, Daymen. It was my

father's, and it meant much to me, but I no longer need it. He would've wanted it to belong to a person who needed and deserved it. You're that person, now that Shai has claimed me."

"Are you sure?" he asked. A strange emotion was in his eyes. Falkris wished that she could interpret it, but it escaped her. At a loss for words, she nodded. He bowed his head to her and sheathed the sword. "You do me honor, Lady. I'll keep it safe. It's a fine old blade, made from Jenestran steel."

"Jenestran?" she said.

"Perhaps, milady, you had a Jenestran ancestor. Either that, or the sword was made in Jenestra and brought to Ravenia before the border between our countries was closed."

"That would have been centuries ago," she said. Why had he reverted to referring to her as nobility? Had she done something to betray his trust, or their friendship? *We are friends, are we not?*

She changed the subject, wondering if it was the talk of weapons that had estranged him. "What we fought was a dragon, wasn't it?"

Daymen nodded. "Yes, milady, it was."

"I thought the last dragon was slain centuries ago."

"In Ravenia, yes," the knight answered, "but we of Jenestra held the dragons sacred, and still do. That's why we created the magic border around our country ... to keep them safe."

"Which is why magic lives on in Jenestra," Falkris mused.

"Yes, Lady. The magic of the priests and priestesses thrives on balance and order. If all the dragons had been slain, the balance would've been destroyed."

"I see."

Daymen studied her for a time, then turned away. "Forgive me, Lady," he said in a soft voice, "but I must take my leave of you for a time. I wish to go for a walk. I have much to consider." Before she could protest or ask him what was wrong, he left the clearing, leaving her alone with Amial and Dax, who were both still asleep.

Falkris rose to her feet and stretched. The sword at her

side shifted until it hung comfortably against her thigh. Adjusting her dress so that it was in place, she looked down at herself. Seeing herself clothed in such a garment was strange. She had not worn a dress since the night that her family had died. To wear one again was both painful and healing. She felt as though she had been born again, as what she would've been had her family not been murdered. A lady. Was that why Daymen was so deferential around her all of a sudden? But no, Shai was there to remind her that all of her painful years as a mercenary, living a strange half-life as neither mercenary nor lady, had truly happened. Neither Rhen's world nor Netria's fit her now. She didn't belong.

Shai whispered into the back of her mind, *"Perhaps you are in a class of your own, Falkris Vilenti. You've become my warrior, the true Blade Singer. You'll see how you are two in one as time passes. You are everything, and yet you are nothing."*

"What?" she asked, trying to understand what the sword was telling her. She could barely hear his voice echoing in her thoughts.

"You will see," Shai promised, but Falkris wasn't certain that she had actually heard him.

Amial awoke as though from a deep sleep. The pounding in her head was terrible, and for a moment she couldn't see. She raised a hand to her forehead, willing her mind to clear of the blazing pain. What had happened?

As her eyes focused, she saw green grass. Where was the snow? Where was the dragon? She sat up, supporting herself with her elbows. The sun was warm on her face, and there was a light, warm breeze making the grass tickle her skin.

When the roaring in her ears subsided, she became aware of another sound, that of a human voice, rising and falling on the wings of song. Amial turned her head to look over her shoulder, trying to locate the source. Though she recognized the voice, she couldn't place it, like listening to echoes from a dream.

At last, she managed to turn herself enough to see the singer, a woman. Her unbound hair was long and dark, the raven-dark color of the glassy mane contrasting with a brilliant white dress. Held in place by a silver chain, a sword hung at the singer's side. The woman's back was to Amial, so the archer couldn't see her face. The woman's voice, though, was like heaven, the sweetest, most beautiful sound Amial had ever heard.

Amial recognized the song, one commonly sung in taverns. This woman, however, made the song into something more, a melody from the heart, a beautiful story of a young woman and her lover. The archer stood there listening, entranced.

She half wondered if she had died and awakened in heaven. The woman could very well have been an angel. Amial longed to sing with her, but couldn't catch her breath long enough to produce a note. She realized that there were tears in her eyes at the sheer beauty of the song.

At last, she managed to calm herself enough to take in a deep breath. She sang softly at first, matching the woman's voice with her own. Then she found harmony to compliment the sweet soprano and sang with more assurance, accompanying the wonderful voice that was so familiar.

The woman turned, and Amial saw that it was Falkris. *Then I am dead,* she thought. *I am dead, and so is she, but at least she has her voice again. To see her sing, to see such joy in her eyes, is the most wonderful thing I've ever felt. This must be heaven.*

They finished the song together, moving closer to one another until they could touch hands, and the air around them was filled with their harmonizing voices. Amial felt wonder grow in her heart and saw it echoed in Falkris' eyes. While she had sung duets before, she'd never encountered a voice that complimented hers like Falkris' did. She could tell that her mentor felt the same. Was it because they were in heaven?

The song ended too soon, and after the glorious sound, the silence was like a great emptiness. Everything was hushed, as though listening. Even the trees were quiet, their leaves making no sound as they swayed in the wind.

Amial felt a presence to her right. Tearing her eyes from Falkris, who glowed with life, was very difficult. Turning her head, Amial saw Daymen standing at the edge of the clearing. Looking at him, Amial saw a solitary tear run down from his left eye and trace its way to his chin.

The knight swallowed. "That was the most beautiful—" He stopped, at a loss for words.

Amial blushed and lowered her eyes. Beside her, Falkris looked away from the knight. After a moment of silence, Amial found the courage to ask the question in her heart. "Are we dead?"

Falkris laughed, a sound like fairy bells, or water splashing; it was beautiful. When she spoke, her voice was rich, and it sang with a melody all its own. "No. But now that you're awake, we must go on. We have the ring, and we must get it back to Lianna."

"Then I've been unconscious for a long time," Amial whispered.

Falkris smiled. "Yes, but it doesn't matter. We're alive, and we have what we came for. That's enough." Without waiting for the others, she set off towards the hill from which they had begun their journey down into the valley. Dax followed her. After a moment, so did the others.

They walked in silence as the day stretched away behind them. They were all hungry and tired, but they refused to stop. Going to the hill was the only thing they knew to do, so they did it.

When the three at last arrived at the top of the hill, most of the day was gone. They looked at the sky, then at one another, but nothing happened. Alihandre didn't transport them back with her magic. Resigning themselves to wait, the weary travelers set up camp. Not a word passed between them, even when Dax wandered off to hunt and brought back a hare for them to cook and eat.

Silence, like the awestruck aftermath of a miracle, covered them. Had they wanted to talk, none of them would've known what to say. Even Falkris' sword was quiet. The world was at peace for that moment, and they were content to wait.

Chapter 39

When Alihandre awoke from her nap, she rose, feeling refreshed. Going at once to the window, she threw open the shutters to check the weather. Though the monastery was surrounded by a ward protecting it from the spell that made the Stormpeaks impassable, it still suffered normal weather. The priestess was disconcerted to find only the darkness of night beyond her window, for it seemed that she'd slept the day away.

Quivering with rage, she went immediately to find the priestess she had told to awaken her. So much rested on each minute that passed. Every hour that Lianna spent under the sway of the drug left her more susceptible to outside influence. Even if Beldaris was prevented from manipulating the girl now, she was still wrapped in his spell, her mind imprisoned in a dream of his making. The stasis had to be broken soon.

After the High Priestess of Truth had rebuked the girl who'd failed to wake her, she went off to find the most powerful of her priestesses. She didn't have to rouse most of them, for the majority had been awakened by the sound of her fury. They followed her into the courtyard without protest, for all recognized her foul mood and had no wish to incur her wrath.

Several of the younger priestesses hurried to light lamps, and Alihandre gathered those she had chosen around her in a circle. As she waited for the courtyard to be illuminated, she explained the situation to the others.

"The Night's Breath has been found, and Beldaris has been apprehended. However, we dare not allow Beldaris to cure Lady Silvian until we're certain that it's our only option. She'll remain more partial to the delusions he has planted into her mind if he's the one to revive her."

Taking a deep breath, she looked around the assembled

circle of women. "We must pray that Sir Aschton has been successful, and that he has the ring. With it and the Night's Breath, we can break the drug's hold on Lianna without aid from Beldaris. The hard part is that we must return Daymen and his party to the monastery. We all know how difficult it is to alter the truth in such a manner, but with our combined wills we should be successful. We'll transport them one at a time, starting with the one we're most familiar with, Sir Aschton. Then, with his aid, we'll bring the others."

The priestesses nodded their understanding, remaining grim and silent in light of their task. Alihandre looked around the circle one more time, making certain that all of the women were prepared. Then, she bowed her head, took the hands of the women on either side of her and closed her eyes.

After a brief moment, she felt the minds of the others join her, reminding her of how they'd combined their wills to protect Lianna. They had failed then; they couldn't fail now. She let her confidence expand to fill the others, and their thoughts mingled, becoming one.

Alihandre directed them with her thoughts. *"Picture Sir Aschton. His dark hair pulled back into the braid of a knight. His dark skin and eyes. A true Jenestran, born and bred. Picture him here, standing in the center of the circle. Try to focus on his face, on his body. Do not try to remember any other details, focus only on that which is important."*

Silence filled their collected consciousness as they shaped the truth, exerting their will over the fabric of the world that surrounded them. When one of the women began to falter in her resolve, Alihandre reassured her gently, urging her to believe in her own abilities. That was her duty as High Priestess of Truth, to guide these women and help them to reach their true potential.

The air began to shift, stirring wildly as something foreign entered it. Then it surged outward as the space that it had filled was occupied by strange mass. Feeling the sudden wind, Alihandre knew that they'd been successful. The others withdrew from the spell a moment after her realization. Without their combined will filling her, she felt very heavy and tired. Too much of her will had gone into the spell, but it had to be worth it. Weary, Alihandre opened her eyes.

Daymen blinked in surprise. A moment ago, he'd been standing watch while Amial and Falkris slept. The wolf had held vigil with him, silent and still. He'd looked down at Falkris sleeping in the moonlight, and the world had bent as a sense of vertigo washed over him.

Suddenly, his feet touched ground more substantial than grass and dirt, one that had the hard, solid feel of stone. He wished the world would stop spinning, but he was tired and his sense of balance was disrupted. Hoping to dispel his confusion, he shook himself.

His vision cleared, and he looked around, finding himself in the courtyard of the monastery. The Priestesses of Truth stood around him in a circle. Turning, he found himself face to face with Alihandre. Without greeting her properly or even acknowledging her, he turned to see if the others were dealing well with the transport. Eager eyes met with empty air. Alarmed, he turned about, searching. At last he looked back to Alihandre. "Where are they?" A nervous quaver crept unbidden into his voice.

Alihandre was startled by his reaction. "Sir Aschton, calm yourself! You've been through so much in the last days, as we all have. Tell me, did you get the ring?"

He wondered what was wrong with this woman, that she was concerned with a stupid ring at a time like this. Falkris and Amial were half a world away, and this woman cared only about a ring. After all they had endured together, almost at the cost of their lives, all the priestesses cared about was that. "Damn the ring!" he growled, his voice rising with anger.

Alihandre blinked in surprise. "Sir knight, I beg your pardon! A woman's life is at stake."

When she invoked his title, it brought him back to himself.

He remembered that he was a knight, and that she was a High Priestess in the very religion that guided his life. He went to his knees. "Forgive me, High Priestess. I am but concerned for my friends ... they've come to mean much to me."

He took a deep, shuddering breath. "Lady Falkris has the ring. It was by her courage and strength that were able to obtain it." He dared to raise his eyes to her face. "Please ... I beg you. Bring her here."

Alihandre's face softened, and a look of understanding that he couldn't quite grasp filled her eyes. "Daymen," she said, her voice kind, the urgency gone, "we'll bring them all. Even the wolf. But you must aid us in our task."

"How?"

"Lend us your memories. Think of your companions, of how solidly they fit in your life. We'll use our powers to bring them here, guided by your thoughts and your heart."

"Aye," he said.

Alihandre gathered her priestesses to her once more and urged him to join their circle. As they directed, he closed his eyes and joined hands with them. Though he had no magic himself, the women still drew him into their spell. Their fatigue was palpable, but it was overshadowed by resolve. Just as he did, the priestesses knew the importance of this task.

Alihandre spoke into his mind. *"Think of them. Picture them here with you, and we'll use our remaining powers to bring them."*

He nodded, and she seemed to sense his movement even though her eyes were closed. Withdrawing from him, she left him to his task. At first, he could think only of the gratitude that he felt. After the completion of this spell, the priestesses would be too exhausted to work magic for some time. Still, they did it.

He turned his thoughts to his friends. To begin, he envisioned Falkris standing before him, tall and strong. The white dress hung around her, and her gray eyes shone at him. Shai hung at her side, held there by the thin silver chain.

Reaching down, she curled a hand in the ruff of fur at Dax's neck. The wolf stood beside her filled with pride, his yellow eyes intelligent as he looked up at the knight. A magnificent beast, but he was willing to bow to his mistress.

On the other side of the canine, Amial stood with her bow slung over her shoulder. Though she seemed so small and helpless, Daymen recognized her strength. Blinded by innocence, she wasn't afraid to face the world.

The two women looked at one another, then down at the wolf. They laughed, the mingling sound of their voices filling his heart. The musical sound reminded him of their singing, of the soaring beauty of their voices as they harmonized.

Falkris came towards him, filling his sight. When she rested one hand on his shoulder, the smell of her filled his senses. "Daymen," she whispered, her voice rich and melodic. This was too real to be a dream.

Opening his eyes, Daymen found her standing before him. Her dark hair framed her face as her mouth curled up in a little smile. "We did it, Daymen."

Her hand was suddenly removed from his shoulder, and Alihandre's bulk interposed itself between them. Daymen stepped back, ready to protest. The High Priestess ignored him as she held up Falkris' hand in triumph. "The ring!"

Falkris, offended with good reason, jerked her hand away. She glared at the priestesses, daring them to come close again. Daymen could tell that she'd been sleeping, for her hair was rumpled and there was a red mark from her bedroll along one side of her face. However, she was still very imposing and alive. The power of her gaze drove the holy women back.

"Yes," she said, her voice strong, "I have the ring, and it's *mine*. *I* fought a dragon for this ring. *I* was burned alive, and *I* was torn to shreds by some sort of elemental creature. I almost died for the damned thing, and you can all go to *hell* if you think you can just take it from me!"

"She's lying," someone said, wisely keeping her identity hidden in the mulling priestesses. "There isn't a mark on her."

Without warning, Alihandre backed up a step, stumbling into Daymen. "Vihenushai," she breathed. "This woman has awakened the legendary sword."

Reverent silence descended. At that moment, Dax gave a sharp bark. Daymen shifted his eyes from Falkris and let them fall on the wolf and Amial, who stood beside him. The canine was studying something across the courtyard, and his tail wagged hesitantly.

Falkris looked down at her wolf, her eyes following his gaze. At that moment, the priestesses all recovered themselves and began to ask a thousand questions at once. Kris ignored them all, a smile spreading across her face, lighting it from within. Pushing her way free of the crowd, she strode across the courtyard.

Daymen followed her after a moment. When he joined her again, she was standing at the edge of a small fenced-in area. Her head was bent, resting against the nose of her horse, Misan. Daymen's own proud black stallion, Vesahn, snorted a greeting and walked over to greet him.

Alihandre soon interrupted the moment of peace. "Forgive me," she said, sounding strained, "but Lianna's mind is at stake. We must act now to restore her from her stasis, before she is lost to us forever."

Falkris nodded. She moved away from Misan, her hand absently ruffling Dax's ears. Grim, she faced the priestess. "Take me to her."

Chapter 40

Netria awoke to moonlight streaming in the window, wondering how she'd managed to sleep the day away. Then again, she hadn't had a decent night of sleep for days and had needed the rest. Climbing from the bed, she stretched. Before she'd be able to fall asleep again, she'd need to go for a walk. *Perhaps Rhen is up,* she thought with a smile. *I wouldn't mind keeping him company for a while at all.* On a mission, she went in search of the handsome lord.

When she passed the courtyard, she saw many people and bright lights, but she continued her quest without stopping. Rhen, social as he was, would still avoid such a place at a time like this. She knew right where he was.

Intercepting a young priestess, she refused to let the girl pass until she paused to answer a few questions. "Where is Lady Lianna Silvian?"

The girl tried to dodge past, but was stopped. Netria had not lived through hundreds of battles and a few wars because she was slow. At last, the priestess resigned herself to hurried directions. Satisfied, Netria left the girl to her work and went in search of her quarry.

She opened the door to Lianna's room without a sound. Rhen was standing with his back to the door, looking down at the lady, his hands at his sides. He didn't give any sign of having heard her open the door, so she slipped in and closed it.

She moved behind him, using her catlike reflexes to keep absolutely soundless. "Look at her, Netria," he whispered.

Though it was the opposite of what she had intended, Netria jumped. "How did you do that?" she demanded.

Rhen laughed low in his chest. "Well, a couple of years with Falkris as my guard taught me a lot about warriors and the way they move." He turned to look at her with his heartbreaking blue eyes. "You have the touch, like she does. But that wasn't what clued me in."

Netria cocked her head. "Oh? Then what?"

He smiled at her. "I could feel you in the air."

She was still trying to decide if that was a good thing when he turned away from her to continue his observation of Lianna. "I wonder," he said, "do you think it's a painful sleep?"

Netria bit her lip, wondering what to do. He obviously cared for Lianna. Still, there was something in the way that he looked at her that made Netria think he cared about *her* too. "Rhen," she said.

Perhaps all of her heart was in her voice, for he turned to look at her. Without a word, he took her hand and drew her near. She came to stand beside him, and together they looked down at Lianna as she slept. The sight of the lady, so beautiful, turned her stomach.

Rhen spoke into the silence, keeping her thoughts from taking self-defeating paths. "I want to tell you that I appreciate all that you've done for me these last days." He looked at her for a moment. "You've come to be ... special to me, Netria." He looked away and swallowed. Was he nervous? "I want to ask you something," he said.

Wanting to jump for joy, she somehow managed to keep her reaction reserved, though she was becoming very warm. She wondered if he'd notice that her palm was sweaty and suddenly wanted to take her hand away before he noticed. Then again, just having her hand there was worth it. "Ask," she prompted.

"Will you stay with me?" he asked.

She looked at him, studying his profile. "What do you mean?"

"You're a mercenary," he said, having difficulty picking his words, "and as such, you move on to different employers. But I don't want that."

"What *do* you want?" she urged, unable to restrain herself.

Rhen looked at her, his blue eyes frank. "I want you with me. Like Falkris was … only different."

Netria grinned. "How so?"

A sudden noise broke the moment, and Netria drew her sword and pushed Rhen behind her. "Who's there?"

Beldaris felt Alihandre's spell weakening. Becoming conscious, he found that he could open his eyes. Darkness surrounded him, and he knew that the priestesses sent to guard him were gone.

Power hummed in the air. Alihandre and her pet priestesses were working a great spell. He could feel it. As they weakened, so did the spells they had put on him to hold him in place. Curious and holding his breath in excitement, he tested the bonds that held him.

Deciding that the risk was worth it, he focused his powers and threw himself against the spells. He felt a great amount of resistance, but he didn't back down. In a moment, the magic that had bound him was gone, and a huge weight lifted from him. After flexing the right muscles to break the mundane ropes that held him, he was free. Triumphant, he sat up.

The hiss of a sword being drawn made him stiffen. "Who's there?" a female voice challenged.

Beldaris smiled and rose to his feet, confident of himself now that he was free. The rest that Alihandre had forced on him had restored much of his strength. Nothing would stand against him now that his power was back. Especially not after he freed Lianna and took her away from this place.

Keeping one eye on the two figures who stood near his beloved, he focused the rest of his being on Lianna. He needed the antidote to awaken her, but it was in the catacombs. If he withdrew now to retrieve it, he'd have to fight off the priestesses upon his return.

Scanning the room, he conjured a small ball of fire to hover over him. He needed light. The fire flared to life, causing the two people to take a step back. Ignoring them, he continued his search. His gaze fell on a small black jar that rested beside Lianna. Could it be?

Beldaris moved towards his sleeping lady, but was brought up short when the warrior woman flung herself at him, sword held ready. He threw up a shield in front of himself just before her sword hit him, and the magical energy deflected the blade.

"Don't take another step!" the woman hissed.

He paused from his mission to get the little black container. Instead, he considered the woman who was attacking his shield with futile strokes of her blade. When he waved a hand at her, the strength of his will molded into a solid force that sent her flying backwards. Much to his surprise, she rolled when she hit the ground and came to her feet. She was reeling from the blow, but could clearly see him as she approached.

The woman's companion, a man, snatched up the black jar and clutched it to his chest. He turned to run for the door, but Beldaris halted him with a second spell. All of the magic he was throwing was bound to attract attention, but he'd deal with that when the time came.

The Priest of Strength concentrated first on the warrior woman, sending another charge of magic into her, this one powerful enough to kill normal people. As she flew backward and slammed against the wall, he heard the distinctive crack of breaking bones and nodded in satisfaction. She would not trouble him anymore.

Approaching the man, with a touch Beldaris knocked him unconscious. Stooping to pick up the little black jar, he spoke a word of power and the ball of fire faded away, leaving moonlight as the only source of light. Beldaris opened the jar. Inside, the glint of silver on triangular leaves shone clearly. The Night's Breath.

In reverence, Beldaris took out one of the leaves. There were enough in the little jar for him to perform the spell that would revive Lianna. The problem was that he'd have to go into a trance to do it. His only hope was to place defensive spells on the room that would keep others out until he was finished.

Grim and determined, he set to work. He took his time, placing the defenses with care. The spells would have to stand against many attacks to give him enough time. With each spell, he left behind some of his own strength. The sacrifice would be worth it.

Beldaris turned to where Lianna lay in the moonlight, looking as though she was sleeping. With great care, he laid out the leaves on various parts of her body, speaking a phrase of power with each leaf.

The first he set on her forehead. "May the light guide you forward from your sleep." When he spoke the words, he felt a light trance settle over him. As he went through the spell, the trance would deepen until he lost all awareness of the world around him. This was necessary.

The second leaf he placed at her feet. "May your feet tread the path away from darkness."

He continued the cycle, placing the leaves with care. As he said the words that accompanied the antidote, he felt her mind stirring, rising to the surface. Awareness of the world faded as his trance deepened, and he became unaware of the words that passed his lips, or of the careful movements with which he placed the leaves.

When at last the spell was done, he felt the strength draining from his body. Trembling from his efforts, he leaned forward to study Lianna. He wanted to look into her cool green eyes the moment that she woke. Her eyelashes fluttered, but she didn't yet awaken.

Hands came down on his shoulders suddenly. With the touch came binding power that held him fast. Still half in a trance, he wasn't aware of his attacker in time to react. He was pulled back, away from his love. As he watched, the leaves of the Night's Breath burst into flames, ending his spell of awakening. All he could do was pray that what he'd done had been enough. He'd trained Lianna well. If she had felt his power calling her, she would break the rest of the spell and come to him.

Unable to worry any longer about his love, he shook himself out of his trance and tried to pull away from his captor. Strong hands held him fast, refusing to let him go. A rich voice spoke in his ear. "Beldaris, we meet again."

"Sister," he hissed. "I wouldn't have thought that *you* would be the one to stop me."

Yellima laughed harshly. "I need Lianna for my own reasons; one of which is to stop fanatics like you from ruining Jenestra forever. If we can end our battles from within, we can stop the Ravenians from spreading their evil powers."

"Lianna and I *will* stop them," he said in reply as he tried to twist out of her grasp.

Running feet echoed down the hall, and his heart sank. Once his sister had help, he wouldn't stand a chance against her. He tried one last desperate time to break free of her, but was held fast. A moment later, her spell on him was strengthened and reinforced by the additional power of others.

He repressed his urge to scream in frustration. Rage was a weakness; he wouldn't let them see the anger that bloomed within him. Reaching out to his love, he cried her name one last time. "Lianna!"

She stirred, her blonde curls shining silver in the moonlight. Slowly, she opened her eyes and looked at him. "Beldaris?"

Chapter 41

Lianna struggled up from the depths of sleep. She felt the weight of a spell all over, but it was weakening. Beldaris was trying to help her; she sensed that. His familiar power signature coated her, giving her comfort. When the touch of his magic broke away, she knew that something had gone horribly wrong, and she fought the remaining enchantment in order to free herself.

At last, she broke the spell, and her senses returned to her. She heard the sounds of a fight across the room and Beldaris calling her name. "Lianna!" That shout jolted her awake, and she managed to open her eyes. A strange ceiling was over her head, but that didn't matter to her. Not when her mentor was in trouble.

Searching for him, she turned her head. Several priestesses were holding him down. "Beldaris?" she cried in confusion. The priestesses had him. As he'd said they would, the holy women had come for him. She had to help him.

A tall, dark woman cursed and hit Beldaris over the head in an attempt to knock him unconscious. Horrified, Lianna struggled to sit up. Her body was very heavy. She must have been sleeping forever, but it seemed like a moment ago she'd been in the catacombs, waiting for Beldaris to return.

"Stop!" she yelled, willing her voice to carry over the chaos in the room. If they heard her, they didn't react. Anger built inside her, growing with each moment. She managed to swing her legs over the edge of the platform she was lying on. "I said stop!" Still, the women ignored her.

Rage gave her the strength to stand. Swaying from the movement, Lianna spread her legs for better balance. She ignored her own discomfort, thinking only of Beldaris and her need to help him. How they were treating him was unfair. After all he'd done for her, he didn't deserve this.

As raw emotions filled her, power welled up inside of her. *Passion can be your greatest weapon. If you believe in something, if you really want it, you can make it come true.* Beldaris had told her this, and she would use it now, to save him.

The power that she needed to save her mentor came to her. As he had taught her, she molded it. Once it had taken shape within her, she released it, letting her opponents feel her wrath. The force of her anger sent them staggering and knocked most of them unconscious. The tall, dark woman was the only one still standing.

Lianna closed her eyes, shutting out the intimidating woman, focusing instead on her magic. Acting quickly, she shaped her raw power.

"Lianna, wait!" the woman shouted. "We're trying to help you!"

"Help me?" Lianna spat, opening her eyes "You're hurting a man who means much to me. I won't allow it." Without waiting for a reply, she released a wave of power that sent the woman flying and broke the spells binding Beldaris.

As he rose to his feet, a proud smile lit his face. Moving to help him, she put one of his arms across her shoulders. She took his weight easily, using her magic to help bear it.

"You shouldn't use your magic so quickly," he warned, though he sounded grateful. "It will tire you."

Lianna gave him a reassuring smile. "Don't worry about it," she said. "I just need to hold up until we're out of this place."

He smiled, and she was reminded of how handsome he was. "Get me to the courtyard, and I'll transport us elsewhere."

"How?" she asked, even as she bent to the task.

"Ever the pupil," he teased. "It's simple, really. I'll exert my strength of will to move us elsewhere." He stopped her from continuing to the door. "I'll need your help. It's a spell that requires much energy, and is usually performed by many people."

She smiled into his dark eyes. "Don't worry, Beldaris. Together, we can do anything." She kissed him, then focused on the door.

Daymen and Falkris followed behind Alihandre as she led the way to the room where Lianna was staying. The sounds of battle reached Daymen's ears, and he stopped short to listen. Falkris reacted with more speed and pushed her way past the rotund priestess. In a moment, she was running down the hall, following the noise.

The knight ran after her. Although she was faster, he managed to keep her in his sight as they ran down several long halls in search of the source of the noise. Ahead of him, Falkris stopped short outside a door. She reached for the handle, but paused, listening.

Daymen also came to a halt, sensing something in the air. Looking down at his arm, he saw that his hair was standing on end. Powerful magic was being worked very near him. He raised his eyes to where Falkris stood. Too late, he opened his mouth to call out a warning.

In that moment, there was an explosion of sound and the door buckled as it was blown outward by an incredible force. Falkris, standing on the other side, was thrown backwards into the wall. He could see nothing but her leg beneath the door as it crashed to the floor.

Lianna herself stepped free of the room, supporting a tall, dark man. Daymen was immediately struck by the beauty and charisma of the couple, but the sensation was gone in a moment, replaced by his concern for Falkris. Lady Silvian paused, looking at him with a mixture of resolve and fear. Did she think he was going to attack her? He shook his head and pushed past her, caring for nothing but Falkris. As he knelt beside the fallen door, he heard Lianna and the man move on.

With shaking hands, he heaved the door aside. Falkris lay beneath it. She appeared unharmed, but was unconscious.

Running his hands over her arms and legs, he checked for broken bones. Her breathing sounded normal, so she didn't have a punctured lung. She would be safe, but bruised. Daymen brushed the dark hair from her face and breathed a sigh of relief.

Alihandre heard an explosion and knew an instant sense of foreboding. Soon after the sharp sound, she came face to face with Beldaris and Lianna. For a heartbeat, the three of them—and seemingly time itself—froze.

Then the young woman burst into action, raising her hand. The arm that swept the priestess aside was powered by a taste of magic. Alihandre slammed against the wall, temporarily too shaken to move or think. By the time she recovered herself, Lianna and Beldaris were already far down the hall.

Alihandre heaved herself to her feet and went after them, cursing her bulk and age with every step. She had to stop Lianna before it was too late and the poor girl was lost to them forever. If Beldaris managed to spirit the lady away now, there'd be no hope of ever rescuing her.

Amial looked up as Lady Silvian entered the courtyard. A dark man was with her, leaning on her for support. Alarmed, the archer brought out her bow and nocked an arrow in one quick move. Beside her, Dax whined. The wolf had been nervous about something; perhaps this was it.

"Stop where you are!" Amial called, trying to muster her courage.

Lianna blinked in an attempt to adjust her eyes to the sun. "Amial Ravenelle, is that you?"

"Lady Silvian," Amial answered, "you don't know what you're doing. Stop there, and go no further. That man is dangerous!" For emphasis, she sighted her arrow on the man, ready to shoot him if necessary.

"That's right," he said, "I am." With that, he stood away from Lianna and rose to his full height.

Amial kept her hand steady and her eye on his heart. She'd fought creatures that seemed to be from a frozen hell. This man was nothing to her. "Don't move, or I'll kill you." Beside her, Dax growled.

The man raised a hand, and with that she loosed an arrow. A scream pierced the air, and Lianna threw herself in front of the man, prepared to take the arrow. When it thudded into her chest with a sickening sound, she fell backward, propelled by the force of the blow. The man, his eyes widening and his mouth opening to cry out, caught her as she fell against him.

Amial, terrified of what she had done, dropped her bow, which clattered to the ground, the sound echoing around the courtyard. Beside her, Dax's growl broke off into a strange whining sound. He took a few steps forward but stopped when the archer sank to her knees, seeming to know that Amial needed him more than anything now.

The man picked Lianna up and cradled her against his chest. With the lady in his arms, he walked towards the center of the courtyard. The priestesses that were near enough tried to stop him, but a wall of force surrounding him repelled their efforts.

When at last he came to the center of the courtyard, no one tried to stop him; even if anyone had tried, they would've been knocked to the ground by the eerie energy that enclosed him in a bubble. He turned to face Amial, and there was such rage and pain in his face that she had trouble breathing when faced with it.

Thankfully, he closed his eyes and placed a gentle kiss on Lianna's forehead. A bright light surrounded him, blinding Amial to what was happening. She threw up an arm to shield herself as pain lanced into her eyes. A whimper of pain escaped her as a strange wind blew across the courtyard, smelling of darkness and dampness.

When she could see again, Amial found that Lianna and the man were gone. Taking a deep breath, she tried to calm herself as she began to shake. Had she killed Lady Silvian? Dax nudged her with his cold nose, trying to reassure her. She looked into his yellow eyes and saw his concern. There was something else there, though, something that was bothering him. Could something have happened to Falkris?

When a hand touched her shoulder, Amial looked up. Alihandre stood over her. There was profound sadness in the woman's eyes, like she had just suffered a great lost. "Don't worry, child. No one expected her to do that. She'll live."

"How can you know that?"

"Because," the priestess answered, "it would take more than an arrow to kill Lianna. That one ... she has the strength to overcome anything." With a sad look on her face, Alihandre turned away. Then she said, so softly that Amial almost didn't hear her, "And now she's gone."

Chapter 42

Falkris woke, opening her eyes cautiously in deference to the terrible headache that assaulted her. The first thing she saw was Daymen, staring down at her, his dark Jenestran eyes focused on her. His hair had come loose from the braid and hung around his face. He looked, for a moment, like some sort of feral beast.

Blinking, she kept her eyes on him for fear that, if she looked away, she would find the world spinning out of control. She couldn't deal with that now, not with so much pain eating away at her forehead. Her entire body ached.

"Lady Falkris," the knight said.

She wasn't certain, but she thought that hurt more than being slammed into a wall by a rampant door. "Sir Aschton," she returned.

He closed his eyes as though pained. She watched as he took a deep breath, then he looked at her again. Tentatively, he reached out a hand to smooth her hair. "Kris."

Falkris smiled. "Much better, Daymen." She at last let her eyes stray from his face. The shattered remains of the doorframe were just beyond him. To her right, the splintered remains of the door rested. She imagined that the knight had heaved the heavy oaken thing off of her.

"Lianna," she said, "is the lady safe?"

"I don't know. She was the one who blew the door open, and when we met she seemed prepared to fight me in order to pass. The man was with her. I think she was trying to leave with him."

"You didn't follow her?" Falkris asked, surprised.

Daymen smiled. "There was another damsel in distress who means much more to me. I've never really met Lady Silvian, but I feel like I've known you forever." His words set her heart beating. "Besides," he added, "it was obvious to me that there was nothing more we could do for her. She was walking free, without the aid of the ring."

"But the man was with her," Falkris whispered, her thoughts spinning. "He must have awakened her himself, and that means she could still be under his control."

"I don't think so. There was quite the will about her, and a charisma I have rarely seen. I think it was the glow of her powers surrounding her."

Falkris let out a deep breath. "Let's hope so. I'd hate to think she was being controlled by another person, no matter what enmity there is between us." She grinned ruefully. "I was starting to like her, before all this mess happened."

She decided to try to rise to her feet. Movement was painful, but she could tell that nothing was broken. Considering the force with which she'd been thrown into the wall, she had been lucky. When Daymen realized what she was doing, he moved back to give her space. Thankfully, he didn't try to help her. Her pride as a warrior wouldn't have allowed assistance.

At last, she managed to struggle to her feet. She leaned against the wall and just stood there for a time. Daymen, unable to help himself, reached out a hand to steady her. She thought of glaring at him, but settled on a grateful smile.

Shai hummed at her side, lending her his strength. Reaching down to touch his hilt, her fingers brushed the sapphire, finding it was warm to the touch. At least she had found her sword and regained her gift of song. Otherwise, the journey to the Temple of Purity would've been in vain.

Falkris lifted her hand and stared at the ring on her finger. The diamond sparkled like it had a life of its own. She wondered what the ring did for its wearer. Having endured far too much to get the relic, she knew that she'd never give it up. Balling her hand into a fist, Falkris wondered if it was worth it.

Netria awoke to find herself sprawled next to Rhen. Beyond

him, she could see the still forms of several priestesses. The nobleman opened his eyes soon after she did, and for an endless moment, they just looked at one another, their noses almost touching. Reluctantly, she started to sit up, but he pulled her back down. She started to protest, but he stopped her words with a kiss. At first she was surprised, but then she returned the kiss with a great deal of passion. When at last they broke apart, she made herself sit up and helped him to do the same.

"Lady Netria," he said breathlessly, "forgive my presumption."

Netria grinned. "No need. I liked it as much as you did."

He smiled, his gorgeous blue eyes taking her in so that she lost the ability to think. "I think that said what I was trying to say earlier, did it not?"

Netria nodded. "Like Falkris, only different." She grinned, filled with mischief. "But I thought that you two were lovers."

Rhen's eyes widened. "Heavens, no. Kris prizes her maidenhood. She's a proud woman."

"I know," she admitted. Then she clapped him on the shoulder. "I was just kidding." Rhen smiled, unoffended by her rough mannerisms.

Netria rose to her feet, wincing in pain. Her sword arm was broken, and more than one of her ribs was cracked, but she had lived through worse. Keeping her priorities straight, she recovered her sword; she didn't want to be caught unarmed. Offering him her hand, she helped Rhen to his feet. He smiled his thanks and started brushing his clothes into place. Though watching Rhen seemed preferable, Netria felt the presence of someone at the door and looked up. What she saw there made her breathe an awed obscenity that got the attention of everyone within hearing.

Rhen was busy brushing some dirt from his fine tunic when Netria cursed beside him. Alarmed, he glanced at her, then shifted his gaze to the doorway. There stood Falkris, but he almost didn't recognize her. She seemed to be a different woman than she had been the last time he'd seen her. While it had been only a few days, it seemed more like years.

Though she was bruised and dirt stained, she was radiant. The fine white dress, something he never would've thought to see her in, lent her an air of elegance. Her long dark hair was let down to hang about her in a glossy cloud. A silver chain at her waist held a fine sword that he'd never seen before.

Netria jostled him, and he closed his mouth. "Fallen for another woman already?" she chided him. Glancing at her in alarm, he saw the grin on her face and smiled. He still hadn't known her long enough to know when she was joking or serious, but he wanted the opportunity to get better acquainted with her.

Falkris smiled in the doorway. "Netria, I see that you've had success." Her voice was musical and rich, like he'd never heard it before. Rhen wondered what she meant even as Netria crowed in delight and vaulted herself across the space between them. The two mercenaries embraced, Netria wincing as she collided with her friend.

"Kris!" Netria cried. "It's you! Like you used to be! Before—"

Falkris nodded as she held her friend at arm's length. "Before I was broken by Lord Silvian."

Netria grinned until it seemed that her face would split. The white scar on her face stood out. Rhen thought it gave her face character. He'd always thought that about Falkris' neck. Now her old scar was gone, as was the woman he had once known.

Netria nearly shook Falkris in her excitement. "Do you remember how the men used to have trouble fighting you? You were so wild and free, they never realized you were carrying a sword until it was too late!"

Falkris smiled, somewhat sadly. "Aye."

"Let me see your sword."

Falkris' face hardened. "I don't think that's a good idea."

Netria sobered. "Why not?"

Beyond Falkris, the Jenestran knight spoke up. "Vihenushai is a magic sword that refuses the touch of any but its owner." Rhen hadn't seen Daymen Aschton standing there until he spoke. He supposed that was why he had to have bodyguards, because of his own negligence.

Netria frowned, but seemed to accept this. "Then can I at least see it?"

Falkris nodded and drew the weapon. Though the light in the room was dim, the white blade sparkled. Having a life of its own, the sword sang as she swung it. A beautiful weapon, Shai was worthy of nobility. Falkris brought her display to a flashy close. "Vihenushai chose me and removed the affects of my old injuries by purifying me."

Netria's eyes widened with intrigue. Rhen smiled as he watched her. "What about the arrow you took for me?" Netria asked. "Is the scar gone?"

Falkris sheathed her sword and shrugged. "I don't know." "Look!" Netria demanded.

Falkris proceeded to pull open her dress to reveal a portion of her chest and upper arm. Rhen, embarrassed, looked away. The knight did the same, though not as quickly. Netria gasped. "It's gone! Now how am I going to tell that story without you to produce the scar?"

Falkris returned her clothing to its proper place. "I don't know, Netria," she said through a smile.

Their pleasant reunion was interrupted by the sound of approaching steps. The three warriors froze and backed into the room, readying their weapons. Netria reached for her sword, the sharp pain in her sword arm forcing her to recall that it was broken. Rhen, feeling helpless as always, moved a few steps back to give the warriors some room. He'd never been any good in a fight. Perhaps Netria could teach him a few things.

Thankfully, the only person to enter the doorway was the rotund little priestess, Alihandre. She walked in as though she carried a great weight on her shoulders. Looking up as she entered, Alihandre's eyes came to rest on the four people in the room, then strayed to where several priestesses lay slumped against the wall.

"So many powerful people," she whispered, "and we couldn't stop her."

"Then, she's gone?" Falkris asked.

Alihandre nodded. "The archer tried to stop Beldaris, but Lianna threw herself in front of him and took the arrow. Beldaris picked Lianna up and transported them to who knows where. May the One God protect us all."

Falkris blanched. "Amial shot Lianna?"

"On accident, yes, though it didn't appear to be a mortal wound."

Not waiting to hear more, Falkris pushed past the priestess and ran down the hall. The Jenestran knight followed after her, both of them white as the first snow. Rhen remembered little of Amial, but he was still concerned for her. A girl like that shouldn't have to endure the turmoil of having shot an innocent person.

Netria came to him. "Rhen, are you going to be okay?" Guardedness was behind her eyes, as though she feared something. He thought he knew what.

He took her hand. "I'll be fine, Netria, because I have *you*. I always liked Lianna, and I thought of it as my duty to protect her. She was endangering herself by her actions, and I felt obligated to defend her. She was a dear *friend*."

Netria smiled and nodded. She appeared quite relieved. "Good."

Alihandre moved further into the room and came to a stop beside one of her priestesses. Kneeling next to the still woman, she checked for a pulse. "I fear that Lianna has been led astray. If only we had all stood together, we may have been able to stop her. Circumstances … circumstances stipulated a different fate for the poor child."

Rhen nodded. "Netria and I tried to stop Beldaris from reviving her, for you said that if he did it would increase his influence over Lianna. We obviously failed."

Alihandre moved on to the next priestess. "We all did, Lord Tahnuil. Now, we must plot our next course of action. I must think on this, and we all must rest. Some of my priestesses are in need of medical attention." She sighed. "We have worked so much magic these last days that I fear my priestesses will be forced to heal with only mundane means to help them."

"We'll remain at the monastery until you can give us further instructions, High Priestess Alihandre," Rhen assured her. He could tell that she was on the edge of a breakdown, and that was the last thing that he wanted for her now. "Netria and I will go and find someone who can send help to you and your priestesses."

"Young man," Alihandre said, looking up at him, "thank you. I am in your debt." Rhen bowed to her. He snagged Netria's hand, and together they left the room in search of help.

Alihandre knelt over the next woman and discovered that it was Yellima. Even the powerful Priestess of Strength had been defeated. "Yellima," she whispered, "what are we to do now?"

The woman, perhaps having heard her, roused. "Alihandre. What happened?"

"Lianna and Beldaris are gone."

"That fool brother of mine," Yellima hissed as she struggled to sit up. "I had him, but the girl broke the spell." She closed her eyes, remembering. "I've never felt such raw power before. It was too much for even me, Alihandre."

"What are we to do?"

"We must go after her," Yellima said. "We must convince her that we're not her enemies. Too much rests on her making an alliance with the priests and priestesses."

"It'll take time for me to locate her again," Alihandre admitted.

"We have time. We must find something that will force her to see the truth, then we must take it to her."

"The artifact guarded at the Temple of Truth," Alihandre breathed.

"Are you certain?" Yellima asked, her eyes intent on Alihandre's face.

"No, but I will be once I consult the texts in the library."

Yellima managed to rise to her feet. "Then it's decided."

"I must tend to my priestesses first, Yellima."

"Then I will search the library myself."

Alihandre nodded her acceptance. "May the One God speed your progress and reveal the truth to you."

Yellima dipped her head. "May He give us all the strength we need to overcome." So saying, she strode from the room.

Chapter 43

Falkris found Amial sitting in the courtyard. She was curled in on herself, convulsing with violent tremors. Dax sat beside her, licking her intently in an effort to rouse her. The warrior rushed to her side and pushed her way between the wolf and the archer. Dax whined a greeting and shifted his ministrations to his mistress. "Amial!"

The archer looked up. "Kris?" Tears streaked her face, making it puffy and red. There was such pain in her eyes that Falkris didn't hesitate to pull the girl towards her.

Amial buried her face in Falkris' shoulder and sobbed. Falkris could feel the moisture of Amial's tears seeping through her dress. She hummed a little lullaby to calm her friend, rocking her and smoothing her hair.

Daymen wrapped his arms around both women so that the archer was held between them. Dax wriggled his way into the embrace, forgetting his dignity for a time. After a short time, Amial calmed. "I killed her," she said, her voice broken by grief.

Falkris smoothed the archer's hair. "No, that's not what happened. Even if she did die, it would be her own fault. She chose to take the arrow."

"Like you did for Netria," Amial whispered.

"Yes."

Amial nodded against her shoulder. "Because Lianna must have cared deeply for that man, however evil he was."

"She must have," Falkris said, keeping her voice soothing. She wondered if Amial was right. What if Lianna had left by her own choice, because she loved Beldaris? Was it really right to interfere if that was the case?

She raised her eyes to look over Amial's head at Daymen.

The knight met her gaze, and she could see that he was thinking the same thing. But Lianna obviously had tremendous power. If that power fell into the wrong hands, it could be very bad.

"What if she dies?" Amial asked, breaking in on Falkris' thoughts.

"I don't think she'll die, Amial."

"But how can you know?"

"I can't," Falkris admitted.

There was absolute silence for a time. Amial's breathing deepened, and Falkris knew that she'd fallen asleep. Daymen met her eye, then he stood and lifted the archer in his arms. Falkris watched as he carried Amial away to a place where she could sleep off her grief.

Falkris was left alone in the courtyard with Dax and the two horses fenced in against the far wall. The wolf watched her with intelligent eyes, waiting to see if she needed him. In response to his gaze, she pulled him closer and buried her face in his fur.

When at last she stood, she was feeling better, but the events of the last days were still weighing heavily on her. She crossed the courtyard and stepped through the fence so she could join Misan on the other side. Her warmare was happy to see her, though they'd only been apart for a few hours.

Without thinking about what she was doing, Falkris saddled her horse and led her out of the paddock, into the courtyard. Needing to get away for a time, to have some peace and quiet, she mounted up and rode Misan across the courtyard. When she opened the front gates, she was confronted with a violent storm. The morning sun was warm on her back, while rain poured just on the other side of the gate. Magic could make inexplicable things happen.

Undaunted, she rode Misan out into the rain. She dismounted for a brief moment to close the gates behind her. Then she was on the mare's back again, riding like mad through the storm. Dax followed her, his tongue lolling with pure joy.

Falkris rode down a steep slope for a time, heading for the

edge of the mountains. She couldn't see very far ahead because of the torrential rain, but she knew that the end had to be there. When she broke free, it was a surprise to all three of them. The sun struck her full on the face, making her blink.

She was faced with gentle foothills, and beyond them, plains. The dark edges of a forest across the plains drew her eye. Reining Misan in, she sat in the saddle and gazed out at Jenestra. A beautiful country, it looked just like Ravenia, but was somehow more exotic, more satisfying to see. Perhaps it was all that she'd gone through to get there.

Vihenushai hummed at her side, and she looked down at the sword. When she unsheathed the beautiful weapon, she held it aloft, looking at the sapphire set in the hilt. If what Daymen said was true, she had already begun her quest to become a legendary warrior. Shai had chosen her and bound her to him. Her soul and his were entwined. This was what she had wanted, what she had come to Jenestra for.

Now that she and her weapon were bound, she wondered what the next step was. What she needed was to go in search of others like her, who understood what it meant to be one with a sword. If only she knew how, she'd talk to Shai and find out what the sword knew. He'd said that her powers were awakened, but that it would take time for her to reach her full potential. At that point, she'd be able to communicate freely with the sword.

After looking at the sword for some time, she sheathed it. Directing Misan, who had been patient while waiting, down the hill, Falkris rode for some time. The foothills rolled up on either side of her, dwarfing her with their gentle presence.

At last, she came to a halt and dismounted. The grass here looked especially soft, and there was a river not far off. Looking around, Falkris nodded. Dax, at her feet, stared up at her questioningly. She smiled and ruffled his ears. "Shall we camp here?"

Dax barked an agreement, and Misan nudged her. She could almost hear them speaking to her, like a tiny buzzing underlying her thoughts. Shai had assured her that one day she would be able to understand and speak with them. Until that time, their companionship would have to be enough.

Daymen laid Amial down on the bed that one of the preoccupied priestesses had directed him to. Hoping that she'd be okay, he stayed by her side for some time. His heart went out to her, for she had been quite shocked by her ordeal. He wished that there was more that he could do, but as always, he was feeling very inadequate.

When he went in search of Rhen and Netria, Daymen was informed that they were sleeping off their ordeal. He wanted to sleep himself, but knew that he wouldn't be able to if he tried, not yet. So he went in search of Falkris. She had the same restless spirit that he did; she wouldn't be sleeping just now, either.

On his way out to the courtyard, Alihandre snagged his arm. "Sir Aschton, where are you going?"

"I was looking for Falkris."

Alihandre nodded. "Well, if you should happen to find her, tell her that I'd like to speak with her on the morrow. There's much to discuss in light of recent events."

"Do you know where she is?" he asked.

Alihandre shook her head. "No one does. She's taken her horse and gone. I can only hope she comes back, for her skills would be a valuable asset to our endeavor."

Daymen started to ask her what she meant, but the High Priestess of Truth was already bustling away, busy with one of her many tasks. The knight stared after her for a moment, then set off towards the courtyard.

When he reached the enclosure that housed the horses, Vesahn glared at him from the other side. The stallion was temperamental after having been neglected and fenced in for so long. Daymen somehow avoided being bitten as he climbed over the fence to join his horse. Vesahn refused to look at him while he saddled the stubborn beast. When he swung up in the saddle, the horse finally looked back at him with one hostile eye and pranced in place, impatient to be going.

Daymen rode across the courtyard and out into the hellish storm that engulfed the Stormpeaks. Letting Vesahn pick his way forward, Daymen preferred to keep his own eyes closed against the storm. When at last he felt fresh air and sunlight strike his face, the knight breathed a sigh of relief.

His first instinct was to search for enemies awaiting his return to Jenestra. The surrounding hills seemed empty of life. At least King Jemis had not set a band of soldiers at the edge of the mountain pass, waiting for his rebellious knight to emerge from the depths of the perpetual storm.

Daymen shaded his eyes and searched the surrounding area. A clear path cut through the thick grass, marking where someone had been recently, most likely Falkris. He followed at a slow pace, keeping alert despite the beauty of the day.

Vesahn came upon the camp around midday. Misan was unsaddled and was grazing peacefully. Dax sat near the horse, his ears perked. He didn't growl as Daymen approached, for the wolf had come to trust the knight. Falkris lay in the shade of a small tree, asleep. Vihenushai was unsheathed and rested beside her where she could reach it if the need arose.

Daymen dismounted and began unsaddling his own mount. He let Vesahn wander free, as Falkris had done for her own mount. Both horses were trained well enough not to run far, and neither would be parted from their masters.

Uncertain of what else to do, Daymen made his way over to Falkris and sat down near her. He didn't make any sound, for he feared waking her and consequently ending up dead. To surprise a warrior while she was sleeping was never wise. He watched her for a time, before drifting off to sleep himself.

Falkris woke when the sun on her face became too warm for comfort. Midday had passed, and the afternoon was waning. As a consequence, the comforting shade of her tree had abandoned her, leaving her to the mercy of the sun.

Dax had settled beside her and was now sleeping with his

head resting on her thigh. When she reached down to stroke his ears, he woke with a start. Though he trusted her and had grown accustomed to the presence of humans, he was still a wolf. He didn't trust humanity as easily as many believed.

Falkris drew in a deep breath, and at that moment realized she was not alone. The smell on the air wasn't her own, nor Dax's, but belonged to a man she knew well. Daymen was very near; she'd know his scent anywhere.

She scanned the camp. Vesahn dozed in the sun not far from her. Misan stood beside the stallion, tolerating him for the moment. The mare was a stubborn horse and cared little for others of her species. That she and the stallion had survived being fenced together these last days was a miracle in itself. That they stood together now, without any sign of violence between them, was another.

Falkris turned her head. Daymen was near her, sleeping with his back against the tree, his head resting on his chest. When a light snore escaped him, she smiled. Though she'd thought to spend this time alone, she found that she welcomed the knight.

Leaving him to sleep in the sun, she rose to her feet and went in search of her bow. While she wasn't an expert with the weapon, it came in handy occasionally, because it was better to kill one's enemies before they were close enough to engage in close range combat. She found the weapon strapped to the side of her saddle.

Falkris checked it over, looking for signs of damage. Both the bow and the arrows appeared to be in decent shape. *Amial might think otherwise, but this will do for me,* she thought. She signaled to Dax, and the two of them departed in search of supper.

Daymen awoke to the smell of hare cooking over a fire, and his mouth watered in reflex. Before rising, he blinked sleep from his eyes and stretched. The sun was setting in the distance, casting a rosy glow over everything. The flames of the fire made the lengthening shadows dance.

Falkris sat beside the fire, carefully turning the meat as it cooked. Beneath the hare, a pan full of herbs and vegetables sizzled. Falkris spared him a glance when he joined her.

He waited for her to say something, but when she didn't, he forced himself to be the first to speak. "Lady Falkris, I—" She glared at him with such vehemence that he ended his sentence before he had truly begun.

"Daymen," she said, "if you wish to continue calling me that, you can leave." Her voice was harsher than the growl it had been before she was healed.

He looked down at the ground rather than into her intense gray eyes. "Kris, to me, you are a lady. I fear that if I referred to you as anything but a lady, it'd make things more difficult for me."

"Difficult how?" she spat. "You would dare to think of me as your friend?"

He swallowed. "More than friends, I fear." Forcing himself to raise his eyes to her face, he saw that she'd frozen as though paralyzed. He almost forgot to breathe. What had he done to her?

At last, she drew in a deep breath and turned the hare. "What do you mean?"

For a moment, he thought she was taunting him, but then he saw how tightly her jaw was clenched. She was as tense as he was, and he realized that she was hanging on his words. "I mean," he answered, "that you've come to mean a great deal to me these last days, Kris." He took another deep breath. "When I thought you were dead, it was as though a part of me died too, and—"

"Don't say it," she whispered.

He searched her face. "Why?"

"Every time I love someone, something happens to them. First it was my family, Bendal, then Amial—" She turned away so that he couldn't see her face. "I'm never strong enough to protect them."

He dared to put a hand on her shoulder. "Falkris, you don't have to protect me. I can protect *you* if you'll let me. I'm a knight; it's what I do."

She smiled. "I'd like that, Daymen."

He returned the smile. "So would I."

Silence fell on the little camp. Grease dripped off the meat and fell into the fire, making it flare up for a moment. Falkris turned the hare one last time before declaring it done. They ate together in the tranquil camp, just enjoying the companionship, and not needing any words between them.

When the meal was finished, Daymen hesitantly said, "Alihandre was looking for you. She wants to speak with you tomorrow."

Falkris nodded. "But that's tomorrow. Tonight, I want to stay here, beneath the stars." Her eyes sought his. "Will you stay with me?"

For a moment, looking at her, he wondered if his honor would be enough to resist the request. "Kris, I really don't think—"

"No," she said, "I just want to know that you're here with me, and that when I wake up in the morning, you'll still be here. I need something solid in my life, just for one night."

Relieved, he nodded. "Then I'd be honored."

Chapter 44

In the morning, Alihandre swept into her office to find it full of people. She sat down with a heavy thud behind her desk, and for a moment just collected herself rather than face the day. Too much rode on what happened next, and on the assembled people.

She looked around the room at last, letting her gaze linger on each person. Yellima stood closest to her. The Priestess of Strength looked resigned to whatever Alihandre had to say.

Beyond Yellima, Rhen stood in the back corner. He looked very worn, and something was different about him. Alihandre realized that the wide-eyed innocence had gone from his blue eyes. On a journey in pursuit of profit and adventure, he'd found something else. For that, he'd paid dearly, but perhaps it was for the best in the end.

Beside him, standing very close, Netria waited. The mercenary had lost some of her rough nature. More serious now, she was resigned to her tasks. Her life had always been harsh, from what Alihandre could gather, but the last days had been enough to take the edge away from her joking approach to life.

Little Amial Ravenelle stood near the door, looking as though she wanted to bolt out of the room. A haunted look was in her eyes. She had not yet come to terms with yesterday's events, and who could blame her? The girl had been through hell, and had ended her journey by almost killing the person she'd risked her life to save. As Amial was discovering, life was never easy.

Daymen stood near Amial, keeping close enough to comfort her if she needed it. The knight looked surprisingly refreshed today. Perhaps, Alihandre reflected, he had fallen in love. The way he looked at Falkris was enough to answer any doubt.

Falkris herself dominated the room with her very presence. Beautiful and with more than a measure of power surrounding her, Falkris had the potential to become truly great, a legend in her own time. All she needed was training. However, time was far too precious to waste, even to train one such as Falkris.

Alihandre took a deep breath before beginning her speech. "As you are all aware, our quest to save Lianna has failed. Yellima and I believe that her actions may still be partially governed by the aftereffects of the spell that held her, and any poisons that Beldaris implanted in her mind. We wish to save her from him for obvious reasons.

"You all know how powerful she is. Even if you didn't see her, she affected you in some manner. Believing that we were against her, she fought us. But, we're not her enemies. We must convince her of that. Her powers are a key element in winning the battle that looms before us. Many of you don't know what it is that we're fighting, and so I will clarify that for you.

"The name of our enemy, so far as we know, is Lord Dracine Silvian. He is a Ravenian noble, and Lianna's father." Marking the alarmed expression on the faces of several in the room, she attributed the reaction to more than Lianna's connection to their enemy. She intended to investigate it later, but forgot about it as she continued with her monologue. "Dracine has been known to work a corrupt form of magic to further his own power. He's also building up a cult of followers. Their intentions, as far as we can perceive, are to subvert the will of the Ravenian people and use them in a war that will build the power of the cult. Their main target is Jenestra and the priests and priestesses that guard it. When we are defeated, nothing will stand in their way.

"Lianna is our only hope. She alone has the power to defeat her father in single combat if she's given the training and time that it will require for her powers to fully awaken and come under her control. We must overcome Beldaris quickly. Since we have little time as it is, the sooner we rescue her, the better.

"We have a simple plan that we pray will work. I will search for Lianna while several of you journey to the Temple of Truth. There, you'll locate the artifact within the temple, a mirror that shows only the truth. I will then transport you to Lianna, where you'll confront her and force her to see the truth.

"The remainder of you will return to Ravenia and monitor Lord Silvian's actions. Both tasks are dangerous, but you're the only ones who can do it." She paused and took a deep breath before looking at them, imploring them. "I am *begging* you to accept my request and to help me. If we fail in this, our last effort, the world as we know it will end and will be replaced by Lord Silvian's dark empire."

Rhen laughed nervously. "Well, you haven't left us a choice, have you?"

Alihandre raised her eyebrows and looked around the room. "Well?"

Yellima snorted. "I'll do it." She turned and prowled towards Falkris. "And so will you. You and I are the only ones in this room with any magical abilities at all. We must each go with one of the teams."

Alihandre repressed a groan. That was the wrong way to approach Falkris, which Yellima didn't understand. "Excuse me?" Falkris growled. "I have my own quest, thank you. It involves these supposed powers of mine, and unlocking them."

The High Priestess of Truth heaved herself to her feet and rushed to interpose herself between the two powerful women. "Falkris, your sword. Its name is Vihenushai, is it not?"

Falkris glared down at her for a moment, but then softened. "Yes."

"Then you're carrying a rare blade, a sword that binds the bearer's soul with its own. Part of coming fully into your powers is to journey to each of the five temples and face the guardians. Once you have passed the five tests, your full powers will be released, and you'll become a true Blade Singer."

Falkris frowned. "Are you lying to get me to do this?"

Alihandre and Yellima both laughed at that. "Falkris," Alihandre said in a gentle voice, "I am a Priestess of *Truth*. I cannot lie."

Falkris smiled. "Then I will go to the Temple of Truth and find your blasted mirror."

Alihandre breathed a sigh of relief. "And the rest of you?"

Rhen stepped forward. "Netria, Keth and I will return to my estates in Ravenia. I think my absence from court shall be ended soon." He smiled conspiratorially.

Falkris stood straighter. "But Rhen, I have to go with you then. I swore that—"

He stopped her. "Falkris, I released you from that vow long ago."

Netria nodded. "I'll protect him with my life, Falkris. You do what you have to, and I'll see that he's safe."

"As will Keth," Rhen assured Falkris.

Falkris stared at him for a time before smiling. "Aye."

Yellima, patience not being one of her strengths, rolled her eyes. "I'm with Rhen and his lot then."

Amial stepped forward. "I'll go with Falkris."

"As will I," Daymen said.

Alihandre smiled. "Then it's settled." She placed her hands on her hips and looked around the room. "You will all depart as soon as possible. My priestesses will provision you and see you off, but that's all that we can do for you. Our powers must be reserved for the healing of our own."

Falkris was standing with the horses when Daymen found her. She looked up at his approach. "I expected that you'd come find me."

"Oh?"

She turned away from him. "Daymen, when we first met, you were being pursued by Jenestran soldiers. If we go into Jenestra, won't your life be endangered? Alihandre said that we must pass through the capitol to reach the Temple of Truth, and someone there will surely recognize you."

He looked down at his boots. "You have the right of it, but I feel ... I feel that it will all turn out right. You and I can do anything, Kris."

Amial spoke up behind him. "I'll be there, too, you know." Falkris turned to face the archer. "Of course, Amial."

The archer lowered her eyes. "I almost killed Lianna—perhaps I even did—but I need to move on. I keep telling myself that I'll never shoot another arrow, but when I think of you two, and everything that you did for me ... well, I know I'd kill to protect both of you." Dax approached and sat down on her foot. He nudged her hand until she fondled his ears. "You too, Dax."

Falkris smiled and climbed from the pen to embrace her friend. Daymen joined them, and for a moment the three of them were lost in a tight hug that was enhanced by the wolf's wet affections. "We've been through so much together," Amial breathed.

"Tomorrow," Falkris said, "it all begins again."

ANGELA DENCKLAU was born in Fort Dodge, Iowa. A proud resident of the Vincent area, where all Dencklaus live, she grew up on a farm. During the long summer days, only her imagination and her brother kept her sane. From the beginning, she found writing as an outlet not only to pass the time, but to find a greater understanding of life.

Her other passion is music. Currently a music education major at Wartburg College, she finds a new source of inspiration in the fine men and women who are her teachers, colleagues, and friends. She will graduate with her BME in 2004.

In the future, Angela hopes to become one of the weird old ladies at the end of the block, writing books and teaching voice lessons. She will not, however, have lots of cats. Feel free to email her at **author@aerisium.com**.